A Novel

DIPLOMACY AND DEATH AT THE UN

Richard Gordon

Cover and book design by Bob Salpeter

This is a work of historical fiction. Some well-known historical figures, events, and places figure in the narrative, but these names, characters, places, and incidents are the products of the author's imagination and are used fictitiously. Any resemblance to actual persons, living or dead, or events or locales, is entirely coincidental.

Printed in the United States of America
ISBN 9781796350067

Praise for Diplomacy and Death at the UN

"A page turning international thriller in the classic tradition of "The Manchurian Candidate" and "The Day of the Jackal." Gordon takes us on a riveting ride from an Israeli kibbutz to the UN in New York--both the institution and the building--and it is clear that he has been there."

H. Claude Shostal,
Former Commissioner of Cultural Affairs in New York City

"A fast-paced thriller which is exceedingly difficult to put down once one is immersed in the plot and characters. The theme, action, and suspense are highly visual and the novel would make a wonderful movie."

Ambi Mani,
Retired Senior Vice-President, Systems & Data Processing, Afco Credit Corporation

"If you think that you are immune to unforeseen twists in the plot of an espionage novel, you will take pleasure in the inventiveness of this thriller as it takes you on journeys from Israel to Paris to Geneva to Nairobi to Beirut to the United Nations, New York."

Dr. William Ryan
Author of "Noah's Flood: The New Scientific Discoveries About the Event That Changed History"

An historical thriller with fascinating characters that moves quickly in surprising ways to create a multi-dimensional plot that both surprises and intrigues the reader.

Nancy Weintraub

"Have you ever read a book that you couldn't put down? If you haven't, this could be the one. A great example of taking historical facts and figures and weaving an exciting suspenseful storyline that keeps one engrossed from beginning to end. A great read."

Richard Young, Documentary
Film Maker; President, The Denan Project

Tout commence en mystique; tout finit en politique. (Everything begins as a mystique/in a mystical way; everything ends in politics.)

Charles Peguy

The most spiritual human beings, if we assume that they are the most courageous, also experience by far the most painful tragedies; but just for that reason they honor life because it pits the greatest opposition against them.

Friedrich Nietzsche, Thus Spake Zarathustra

There's no one thing that's true. It's all true."

Ernest Hemingway

Prologue

On September 12, 1978 the United Nations General Assembly hall filled to capacity with delegates and observers from 151 member states. The Palestinian Liberation Organization was about to become a full member of the U.N. General Assembly, and PLO leader Yasser Arafat was standing at the podium ready to outline the steps he would take to create a Palestinian state. Then he would denounce Israel for founding 'illegal settlements' in the West Bank, as well as repressing and impoverishing the Palestinian people. These accusations had been heard many times before. What was new was that the Security Council, after extensive diplomatic maneuvers, had voted in favor of the PLO joining the General Assembly.

As 10 a.m. approached, the frantic buzz of conversation among the delegates suddenly stopped. Chairs were brought onto the podium for Arafat and his colleagues. Then the President of the General Assembly took the stage with Arafat, the Middle East delegations erupting in applause. In the predictable charade, the Israeli delegation would leave the hall as soon as Arafat began his oration.

Behind the scenes a very different drama was taking place. A professional assassin seeking to murder the PLO leader was circulating within the United Nations. In fact, U.N. Security had recently learned that two separate assassins had been recruited to kill the PLO leader. The world's top security agencies--American, Chinese, Russian, French, British, Israeli, Iranian, and Interpol--had been mobilized by the United Nations to work together to prevent the assassination. Given the danger, Secretary-General Kurt Waldheim had pleaded with Arafat not to appear in the General Assembly, but hold small closed-door meetings instead. Wanting to savor his moment of personal and political triumph, hower, the PLO leader had insisted on addressing the General Assembly.

At the podium, Arafat waved his arms to quiet the applause. Then he began speaking.

Security officers in uniform and plain clothes scrutinized the mass of delegates, translators, and observers on the main level, as well as interpreters in booths above the hall. They knew that a potential assassin could mask his identity, posing as a delegate or staff member, stationing himself in any number of sites on or above the General Assembly hall.

How had this precarious situation come about? It began two years earlier in a remote Israeli settlement in the West Bank.

United Nations

Chapter 1

January 6, 1977, West Bank, Israel

A car inched forward in the early evening half-light along a single-track path in the low-slung hills above a group of buildings dotted with lights. When the car stopped, four men emerged, leaving the vehicle doors slightly ajar.

Three youthful men gathered around a much older one. Around each of their waists hung a thick belt into which were inserted a container of water, two short-bladed knives and a revolver.

"We wait until complete darkness," the older man whispered in Arabic. Pointing to the left, he muttered: "You see the path we take to get down there?"

The other three looked impassively in the direction his finger pointed and nodded assent.

"El-Fazi stays here with the car," he continued. "Abdul and Georges come with me. Understand?"

Again they nodded.

"So we wait, and when I give the signal, we move."

He sat down on a rock, the others following suit. Sipping water, they looked up at a sky that was beginning to display a panoply of light.

In the settlement below, outside the half-completed communal hall, seven men gathered to decide the order of sentries for the evening's watch. A youthful, bearded settler held out the thin sticks, and Danny Ben-David, to his annoyance, pulled the short one. This meant five hours of sentry duty starting at nine o'clock. Shrugging, he walked slowly towards the small cabin situated near the outskirts of the settlement.

Inside the dwelling, a young woman was preparing the evening meal. Blonde and blue-eyed, she wore a stylish maternity dress, sapphire earrings, and red shoes. A shiny silver bracelet with an image of the Sacre Coeur cathedral in Paris gleamed on her left wrist. With her pink lipstick and stylish hairdo, Julie Ben-David looked ready for dinner at a three-star Parisian restaurant rather than for a makeshift meal in an isolated settlement in biblical wilderness.

The door opened, and her husband entered, bringing in a cloud of dust. Danny Ben-David was tall, broad-shouldered, and bearded. A purple wool skullcap that Julie had knitted for him lay snugly on the back of his head, with black curly hair protruding from the rim. Removing the skullcap, he placed it on a metal table to the right of the door.

His wife greeted him in French from the stove where she was sampling a taste of the nearly cooked chicken. Adding a pinch of rosemary, she walked over to embrace him.

Placing his Uzi against the wall, he marveled at how elegant she looked in contrast to the dowdy, unattractive wives of the other settlers.

"What's for dinner, love?" he asked in Hebrew.

"Desert coq au vin," she answered. "Nearly ready." She moved back to the small stove to stir. The fire had gone out again.

"Zut alors," she exclaimed, frowning. "It's impossible."

Danny came behind her as she re-lit the burner.

"How is my son doing today?" he asked, encircling his arms around her large belly.

"You're such a male chauvinist," she said, smiling. "It could be a girl, you know."

"Not possible. We Israeli sabras always have a firstborn son; then three or four girls in succession."

"Are you joking"? she asked, touching her eyelid. "You want to keep me permanently pregnant"?

"Sure, why not?" Danny said, laughing loudly. "Israeli men like big families, because that means a lot of sex."

"As if you are deprived, my poor, sex-starved husband. Let's have the first baby, and then we will negotiate."

Julie served the meal, and he ate ravenously. They spoke in French, with Danny inserting some Hebrew expressions. Her Hebrew was clumsy, rudimentary. Patiently he coached her, but she frequently lapsed back into her native tongue. Julie would learn his language, as she promised, but in her own good time. He told her what he had done in the orchard that afternoon, embellishing his tale with amusing comments about the eccentricities of the other settlers.

Today's work, which included hoeing and weeding the orchard, digging ditches, and implanting heavy water pipes throughout the settlement, had been especially difficult. Both men and women carried tools in their hands and automatic rifles slung over their shoulders. When their work ended in semi-darkness around 5 p.m., the settlers straggled to their cabins, thinking only of supper and sleep. Walking to their dwellings, the settlers glanced warily at the picturesque hills in the background, as if the jagged rocks and thin-trunked trees with rust-colored branches might suddenly spring to life and threaten them.

"It's too dangerous here," the army captain had warned. "Build your settlement farther south, closer to our base." After he left, the settlers discussed whether his warning should be taken seriously, whether they should ask the organization to move the settlement closer to army protection.

But Gush Emunim (Bloc of the Faithful), the conservative political organization dedicated to promoting Israeli settlements in territories acquired in the victorious 1967 war, wanted to prove that this part of the West Bank, though isolated and exposed, was ripe for Jewish colonization. If Yad Yehudah could survive and flourish, other settlements would follow. A meeting was held with a Gush Emunim representative, and the majority of settlers, including Danny Ben-David, voted to remain where they were. They did ask for additional handguns, Uzis, and small rocket launchers which the organization procured for them. Security measures and patrols were intensified, especially at night. The settlers continued their work, but many of them felt less secure than when they had first arrived.

Within four months, the settlers had constructed their primitive homes and the communal hall that would serve both for meetings and for prayer, cleared the fields of weeds and rocks, and begun planting the figs, grapes, and almonds to be marketed in the major cities of Israel. The only interlopers who approached them were a few Bedouins on donkeys who scurried away when they saw who they were. Yad Yehudah, having generated so much political controversy at its inception, was now a fait accompli, a rudimentary settlement on its way to permanence like many earlier ones established in the West Bank and in Gaza.

In their cabin, Danny and Julie ate slowly, sipping savory French wine they had brought from Tel Aviv.

"Well, do you like my chicken?"

Danny stopped eating and smiled at her. "I love the chicken, but I love you more."

"Quite the charmer, aren't you? You must have had abundant practice with women you knew before me."

"Hey, what is this?" Danny asked. "Do I detect a note of jealousy here? No reason for that."

"Sorry, love. I'm just bantering. I've been inside most of today and my mind jumps all over the place."

"Julie, it isn't healthy for you to isolate yourself so much. You should visit the other women more often. Rebeccah, Sarah, others...and they could come to see you. We've talked about this."

"I like the women, but I can't communicate with them. When they are with me, they try to talk slowly in Hebrew, but it's still incomprehensible to me."

"You were doing well with a tutor in Jerusalem," Danny said. "I'm going to speak with Rebeccah. She knows a little French, and maybe you two could exchange lessons."

Julie frowned.

"Come on. You like her. Give it a try."

"Okay, you win. I'll give it a try."

"Good. I'll speak with her tomorrow. Now let's talk again about a name for our baby. I am going to throw out a few names, and you tell me what you think. Okay?

"Throw in some girl's names too, please," Julie said mockingly. "I know that Israeli men are pretty chauvinistic, but I thought that my broad-minded husband was an exception. I've been around enough macho French bastards, and that's why I married a tolerant Israeli like you." She raised her wine glass to him.

Danny stared at her. " Wow, you're coming on pretty strong. I'm no dictator, not even a benevolent one. In my view, you and I have a perfectly democratic marriage. Don't you agree?"

Julie smiled at him and said calmly: "We're doing fine, but let's consider some girls' names, please." She pulled out a piece of paper from her pocket. "I also made a list."

"Fine. But I'm going to surprise you, because I have a number of girl's names on my list…But I'm still hungry. Can we finish our meal, and then discuss babies' names?"

She nodded. Reaching into the pot with a big spoon, Danny put a generous helping of chicken and rice on each of their plates.

Sitting at the table with her husband, Julie suddenly thought of the curious, even incredible path her life had taken. For this she had her brother to thank and to blame. Over a year ago in Paris, her love life had gone sour. Her married lover, after many promises, had refused in the end to leave his wife and teen-age son, and her design job at the fashion magazine had lost its initial allure in the face of tight budgets and the appearance of a new nasty, demanding boss. Her brother, Robert, had rescued her by offering enough money for a long holiday anywhere in the world she wanted to go.

"Non, non, Robert," she had said. "You're trying to save me, as usual, but I shouldn't run away from my responsibilities."

They were having dinner at a small Algerian restaurant on the Avenue Wagram famous for the best cous cous in Paris.

Blond, blue-eyed, and muscular, Robert Sebastian wore a blazer and tie that gave him a youthful elegant look. His hair was cut short in military style, a leftover from his time in the French army. At thirty-two, he was five years older than his sister.

"In my view, Julie," he said softly, "you're overburdened with responsibility, both in your job and in your personal life." He poured more red wine into both glasses. "Love and work, Freud said. The two main pillars of life…and right now in your case, both are a little shaky."

"'Shaky', hah. That's an understatement. That prick, Rodolf. I spent so much time trying to establish good rapport with his son, and I think that I got close to succeeding."

"What the hell happened then?"

"A few days ago he announced to me that he couldn't leave his marriage. He didn't want to harm his son, he said. "

"And his wife took him back?" Robert asked.

"Yes, even knowing about us, the silly bitch. He told me that his wife was very inse-cure, very dependent on him both emotionally and financially. And, according to him, she was lousy, 'zero' in bed, as he put it."

"That's ridiculous. How could he choose marriage with a weak, ineffectual woman like her when he could have had a strong and sexy woman like you?"

"You flatter me as usual, Robert. I'm not so sure how strong I am…First I cried, and then I was angry as hell. I returned all his letters, called him a louse and a coward. The worst thing of all was that the bastard agreed with me. Didn't even let me have my little victory over his behavior…"

Sebastian laughed. "That's my sister Julie--full of fire and energy. Your strong char-acter will get you through this." He raised his glass in toast to Julie who clicked hers and sipped the remainder of her wine. Her brother poured some more.

"And what about the job?"

"Oh, Bruno, the fucking new boss. He's never satisfied. Makes us work on projects late into the evening. And last week I produced something really exceptional, an abstract design for the cover of our magazine, and he took it from me and put his name on it."

"What? That's outrageous."

"Maybe so. But he's the cousin of the owner of the agency. So what can I do? I have no leverage at all."

"I have some leverage," her brother said, pulling aside his sport jacket lapel and revealing a holster and gun. "Maybe I should see Bruno and give him a little warning about stealing your work." His face took on a taut, fierce look.

Julie had seen her brother's 'self-protective' gun before. She pressed down hard on his arm. "No, Robert. It's not worth it. What would you do, tell Bruno that you're my rough, tough brother, and if he doesn't shape up, you'll plug him? No, no," Julie said laughing. "Although if it did happen, I would certainly like to be there to see his expression."

"Look, Julie. You're having a difficult time now in both love and work. Me, I believe in destiny. I think that this conjuncture of bad stuff is a sign for you, a sign that you need to get away from all this unpleasantness."

"What are you saying?"

"I think that you should get the hell out of Paris for awhile. Get away from the double misery currently afflicting your life. Go somewhere exciting, exotic, a place that will take your mind off things. Then come back and start a new life. I was going to give you a nice monetary gift for your birthday. Now I'll just add to it."

"My birthday isn't until two months from now."

"That's okay. We'll accelerate. Today is Friday. Why don't you think about where you would like to go? And let's meet here on Sunday or Monday and see what you have decided."

"Okay, Monday. Ironically I'm going museum hopping on Sunday with my friend Denise. I'll talk with her about it." Julie took his hands in hers. "Oh, Robert, you're the best. The one person who loves me unconditionally..."

"There are many others, I'm sure," Sebastian said softly. "On Monday you'll tell me where you've decided to go, and then you can give notice to your job. Meanwhile I will rack my brains over the weekend trying to guess what destination my sister will choose— South America, Asia, Africa, the Magreb, Fiji..."

She chose Africa. Starting in the former French colonies in West Africa, Julie basked on the sunny beaches of Senegal south of Dakar, rode on camels in the hills of northern Mali outside of Timbuctu, visited a cousin living in the petrol-rich capital of Libreville, Gabon, and learned to carve expressive ebony figures by imitating native craftsmen in the art markets of Yaounde, Cameroon. It was a nonstop whirl, perfect therapy for Julie.

To make the situation even better, her friend Denise joined her in Mali and then traveled with her to Libreville and Yaounde. Denise was Julie's closest friend, someone with whom she could share her innermost thoughts. Blessed with flowing brown hair, an extremely pretty face, and a thin, yet full figure, Denise had studied anthropology at university, intending to teach at the lycee level. However, one day while strolling along the Boulevard St. Germain, a well-dressed man accosted her and said that he was an agent for fashion models. Praising her looks, he invited her to come to his agency the next day to appear before a camera. Intrigued, Denise went and impressed the agent, his underlings, and the cameraman. The agent found sporadic modeling gigs for her, but nothing exceptional, and he implied that if she wanted higher-level work, she would have to go to bed with him. Bolting the agency, she signed with a more prestigious modeling firm, and her career began to blossom. She wasn't at the top level yet, but she had reasonably steady work without having to compromise herself.

Denise and Julie had met six years ago at a fashion-related party where they ended up talking exclusively to one another about the men in their lives and the flamboyant, competitive characters in contemporary French fashion. They began to see each other regularly, and each introduced her boyfriends to the other for scrutiny and advice.

Julie wanted to introduce her brother to Denise, but he gave the excuse of frequent travel for his work as an international financial consultant. Before Julie had left on her trip, she asked Robert to join the two women for dinner, but Robert told her that he would be on an assignment in Prague. He returned the day before Julie's departure, feting her at the extravagant 18th century restaurant Grand Vefour on the perimeter of the Palais Royal.

After their stay in Yaoundé, Cameroon, the women were scheduled to fly to Lome, Togo and then return to Paris. Sitting at the pool at the elegant Hotel Mont Febe in

Yaounde on a sultry hot afternoon, Julie and Denise languidly sipped cocktails, while glancing at their paperback novels and Parisian newspapers.

"The heat's devastating, Denise. I'm so tired that I can't even read."

" Let's jump in the pool, Julie. That'll cool us off." After a long stay in the pool, they returned to their chairs.

"Denise, look over there," Julie suddenly said. "Those two men across the pool were looking at us, and now they're coming in our direction." She put on her sunglasses.

The men walked near their seats. "Bonjour, Madame," the tall one said. "Je veux, je voudr...Oh damn, my French is lousy and that's the sum of it."

"You are British or American then?" Denise said in English with a heavy French accent.

"British. We're photographers based in London doing a shoot about expatriate life in the capitals of Cameroon, Nigeria, and Ghana. We came here two days ago from Accra. I'm Richard and this is Simon."

"Just a minute. I have to interpret for my friend." Denise told Julie that they were British and didn't speak any French.

"Merde," said Julie. "I cannot understand any of their English gibberish. Tell them that."

"My friend says that she cannot communicate with you in English. She knows only French. We're both French, living in Paris."

"That's very nice," Richard said to her. "I'll be honest with you. We've seen you at the pool and in the dining room the last two days, and if you are alone like us, we would like to ask you to come to dinner with us this evening. I hear that there is quite a good Indian restaurant near the legislature. I can promise you three things—one, we are gentlemen; two, you will enjoy yourselves; and three, we will happily pay for your dinner."

Denise interpreted what he had said, and Julie suggested that they meet for a drink at 6 p.m. in the hotel bar and then decide about going out to dinner with them.

They met for drinks, and Denise decided that she liked Richard's looks and general demeanor, and so she proposed to Julie that they go to dinner with the men. At the Indian restaurant they consumed lamb curry and fish birani with rice and vegetables and sipped Kingfisher beer. During dinner the shorter man, Simon, tried to engage Julie in conversation, and Denise laboriously interpreted until Julie interrupted: "It's okay, my dear. It's too much of a strain for me to talk to this guy with you interpreting. You clearly like the tall one, and so you just go ahead and flirt with him. You can talk about the Hundred Years War between England and France (remind him that we won) or how deGaulle wouldn't permit the Brits to come into the Common Market in 1963."

"Oh, you are naughty," Denise said, laughing. "But you've just given me some political topics to impress the Brits, as you call them."

"Well, good luck. And don't worry about me. After dinner, let's go back to the hotel, and you can go off with your tall guy, and I will go to sleep. You can tell Simon that it's just too much of an effort for me to talk in English."

"Okay, Julie." She apologized to Simon on Julie's behalf, and he nodded his head in sympathy.

After the meal, the four returned to the hotel, and Julie went up to her room, taking some time to fall asleep. The next morning, at the breakfast table, she looked inquisitively at Denise who simply smiled enigmatically.

"So you won't tell me anything, Denise? Not fair. I'd tell you, if the situation were reversed."

"Let's just say that when he said that he was a 'gentleman', he meant it. He was very 'correct'. If he had been more aggressive, I probably would have jumped into bed with him, but after we smooched a bit, he excused himself, saying that they had to get up early this morning." Denise laughed. "He promised to see me the next time that he comes to Paris, probably in 2-3 months. So my great chance for a love affair in Africa has proven to be a dud. That's how life goes, n'est-ce pas?"

"You're philosophical about it. That's good."

Denise shrugged. "Hey, we're off to Togo tomorrow, and why would I let a man, especially an Englishman, ruin my superb time in Africa with you?"

Julie hugged her. "You know, Denise, I've been thinking about things, specifically my mediocre English language skills. The little that I learned in school has withered away. And that was a handicap at my last two jobs when I had to turn down assignments in London and New York because I couldn't speak the damned language. I probably should have spent more time with my father after he divorced my mother and returned to the U.S., but I was too angry with him."

"And so?"

"And so I stayed up last night thinking that I have the time now to do an immersion course in English for a month or two. I don't see the point of going to another French-speaking country when I can go to an English-speaking one, do an intensive course and practice conversational English. I can read the language reasonably well, but my oral skills are pure shit. I get intimidated, but it's time for me to conquer my language demons. Speaking English could be useful in any future job that I have."

"Does that mean that you want to cancel Togo and go to an English-speaking country. Which one-- Ghana, Liberia, Nigeria?"

"Actually I was thinking of going across the continent to East Africa. We've 'done' West Africa. Why not go to the other side?"

"So that would mean places like Uganda, Tanzania, Kenya, or even South Africa?"

"Wow, you really know your African geography, Denise. Someone in my office went to Nairobi on holiday and had a great time. Let's go there…Would you come with me to Kenya and leave for Paris from there?"

"Hmm…Why not? I've never been to Nairobi and I've heard that it's fascinating culturally. Sure, I'll go with you. It would also be good for me to practice my English conversation. While you go to class, I'll wander the streets, talk English, and check out African dress and artwork. We can meet up in the evenings for dinner."

"Great. Let's go to Air France after breakfast and see about changing our tickets."

The next day Denise and Julie flew from Yaounde to Dakar and then across the continent to Nairobi. They found a charming flat in the Indian section of the city. Enrolling in an English language school run by an old expatriate British couple, Julie spent her days in class and her evenings pouring over grammar and vocabulary exercises. Denise wandered the city, stopping frequently at the French Embassy to read the Paris press and attend lectures. There she met an older woman from Lyon who was chatty and intelligent, and the two met up daily for long walks and visits to art galleries. In the evenings Denise joined Julie for dinner. Enjoying this routine, Denise extended her stay in Nairobi by a week.

Julie tried dutifully to learn to improve her linguistic skills, but after ten days of repetitive, painful practice, she decided that her attempt to master spoken English in a short time was unrealistic, if not futile. The intensive program was giving her migraine headaches, and she told the English couple that she needed to leave the program "to protect my health."

"What could I do, Denise?" Julie said at dinner that evening. "I can't learn English with a sharp headache. It's best that I stop now. I've made some decent progress. I can order simple food in a restaurant. I can say 'Hello. How are you? Where is the toilet? So when I go to London, I will be able to eat and to relieve myself."

Denise laughed. "Fine, fine. Your basic needs will be taken care of in an Anglophone atmosphere. What more can you possibly wish for? Have you learned to say 'faire l'amour' in English? 'Make love'."

"I knew that already, you silly 'twit'. I learned that insult in my class. Basically speaking I'm happy with my little progress here in English, and when I get back to Paris, I'll enroll in an evening course. Mercifully it will not be an intensive one."

"Good idea. So what happens now?"

"I was thinking of travelling across the continent to see the pyramids in Egypt that I have dreamt about since childhood, but I don't think that I should do this on my own. Maybe you'll come with me next year."

"Sure. Why not? You're great to travel with. Count me in."

"I'll go back to Paris with you on Tuesday. Until then, if you don't mind, I'll join Cecile and you on your walks to the galleries and around the city. I can try out my meager English on the African and Indian merchants…Hoorah. I feel liberated already. My headache is gone, and next Tuesday I'll be back in Paris."

But Julie never made it out of Nairobi. Three days before their flight to Paris, on Saturday, December 3, 1975, a date that she would never forget, Julie came downstairs from her room in mid-morning to the elegant hotel restaurant. Sitting at a table at the back, she ordered coffee and a pastry. Suddenly she noticed a husky handsome man with black curly hair and muscular arms at the next table carrying on an animated conversation in a language she didn't recognize. After several minutes, he walked over to her table and began speaking in English. Her halting response in French-accented English prompted him to ask if she were French, and receiving an affirmative reply, he began speaking to Julie in her own language.

"Est-ce que je peux m'assoir?" ('May I sit down?') he asked.

Julie looked closely at him, finding his sun-tanned face and dark hair attractive. "Oui, bien sur," ('Certainly.') she replied. "Vous etes d'ou?" ('Where are you from'?)

"Israel, mais j'habite ici a Nairobi. Et vous?" ('Israeli, but I live here in Nairobi. And you'?)

"La France. Je suis de passage, une touriste. Je suis avec mon amie Denise qui va me rejoindre l'instant. Voici Denise." ('France. I am just passing through, a tourist. I'm here with my friend Denise who is going to join me in a minute. Here she is.')

Approaching the table, Denise was surprised to see a man sitting there. She took the seat next to Julie.

"Excuse me, " he said, standing up. "May I introduce myself? My name is Danny Ben-David. I'm Israeli and I work for the United Nations Environment Agency in Nairobi. May I ask your names?"

"Julie...Denise."

"I'll be honest. I must seem like an intruder. There I was with my Israeli friend, and suddenly I see a very attractive blond woman alone at the next table. So I decide spontaneously to approach her, and while this may appear clumsy on my part, it's the simple, unblemished truth." He flashed a big smile.

"Very nice," Julie said. "I should be flattered, but now you see my beautiful friend Denise and maybe you would like to focus on her."

"You're very funny," said Danny. "This isn't a lottery, is it? Maybe I was a bit aggressive in approaching you, but something attracted me and the fact that you are French, that you are both French, suits me very well, since I went to university in Paris and I love French culture and France itself. My friend Benjamin doesn't speak French. He's a businessman in Nairobi and so he speaks English. Therefore he wouldn't be able to communicate with us. Correct"?

"Well," Denise said. "I speak reasonable English, but I'm not looking to practice with an Israeli guy in Nairobi."

"Let me talk with Benjamin for a minute. I have an idea that could be pleasing to you both." He walked to the next table and began chatting with his friend in Hebrew.

"You little fox. I can't leave you alone for a minute," said Denise, smiling. "I come downstairs and here is this Israeli guy all over you. Have you no shame, woman?"

"Denise, he came over to talk with me literally a minute before you arrived. He's attractive, don't you think? Plus…"

Danny returned to their table. "Benjamin and I would like to invite you both for a stroll through the city. As tourists, you undoubtedly have seen the usual places. But we've worked here for several years, and we can show you the inner pulse of Nairobi as well as any Kenyan. So we can walk for a couple of hours and then have lunch at the best African restaurant in the city, a place that you would never find on your own or even with a tourist guide. What do you say?" Seeing them look at each other, he added: "I'll move away and let you decide if you would like to accept our offer. I hope so."

He sat down at the adjoining table, while Julie and Denise conferred. Denise was hesitant, but seeing her friend eager to join the men, she relented. Denise stood up and approached the two men.

"Okay, we'll accept your offer," she said in English. "Your friend said that your name is Benjamin. Mine is Denise." They shook hands. "It looks as if you and I will mainly be talking together, while…Danny, is it?…will be conversing with my friend Julie in French. We'll finish our coffee and then go back to our rooms. We'll join you in the lobby of the hotel in thirty minutes. Okay?"

"Fine," Benjamin said. Watching Denise walk away, he remarked to Danny: "She's beautiful…too bad I have a fiancée. I think that I'll tell her that up front…out of fairness. Not that she will find me anything special…"

"Yeah, you should tell her about Sarah," Danny replied. "In my case, I have no such restrictions, because as I've told you, Miriam and I decided that the distance between Haifa and Nairobi is too great and we should begin to see other people." He hesitated and then said: "I tell you, Benjamin. You may find her friend a beauty, but I'm impressed with the blond. She's charming and good-humored." He mentioned Julie's attempt to fob him off on Denise. "I've got a hunch that I'm going to get along quite well with that woman."

"You're crazy. How would you know? You just met her five minutes ago."

"On verra bien."

"What the hell does that mean?"

"We shall see," said Danny, smiling.

The men moved to chairs in the hotel lobby. When the women returned, they began to walk along Kenyatta Avenue, Danny and Julie leading the way. Behind them Denise and Benjamin conversed in English, with the Israeli telling her about his fiancée in Israel and asking her if she was involved with anyone.

"Not right now," Denise replied. "I met an Englishman in Cameroon who said that he would come to see me in Paris, but probably nothing will happen with him. In France I have no one at the moment, but things can change quickly, if I let it. But let's not talk about this sort of thing. Talk to me about Nairobi or about Israel. I almost went there on a fashion assignment last year, but it got cancelled at the last moment. A pity that I missed seeing the holy land…"

"Tell me about Israel, a country that I don't know at all," Julie said, as Danny led her down a narrow street dotted by small stores and booths displaying exquisite colored cloths.

"That will be a pleasure," he said. "I'll try not to bore you." And Danny began to talk about his life in Israel and his adventures up and down East Africa from Addis Ababa to Capetown. Julie found him charming and intense, as he regaled her with stories about his trip to Victoria Falls and to game parks in Botswana, South Africa, and Tanzania. She liked Danny's self-deprecating sense of humor, as he told her about his military service in the 1967 War and the Yom Kippur War of 1973, his two-year stint at the Sorbonne studying existentialist philosophy and French literature, and then his escape to the United Nations Environment Agency, Habitat, in Nairobi two years ago from a claustrophobic job in Tel Aviv. "During the day I work on urban environmental issues for Habitat, but in my spare time, I'm helping Benjamin set up an export business in precious metals."

"Very interesting. The only UN agency I know is UNESCO in Paris where a girl friend of mine works to preserve ancient monuments. I had lunch with her in the cafeteria and I was amazed by the dazzling profusion of nationalities."

"That's how it is in Habitat. I'll invite you to lunch there." Danny looked back, but didn't see Benjamin and Denise. "We've lost them, but it doesn't matter. Benjamin knows the restaurant where we're going for lunch. We'll see them there. Now, please, you talk. I've been uttering a lot of blah blah trying to impress you with my worldliness and sophistication, an impossibility with a Parisian woman."

"You're doing a pretty good job of it," Julie said. "I've learned a lot about Africa and Israel in a short time."

"You're nice to humor me, Julie, but it's your turn now. Please. I want to get to know you."

As they strolled, she told him about her life in Paris; her brother Robert whom she described as her confidante and protector; her Parisian friends; a couple of old boyfriends, (omitting any mention of the married lover); her design studies; and her recent unpleasant job from which she had escaped to Africa, thanks to the generosity of her brother. Then Julie mentioned that Denise and she were returning to Paris in three days time.

He turned pale. "Non, non. Please don't go. Now that we've met, we must have some time to get to know each other. Please cancel your trip and stay here for a longer time.

If Nairobi becomes boring, we can go to Mombassa."

"Where is Mombassa?"

"On the Kenyan coast. Second largest city, with beautiful beaches on the Indian Ocean. You'd love it. Don't worry…separate rooms for us."

Julie gave him a skeptical look. "I'll see you in Nairobi now, and then I'll make a decision about returning to Paris with Denise or staying for a while longer."

"That's reasonable, I guess."

They met Denise and Benjamin at the restaurant and had a sumptuous lunch of heavily seasoned goat, chicken, and vegetables. In the afternoon the Israelis took the women to some out-of-the-way small art galleries. Escorting them back to the hotel, they made plans to have dinner at an exclusive businessmen's club that Benjamin belonged to.

"Well," asked Julie when they were alone. "Was Benjamin a big bore?"

"No. He's nice. But it's a strain for me to speak English continuously. And how was your interaction with the muscular Danny?"

"Well, he's very intelligent, studied at the Sorbonne…He's been all over East Africa and has had an interesting life in Israel, and he fought in the wars of '67 and '73."

"Benjamin also mentioned fighting in wars, but didn't go into detail. Oh, by the way, he confessed right away that he is engaged to an Israeli woman. This made me happy, since I have no romantic interest in him. But, dear Julie, can you say the same?"

Julie's face reddened. "You know me so well, Denise. There's something about Danny that I like. Maybe it's his masculine authority. He's so different from Rodolf or any of my previous boy friends. He speaks French like a native, and he knows French literature, art, philosophy…" Hesitating an instant, she added: "When I told him that I was intending to return to Paris in a few days, he got pretty upset. He asked me to cancel my trip and stay on in Kenya for awhile, maybe go to a coastal city called Mombassa with him."

"What? What nerve. What did you tell him?"

"I told him that I would see him in Nairobi now and then make the decision about returning to Paris or staying here a while longer."

"You're crazy. You hardly know him."

"That's true, Denise. But I'll get to know him better in the next two days and then I'll see. What's wrong with that?"

Denise shook her head. "You know the reputation of Israeli men, don't you? They're Jewish, of course, and when they go out with Catholic girls in France or Protestant women in England, I would imagine, they screw the hell out of them, make all sorts of promises, and then return to Israel to hook up with the nice traditional Jewish woman that their mothers have picked out for them."

"I've heard about that. Look, I have two choices—return to Paris with you and probably never see him again, or stay here for awhile and see if there is any magic in this."

"Magic? Oh, Julie, you're completely dreaming now."

"Denise, I'm not going to rush into anything with this guy. I promise you that."

"Promises, promises. Words, words. Okay, Julie, have it your way."

That evening the two men appeared in elegant suits and the women wore fancy dresses to Benjamin's club. Conversation between Denise and Benjamin faltered, and soon Denise was conversing with Danny and Julie in French, and Denise began to appreciate Danny's charm and humor, as he told funny stories about cultural differences between France and Israel. He appeared to be the opposite of egocentric, asking Denise and Julie a number of questions about their lives in Paris, particularly their families and their careers. Since Benjamin was busy with work the next day, Danny invited the two women on a drive to the Nairobi National Park to see the mélange of wildlife--lions, leopards, cheetahs, hyenas, giraffes, exotic bird species.

"This is amazing," said Denise, gazing at two large giraffes with an adorable baby behind a barrier.

"I can understand your enthusiasm," said Danny, "but, trust me, this is nothing. The real safari parks, much bigger and with a multitude of animals, are several hours' drive from Nairobi. The best ones are in northern Tanzania, quite a drive, but well worth the effort."

Julie walked to the aviary with her camera and began to take photos of brightly colored birds.

Denise suddenly turned to Danny: "I hear that you asked Julie to stay on in Kenya."

He saw the angry expression on her face. "Yes, that's true."

"Isn't that ridiculous?" Denise said loudly. "You meet someone for the first time, and you immediately pressure her."

"Ah, I understand; you're protecting your friend. That's a good thing."

"I'm not sure that I would use the word 'protect', but it makes me angry to see a man come crashing in and after a day, actually after a few hours in fact, he proposes that she stay in Nairobi with him. It's ridiculous and I'm going to advise her against it."

"Denise, I understand what you are saying. I wish that Julie lived in Nairobi, but she lives in Paris, and I would like her to stay here for a while so that we can get to know each other better. What's wrong with that?"

"You make it sound so sweet and normal. But I think that it's nuts, and I'm going to advise her to return to Paris with me on Wednesday."

Danny sighed. "Denise, I don't want to be your enemy. I want to be your friend. I like Julie and I think that we should get to know each other. I'm not looking for a momentary fling. So I'm promising you that if Julie doesn't stay here now, I'm going to ask her if I can come to see her in Paris in a few months. And, of course, I would like to see you as well when I come to Paris."

"We'll see about that," said Denise. "At least you and I know where we stand on this. Enough...Julie is coming."

That evening Denise strongly advised Julie to return to Paris with her.

"I'm thinking, Denise. I haven't made a decision yet. I'll see him tomorrow and decide."

"Then why don't you see him on your own tomorrow?"

"No, Denise. It's the last day of our trip to Africa. You come with us, and I'll have a drink with him before dinner and tell him my decision."

The next day Danny took Denise and Julie to an art exhibit of the countries of the East African Community, featuring ebony carvings from Kenya, brass and copper figures from Uganda, and wildly expressive paintings from Tanzania. When Denise expressed interest in a colorful painting of African women, Danny negotiated with the artist who lowered his price by two-thirds.

Over lunch he explained the differences between the three countries in terms of history, politics, culture, food, and art. "Although they were all British colonies, their post-colonial history has been remarkably different," he said. "Uganda is known for having the intellectuals, Tanzanian the politicians, mainly socialists, and Kenya the businessmen. A hodgepodge of distinct cultures, and it's not at all certain that the Community will survive. Particularly with that crazy man Idi Amin creating havoc in Uganda."

Returning to the hotel, Denise walked to her room, while Julie and Danny went to the hotel bar and ordered glasses of wine.

"Well, Julie. You're scheduled to leave for Paris tomorrow, but I hope that you'll stay here longer. However, it's your decision." He nervously looked into her eyes. "So what is it?"

"Can you guess?" she asked, smiling at his nervousness.

"Well, if I interpret your smile correctly, you're staying here in Kenya."

"Smart man. You're right. I'm willing to stay here a little while longer."

"Oh, that's great," he said, hugging her tightly.

"Denise won't be too happy about this. Let me go upstairs and tell her."

"Fine. I'll be back at 8 p.m. to take you both to a special place."

Danny took them to a nightclub featuring delicious local food, loud African music, noisy drums, and sexy dancing. The dance floor was packed, but Danny managed to find space to dance with both Julie and Denise who emulated the movement of the African women gyrating next to them. Two Kenyan women clapped and began to dance with them.

At one point Denise signaled to Danny to follow her outside.

"Julie told me that she is staying," she said coldly.

"Yes," he said. "But you needn't worry. I will take good care of her."

"Listen closely. If you mess her up, I promise you that I'll come after you, and you will pay a big price."

"Wow," said Danny. "You're a great friend, protector, bodyguard even. Look, I'm entranced with Julie and want to see where this will go. I think that she may feel the same."

"Maybe so, but I'm telling you that you had better heed my warning."

He took Denise's hands. "I promise you, Denise, that I am operating from the best intentions regarding Julie. You understand?"

Denise nodded reluctantly, and they returned to the dance floor.

The next day Danny and Julie drove Denise to the Nairobi airport. As Denise moved to the gate, she whispered in Julie's ear: "You be careful, babe, you hear me?"

"I know what I'm doing, Denise," Julie said, kissing her on both cheeks. "Have a safe flight, and thanks for being such a great friend and traveling companion."

Denise waved and moved to passport control.

"Some woman!" said Danny.

"Yes, she's an amazing friend. Did she threaten you to behave with me or else she would murder you?"

"Yes, more or less, but I promised her that my intentions were honorable. Let's move along. I'll drop you at the hotel and go to my office for the afternoon to clear up some things. Then I'll pick you up at the hotel around 7:30 p.m., and we'll go back to Benjamin's club for some fine dining. He's busy, but he made a reservation for us at 8 p.m."

"Oh, that means that I have to dress up again."

"Not really. I'm going to wear a safari suit."

"Then I'll wear the African dress that I bought in Mali."

They spent the weekend in Nairobi strolling through remote African and Indian districts, visiting museums and galleries, and discussing a myriad of subjects, including their tastes in art and literature, their families and friends. Whenever Danny saw Julie, he kissed her on her cheek and gave her a light hug.

"Let's just be good friends right now," he said to her at one moment.

"Perfect," she replied, and they shook hands on it.

Slowly they came to the decision to go to Mombassa on the Indian Ocean.

They dove into gentle waves and lay side by side on the steamy hot sand of an endlessly stretching beach. The town center, as well as parts of the beach, was filled with prostitutes frequented by men from Western Europe and Australia, but Danny and Julie found isolated spots to sunbathe and jump into the ocean. They took long walks, ate delicious mutton and fresh fish in coconut juice in the hotel restaurant, and read French poetry to each other. Danny had arranged separate rooms for them, but in the afternoon of the third day, he suddenly kissed her on the deserted beach and she responded willingly. Their arms encircling each other, they walked slowly to the hotel. He guided her to his room where they made love, passionate love, for several hours. At dinner they looked starry-eyed at each other across the dinner table, and that night they slept together in his room. The following morning he told her that he loved her.

"Mon Dieu," she exclaimed. "After only a week?"

"After a day," he retorted. "But I kept it a secret until now. Didn't you guess?" Playing with her blond hair, he placed some strands in his mouth.

"No," Julie answered, looking at him with a serious expression. "I thought that you simply wanted to find a French woman to seduce with your superb language skills. Since you were a student in Paris, I'm obviously not your first French conquest. You must know that Israeli men have a bad reputation. They come to have sex with French Catholic girls, brag to other Israelis about deflowering them, and then they return home to marry the nice Jewish girl that their mama has chosen for them."

"In my case, that's a bunch of merde. I'm my own man, and I choose my own woman," Danny proclaimed, looking fixedly at her. "Listen, we've just met and we've just made love. We're happy together, but let's take it slowly." To accentuate his point, he moved a few inches away from her on the bed.

"You call this slowly," she said, laughing, and jumped on him.

Making love twice a day, they found time to take long walks on the beach, lie naked on the sand to suntan their bodies, cool off in the ocean, and go out on a fishing boat to catch yellow fin tuna and dorado to be grilled for their dinner.

"Bed or beach?" became Danny's morning mantra-question to her.

"Both," Julie would shout.

After a delightful week in Mombassa, they returned to Nairobi. Danny asked for additional vacation time from his job, and they drove north towards Arusha across the border in Tanzania. En route they saw a herd of giraffes in the high grass prancing by the side of the road. Julie asked Danny to stop the car.

"Magnifique, magnifique," she said, taking dozens of photos of giraffes, as well as of frolicking black and white-faced colubus monkeys and duller-looking wildebeests grazing along the sides of the road.

Arriving in Tanzania, they hiked part of the way up Mount Kilimanjaro and then bumped along an uneven pockmarked, muddy road to Ngoro Ngoro Crater on the way to Serenghetti. Descending the crater, they observed a fascinating array of animals, including lions, hippos, rhinos, monkeys, exotic birds, and ugly vultures flying low on the horizon. Julie took photos of sleeping lions, chattering monkeys, and hippo heads emerging from the muddy water of a small lake.

A group of Masai men and women dressed in colorful costumes ambled by their land rover herding their scrawny cattle to a water hole a few hundred feet away. Fascinated by the costumes and serious demeanor of two teenage boys holding long sticks, Julie pointed her camera at them. The boys hid their faces. It was close to mid-day, and the sun was at its peak, causing Julie to sweat profusely. Reaching into her bag, she pulled out a handkerchief to wipe off her forehead. Then she moved the camera upward again, pointing it directly at the Masai boys who were now waving their arms and gesticulating "no" emphatically. One of them reached down to touch the top of his knife.

Danny grabbed the camera from her hand. "You cannot do that, Julie. He thinks that you are stealing his soul, and if a Masai warrior takes out his knife, he is obliged in his culture to follow through and stab you."

Julie shuddered. "You saved my life, then," she said wanly. "What an idiot I am."

"No, no, ma cherie. How could you know their culture? But I saved both our lives, because I would have put my body in front of yours if the boys had become aggressive with their knives. A lot of French and Israeli blood would have mixed together on the ground right here. Beautiful color red, I'm sure, but it would not have been a pretty sight."

Shuddering, Julie bowed to the boys in apology.

They bowed back, smiling, and gestured that Julie could take some photos of them, if she wished.

She took a few photos and gave the boys some Kenyan shillings. One of the boys ran to the Masai group nearby and returned with a large multi-colored broad woman's necklace that he offered to Julie. She accepted it with a big smile, and the boys ran off.

Danny was charmed. That night he proposed to Julie.

Two weeks later Julie returned to Paris to tell her brother Robert that however trite it might sound, she had met the man of her dreams, an Israeli who had proposed to her in Tanzania on a moonlit night at the rim of Ngoro Ngoro Crater, with lions, rhinos, and hyenas braying loudly below.

Robert Sebastian was skeptical. "You barely know him," he said pointedly. "You meet this guy, he takes you to the beach and to a game park to impress you, and then he proposes after knowing you not even a month. Ridiculous. Absurd. It's too rushed. Maybe you're choosing him on the rebound," referring to her painful experience with the married lover. He looked into Julie's eyes for her reaction.

They were having an afternoon glass of wine at the Café Les Deux Magots on the Boulevard Saint Germain, Robert Sebastian's favorite haunt ever since, ten years earlier, he had seen his intellectual heroes Jean-Paul Sartre and Simone de Beauvoir sitting in a booth opposite him conversing intensively, smoking nonstop.

"Non, non, my dear Robert. Danny is nothing like that cretin who made promises to me and then couldn't follow through. Or like Hassan, the Moroccan law student you saved me from…"

Sebastian winced. "I still feel a little guilty about that." After meeting the Moroccan, Sebastian had a funny feeling, and following him for a couple of days, saw him embrace a pretty Arab woman on two different occasions. Without consulting Julie, Sebastian confronted the Moroccan and not receiving a suitable answer to his questions, had twisted Hassan's arm to the point of breaking it. Hassan later told Julie that the woman was his 'cousin', but he was sufficiently frightened of her brother that he stopped seeing her.

"Maybe I overreacted," Sebastian said, sipping his wine.

"Non, non, Robert. You were protecting me, and you did the right thing. I know that I've not always chosen wisely," Julie continued, "but now I've finally met a man who is perfect for me. Danny is very intellligent, serious, and thoughtful. He acts in a loving way, he says all the right things, and he wants me to be his wife. Look at his photo. Isn't he handsome and strong? Not as athletic and strong as you, of course…" She knew that her brother, a former gymnast and rugby player, prided himself on his athletic ability and strength. Always in excellent shape, Robert sometimes dragged Julie to his gym. Although hating gyms, she went along to please him, with her efforts invariably rewarded by a delicious meal in a Moroccan or Vietnamese restaurant close to the Bibliotheque Nationale where Julie had done research on the history of art and design in her student days.

Sebastion glanced at the photo. "I'm suspicious. It's my nature. And you know that with our father gone and our mother in a 'loony bin', I feel responsible for you. I wish that I could meet your Danny and talk with him."

"Have you seen Maman lately?" Julie asked, her face tightening.

"A month or so ago. I try to go to the hospital every four to six weeks." Their mother was in a private hospital-asylum for 'mentally challenged adults' in the north of France on the Atlantic coast.

"I really should go to see her," Julie said.

"It will depress you, but since you're planning to leave Paris soon, you should." They made plans to go the following Sunday.

"Let's get back to the subject we were discussing," Sebastian said. "To be honest, I wish that I could meet your Danny to probe his intentions further."

"Take this," Julie said, handing him an envelope. "It's from Danny to you." In a letter written in excellent French, Danny spoke about his love for Julie and his fervent wish for her to become his wife. He asked Robert as the man in their family to give his blessing to their marriage and to come to Nairobi to visit them as soon as he could.

"Well, he can at least write decently in French," Sebastion said half-heartedly.

"I can list some of his other good qualities, if you like, dear brother," Julie said, smiling.

"Another day. Now let's go see the Godard film at the Theatre Odeon that we're both dying to see."

The next day she went to dinner with Denise. Julie had already written to her from Nairobi announcing Danny's marriage proposal and her acceptance.

"I have to tell you, dear Julie, that I was stunned when I received your letter. In Nairobi your Israeli did tell me that his intentions towards you were 'honorable', as he put it. But I wouldn't have guessed this in a hundred years." Smiling, she told Julie that she had threatened Danny in Nairobi. "Maybe he felt that he had to propose or else I would cut off his balls."

"He does have them, I assure you," Julie said, both women laughing loudly. "And since he and I both need them, please don't cut them off."

"Okay. You have my word on that. But tell me, Julie, you haven't known him for very long. Do you really love him?"

"Yes. Completely. But don't worry. We are going to live together for awhile and definitely not get married until we're absolutely sure about it. At least a year, and maybe two or three."

"But what will you do in Nairobi?"

"Learn English, I guess, no matter how painful it may be. And hopefully do some design work. I've spoken to a couple of Anglo-African design firms in Nairobi, and one of them is willing to give me a tryout."

"Okay, that's good."

"Now, Denise, tell me about your life. Did that Englishman Richard come to see you yet? "

"No, not yet. But he has written and called me, and he promises to come to Paris in the next three weeks, if not sooner."

"Anybody on the horizon here?"

"No, not really. Men flirt with me a lot, but no one really attracts me right now. And I'm fine with that. I've taken on extra modeling work, and I'm scheduled to appear in fashion weeks in Rome and Berlin in the near future. So my modeling career is going really well."

"Good. I'm going to see my mother this weekend. My brother is driving us, and I'll ask him again about the three of us getting together."

"You can, of course, Julie, but I think that your brother is a lost cause for me."

On Sunday Robert drove Julie to visit their mother. He had telephoned a day in advance to inform her that they would be coming. Her response was phlegmatic, but the nurse on duty promised to list the visit in the guest book and make sure that their mother was properly dressed.

The Center for Challenged Adults (Le Centre pour les Adultes Semi-Fonctionnels), a large sprawling building poised above the Atlantic Ocean in Brittany, had a deceptively cheerful look. Green lawns with walkways, benches, and seats overlooking the ocean gave the appearance of a well-designed country club. It was an expensive facility, one of the best in France, well beyond the means of most people. Businessmen and movie stars placed their dysfunctional relatives here for treatment and in many cases, for long periods of safekeeping. The care by the doctors and staff was considered excellent, but the national insurance was in no way adequate to support a patient at the Center, and when Robert Sebastian had transferred his mother from an inferior facility thirty miles from Paris to the Center in northern France, he was obliged to pay a large sum each month.

"Hello, Maman," Julie said softly to their mother as they entered her room. "How are you?" She embraced her tightly. Her mother had been an elegant woman many years ago, but now she could have passed for an impoverished chambermaid. She wore a blue and white pastel dress of ancient vintage and had a faint trace of make-up on a tired-looking face. Whenever Julie saw her mother, she shuddered inwardly at the contrast between the memory of her attractive past and the tawdry present. Her mother wasn't young, but in her right mind, Julie believed, she would have taken better care of herself. In her depressed state she seemed unaware of her appearance and the effect it had on her children.

Her mother grunted an inaudible reply. She held tightly to a rosary on a gold chain. Her expression was impassive, but her eyes shone brightly at the sight of her daughter.

Julie sat down on the bed, taking her mother's hands in her own. After some desultory conversation, Julie said quietly: "Maman, I have something important to tell you. I am leaving Paris in a few days to go to live in Nairobi, Kenya in Africa."

"Africa?" her mother stammered. "Why Africa?"

"I was traveling in Africa for several weeks. Do you remember my telling you that before I left about two and a half months ago?"

"Not really," said her mother, looking confused.

"Well, I took a fantastic trip to Africa, thanks to the generosity of your son Robert here. And then, in Nairobi, I met a wonderful man and I've fallen in love with him. He has asked me to marry him, and I accepted. We will get married some time in the future, but for now I am going to live with him in Nairobi." Hesitating, Julie then said: "He's an Israeli, Maman."

"An Israeli," she muttered. "An Israeli? Does that mean that he is Jewish?"

"Yes, Maman."

"There are so many Catholic boys in France. Can't you find a nice Catholic boy?" She went to the sink and spit in it. "An Israeli, a Jew," she said, shaking her head.

"Maman, I have had many boyfriends, but this is the first time that I feel really in love. I don't care if he is Israeli or Jewish or even if he were a black African. I love him for himself."

Robert took his mother's hand and said: "Maman, don't be prejudiced. Our father was Jewish. Don't you remember? You married a Jewish man. I know that it didn't work out, but you had many good years with him."

"I don't remember," their mother said.

"Well, you did. Julie and I remember. So Julie is entitled to make the choice that suits her best, as you did long ago."

Julie smiled gratefully at her brother.

"I suppose so…but still, another Jew. I don't know.'

"Maman," Julie intervened. "How are you doing here? Robert has told me that there are many activities and that you are well taken care of."

"I suppose so…where else would I go? I have a few friends here. We play cards together. We sit at the dinner table together at night.'

"That's very nice, Maman. I would be happy to meet some of your friends."

"Oh, they don't talk very much. Maybe the next time you come."

After an hour Robert suddenly stood up, signaling to Julie that it was time to leave.

"Bye, Maman. I will see you next time I come to Paris. Robert gives me good reports about you, and so I always know how you are doing."

"Merci, my little daughter." And then she said quietly, shaking her head: "Mon Dieu, a Jew?"

After embracing their mother, Robert and Julie left the room.

"Frustrating woman," Robert said as they got in the car. "There's a decent bistro a few kilometers from here. I could use a stiff drink and some food right now."

"Okay, Robert. I'll have only one glass of wine so that I can drive in case you get tipsy."

He smiled. "Me tipsy? Very doubtful. But maybe the fiancée of the Jew should try purposely to get tipsy."

During the next ten days, Robert and Julie met several times for meals, as well as for movies, and they invariably discussed the subject of Danny and Julie's desire to marry him.

"Julie, you have worn me down," he said resignedly in their last meeting on the day before her departure from Paris. "I surrender. I accept your assertions of love for this Israeli character. You have my consent, but do me one favor, please. Don't rush into marriage. Spend more time with him before taking the vow. Okay"

"Yes, Robert, yes," Julie said, her face beaming now that her brother had given his sanction to her marriage. "I won't rush into marriage, I promise. You can be at ease."

She stared into her brother's eyes. "Now what about you? I've tried to introduce you to Denise, but you always have some excuse. Are you still seeing that beautiful blond graduate student?"

"No, not really. She got fed up with my constant traveling." Sebastian's expression tightened noticeably.

"Your business is going well, then. The international investing?"

"I'm not doing the investing, Julie. I'm only 'advising'. I'm just a financial consultant to some big international companies. As a middle man, I can avoid the boring corporate responsibilities and yet roam around the world, hobnobbing with big executives and earning very well."

"It sounds great, Robert. However, you are moving up in your 30's, and maybe you should find someone to settle down with while you still have your good looks. They won't last forever, you know."

Robert smiled at his sister's concern. "Don't you worry, little sister. If I start getting ugly, I'll get some plastic surgery." Julie laughed and slapped his arm. "And, like you, when I meet the right person, I'll know it. Until then, I shall clip the coupons—that is, work in distant lands, enrich my bank account, and meet exotic women."

"Okay, big brother. One day, though, just as you are seeing me madly in love, I want to see you experience the same thing."

"Que sera, sera, my romantic sister…You find me a beautiful African woman or a gorgeous Israeli lady. See if your Danny has some good-looking cousins. But please check them out first before inflicting any ugly duckling on me. D'accord?"

"Oui, Robert. I think that you can do perfectly fine on your own, but my eyes will be open. One never knows. Look at how I met Danny in Nairobi…Now, mon cher, I must go to my apartment to pack, greet the new tenant, and get to sleep early. You know that I am going to the airport early tomorrow morning."

"Can't I drive you?" He had asked her three times already.

"Non. non. Good-byes at airports are too sad. We'll say good-bye now, and I'll see you soon in Nairobi." A final hug, and she was gone.

Robert Sebastian sat in the corner booth of the bistro where they had just had lunch. He ordered another glass of wine and lit a cigarette. He thought about his sister, his lovely, dreamy sister. He was happy for her, but given his cynical nature, he reserved judgment about her chances for success in marrying a man like Danny from an entirely different culture. Sebastian had had some experiences with Israeli men, and he had found them intelligent and affable, but also tough-minded and aggressive. Of course, they had to be self-protective, given their turbulent history and encirclement by enemies. He thought about the affluent Israeli businessman based in Zurich who had given him a couple of jobs in the last few years. After the first venture, he had tried to cheat Sebastian out of part of his fee. The Frenchman took out a small revolver and placed it on the table separating the two men. Seeing the look in Sebastian's eyes, the Israeli immediately backed down and never repeated such a folly.

What would Julie think if she knew her brother's real profession? Sebastian ruminated, sipping his wine. He had hinted at it once, but she had laughed and had accused him of making a poor joke. So it remained his secret, and it was clearly better this way. Keep Julie innocent and not let her worry about him.

His profession was simple… hit man, contract killer. The words sounded fierce, but it was professional work like any other occupation with its advantages and its constraints. Sebastian saw himself as a conventional man with an unconventional profession. For this he had the French army to thank or to blame. After going to university in the U.S., he had returned to France, and given the policy of compulsory military conscription, he had enlisted. Seeing his expertise in marksmanship (his father had frequently taken him hunting in both France and the United States), as well as his prowess in the difficult physical exercises (thanks to his decathlon training in the U.S. and rugby playing in France), his superiors put Sebastian into an elite army unit that was created to do some nasty things to certain elements of the native population in Algeria.

In the late 1950s and early 60s, the brutal Algerian war was in its bloodiest phase. Having "lost" their colony of Vietnam in 1954, the French were determined to hold on to Algeria, a colony since 1830, and technically a department of France. However, Algerian "freedom fighters" seeking independence carried out assassinations and planted bombs in French cafes in Algiers, eliciting a correspondingly brutal reaction by the French military forces. (When Sebastian saw the film, "The Battle of Algiers," in the late 60s, he could identify with the torture and brutality inflicted on the native population by French soldiers, and he left the theatre with tears in his eyes.)

With France divided between those who wanted to hold on to Algeria at any cost and those who favored Algerian independence, the country summoned WW II hero Charles deGaulle to power in 1958. DeGaulle immediately established the powerful presidential regime of the Fifth Republic. When it became evident a year or so later that deGaulle was planning to permit Algeria to become independent, a right-wing reaction arose in the form of the Organisation de l'armee secrete (OAS) dedicated to keeping Algeria permanently French. Robert Sebastian became an integral part of an elite unit set up to combat the OAS , given the assignment of infiltrating the clandestine organization and eliminating some key OAS figures. This went on for ten months until an OAS message casting doubt on Sebastian's 'colonial loyalties' was intercepted, and he was ordered by his superiors to 'disappear'. He was given an honorable discharge, along with two hundred thousand francs.

Considering it too dangerous to stay in France while the Algerian issue was burning, Sebastian went to Brazzaville in the French Congo, where he hung out in cafes frequented by ex-military types and soldiers of fortune. One day a buddy mentioned that Katanga Province of the newly liberated Belgian Congo was hiring mercenaries to resist the incorporation of the mineral-rich province into the new nation of the Congo. He joined up, and with other soldiers-for-hire of different nationalities, committed some violent acts on behalf of Katangan independence against the weak central government. However, international pressure caused Katanga to capitulate and become part of the Congo (later Zaire) in 1964. And with the Algerian War finally resolved in 1963, Algeria became an independent nation, and the OAS. leaders were either in jail or in hiding in Spain and South America.

Sebastian returned to France. He loafed around for a few months, seeing Julie frequently, hanging out in casinos and bars, uncertain what to do with his life. Since he had always been strong in languages and in economics, his college major at the University of Virginia, he decided to enhance his skills in each area in order to acquire international business skills. Already fluent in French and English (thanks to his French mother and American father), he enrolled at the Ecole des Langues to perfect his knowledge of Italian and Spanish, two languages that he knew marginally, as well as attain a conversational knowledge of German, completely new for him. Thinking that it could be useful, he took courses in simultaneous interpretation, French and English, and even got a few small assignments as a fill-in at UNESCO. Simultaneously he audited some courses in economics at the Sorbonne and read extensively in libraries in order to master the basic elements of international trade and finance.

In his off hours away from courses and libraries, he began to nose around on the fringes of the fast-paced gambling world of Paris. Becoming a regular at the bar in a large, elegant casino on the Ile St. Louis, "Les Enfants du Paradis," he met the owners, the Melachi brothers, Armand and Bertrand, who took a liking to him. One day Armand quietly mentioned that one of his regulars in the casino, an important businessman, had asked if Armand knew anyone who could "eliminate" his business partner who was threatening legal action against the businessman for allegedly skimming funds to pay for his gambling debts. Sebastian was interested. Having witnessed the unsuccessful attempts on the life of President Charles de Gaulle in the early 1960s by both political and hired assassins (encapsulated in the novel, "The Day of the Jackal," by Frederick Forsyth, which Sebastian devoured in a day and a half), he imagined the life of a contract killer as something both adventurous and lucrative. An agreement was made for 300,000 francs, the Melachis receiving 20% as their commission. Sebastian followed the partner, observing his habits, and when he was alone in his apartment, Sebastian surreptitiously entered, put a gun to the man's head and poured poison down his throat, leaving a 'suicide note'.

After this "success", the Melachis found more clients for Sebastian-- a jealous wife furious with her philandering husband; an assignment in Senegal for a Senegalese army colonel who found his way to the top of the general staff blocked by an aggressive competitor; a pair of brothers whose father had told them that they were good-for-nothings and that he was going to leave his fortune to his third wife. In most cases Sebastian arranged 'accidents' or suicides. The Senegalese military competitor was dispatched with a bullet from his own revolver, with a suicide note appearing by the body. The philandering husband "drowned" in the Seine. Sebastian branched out beyond the Melachi brothers, obtaining assignments from a certain class of wealthy underworld figures in France and in other countries. He worked mainly in Europe and Africa, although he ventured as far as Tokyo for one assignment, the elimination of a rival yakusa gangster. He began to be selective in his acceptance of jobs, refusing those that did not provide lucrative paydays. He hadn't worked in four months, but the Melachi brothers had left him a message to come to their casino in the Ile St. Louis that evening to discuss a prospective assignment.

Julie returned to Nairobi to be with Danny. He continued to work at Habitat, and as often as he could, he invited Julie to lunch in the staff cafeteria to meet his colleagues and friends. However, her limited English made it difficult for her to communicate, and at interviews with a couple of design firms, she was asked to return when her English improved. Danny found an Englishwoman from Liverpool in the interpretation section at Habitat to speak with Julie in English twice a week.

However, she spent most of her time alone wandering around the local art galleries and reading French novels. Occasionally she went to a lecture at the French Embassy, but most of the time she was bored and constantly worried about Danny's safety. Outside of his job, Danny was carrying on a profitable trade in precious metals with Benjamin and another Israeli friend. The ruling Kenyatta family, however, had a monopoly in precious metal exploration and commerce, and they reacted violently against competition. One weekend night Danny was badly beaten in a game park near Lake Victoria and told to leave Kenya. Julie pleaded with him, and he agreed only after it was certain that she was pregnant.

Danny resigned from his job and took Julie to his parents' home in Jerusalem. She did her best to charm them by smiling a lot and helping with the household chores, but there was no common language for them to speak, and they were skeptical about the intrusion of this unknown French shiksa into their lives. They began to mellow once Danny told them how much he loved Julie, mentioning that she would soon begin taking lessons from their rabbi to convert to Judaism. In the meantime, since Julie was pregnant, they were eager to get married, but Danny had to explain to her that their marriage could not take place in Israel.

"What are you saying? Julie asked incredulously. "We can't get married in Israel? That's crazy. Why not?" They were sitting in the coffee shop of the King David Hotel in downtown Jerusalem sipping cappucino and sharing a chocolate bun.

"Because, my dear Julie, the Orthodox control all the marriages in Israel. I'm not Orthodox, you're not Jewish yet, and therefore we have to have a secular marriage. The Orthodox, with their monopoly, do not permit civil or secular marriages to take place in Israel."

Julie shook her head in exasperation. "Danny, it will take me several months to learn everything that is required for me to become Jewish. Do you want us to have our marriage and our baby delivery on the same day?"

Danny smiled and touched her arm gently. "Don't worry, ma cherie. There is a good solution. Do you think we are the only couple in Israel that wants to or needs to have a secular or civil marriage? There are thousands every year, and with our good Yiddishe kopf—that means Jewish brainpower--couples fly to Cyprus to combine their marriage with a nice vacation."

"Cyprus?" Julie mused for a moment. "Why not in Paris? Then my brother could attend the wedding and give me away."

"That's another option for us. I thought of it. But if we have our wedding in Paris, my parents, my sister, my cousins, and my close friends Yoram and Miriam and Sammy and Rebecca would not be able to come because of the cost. They would come to Cyprus, however. There are great deals on flights, hotels, catering services, and secular-civil marriage authorities in Cyprus. The Cypriots and the Israelis have created a virtual shuttle service between Tel Aviv and Larnaca Airport, and marriage in Cyprus is like a cottage industry beneficial to both countries. We can have a fabulous wedding on the beach there."

Julie rolled her eyes and looked up at the ceiling. "I don't know. It seems weird, but if the Orthodox control all the marriages here, then…."

Danny interrupted her. "I hear you sighing…I know that you're surprised by this development and not happy about it. But here's a thought for you, sweetheart. Ask your brother to come to Cyprus for our wedding. You've talked endlessly about what a great guy, what a superb human being, Robert is, and I would finally be able to meet this French Superman to see if the reality matches your description, and you'd be a very happy bride with your brother at your side giving you away at our marriage."

Julie thought for a few minutes, wondering if she should press the idea of their getting married in Paris so that not only Robert, but Denise and some other close friends could attend. But the main person was Robert. He had to be there.

"Okay, tell me how soon the wedding could take place. Then I'll call my brother. But I'm telling you now that if he can't come to Cyprus, I'm going to revive the notion of our getting married in Paris. You understand that?" Julie gave him a stern look.

"Of course, darling. Call your brother and tell him that you and I could arrange our marriage in Cyprus between May 1 and 14. The ceremony and festivities will take 3-4 days. Oh, yes…tell Robert that I am very excited to meet him finally and to have him give you away at our wedding."

Chapter 2

Cyprus, May 9, 1976

The Air France plane taxied to the gate at Larnaca International Airport in the Greek section of Cyprus. Inside the terminal, anxiously awaiting the arrival of her brother and five of her friends from Paris, Julie studied the passengers lined up at passport control.

"That's him," Julie shouted. "Robert, Robert." She ran into his arms as he came into the terminal.

"This is Robert, Danny," she said, tightly holding her brother's arm.

"Enfin. Enfin," Danny said, smiling. "Finally we meet, Robert." They shook hands firmly.

Studying Danny's face and gestures, Robert said: "I'm very happy to meet you, Danny. Julie has said some very nice things about you."

"Well, Robert," said Danny. "Nothing that she said about me could have approached what Julie has told me about you. She has painted you as a mythical creature of brains and brawn, someone with the strength of a Sampson and the intelligence of a Camus or Sartre. I have been very intimidated by the thought of meeting you."

"Julie exaggerates, as usual," Sebastian said, laughing. He looked as his sister ran to greet her Parisian friends now coming into the terminal.

"And, oh yes," Danny added, looking into Sebastian's eyes. "Julie also told me never to get on your wrong side. She didn't tell me why."

Robert gazed blankly at him. "As long as we both love Julie, we'll be the best of friends."

"A wonderful way to express it," Danny answered. "We'll never have a problem then, that's for sure." He shook Sebastian's hand again.

"Julie, Julie," some voices shouted. Three of her close friends from Paris, including Denise, had just appeared. As Julie embraced Denise, the latter whispered in her ear: "Your brother, he's quite a hunk. He must be taken."

"Non, non," Julie whispered back. "I told you that he was special. I don't think that he's seeing anyone right now. Go for it."

Danny had rented a mini bus to drive everyone from the airport to the hotel where they were all staying. His parents, sister, aunt and uncle, and Israeli friends had arrived the previous day.

That evening Julie and Danny had arranged a pre-wedding dinner for the group of twenty-seven wedding participants and guests, all coming from Israel and France.

The music blared. An accordion, violin, piano, and drum were playing a variety of musical pieces, and the guests started dancing slowly and then moving on to fast rock and suddenly the hora, as couples, their hands clapping above their heads, were prancing in a semi-circle around four tables filled with copious amounts of lamb, chicken, cous cous, vegetables, champagne and wine bottles. At the head of the line were Danny and Julie, followed by Danny's parents and then Robert Sebastian and Denise, who had asked Julie to seat her next to him.

"Are you happy that your sister is finally getting married?" Denise asked Robert, looking directly in his eyes, when they were seated at their table sipping champagne.

"Well, I would say that I am happy about whom she's marrying," he replied softly.

"I understand very well," Denise said. "She's gone out with some less than desirable types. I think that we both know that."

Robert winced. "You have obviously met or heard about a few of them…Danny seems to be another story…a solid guy who is crazy about her, and, as far as I can see, vice versa."

"Yes, I met Danny in Nairobi and was initially suspicious of his intentions, but I liked him a lot even as I threatened him with mayhem if he messed Julie up," Denise said, smiling at the memory. "Charming, sweet, and yet very masculine. Quite ethnic, of course, but if Julie is willing to live in Israel and even become Jewish, it should be a good life for her."

Looking at Denise, Sebastian said: "You probably don't know this, but our father was Jewish. Non-practicing, but American Jewish in origin. So she has some knowledge of Judaism, although we were raised Catholic, the religion of our mother. If Julie wants to convert, so be it. The main thing is that her marriage brings her stability and, I hope, a couple of kids."

"Are you the uncle type, Robert?" Denise asked softly. Her brown hair flowed onto her shoulders, and with her vibrant green eyes and angular face, Sebastian found her very attractive, and the fact that she was Julie's closest friend added to her allure. "I'm being inquisitive, I know. But I've just met you and so I don't know much about you other than what Julie has said. Of course she always praises you to the skies." Denise paused for a moment. "I will tell you one thing, though. My brother, Richard, has been married for about a decade, and he has a six-year old son and three-year old daughter. I love going to visit them and playing the role of adoring aunt…Of course, they live close by, in Neuilly."

"You're lucky, Denise. It looks as if I'll have to make the trek to Israel to see Julie and her eventual children. But I'll do it…a couple of times a year, I figure…And get them to come to Paris as well."

They reached over with their plates to get some food, and Sebastian poured red wine into their glasses. Extricating herself from a lively conversation with her friends at a nearby table, Julie made her way over to them. Draping her left arm around her brother's shoulder and her right around Denise, she smiled at them. "So how are my favorite brother and my best friend from the Left Bank doing?"

"Excellent. Excellent," said Robert. "Denise and I were just talking about Danny and you and your new life in Israel."

"We're so happy for you," said Denise, hugging her.

Julie embraced them both and then moved towards Danny, who was beckoning her to join him and his Israeli friends.

"Julie and you are extremely close, n'est-ce pas? Denise said, turning to look at Robert.

"Yes," he said. "It's no secret. When our parents divorced, our father moved back to America and our mother stayed in France, but she became pretty unstable. I visited my father frequently in New York and went to university in America, but Julie never got over the fact that he had caused so much pain to our mother, and she rarely went to see him. So with my sister, I had--rather, chose--to fill the roles of big brother, surrogate parent, advisor, and protector. And, believe me, it wasn't always easy...I lost a lot of sleep worrying about her, but now I can sleep well knowing that Danny and she will be together in Israel."

Denise looked at Robert wistfully, tears forming in her eyes. "Julie is very lucky. My older brother is 'correct', even affectionate occasionally, but nothing like you. I wish that I had a big brother like Julie has."

"You're very sweet, Denise," he said, reaching over and touching her arm. She put her hand on his.

"Ladies and Gentlemen, Mesdames et Monsieurs," a voice suddenly boomed, first in Hebrew and then in French. It was Danny standing with a wine glass in his hand. "We have eaten a Cypriot feast, drunk French champagne and wine, and danced the Israeli hora. Very multi-cultural, I would say...Let me remind you that this is my last night as a single man, a man going happily to his fate tomorrow. But I remain a bachelor tonight, and so I will take the liberty of proclaiming this event as my bachelor party and as Julie's as well. So let us tell stories, tell jokes, in French and in Hebrew. I will interpret. Who will begin?" He looked around the room. Everyone was smiling, but no one spoke.

"Okay, then. I, a modest man, will have to begin." One of his Israeli friends groaned loudly at the word 'modest'.

"Yes, modest, you Israeli doubters. I'll tell you all a joke, and then anyone, everyone, can follow me. If you don't, you will hear my clumsy voice and bad jokes for the next two hours. So you had better chime in quickly...Let me begin by telling you the story of the oversexed Bedouin warrior and his lusty camel..."

Someone shouted: "No, not that one," but Danny continued, unstoppable.

Robert Sebastian whispered in Denise's ear, and when Danny's head was turned, they skipped away and headed for the path leading to the beach at the back of the hotel.

Chapter 3

The Following Day

"Do you, Danny Ben-David, take this woman to be your lawful wedded wife in sickness and in health, in happiness and in sorrow, until death do you part?" The civil officer, speaking in Hebrew and in English, looked into Danny's eyes.

"I do." Danny stood facing Julie, a solemn expression on his face.

"And do you, Julie…."

"I do," said Julie, smiling.

"The rings, please."

Robert Sebastian held out an open ring box for Danny to take a gold ring and place it on Julie's finger. Danny's friend Yoram did the same for Julie to place on Danny's finger.

A month earlier Robert Sebastian had offered to have the rings made in Paris. Julie had sent him their ring sizes, and he had the rings made by an expensive jeweler on the Rue de Rivoli and brought them to Cyprus. They were part of his wedding present. He had told Julie that he wanted to pay for the pre-nuptial dinner, the ceremony, and the flowers. On the morning of the ceremony, he had taken Julie for a walk on the beach and handed her a large envelope containing a stack of hundred dollar bills.

"It's too much, Robert," she said after counting out thirty-five thousand dollars.

"No, it's not, ma petite soeur. Once in a lifetime, for your wedding. I brought dollars instead of francs, since they are more acceptable in Cyprus, I was told. Use whatever is left when you return to Israel."

"Oh, Robert. You've always taken such good care of me. And I do so little for you, except give you worries," Julie said, tears forming in her eyes.

Robert laughed loudly. "No, no. Stop crying. What you are saying is 'bullshit', using an English word. He took a flat rock and skimmed it several times in the ocean. "You do plenty for me, Julie. You're my sister, my only real family…It goes both ways. I'm so lucky to have you. But if I think about it, I will tell you what you can do for me. Have a baby boy, a big strapping boy so that I can teach him to play rugby. That's not asking too much, is it?" He put his hand on her shoulder playfully.

"But what if I have a girl?" she asked dolefully.

"I'm joking, Julie. A girl would be just fine. I will teach her more gentle rugby or maybe gymnastics and tennis. And you can try again for a boy or another girl. I will wait patiently for whoever appears."

"Oh, Robert…"She hugged him tightly.

"One more thing," he said. "So that you don't forget Paris, here is my personal wedding present to you." He handed her an elegant box with a red ribbon around it.

Opening it, she saw a gleaming silver bracelet with a representation of the Sacre Coeur Cathedral on the front and Julie's name on the back. "I had this specially made," he said. "You remember that our mother used to take us to the Sacre Coeur when we were young, sometimes on Sunday, but always on Easter and Christmas Midnight Mass for many years. It's a link between our mother, you, and me. A symbol of the time when she was happy and doing well, and when we three were together and happy. I hope that you like the link between the cathedral image and your name."

"It's beautiful, Robert. I'll never take it off. I will think of Maman, of course, but mainly it will remind me of you." She put the bracelet on her left wrist.

Robert smiled at her. "You had better take it off some of the time. Especially in bed. Otherwise Danny will become jealous…"

"Okay, okay, maybe when we're making love or trying for another baby, I'll remove it in advance."

"Perfect," Sebastian said. "I accept that condition."

They had been walking for almost an hour and had now meandered back to the beach in front of the hotel. "I'd better go to put on my wedding dress," Julie said. "Denise and Simone are helping me. Denise seems to like you, my dear. None of my business, of course, but what do you think of her?"

"You nosy creature, you," Robert said in a jocular tone, as he lit a cigarette. "Okay. Just to satisfy your inquisitive, dirty mind, Denise and I have agreed to stay in Cyprus for a few days after the wedding to explore the antiquities and beaches on the island…All very cultural and innocent, of course."

"Mon oeil," Julie said, laughing. "I'm delighted. Who knows, maybe we'll all come back to Cyprus next year to witness Denise and you getting…"

Sebastian put his hand gently over Julie's mouth. "Doucement, doucement, ma petite soeur. ('Easy, easy, my little sister.') I like Denise, but I'm not thunderstruck like you and Danny. One step at a time, please. It's so funny how the tables are turning. I used to be your advisor about the opposite sex, and now that you're becoming a married woman, you're advising me on that subject. Pretty funny, isn't it?"

"Yes, it's funny, big brother. With my newfound marital maturity, you can come to me any time for advice about women…but please, give Denise a chance. She's not only beautiful, but also educated and smart. She's one of the best."

"Okay, little sister. I'll keep an open mind…Now let's get you ready for a wedding."

After the wedding ceremony, the group went to a large restaurant featuring Greek and Lebanese delicacies. Again there was drinking, feasting, music, and dancing.

"Ladies and gentlemen," a voice suddenly shouted in Hebrew-accented English. It was Yoram, Danny's closest friend. "Danny, please interpret into French, for I will now speak in Hebrew. As the best man, I have the right to praise and to ridicule my newly married friend. And I shall do both, if you will permit me."

He stopped after each sentence to allow Danny to interpret into French. Before Danny began, he whispered in Yoram's ear: "You're asking the Jew to put his head into the lion's mouth. Isn't that for the Christians?"

Laughing wildly, Yoram shouted: "Okay, Danny, wise guy. Now interpret exactly what you just said to me."

And Danny had no choice but to do so…first in Hebrew and then in French. Everyone laughed. Then Yoram began to describe some childhood experiences that he had shared with Danny, mentioning a couple of embarrassing moments at school and in Danny's relations with girls. "You were a nasty little boy and then a wild and arrogant teenager. I cannot even count the scrapes that I got you out of at school and then a couple of times in the army when we served together." In a more serious vein, he mentioned Danny's military service and the decoration he had received in the Yom Kippur War of October '73. He ended with a flourish by praising Danny's "transcendentally excellent judgment" in approaching Julie at the restaueant in Nairobi where he had undoubtedly used every verbal trick at his command to persuade her to cancel her return trip to Paris. "You have made the best decision of your life, my dear friend. Julie is not only beautiful in looks and in soul; she has intelligence and culture; and she also had the superlative good sense to allow a wild, funny Israeli to charm her. Today is the result of your unusual meeting leading to the start of your magnificent marriage pilgrimage. Your beautiful life together is just beginning, and I wish you both the very best of happiness in your marriage and in your lives." Yoram raised his glass of champagne, but he had to wait until Danny interpreted his Hebrew words and sentences into French. Danny hugged Yoram tightly, as did Julie… and everyone raised their glasses to the newlyweds.

Then Robert Sebastian rose from his seat. "Excuse me, everyone, but as Julie's brother and only family member here, I would also like to say a few words. I'm speaking French now, but if it helps, I can talk in English. Would that work, Julie and Danny?"

"Danny's parents and many others won't understand English," Julie said to Robert in French. "We'll have to make Danny work again in Hebrew."

"It will be my pleasure to do so, Robert," Danny said.

"Okay, thank you, Danny. I'll try to be brief, and I'll certainly be less entertaining than Yoram. But I must tell you, one and all, that Julie is my precious younger sister. We have been together from birth through all the advantages and hardships of life up to this moment. We are the closest of siblings, the best of friends, soul mates, even the guardians of each other. As her older sibling and big brother, I have always felt a special love and responsibility towards Julie, a desire to guide and protect her. Many younger sisters would have rebelled, would have told an overprotective big brother to shut up, stop advising, stop hounding her. But Julie never did that. She always heard me out, listened to what I had to say, even if she felt it was nonsense and off the mark. And, I must say, whatever advice I gave to Julie over the years, she always made up her own mind, always chose her own path."

Sebastian hesitated after each sentence to permit Danny to interpret.

"This applies even to Julie meeting Danny in Nairobi and accepting his marriage proposal," he continued. "I see now what a wonderful guy Danny is, but when Julie first talked to me about him, he was a complete abstraction, an unknown to me. Julie was in love; that was evident. But I was skeptical. I didn't know a thing about this Israeli warrior who had fought in battle and yet was working for the peace-loving United Nations in Nairobi. Who was the human being behind the abstraction? Was Julie making the right choice? I reserved judgment. In fact, I wasn't very positive initially. I tried to get Julie to wait until she knew Danny better. Finally two factors persuaded me. The first was Julie's devotion and love for Danny, and the second was Danny's note to me explaining how much he loved Julie and asking me to consent to their marriage. An old fashioned approach, maybe, but I became convinced of his sincerity, and here we all are today in beautiful Cyprus to witness and participate in their marriage.

"So, Danny, as Julie's older brother, I willingly give her to you. You have already made her very happy, and I know that you will continue to do so. And with respect to Julie, I have no doubt that she will continue to make you the happiest of men."

He raised his glass and said: "To Julie and Danny. May they live and love forever."

After interpreting, Danny and Julie went over to hug Robert. With tears in her eyes, Julie whispered in Sebastian's ear: "That was so beautiful, Robert. You are the best, best brother that anyone could have."

Brother and sister hugged each other, with Danny's arms encircling them both.

Chapter 4

After a five-day honeymoon in southern Italy, Danny and Julie returned to Israel. Danny's cousins in Tel Aviv offered to lodge them until they found a residence of their own. But the cousins were rigidly 'old school', and they communicated their disapproval of Danny's fancy French wife in a thousand small, cruel ways.

Having lived in Kenya for the last five years, Danny was out of touch with and even appalled by the fast pace, cacophony, and materialism of urban Tel Aviv. He applied for a job with the Social Affairs Agency branch in Jerusalem, but was told that there was nothing available right now and that he should reapply in six months. His experience at the U.N. Environment Agency seemed useless in Israel. While their expenses were low and they lived off their wedding presents, particularly Robert Sebastian's money gift, Danny became depressed when he couldn't find any work that was challenging or meaningful to him.

"Maybe we should go back to Nairobi," he said to Julie one day. "I can try to revive my job at Habitat."

"No way," said Julie. "You'll be tempted to go back into the illegal jewelry trade. And I don't want our son or daughter to live in filthy conditions in Africa. So just forget about it."

"Who is ruling the roost, now?" Danny said, wanly smiling. "The Israeli husband cannot even get his own way in Israel, it seems."

"Be patient, Danny. Something will come up. Be positive. I certainly am."

Yet Danny felt unfulfilled, uncertain about the future, a feeling that had never occurred to him before. Some days he wandered on the beach staring at the ocean for several hours without telling Julie. His status as an unemployed husband and soon to be father was puzzling to him. He had always been decisive before, but now he didn't see what he could do in terms of finding satisfying work in Israel.

Then one day Yoram told Danny that his wife and he were going to be pioneers in a new settlement sponsored by the Gush Emunim organization in the northern part of the West Bank. "Why don't Julie and you come with us?"

"Yoram, you know that I'm a Labor Party guy. And that I detest these messianic, fanatical diehards, these right-wing pea brains proclaiming that the entire West Bank is ancient Jewish land. We know that the West Bank was captured in the '67 war, thanks to the stupidity of King Hussein in bringing Jordan into the war. And that's the only reason that we have it. We grabbed it in battle, not from the Bible, even though the fanatics look for evidence in the Torah and the Old Testament." Danny's voice became agitated.

"I know, Danny, I know," Yoram said with a sigh. "However, this new settlement will start off in a secular way. No biblical bullshit or messianic behavior; just practical work to get it established. So you can calm down about that." He put his arms on Danny's shoulders. "Do me a favor, will you? Go to the recruiting office and talk with them. In fact, I'll drive you there."

Two days later Yoram drove Danny to the Gush Emunim recruitment center in downtown Tel Aviv.

"I don't know if Yoram told you," Danny said to a middle-aged bearded man behind the desk, "but I'm a liberal and not at all a believer in your messianic notions. I don't give a hoot about Judea and Samaria. And I despise violent activists like Meir Kahane who want to dispossess the Arabs from their land. So I really don't think I'm a good candidate for you."

The Gush Emunim official sighed, touched his skullcap, and then smiled at Danny. "Yoram told us about your political beliefs. It doesn't matter. We're looking for men and women who are willing to work hard to get Yad Yehudah established. There is no ideology in hard work. There is no violence in cultivating the land and making it spring forth with vegetables and fruit. Yoram gave us a glowing report of your character. Come to Yad Yehudah and try it for a year. If you and your wife are not happy there, if you find it too 'messianic', you can leave, and we'll help you relocate to Jerusalem or Haifa. We will even arrange for a low-interest loan for a house for you."

"I don't know," Danny said. "I came here as a favor to Yoram, and now you are trying to seduce me to be a new settler. It sounds intriguing, but I can't decide on my own. I have to consult my wife."

"Of course, of course. If she would like to meet us, that would be fine as well. But please, you need to give us a decision within two weeks."

When Danny related to Julie what the conditions would be in the new settlement, she became excited. "I like it. It could be a great adventure for us…and for the new baby. Here with your cousins, it's pure shit ("c'est de la merde totale"). We have to get out of here or I'll go crazy. I say that we give it a try. A year is a short time. They said that we could leave after a year and that they would help us to buy a house wherever we like."

Julie went with Danny to meet the Gush Enumin recruiters. They did not hide the fact that it would be hard work, but they insisted that the settlers would be pioneers in creating something communal and imaginative. "It would be like establishing a kibbutz in the wilderness," the recruiters stated. In the end, Danny and Julie agreed to join with twenty others in founding the new settlement.

"It's a Godsend," Julie said to him on the street outside the office. "Au revoir, terrible cousins."

Danny shrugged. "I hope that you're right."

Two months later, in October 1976, they arrived in Yad Yehudah with the other settlers. They lived in arduous conditions, but Julie was content. She got along well with Yoram's wife and with the other women even though she couldn't communicate well in Hebrew. Now visibly pregnant, Julie worked with the others a few hours a day until her seventh month. And Danny enjoyed the hard labor in the fields, much as he had during a number of summers working on kibutzim when he was a teenager and in his early 20's. He even enjoyed the Friday night religious service ('orthodox light', someone called it), leading the group in singing and spirited dancing after the service.

"Julie, Julie," Danny said loudly, interrupting her reverie. "You've been so quiet while I've been munching away. Are you okay?"

"Yes, yes. I was day-dreaming, actually night-dreaming, about how we met in Narobi and our wonderful time together ever since that moment," she said, smiling at him.

"Well, I can relate to that...But I forgot to tell you. I'm going on guard duty later."

"When?" asked Julie, disappointed.

"After dinner. Only for a few hours. I'll wash the dishes, and then let's hug until I have to leave."

Alone, Julie combed her hair and prepared for bed.

She saw in the hand mirror how tanned and healthy she looked. She was flourishing here. Now if only the baby came out healthy...She gently rubbed her protruding stomach.

Then Julie settled in bed with a Francoise Sagan novel, reading by candlelight. When the flame flickered down, she closed her eyes. She did not hear Danny come in at 2 a.m. and lie down on the bed next to her.

Outside, the night was chilly. The sentry shivered and lit a cigarette. Hearing a slight noise a few yards away, he turned to investigate. A clammy hand covered his mouth to prevent him from screaming when the knife penetrated his upper back.

Three men in battle fatigues rushed to the hut. Through the window they saw two sleeping forms illuminated by the moonlight. One of the men signaled, and they moved to the door that creaked as they entered.

Julie Ben-David sat up, startled from a pleasant dream. "Danny," she mumbled, as one of the men rushed over and held her roughly. She tried to scream, but no sound came from her mouth. She was terrified.

As Danny woke, he felt the metal point of a revolver pressed to his temple.

Seeing the woman was pregnant, the third man, the leader, made an immediate decision. He ordered his comrade to bring Julie towards the moonlit window where Danny could see. Calmly lifting his rifle, he shoved the bayonet into Julie's stomach. She gave a piercing cry as she dropped her hands over her stomach to stop the spurting blood. She grabbed at the blade and saw blood seep over her hands. The leader twisted the blade sharply downwards. Then he withdrew it. Blood spattered from her hands and body onto the floor.

A thin film of gauze-like flesh emerged from her lower abdomen. In the last seconds of her life, Julie saw the umbilical cord and knew that her unborn baby was dead. "NON...NON," she cried, as she crumpled to the floor.

Danny yelled and rushed forward, but the leader smashed his face with the rifle butt. Then he ordered his men to flee. Already there were noises outside.

Passing the small table near the door, the leader saw the gleam of a silver bracelet. He stuffed it into his pocket as he ran into the darkness.

Within minutes they were in the hills outside Hebron where they drove for an hour, abandoned the car, and hid overnight. The next morning a truck wended its way into the hills, picked up the three men, and drove them to the border. When they arrived safely inside Jordan, Hassan Barka congratulated his men on a job well done.

Chapter 5

Jerusalem Post

TRAGEDY AT YAD YEHUDAH SETTLEMENT

"At 4 a.m. yesterday, Arab terrorists murdered Moshe Lebowitz and Julie Ben-David at the controversial Gush Emunim settlement of Yad Yehudah in the northern West Bank. Mr. Lebowitz was killed on guard duty and Mrs. Ben-David in her home. Mrs. Ben-David's husband, Daniel, suffered a fractured jaw and remains in a state of shock. Mrs. Ben-David, a French national, was seven months pregnant with their first child. Mr. Lebowitz leaves a wife, Miriam, and one year old son, Yehuda. He was the son-in-law of Eli Berger, famed Irgun leader and confidente of Prime Minister Menachem Begin.

"Prime Minister Begin called the murders "senseless and barbarous." He promised reprisals against Arab terrorists sheltered by other countries. In Beirut a spokesman for the Palestinian Liberation Organization denied responsibility for the incident.

"A Gush Emunim official in Jerusalem stated that the Yad Yehudah experiment would continue. "This foul act will not prevent our return to Judea and Samaria," he said. "We are sending more colonizers to Yad Yehudah, with increased protection for them." The official also noted that Moshe Lebowitz and Julie Ben-David, "martyred at Yad Yehudah," would be buried tomorrow in the settlement. The government will send a delegation to the funeral led by the Minister for Foreign Affairs, Moshe Dayan. The French Ambassador will reportedly attend the funeral of Julie Ben-David."

Two days later, a tall stranger wearing a blue blazer and thick sunglasses, arrived at Yad Yehudah. With security tight, he had to explain over and over that he was not a reporter. Finally he identified himself, and they pointed out the hut.

Knocking softly, he entered into semi-darkness. The room had a musty smell. In the corner a nurse sat knitting. He saw a figure on the bed, heavily bandaged, either sleeping or sedated.

"Most of the time he is delirious," the nurse said. "Blames himself for what occurred. But what could he have done?" She shrugged.

"I'm her brother, Julie's brother."

The nurse nodded, expressionless, as if nothing that happened could ever surprise her.

Robert Sebastian asked how Julie died. She wanted to spare him the details, but he insisted. Even before the nurse finished, his fists were clenched and shaking. Without a word, he stumbled out into the open air. A small crowd had gathered in front, morose-looking men, and teary-eyed women clutching small children. He brushed someone off who tried to offer a word of sympathy.

Her freshly dug grave was located in a patch of rocky ground near the orchard. It was marked by a Christian cross and a Jewish star. The inscription read:

> Julie Ben-David
> Born: Paris, France 1951.
> Died: Yad Yehudah, Israel 1977.

A beautiful woman, martyred, and buried here with her unborn daughter.

Robert Sebastian spent hours staring at the freshly dug mound of earth. Once he grabbed some dirt and flung it hard against a rock. He paced back and forth at the grave's edge, but mostly he just stood and stared. He tried futilely in his mind to bring Julie to life, the Julie he remembered from Paris, from Cyprus in May last year. He couldn't accept the fact that his sister was dead, an innocent victim of a war not of her own making. At the end, he made a vow to avenge her.

Returning to the dwelling, Robert Sebastian handed an envelope to the nurse. He told her to give it to Danny Ben-David when he became more lucid. The letter it contained was in Julie's handwriting:

December 15, 1976

Mon Cher Robert,

Forgive me for not writing these last few weeks, but I seem to have precious little time for anything but the basic necessities of life. Everything takes so much longer here. Even making a simple cup of coffee can take half an hour.

Our hut is so small that Danny and I would bump into each other every other minute if we're not careful. With my stomach so big, I have to maneuver my way in and out of the door. But do not laugh or pity me, dear Robert. I have been compelled to spend time with myself, and I have changed quite a bit. I am no longer the melancholy creature you used to meet at the Cafe Les Deux Magots and had to cheer up with funny stories. That egoistic person, so full of herself, has become an individual who can now think of others. I have Danny and my future baby to consider now, and we are making plans for his/her upbringing that include a Bar/Bat Mitzvah and a lycee education. Thinking of the future helps me to forget the harsh life here.

Danny is really a wonderful husband. You remember him from our wedding in Cyprus, of course. You must come to visit us after the baby is born. And no excuses about your work. Please, Robert, come in the early spring. I miss you terribly.

You asked whether the Arab-Israeli tension affects us at Yad Yehudah. Not at all. The men and women carry guns all the time, but we really have the feeling of peace and security. I wear the maternity dresses you sent to me all the time to remind me of you. And I have set up a 'Robert' toy corner next to the crib that Danny's parents bought for us.

I had better stop now to get this in the weekly mail run. Have a wonderful Christmas and New Year's, and do not forget your little sister now so far away from you.

Julie

Chapter 6

Robert Sebastian walked the beach of Tel Aviv angry and depressed, mired in sad thoughts about Julie. He couldn't accept the fact that his innocent, lovely sister was gone. It was too much to bear. Running incessantly through his mind was the question of how his sister could have become a victim of the Israeli-Palestinian conflict. He wanted desperately to strike out at her killers, but of course he was impotent to do so. Several times he sat down on the beach, his body shaking and his eyes full of tears.

Finally, after three days, he decided to return to Paris. With fog enveloping DeGaulle Airport, the plane had to circle for an hour before landing. Outside the terminal a freezing rain hit his face. He retrieved his black Mercedes, and, driving quickly on the highway and ring road around Paris, arrived at the Rue Greuze, a clean, narrow street in the 16th arrondissement near the Trocadero shortly after dark.

Unlocking an iron gate, he maneuvered his car into the courtyard and slammed the gate shut. Wedged into the iron gating was an envelope addressed to him. It was a message of sympathy from Denise about the "terrible, inexcusable loss" of Julie. Sebastian had seen Denise in Paris several times since their original meeting in Cyprus. They had become lovers and had talked of traveling to the Swiss Alps in late January to ski together. In her note, she asked Robert to contact her as soon as he returned from Israel.

He walked slowly into the house, dripping water onto the floor. The place smelled musty. After receiving the telegram, he had forgotten or neglected to open any windows. It felt like a funeral parlor, suitable for mourning. The house was soundproofed, and the silence, once hospitable, now hung over him like a suffocating cloak.

He didn't dare turn on the light, for he knew that Julie's picture, the one taken on the boat trip on the Seine three years ago, would stare at him from the mantle above the fireplace.

Someone knocked on his door. It was the concierge returning his cat. She mumbled some pleasantries, but seeing his ashen face, retreated quickly.

Sitting in the beige armchair near the tall glass case containing a collection of guns of various sizes and dimensions, he began to doze. At one moment the cat, a large white Angora, must have jumped on his lap, for he was conscious of reflexively hurling her across the room and stumbling into the bedroom. Sleep was fitful. He was besieged by frightening dreams of bizarre creatures engaging in dance-like battle. When a huge red bird dripping blood pecked at the womb of a young woman with flowing yellow hair and a witch's face, Sebastian awoke to the sound of his screaming voice.

Light streaked in through the vertical white blinds. He lay motionless on the bed, the half-wet clothes clammy against his skin. Somehow he managed to lift himself up to drink water and defrost some old croissants. Then he collapsed again. For the next two days he was in a trancelike state, where day and night merged, and sleep and wakefulness lost all distinction. In a dreamlike condition, memories and images of Julie flitted through his mind—Julie at ten disconsolate on the day their father left the family and moved back to the United States; Julie and he taking long walks after school, playing in the forest near their uncle's farm in Provence; the two of them visiting their father in New York and traipsing around Manhattan together; Julie at thirteen disclosing that the man living with their mother had tried to molest her, and then her tortured expression when Robert told her that he had beaten the man and ordered him to leave their apartment; Julie trying to console their mother who reacted in a fitful state and needed to spend some months in a rest home; Julie at sixteen ecstatically greeting him at the railroad station following his two year absence from Paris; the melancholy moment when Julie and he took their mother from her apartment to the Center for Challenged Adults in Brittany; Julie visiting Robert in the U.S. while he was pursuing his college studies in Virginia; Julie coming to the funeral of their father during his junior year in college; their years in Paris seeing each other so frequently; Julie last summer on the verge of returning to Nairobi to Danny Ben-David, tearfully saying good-bye; and finally the exquisite moments of their marriage in Cyprus when Danny and she were so ecstatic. It was the last time that he had seen Julie alive.

On the third day after his return from Israel, Robert Sebastian got up and slowly dressed. He went outside to a nearby cafe and ate some soup and chicken. Then, returning home, he locked up the house, gave his cat to the concierge at the Thai Embassy across the street, and left Paris.

Driving nonstop towards Switzerland, he crossed the frontier near Geneva and headed to Loeches-les-Bains, where he had taken Julie climbing three years before. He rode the cable car high up the mountain. It was a crisp, clear day, with the sun's rays reflecting crystals off the packed snow. At the peak Robert left the ski slope and walked along a narrow path leading to the precipice. Edging towards a jagged rock uncovered by snow drifts, he sat on a ledge and through gently moving clouds, looked down a thousand feet. The wind howled in his ear; snowflakes swirled around his face. One move and he could end the excruciating pain in his head...Join Julie. His lovely, now dead sister would forgive him, but could he forgive himself if he failed to avenge her? There was only one way to 'join' her, to overcome the feelings of misery in his brain and pain in his heart, and that was to put a bullet in the head of her killer. Slowly he walked away from the precipice.

The next day Robert Sebastian returned to Paris. The city was unbearable. Every building, every street corner, every cafe, reminded him of his sister—of visits to museums and concerts they had gone to, of meals and moments they had spent together. Day and night her memory haunted him, and he sank into depression. Denise left another message, and he sent her a reply saying that he was "devastated" by Julie's death and would contact her when he felt able to do so. After a week he decided to travel to escape from the immediacy of his vivid, sad Parisian memories. He went first to familiar places--to Italy, Greece, and Turkey. Then after a short stay back in Paris, he flew to Lima, Peru, spending a few days on the beach and then driving on narrow roads in the Andes. After two weeks he arrived in Cusco where he bought a book illustrating the history of Macchu Pichu and went by train to see the scene of an advanced, yet primitive, civilization that had built this extraordinary mountainous fortress that had collapsed mysteriously at its height. Then he went to the Yucatan Peninsula of Mexico to view ruins of another complex ancient civilization near Merida which had succumbed to the colonizing brutality of the Spanish invasion. And finally he went to the United States, landing in Washington, D.C. to lose himself in exploring the Washington and Lincoln monuments and government buildings, then driving to Charlottesvile, Virginia to to wander around his former university, to North Carolina to walk on the beaches of the Outer Banks, and finally ending up in New York, where he stayed in the Plaza Hotel and made a practical decision to overcome his depression and to try to heal himself. He ate copiously to put back the weight he had lost, jogged the six mile loop of Central Park daily, spent hours in the hotel gym, and eventually summoned up the mental and emotional strength to return to Paris.

The city stirred up memories of Julie, but he was now determined to overcome his wanderlust. Closing down his house on the Rue Greuze, he moved to a shabby pied-a-terre on the Rue Juge off the Boulevard de Grenelle in the 15th arrondissement, a nondescript area frequented mainly by Arabs. He lived in a tarnished red brick building above a seedy Algerian cafe called "Le Rugbyman" from which Arabic music wailed each evening. The place was minimally furnished—wooden chairs, folding table, old throw rugs, a narrow bed, and a few lamps. He kept the interior dark, never opening the brown curtains over the single window.

Every day, regardless of the weather, he put on his sneakers and did an 8-10 kilometer run along the Seine, in the Bois de Boulogne, or on grimy streets in his neighborhood. Then he exercised on the living-room rug—calisthenics, weight lifting, and yoga, tuning his body and getting back into what he termed his 'fighting shape'. Often he read late into the night—Nietzsche, Spengler, Celine, and Genet; Freud and Jung; Camus, Malraux, and Sartre. He read books focusing on death and reincarnation, existentialism and spirituality--novels, philosophical works, and psychological treatises.

Over his bed he taped to the wall a quote from Ralph Waldo Emerson:

> The Great Man is He Who in the Midst of the Crowd Keeps
> With Perfect Sweetness the Independence of Solitude

Sebastian became slowly aware that his psychological state had altered from deep despair to a more manageable grief, permitting him to think and to function rationally. Though desperate to lessen the pain in his head and in his heart, he felt that the presence of the pain had a positive aspect--a reminder of and direct link to Julie.

One day he made the decision to examine his mental condition more clinically. He began to read psychological works on the subject of loss and death, developing a theory of successive phases of psychological and physical changes in response to loss. First, the sheer shock and incredulity; then deep, prolonged grief and emotional numbness, accompanied by an obsessive probing of memories and constant visualization of the 'lost one'. This painful phase could continue for a long time, but eventually there would be the emergence of what could banally be termed a 'partial recovery', that is, an ability to alter the focus from the lost one to oneself. The harsh pain would diminish, replaced by a numbness and a slow restoration of psychological health. Every day Sebastian wrote down his feelings and thoughts, observing both the overt and subtle changes in his psyche over time. Slowly he moved from an obsessive focus on past memories of Julie to an evolving acceptance of her physical loss and awareness of his present psychological condition that was calmer, less painful. Furthermore, he could rationally think of a time period that he mentally labeled 'the future'.

Each evening, around 8 p.m., he went to a seedy bistro around the corner, ordering the daily specialty with vin rouge ordinaire. La Petite Normandie was owned by a Norman family named Boulot, with the pot-bellied husband serving as chef, the garrulous wife as waitress, and the fish-eyed daughter as dishwasher. Once Sebastian became a regular, M. Boulot gave him the back corner table, serving him efficiently and avoiding all but essential conversation. His wife and he imagined Sebastian a fallen aristocrat, a déclassé gentleman who, through life's misadventures, had sunk to the point where all he could afford was the evening meal in La Petite Normandie.

After dinner Sebastian walked the neighborhood, strolling down narrow streets lined with unattractive shops, grocery stalls, and small cafes. The few people out at night were mainly Arabs, since the area bordered an Algerian district. His reason for moving here was to study the behavior of Arabs, the people who had killed his sister. As he observed their faces and mannerisms, Sebastian found himself despising them, believing them all guilty, suppressing the urge to strike out at everyone he saw.

One night he came upon a man hitting an Arab boy in the hallway of a poorly lit building. His inclination was to pass by, but hearing the boy whimper like a beaten cur, he suddenly took hold of the man and banged his head against the lobby wall, knocking him unconscious.

Wiping blood from the side of his mouth, the boy looked at Sebastian and said,

"That's my father. He'll kick the shit out of me later."

"If he tries anything," Sebastian said quietly, "tell him that the guy who hit him lives nearby and will break every bone in his body if he harms you again. Understand?

"Oui, monsieur."

Sebastian walked away, the boy following. Turning around, Sebastian said, almost growling: "Piss off, kid."

Two nights later Sebastian walked down the same street. The boy was waiting. He fell in step. They walked for a few minutes without speaking. Sebastian saw how thin, even emaciated, the boy was.

Finally Sebastian asked: "What is your name?"

"Bekir."

"Your father behaving, Bekir?"

The boy grinned broadly. "I gave him your message, and he's scared shitless."

"Bekir, you look as if you could use a good meal. Want to have dinner with me?

"Oui, Monsieur."

Sebastian brought him to the restaurant and watched the boy wolf down his food.

Most evenings thereafter Sebastian met Bekir either before or just after his meal. Sitting together at La Petite Normandie, he asked the boy about his family, when they had left Algeria, how they lived in Paris, if they identified with Algeria or with France.

"You ask me too many questions," Bekir said to Sebastian one night.

"Sorry. I'm trying to understand how Arabs live and behave here, and you're my only source."

"Maybe so, but I'm only a kid," Bekir replied. "What do I know? Little that would interest you."

"You'd be surprised, mon petit. But I understand; no more questions." Sebastian tousled Bekir's hair and began to talk about his recent trip to Spain.

Some nights they ate in complete silence, each of them lost in thought. Sebastian developed a strong affection for Bekir, and he informed the boy whenever he left Paris. He brought him back small souvenirs from Italy, Spain, and the U.S.-- T-shirts and other mementos of the places he visited.

Once Sebastian asked Bekir if he wanted to come mountain climbing with him. The boy declined, saying that he would have too much trouble with his father if he did. Sebastian went alone to the Austrian Alps. Whenever Paris became too oppressive for him, Sebastian went climbing, choosing hazardous areas where he knew he would be alone.

One day a letter arrived from Tel Aviv. Danny Ben-David began by saying that he had recovered from his head wound. He went on to describe Julie's grave as a "secular shrine adorning her everlasting memory." He brought flowers to the site every week, he said. The letter concluded: "Since you, her brother, and I, her husband, were the two people she loved most, I wonder if we might correspond. When I met you in Cyprus, I liked you very much and was hoping that you would come to visit us in Israel. I look forward to hearing from you and, God willing, seeing you here or in Paris one day." Sebastian tore up the letter. Then he gulped down a large glass of whiskey. He stayed up very late that night.

The next morning Robert Sebastian ventured outside the 15th arrondissement. Crossing the Seine, he walked along the Tuileries Garden to the Rue de Rivoli. He gazed at the crowds and into shop windows, stopping before a collection of war medals commemorating the Napoleonic era and France's wars in the 19th and 20th centuries. He thought of buying a Franco-Prussian War medallion for Bekir, but hesitated and walked on.

Passing by the Ministry of Culture, he cut into the long, narrow garden of the Palais Royal. A few people sat on benches reading newspapers or books. Off to the side, a white-haired woman wearing rags threw breadcrumbs at a flock of pigeons.

Halfway down the path, he crossed under the archway and stopped to look in the window of a small, cluttered shop featuring old war medals.

At that moment an elegantly dressed man, wearing a red boutiniere in his lapel, approached Sebastian.

"I thought that you were dead, mon petit," the man said, holding out a hand adorned with a gold chain bracelet. He had thick black wavy hair and a prominent gold tooth that reflected in the sunlight as he smiled with practiced charm at Sebastian. His voice was low and gravelly. "Happy to see you alive. Where have you been?"

"Out of circulation"

"Armand and I have work for you if you want it."

"Not this time, Bernard," said Sebastian.

"A good payday."

"I know where to reach you if I am interested," Sebastian said, moving abruptly away. At the end of the Palais Royal, he walked up some stone steps and headed to the Rue de Richelieu towards the Bibliotheque Nationale. There he spent the rest of the day scanning the card catalogue and reading a book entitled "Israel and the Palestinian Problem." On his way home, as he did every day, he bought copies of Le Figaro, Le Monde, International Herald Tribune, and the Manchester Guardian, which he scrutinized for articles on the Middle East. He searched, in particular, for writings on the Palestinian Liberation Organization and its head, Yasser Arafat.

He called Denise and said that he would meet her for a drink at Les Deux Magots. He wore dark glasses shielding his eyes.

"Robert, Robert," Denise said, sitting across from him and clasping his hands. "I've been so worried about you. I know what a loss it has been. I've also been suffering, suffering immensely." Tears appeared in her eyes.

Sebastian took her hand, then withdrew his own. "I know, Denise. I know," he said quietly. "I cannot believe that I was sitting in this very place with Julie when she announced her marriage plans with Danny to me. Then the wedding…and then, the catastrophe…" He folded his hands on the table.

"I wish you would let me share it with you. She was my best friend, as you well know." Denise took his hand which remained limp and unresponsive. "I lost her. I don't want to lose you, Robert."

"Denise, I need time. I've been absolutely devastated, as you can understand." He asked the waiter for a refill of their wine glasses. "I mourned, I brooded, I traveled. I changed where I lived in order to escape from all the memories of Julie. I couldn't function; now I function partially. I know that you've suffered a great loss too, and, as you say, you want to share it with me. But I need more time before I can see you again. I'm going to travel, to try to sort things out in my mind. I will not ask you to wait for me, although I will promise you that I will not see any other woman. But I must isolate myself now until I can attain an inner balance and calm. Then I will come back to you and we can see how things are. For now, I have to do things on my own. Tu comprends?" ('You understand'?)

"Oui, Robert. I understand. I would like to accompany you on your journey right now, but if you need the time and the solitude, I will have to accept it." Denise began crying.

"Denise, I'm sorry…"

"Robert, I had better leave. I'm getting too emotional. Please contact me when you can. Don't erase me from your life." She got up and quickly left the café.

"Bernard, it's me." Sebastian sat in a telephone kiosk in the Gare de Lyon a week later. "That job still on?"

"Situation is quiet, but I will try to revive it. Give me two days. You want to come here?"

"No. At the bench in the Luxembourg Gardens. Three days from now at 4 p.m. Ciao."

It would be the first time he had worked in over a year. After Julie's death, he had closed down the house in Nice and the apartment in London. Letters piled up in his box in Paris containing hints of interesting offers, but Sebastian never responded. His contacts dried up, thinking him underground or dead. Even now he would not have worked had it not been for his state of mind. He felt increasingly frustrated and impotent. Realizing that he would never identify Julie's actual killers, he focused his rage on Yasser Arafat, who was ultimately responsible for the PLO attack on Yad Yehudah. But there was no conceivable way he could get at Arafat. Feeling weak and helpless, Sebastian was consumed by strong guilt feelings that only increased his turmoil. A job might distract him, divert or channel the feelings of frustration he was experiencing.

A week later, as planned with Bernard, Sebastian went to a cafe off the Boulevard Wagram to meet a wealthy wine merchant from Seville named Francisco Albornoz.

"You can speak Spanish, Senor Albornoz," Sebastian said, drinking a glass of red wine.

Between sips of coffee Albornoz nervously related details of his wife's infidelity with a prominent official of the local Phalangist Party in Seville. He brought out photos. The evidence was indisputable.

Albornoz's face turned red. He stood up abruptly and shouted: "Yo soy furioso, furioso. Sobre le sangre de mi madre….she will pay. How could she? How could she? The slut…Will you do it?" he asked, sitting down again.

"I see your problem, Senor Albornoz. Yes, I will take the job."

"Good." Here is the initial payment. Albornoz passed over a large envelope containing two hundred thousand francs. An equivalent amount would be given to Bernard afterwards.

Chapter 7

Four days later Sebastian flew to Seville and rented a car under another name at the airport. Discreetly following Senora Albornoz, a heavy-set, elegantly dressed woman wearing expensive jewelry, he observed that she shopped daily in town, met friends for lunch and afternoon tea, and twice a week, punctually at noon on Tuesdays and Fridays, drove to an apartment complex on the Cordoba road where she spent approximately two hours and then drove back to the central city. Arriving early one Friday, Sebastian saw the man in Senor Albornoz's photos drive up in a Citroen and enter the building. He was tall, well dressed, and walked with an assured air. From the hallway below, Sebastian heard an apartment door slam shut on the third floor. Waiting on the landing behind the stairwell, Sebastian watched Senora Albornoz stride up and open the door with a key.

That evening Sebastian met Senor Albornoz in an elegant restaurant near the Museo de Bellas Artes de Seville.

"I followed them. No doubt about it."

Senor Albornoz simply shrugged.

"Find the key to that apartment in your wife's possessions, and make a copy for me," Sebastian said. "Let us meet in the Café Central at 5 p.m. in two days time. One more thing. I will need a specimen of your wife's handwriting. Once you deliver the key and the handwriting to me, you leave Seville on an extended business trip in the company of some associates. You understand?"

"Si, Senor."

These matters were duly arranged. Sebastian noticed that the lovers' twice a week routine did not vary during Senor Albornoz's absence.

Entering the apartment early one Tuesday morning, he hid in the closet of the spare bedroom. When he could hear the lovers audibly engaged in the next room, Sebastian crept up to the open door and watched them for a few seconds, a thin man and a chubby woman gyrating on the bed, Senora Albornoz panting loudly and emitting screams of pleasure. Shrugging, Sebastian entered the room and without saying a word, shot them at close range with a pistol equipped with a silencer. Unscrewing the silencer, he opened Senora Albornoz's right hand and clutched her fingers around the gun. In her handbag he placed a note in Spanish, forged in her handwriting, saying that inasmuch as her lover refused to divorce his wife, she, Senora Albornoz, "unable to bear the pain of living apart," had decided to end their lives. She prayed to "Almighty God for Forgiveness." Within the hour Sebastian was at the airport, and the next morning in Paris read newspaper accounts of the sensational murder-suicide in Seville.

Paris still summoned up painful reminders of Julie, and within a short time he took a two-week trip away from France. This was to become his pattern for the next year and a quarter. When Bernard had work for him or when he was bored abroad, Sebastian returned to Paris.

On his trips he sent post cards to Bekir and a few times to Denise. Back in Paris in March 1978, he asked the boy to join him on a hiking trip. Bekir, now almost 16, got his father's permission to go hiking with Sebastian in the eastern Pyrenees. Walking long distances in rugged terrain, they swam and fished in small streams and slept in a tent at night. Sebastian let Bekir shoot his revolver at squirrels and birds. At Perpignan he took the boy on his first plane ride back to the capital. During the three week trip Sebastian felt relaxed and even carefree; once in Paris, he was as restless as ever.

The jobs Bernard arranged were ones that Sebastian in the past would have refused because of low pay or high risk or both. Now he gave little thought to such factors; the main thing was to keep occupied. During this period he accepted contracts on a restaurant owner in Lyon, a colonel in the Moroccan army, and a Greek Communist Party official.

These events took him away from Paris and its vivid, painful memories of Julie. In late May 1978 Robert Sebastian made a routine phone call to Bernard from Athens.

"Jesus, mon vieux, where have you been? You were supposed to call last month."

"I was tied up," Sebastian said flatly.

"Well, untie yourself. I've got a big one for us, a real big one."

Sebastian said nothing.

"When will you be back?"

"In a week or two."

"Make it sooner, will you?"

Bernard and his brother Armand ran a large opulent gambling casino on the Ile. St. Louis where politicians and film stars mingled with professional gamblers. The casino had three levels--the first featuring a huge bar and hors d'oeuvres tables which were always filled with 'important people' and hangers-on; the second level, a casino open to the public; and the third level, private offices and a large room decorated in red and black where those deemed 'serious' gamblers were invited to spend their time and hopefully lose a bundle of money to the casino.

Sitting in the back of the first floor of the darkened casino late in the afternoon of May 30, 1978, Bernard drank campari and told Sebastian of the latest opportunity. "Rene in Marseilles was approached by Gilles Lafonte of Toulouse. Rene owes me a favor, and he knows that I have solid connections to a pro. So he threw it my way, and we—especially you—stand to make a killing. There is only one thing," he added.

"What's that?"

"I've got to give Rene something, so this time I need 25% of the action."

Sebastian's jaw tightened as he looked coldly at the other man.

"Look, if it's too much..." Bernard said quickly.

"No, it's okay. 25% for you and Rene if I take the job." Sebastian stared off into space.

"I've set up a meeting for Thursday at 11 a.m. by the pool in the Luxembourg Gardens. A man and a woman. The man will carry a copy of Canard Enchaine. Contact name Benson. Oh yes, one other thing," Bernard added. "They're Arabs."

"What did you say?" Sebastian asked, clutching Bernard's forearm.

Bernard winced. "They are Palestinians. You...are....hurting me."

"I don't like Arabs." He let go.

Bernard moved back from the table, rubbing his arm. "You'll like these Arabs when you hear what they are offering."

"What's that?"

"Five million. Dollars, not francs."

Sebastian looked blankly at him. "For whom?"

"He didn't say. My guess is some oil sheik."

"We'll see," Sebastian said vaguely, his face somewhat flushed. He got up and left the casino.

That evening he strolled along the Seine with Bekir.

At one point, as they threw stones into the water and watched the expanding ripples, the boy asked if anything was wrong.

"No. Why?" Sebastian asked, staring blankly at the flickering waves.

"You are quieter than usual, that's all."

A few minutes later Bekir mentioned that his father was returning to Oran. "I told him I wouldn't go. He is not happy about it, but screw him. He can't force me."

"What will you do here?"

"When I'm sixteen in a couple of months, I'll quit school and go to work. I'll find something." Then he said as an afterthought. "There is another reason. I don't want to leave you."

"It's tough for Algerians in France. Maybe you should go with your father."

Bekir turned away and said nothing.

Chapter 8

Two days later, at 10:30 a.m., Sebastian entered the Luxembourg Gardens and made his way under overhanging trees towards the large circular artificial lake in the center. Sitting in a metal chair by the monument to Auguste Scheurer-Kestner, former President of the French Senate and key supporter of Dreyfus during the "Affair," Sebastian, wearing thick-rimmed sunglasses, watched tourists strolling by the lake. Glancing at the tricolor flag fluttering in the breeze over the grey-white Senate building, he saw a middle-aged man and young woman edging their way through the crowd. The man carried a copy of the newspaper Canard Enchaine. Thin-boned with a thick mustache, he wore a dark blue summer suit. The woman had long, flowing black hair, a touch of make-up, and high cheekbones. Dark-skinned, they were obviously Arabs, causing Robert Sebastian's stomach to tighten and make him think of leaving without making contact. Finally, at 11:05 a.m. he approached them.

"Monsieur Benson?" he asked.

"Oui," said the young woman. "And you are Monsieur Sebastian."

He nodded.

"I am Lydia Ahmed. This is Hassan Barka. He doesn't speak French, so I will interpret."

"Come with me. We are leaving."

Leading them along a path bordered by manicured lawns and a row of red and violet flowers, Sebastian exited by the main gate. As they walked down the Boulevard Saint Michel towards the Boulevard Saint Germain, he stopped every so often to window-shop in boutiques, discreetly checking to see if they were being followed. Satisfied, he crossed the Seine by the Petit Pont and turned right at the cathedral of Notre Dame, proceeding to the far tip of the Ile de la Cite into a small, enclosed park containing a memorial to the "200,000 French Martyrs Dead in the Deportation Camps, 1940-1945."

Facing the tall, blackened spires of Notre Dame, Sebastian broke the silence. "Tell me what you want, Monsieur Benson or Barka."

Lydia Ahmed translated into Arabic, but before Barka could reply, Sebastian said in English: "I do not like indirect conversations. Does he speak English?"

"Yes," Barka replied, looking sourly at Lydia Ahmed.

"Then go ahead."

"Four years ago," Barka began, "someone killed the Crown Prince of Saudi Arabia's cousin in Zurich. It was rumored that a French assassin was responsible. A year afterward a business competitor of the cousin poisoned himself, but before dying, he left a note saying that he had hired the killer in France."

"I don't recall," said Sebastian.

"These events were hushed up and kept out of the papers." Hesitating a moment, Barka continued: "I bring this matter up only because I have been looking for a professional for a very difficult assignment. I believe that I am talking with one of the most competent professionals I could find."

"So?"

"Are you free for the assignment?"

"That depends."

"How does five million dollars sound to you?"

 "Who could possibly be that important?"

Barka looked him straight in the eye. "Yasser Arafat."

Pain shot through Sebastian's head. "Julie," he thought.

Barka started to speak, but Sebastian waved him quiet and walked to the wall overlooking the water. He fought to control his emotions.

"It's impossible," he said, when he returned. "Arafat is guarded day and night. His movements are secret. No outsider could get through. An Arab maybe."

"Arabs have tried and failed. It's time for an outsider."

Sebastian looked away, staring at the Seine.

Barka continued. "In September Arafat is coming to address the United Nations in New York. He will be at his most vulnerable then." Turning to Lydia Ahmed, he said: "Lydia works at the U.N. She will help you."

"I always work alone."

"For this job you will need her assistance. We have formulated a plan to get you close to Arafat. Will you listen?

"Go ahead."

Sebastian listened to the plan. When Barka finished, he said: "It is hardly foolproof, your idea. But it could be modified." He walked near the white marble monument, feigning deep thought.

"Before I say if I will do it, let me ask you a question. Why do you, a Palestinian, want Arafat dead?"

Barka looked directly at Sebastian. "It is really not your business. However, I will say that both Lydia and I consider Arafat to be a nullity, a useless creature who pretends to be a leader, but cannot even wipe his own ass correctly. Long ago he may have been earnest about Palestinian statehood, but now he shrinks from action. He lets the Israelis control the West Bank and Gaza, and he will not hit at them. He is sucking the life out of the resistance movement. He is not worthy of living. Once he is dead, we will find someone who is strong and militant, someone who will not hesitate to attack and take back what is rightfully ours." Barka stopped talking. He wiped his mouth with his sleeve. "I have said too much about my motives. It doesn't concern you. I need to know now if you will take the job."

Sebastian walked in a circle, feigning pensiveness. Finally he spoke. "Okay," he said. "The money is good. I will do it."

"There are some details we must iron out first," said Barka, studying Sebastian. "I'll let you know within the week. May I call you directly?"

"Use the same method as before."

"I don't like intermediaries."

"And I don't like accomplices," Sebastian said, moving away. He walked past the cathedral, crossed the Petit Pont, and headed towards the 15th arrondissement. Suddenly out of breath, he leaned against a parked car to steady himself.

An old man, wearing a beret and holding a cane, came up to offer assistance, but seeing the expression on Sebastian's face, limped away as fast as he could.

Sebastian tried to compose himself. He stopped in a cafe for a whiskey. The liquid burned his throat. He clenched his fists tightly. In his mind he visualized Julie's gravesite and the dark hut in which her husband lay nursing his injuries. Julie, Julie...He thought of her wry smile, her silken yellow hair. Opening his wallet, he stared at her picture enclosed in the last letter she had sent him from Israel. His world had collapsed after her death. Now, unexpectedly, he was being given the chance to avenge Julie and perhaps live normally once again. With some difficulty he stood up and left the cafe to go to his apartment.

That evening he met Bekir at La Petite Normandie. Near the end of the meal he said casually: "I may be leaving soon and staying away for awhile."

"When?"

"In a week or two."

Sebastian poured another glass of wine for Bekir. "I've been thinking. You should stay in Paris."

"You didn't say that the last time."

"Oh, forget that. Now listen. I have spoken about you to a friend who owns a casino. He has found a job for you with one of his clients, a part owner of the department store Galeries Lafayette. Here is the name and address." Sebastian passed over a piece of paper.

"You will pack at first and do menial jobs, but if you work out, he is prepared to promote you to selling."

Bekir's face turned scarlet. "I...I..."

"Keep quiet for a minute. In this life you never know what will work and what will not. So I have some insurance for you in case anybody screws you around because you are Algerian." Under the table he handed Bekir the pistol that the boy had shot in the Pyrenees a few months before. "Only for an emergency. Understand?"

The boy nodded and put the gun in his bag.

"And here is something else. To tide you over if you muck up on the job or if the boss turns out to be a piece of shit." He handed Bekir an envelope.

Opening it, Bekir saw a thick stack of one hundred franc notes. Tears formed in his eyes. "I don't know what... to say."

"Nothing, mon petit. Now bugger off and let me think. You can come to the restaurant here over the next couple of weeks to see me while I'm still here."

Alone, Sebastian considered the matter he would soon be undertaking. He decided that starting tomorrow he would call Bernard daily to see if Hassan Barka had contacted him. He was grateful to Barka for providing the opportunity he had thought about almost exclusively since Julie's death.

But Hassan Barka was not altogether convinced that the French assassin, Robert Sebastian, was right for the job. From the contacts that Barka had made, Sebastian seemingly had imposing credentials; in person he came off as tough and resourceful. But at the same time, Barka felt that the Frenchman might be difficult to control. Lydia Ahmed thought him nervous, arrogant, and potentially unmanageable.

Barka decided therefore to contact his second choice in Europe, an Italian named Giuseppe Marcellini, who went by the nickname, the "Sicilian." Barka's year-long search for the world's key hit men had produced five outstanding prospects: a South African named Roy Harper; an Israeli with the pseudonym Benny Simpson; an American named Charles Browning; Robert Sebastian; and the Sicilian. Harper, engaged on a long-term basis by the newly established Zimbabwe government, was unavailable. Interviewing Simpson off the Cyprus coast, Barka was generally favorable; yet he ruled him out because of fears that the Israeli might have connections to his government. The American Browning had not responded to the contact that Barka had initiated in New York a few weeks ago. So Barka appproached Sebastian, taking Lydia Ahmed along to interpret on the mistaken belief that the Frenchman was only French-speaking. With Sebastian now judged suitable in some respects, but less than perfect in others, Barka decided to interview the Sicilian.

After sending Lydia Ahmed back to New York, he cabled the contact point in Livorno, requesting a meeting in Geneva. Over lunch of cheese fondue and cider in the open-air dining room of a tourist boat cruising the lake, Barka looked intensely at the Italian.

The Sicilian was dark-haired, with a narrow bony nose and deep pockmarks on his cheeks. He was dressed in a tight-fitting white suit, blue cameo shirt, and Hermes lavender silk scarf. Compared to Sebastian, he was courteous and attentive as Barka disclosed his need to obtain a professional "to eliminate a leading personality in the Arab world." Aside from using a switchblade to peel and quarter an orange, the Sicilian was a model of decorum, and Barka felt that he would be easier to work with than Sebastian. Yet he seemed to lack a certain spark, and Barka wondered how intelligent or imaginative he was. So Barka decided to test him.

"The people I represent want to be certain that you are the right man for the job."

"So?" asked the Sicilian.

"The man must have not only the required skills, but also judgment and the ability to cooperate and follow orders. We are investing a lot of money in anyone we choose. We don't want the job bungled or have any trace of guilt pointed at us."

The Sicilian glanced out the window at a scene of a verdant private park and chateau belonging to one of the municipality's leading citizens. He spoke Italian-accented English in a scratchy voice that was soft, but distinct. "I know you do not mean it, but you insult my brains," he said in a calm, affable tone. "I work in strictest secrecy, and I never, how you say, implicate anyone else. Should anything go wrong, I take blame myself. Rest assured, though, nothing ever goes wrong." He popped a slice of orange into his mouth.

"I think that you are the man we want. Let us just say that as a sign of good faith, you will agree to my request." Hunching closer, Barka continued. "You will be well paid for eliminating this one first." He showed the Sicilian a photo of a youngish man with aquiline nose, thin mustache, and long dark hair. "Two hundred thousand dollars. Half now; the rest afterwards. Do this within four days, and then we will talk about the big job. Okay?"

The Sicilian shrugged. "Okay, tell me more."

"He is here in Geneva. His name is Selim el-Nuseury. He is sitting in UNCTAD Conference Room 6 at the Palais des Nations. Make it look like he got in the way of a robbery. Nothing political. You understand?"

The Sicilian nodded and Barka handed him a thick envelope containing one hundred thousand dollars.

When the boat docked, the Sicilian took a taxi to the Palais des Nations, located off the Avenue de la Paix. The Palais was the second largest complex in the U.N. system after New York. The building had been constructed after World War I to house the League of Nations, the global dream of President Woodrow Wilson, accepted at the Versailles Peace Conference in 1919, but rejected by the Republicans in Congress, ensuring that the United States would not sign the Versailles Peace Treaty nor join the League of Nations. The outcast nations Germany and the Soviet Union eventually joined, but the League was inherently weak, and after suffering the withdrawal of Hirohito's Japan, Mussolini's Italy, and Hitler's Germany in the 1930s, the League of Nations became a hollow shell, helpless to prevent the onslaught of World War II in September 1939. After the war, with the victorious powers subscribing to the new dream of President Franklin D. Roosevelt, the League of Nations morphed into the United Nations, with the faded existing buildings of the Palais serving as the U.N. headquarters in Geneva.

The Palais was immense, consisting of elongated rectangular buildings grafted onto a main base, with straight pathways running off at 90-degree angles. Just above the Palais perched the buildings of the World Health Organization and International Red Cross; below it stood other UN agencies and offices. The dominant color of the buildings was gray, representing the faded past of the challenges and failures of the post-WWI period. The Sicilian knew the layout, having contracted on a Vietnamese ex-general working in the international community in Geneva five years earlier.

Entering the Palais by the tourist gate, he followed signs that pointed to UNCTAD Conference Room 6 where the "Governing Council Meeting— United Nations Development Programme (UNDP)" was being held. The Sicilian took a seat in the visitors' gallery at the rear. Scanning the scene below, he saw row upon row of delegates representing various countries, international agencies, regional groupings, nongovernmental organizations, and the Palestinian Liberation Organization. At the PLO desk three men sat with headphones, with the man in the photo, Selim el-Nuseury, intensely taking notes.

On the rostrum, a delegate was speaking passionately in Spanish. Putting on the interpretation headpiece, the Sicilian heard a plea for additional funds to combat starvation in Bangladesh and in the Sahel region of North Africa. After a minute, he stifled the rhetoric by turning the button to "off."

The meeting ended in the late afternoon. The three PLO delegation members, including el-Nuseury, left the conference room and headed for the main exit. The Sicilian followed them on foot to the Hotel Inter Continental a few blocks away. Accompanying them on the elevator to the ninth floor, he noticed which room el-Nuseury entered.

At 9:00 the next morning, sitting in a parked car across the hotel, the Sicilian saw el-Nuseury, tall and thin with a full mustache, enter a taxi and head for central Geneva. The Sicilian followed him to the jewelry district across the Pont du Mont-Blanc. Pretending to window-shop, he watched el-Nuseury buy some gold watches at an expensive watch boutique. Then he followed the taxi to the Palais.

After the day's meeting, the Palestinians returned to their hotel. In a darkened bar off the main lobby, they smoked cigars, sipped cocktails, and chatted with other U.N. diplomats. Then they went into the dining room. After a sumptuous meal of filet mignon, roast potatoes, petits pois, and some excellent French cheeses, washed down with three bottles of red wine, they beckoned the maitre d', whispered in his ear, and returned to the bar.

Half an hour later, two heavily made-up, buxom young women joined them. One was a brunette with high Slavic cheekbones, the other a Scandavian blond with pale blue eye shadow. The men drank champagne and toasted each other lavishly in Arabic. Then the three men and the two women headed for the elevator.

"Selim," said one of the Palestinians in Arabic as they rode up. "Since it is your birthday today, Hamid and I have decided that you can have them both first."

"To... together?" asked el-Nuseury, slightly inebriated.

"That's right, brother. What greater sacrifice can we make for you?" said Hamid, who handed each of the women a five hundred Swiss franc note and told them to get off with el-Nuseury.

In his room the three undressed. One of the women asked if she might put the air-conditioner on low. El-Nuseury nodded. He stared at the two of them standing naked near the bed. Fondling the blond, he felt himself getting excited by the brunette's hands on his body.

Just then there was a soft knock at the door. Cursing in Arabic, he ran over and asked who it was.

"Room service, monsieur."

"Go away."

"Champagne for you, monsieur. Courtesy of your friends." El-Nuseury laughed and unlocked the door, opening it slightly. A champagne bottle, nicely chilled, was thrust through. He reached for the bottle.

Then he was on the floor, bowled over by the swift motion of the door, as a man wearing a white hood stood over him shooting at his naked body. One of the women screamed, the other fainted. Pointing his gun at the screaming blond, the Sicilian pulled the trigger once. Then he ran to the chest of drawers to look for the watches that el-Nuseury had bought that morning. Unable to find them, he took el-Nuseury's wallet from his pants pocket, as well as some money from the top drawer, and hurried out the door.

"He bungled it," Hassan Barka shouted into the telephone. "The idiot killed the girl as well." He was staring at the headline of the Journal de Geneve spread out on the bed:

"PALESTINIAN AND PROSTITUTE SLAIN: NO CLUES."

"Where does it leave us?" asked Lydia Ahmed.

"I'm flying back to Paris today. Before I make it definite, though, I need to have Sebastian's assurance that he will work with you."

"Do you want me to come over?"

"No. You stay there. Anything new?"

"There is talk that Waldheim will go to Washington in the next few days to try to persuade President Carter not to veto the PLO entry when the resolution is proposed."

"What are his chances?"

"Some say good; others are unsure."

"He must succeed. Otherwise Arafat will not attend."

"Hassan. I have told you before. He will attend. No matter what."

"I would still feel better if..." He did not finish the sentence.

"Trust me," she said. "He will come. You know him. He is desperate for the spotlight and the glory."

"There is one consolation, though," Barka said.

"What is that?"

"At least we are rid of that worm el-Nuseury."

After he hung up, he composed a cable which he sent from the hotel desk:

Franco Zampert, c/o Abruzzi, Via Appia, Livorno, Italy. Your services no longer required Stop Remainder resources follow JOYOUS

Chapter 9

They sat in a cafe in a back street off the Bastille. It was late afternoon and a light rain was falling outside. Sebastian drank an aperitif, Barka strong tea.

"Before we agree on anything," Barka said, "we have to understand each other a little better."

"Go ahead."

"The matter we are discussing is extraordinarily important to me. That is why I pay such big money." He wiped his forehead with a handkerchief. Arafat is a traitor to the Palestinian cause. He is selling us out to the Israelis for his own glory and power. I do not expect you to understand the politics of it. Just believe me."

"I understand," said Sebastian, sipping his drink.

"There have been many attempts to kill him; none of them have come close to success. He is intelligent, elusive, heavily protected. He has frustrated every attempt, eliminated opponents, isolated dissidents, and consolidated his rule. Do not underestimate him."

Sebastian nodded.

"But he's a man who is mortal and can die like any other. The other day you criticized our plan."

Sebastian tried to intervene, but Barka cut him off. "No, let me finish. The plan is not foolproof, but if the chain of circumstances that I anticipate occurs, then it is the best plan. It only needs the right man to execute it. Understand?"

"Yes."

"The man must not only be purposeful, resourceful, accurate with a weapon. He must also be flexible, willing to bend if circumstances change. And he must be able to work in tandem with somebody else, even if it goes against his ingrained habits."

"You are talking about Lydia Ahmed?"

"Yes."

"I am glad you brought that up," said Sebastian. "I have reflected on the matter. The assignment is an exceedingly difficult one. I have thought about ways to accomplish it. And the more I think about it, if it is to take place at the U.N., then I will need her assistance."

"You did not react this way the first time we spoke," said Barka, looking at the Frenchman.

"Now you must understand me," Sebastian said. "I have a suspicious, even cynical, nature for obvious reasons. I work alone. And there you were, ordering me about like a subaltern to collaborate with someone I don't know."

"And now you agree?"

"Yes."

"The money is acceptable?"

"Yes."

"One half down; the rest later."

"Fine" indicated Sebastian.

"There are two stipulations to this. Should Arafat not appear at the U.N., we will arrange something else as soon as feasible. Secondly, I expect you to carry out the assignment whatever else may occur. Only my personal intervention should cause you to change or abandon it."

"Rest assured," said Sebastian, folding his hands tightly. "I swear to you that I will hunt down Yasser Arafat at the U.N. or wherever else he may go on this earth."

Barka flew to Damascus the next day. Two of his men met him at the airport. They drove north for three hours into the mountains, crossing the Lebanese border by a narrow unguarded road, and proceeding to a hillside village eighty miles southwest of Beirut. Barka went to a safe house that he used periodically. He would stay here a few days, then move to another location. Until Arafat died, he intended to remain mobile and out of sight. There was a message that his friend, Shukri Kamal, wanted to see him urgently. Barka told a lieutenant to inform Kamal to come at noon the following day. Then he lay down and fell into a deep sleep.

When Kamal arrived, Barka greeted him effusively. They had known each other as children in Jerusalem. On the day the Palmach soldier killed his father, Barka had run to Kamal's house where he was welcomed into the family and lived for many years. Later Shukri and he joined the underground movement together, and afterwards the PLO.

Kamal had a round, moon face, with bushy eyebrows and a droopy chin, concealing a keen intelligence. He smiled frequently at his childhood friend. "Where you been hiding these past weeks, Hassan? You too busy to see your old brother?"

"Nonsense, Shukri. Stop your feeble complaining and come in for lunch."

They sat on hard wooden chairs around a small table. Barka's cook served them mutton, rice, pita bread, and strong tea.

"You eat better here than I do in Beirut," said Kamal near the end of the meal.

"Then there is only one solution, Shukri. Join me here."

Kamal laughed loudly. "That is really ironic, when I have come to this godforsaken retreat to ask you to join me in Beirut."

Barka looked sourly at Kamal. "That's a poor joke, Shukri."

Suddenly gesticulating with his hands, Kamal said emotionally: "Everything is different now, Hassan. We are no longer sullen dogs in the wilderness. Our stock has never been higher—in the Middle East, in the Third World, even in Europe. Soon we will be joining the United Nations General Assembly. So what is the use of remaining an outcast? You had a grievance, as we know. You organized a band of radicals, called yourselves 'Black September'. You had your moments of glory in killing the Israeli athletes at the Munich Olympics, carrying out diversionary attacks on Israeli settlements, putting the blame on us, embarrassing Arafat. Where did it get you? Israeli reprisals after Munich, most of your men picked off and killed, and then continued isolation and impotence in the wilderness." Kamal made a sweeping gesture with his arm towards the barren valley below.

"What the hell are you getting at, Shukri?" Barka had rarely seen his normally calm friend so vehement.

"You, Habash, and Nasser constitute the left wing opposition to the PLO. The so-called 'rejection front'. But you're wasting your time. You're a tiny group isolated in the wilderness and cannot do anything except commit senseless murders. Give it up and come back to us." He paused for a moment. "An approach has been made to Habash. Arafat sent me here to sound you out. The Central Committee agreed."

"Sound me out for what?" Barka stopped eating.

"To come back into the fold."

"With Arafat as head?"

"What do you think?"

Barka made an obscene gesture. "Take that back to the Central Committee."

"Hassan, you were his protege. He took you from the battlefield into his inner circle, made you one of his closest advisers. I knew you before, do not forget. You were a ferocious fighter--reckless, courageous, but irrepressible and wild. Yet Arafat sensed that something more existed in you. Something he could mould and develop. He trained you politically, took you with him around the Middle East and to Europe. He treated you like a son, and I am convinced that he was grooming you to replace him one day."

"Garbage, Shukri. Absolute shit and garbage. He humiliated me. Rooted me out of the PLO."

"He had no choice, Hassan. You defied him. You kept talking about a religious crusade. Advocated 'intifada' when it was politically useless, counter-productive even."

Barka leaned back in his chair, his fists clenched. "Arafat became moderate, mis-guided, weak. He vetoed the suicide missions, undercut the intifada, curbed the military commanders, abandoned terrorism as a policy. And why, Shukri? Why? To get money from Saudi Arabia and love from Sadat. And most important for the swine--the respect of the so-called civilized world, of Europe and America."

"It's a policy, Hassan. And a strategy, if you like. A realistic one." Sipping his tea, Kamal added more sugar.

"Well, it's a ruinous one," Barka said loudly. "The Zionists live in security, and we're no closer to a state than before. Arafat's strategy, as you call it, guarantees us isolation and second-class status."

"Arafat is not as moderate as you think," said Kamal. "He's got some military aces up his sleeve."

"They're well-concealed, Shukri. His sleeves are empty. I can tell you that."

"Hassan. If he can forget, forgive, why can't you?"

"Shukri. Almost three years ago he had his bodyguards armed with machine guns drag me to him. He called me a traitor, a 'radical deviationist', threatened to shoot me." Barka, looking off into space, shook his head. "I will never forget it. I thought that I was a dead man."

"Hassan," Kamal interjected. "You were not only undertaking unsanctioned terrorist missions, but also secretly conspiring with Syrian generals behind his back against Assad."

"Assad is a weakling and couldn't care less about the Palestinians."

"After the successful '73 war against the Zionists, Assad is simply not ready for another war. That is why he insisted that we terminate our assaults from Syrian territory into Israel."

"If I had had my way," Barka said, "Assad would have been deposed by a general who would have backed us to the hilt." He sipped his tea, adding hot water to the cup.

"It was a desperate maneuver, Hassan," said Kamal, his tone becoming softer. "The struggle has made you warped. Look at the results of Arafat's policy. Daily we are gaining support, attracting funds, exposing the imperialist nature of Israeli policy to the world. Time is on our side, if only we act shrewdly."

"He said I was fragmenting the movement," shouted Barka, ignoring what Kamal had just said. "'Radical deviationism'; worse than 'bourgeois individualism', he told me. 'Black September' divides the movement, only helps our enemies', he said."

"But he let you live, Hassan. Your past service restrained him. He told us that in committee."

"He will regret it," said Barka.

"It's hopeless, Hassan, just hopeless. You are poisoned against him for what happened three years ago. Let us eat the rest of our meal in peace."

As they walked back to Kamal's car, Barka asked how Habash had reacted to the proposal of reconciliation.

"He was noncommittal, I am told. But he didn't say 'no'. You know that Habash is his own man. He has even refused ties with the Iraquis, despite all their oil money. He is a visionary, sitting there in Bagdad reading Lenin and concocting fantastic schemes. But it never comes to anything."

"He has got the quality of persistence which I share and the virtue of patience which I lack," said Barka.

"He will come around, I am certain."

"How much shall we bet, Shukri?"

"No bets, Hassan. I am just waiting for you to soften up a bit."

"You will be a toothless old man with white hair before I do, Shukri." He hugged Kamal and wished him well.

"Good-bye, brother."

Chapter 10

NEW YORK TIMES, New York, July 2, 1978 "A spokesman for United Nations Secretary-General Kurt Waldheim announced today that Yasser Arafat, leader of the Palestinian Liberation Organization, will visit the United Nations in September to mark the expected entry of the PLO into the General Assembly. The Security Council will vote on the issue of PLO admission in late August or early September. In Jerusalem, an Israeli Foreign Ministry official denounced the proposed upgrading of the PLO from Observer Status to U.N. membership in the General Assembly, calling it an 'unworthy act' which Israel 'will do everything in her power to prevent'."

The procession entered Cedarcrest Cemetery in Forest Hills, Queens, New York, just before noon. Two black limousines transporting the family of the deceased led a line of cars carrying friends and relatives to the site that would soon contain the mortal remains of Samuel Kaplan, who had died two days earlier of lung cancer at age 87.

As a multitude of people gathered around the gravesite, the immediate family huddled before freshly unearthed mounds of dirt. Kaplan's wife, a sparrow of a woman, was supported by two large sons and a sturdy daughter holding her arms tightly to keep her wobbly legs from collapsing altogether. Someone leaned over to offer smelling salts, but she shook her head.

The oak coffin lay suspended on elastic cloth treads. In the hole, a baseball-capped workman labored frantically to repair the pulley system that would lower the coffin.

When he finished, the black-clothed rabbi from Kaplan's synagogue, the prominent Temple Emmanuel on Fifth Avenue across from Central Park, whispered to the family that he would begin. In a high-pitched, reedy voice, he chanted the ancient Hebrew prayer for the dead. Then mournfully gazing at the coffin, the rabbi began his eulogy. Identifying Kaplan as a religious man, a devoted husband and father, a successful businessman, and a huge benefactor of Israel, he raised his voice to say: "Prime Minister Begin of Israel has cabled his deep personal regrets to the family and has asked the Israeli ambassador to the United Nations to represent him here today. Will Mrs. Sonia Berenson please step forward?"

A striking woman in her mid forties moved near the coffin on the side facing the family. Her jet-black hair, expertly coiffed into a thick bun, was pulled back on her head. She wore a black chiffon dress that hugged a slightly spreading waist and full bosom. Buzzing noisily, the crowd pressed forward to glimpse a celebrity that most had seen only on television. Removing her sunglasses, she signaled for the gathering to be silent.

"Samuel Kaplan," she began, "was a true friend of Israel. Before the State of Israel was born, he worked tirelessly in this country—organizing meetings, addressing rallies, lobbying politicians." Across the way, the dead man's wife hunched her shoulders and began to weep.

"When President Truman announced United States' recognition of Israel in 1948, Samuel Kaplan was invited to attend the ceremony in Washington, DC. After independence, he secretly channeled guns, bullets, planes, and money to us. He was crucial to our survival. Today I am privileged to announce that the Israeli government has established a chair in ancient history at Jerusalem University in his hon..."

Suddenly, across the grave, Mrs. Kaplan fainted. Somebody screamed, and people rushed closer to help. "Back, back," shouted the rabbi. "Give her air."

In the shadows of a large chapel located on a hill a hundred yards away, two men talked quietly. The sun filtered through rusted iron bars, casting light on the flattened gravestones inside. Elaborate latticework in the form of Hebrew letters attached to the fingers of a cherubic young boy with flowing tresses fringed the outside of this ornate monument to a hotel owner, his wife, and three children who had perished in a fire early in the century.

"Well, Browning?" asked David Arovitch, a tall, husky man in his mid thirties. "Have you considered our offer? Will you do it?"

The other man, around the same age, blond and well built, stared at a photo of an Arab in headdress. Finally, almost rhetorically, he said: "It's no ordinary job."

"That is why we sought you out," said Arovitch.

"The man is in his own backyard. He is never alone; probably sleeps with five bodyguards. Any misjudgment would be fatal--to me." Bending down, Charles Browning rubbed his fingers gently over the faded numerals of patchwork gravestones. Then abruptly he stood up and handed back the photo. "It would require elaborate planning, perfect timing, and incredible luck. No way, not with the money you are offering. Too many risks involved for a tiny payday."

"We are offering you a small fortune, Browning. Seven hundred thousand dollars."

"Small is right. In normal circumstances, I would say you were being reasonable, maybe even generous. But for this," he added, shaking his head, "the money has to be so great that I would be a fool to pass it up."

"I am not authorized to offer more."

"Then our discussion is over." Browning started to move away.

"Wait." Arovitch's face was flushed. Their American contact, a corporate lawyer named Sol Reiner, had used Browning's services once before and had identified him as the best professional assassin in the western hemisphere, maybe the world. "How much more would you require?"

"Three million. Half down-payment, the rest afterwards."

Arovitch gasped. "That is a fantastic sum. I doubt we can raise it."

"That's your affair," Browning said laconically. "If you're convinced that Arafat is a threat to your country, you will raise the money." He hesitated a moment. "I thought that the problem for you people was survival, not money. Where I come from, I learned that you people were dripping in it. Maybe I was wrong about that."

Arovitch's jaw tightened and his fists clenched. He took a deep breath. "Where can I reach you?" he asked.

Browning scribbled some figures on a paper. "I will give you three days to decide. After that you won't find me."

Arovitch walked down the hill towards Samuel Kaplan's grave, into which two workmen were shoveling mounds of dirt. He joined the queue of mourners, headed by the dead man's family, moving towards the row of parked cars along the roadway.

The dark blue Lincoln Continental with DPL diplomatic plates was the fifth in line. The chauffeur, who doubled as bodyguard, opened the rear door for Arovitch to climb in.

Sonia Berenson, wearing thick-rimmed reading glasses and perusing some documents at the other end of the seat, looked up as he entered. Arovitch took his place next to the window, gazing blankly ahead.

As their limousine edged along, Sonia Berenson held out her hand, and David Arovitch took it. He moved close to her, and their fingers interlocked tightly.

Off to the side, Charles Browning lit a cigarette and watched the procession exit from the cemetery.

Chapter 11

The next morning Charles Browning entered the offices of Sherry Netherlands Wine Distributors on Madison Avenue. A small portly bald-headed man named Jerry ushered him into a large, map-lined conference room where a striking young black woman was sitting.

"Charles, meet Cynthia Sherman," Jerry said in a raspy voice. "Cynthia is handling auction and lot agents for us now. Cynthia, Charles is the best free-lancer in the business. He's got a proposition for us that you're gonna like. See you kids later." He left the room.

"What do you have, Mr. Browning?"

"Chateau Lafite '53', Miss Sherman. My sources tell me that Christie's is going to offer it in medium-size lots at its auction next Friday in London. Interested?"

"Depends on the price, I would say." She looked at a catalogue and some handwritten notes.

"How does $575 maximum per lot sound?"

After doing some calculations on a mini-calculator, she said: "Make it $545 maximum, and you have a deal."

"You're not giving me much latitude, I would say."

She folded her hands on the table and smiled at him.

"It's the best that I can do. See Jerry if you want to haggle."

"I wouldn't dream of it," Browning said. "I'll take it."

After negotiating quantity and commission, she said: "Cable us from London if you consummate the purchase."

"Not 'if'… 'when.' But that's all right, Miss Sherman. I like healthy skepticism. Makes it more of a challenge." He studied her closely. "How come I haven't seen you around here before?"

"Because I'm new. They pried me loose from a competitor three months ago."

"And before that?"

"College and grad school."

"I detect an accent. The South?"

"Grew up in Mobile, but went to school on the West Coast. Pepperdine B.A. and then Stanford M.B.A." She reached for a filtered cigarette. Browning pulled out his lighter.

"Thanks," she said laconically.

"With that background," Browning continued, "how did you happen to grace the wine and liquor business with your presence when you could have gone anywhere—Credit

Lyonnais, IBM, the World Bank, even the U.S. Treasury Department?"

"That's a long story," she said, gathering up her papers.

"Tell it to me tonight at dinner."

She looked inquisitively at him. "You're pretty aggressive, aren't you?"

"Cynthia, you ever been to a really high class wine tasting?"

"Of course I have. Many times."

"But my guess is that you have never been to one like the tasting being put on at the Explorers Club tonight. Strictly by invitation. The biggest growers in France and Italy will be there. Come with me, and then we'll have dinner afterwards at a nice little place in the Village."

Hesitating, she finally answered: "Okay, babe. We have wine in common, and I like challenges. I'll meet you in the lobby of the Explorers Club at 7:30."

On the street, Charles Browning took a taxi to a small white-brick building on 56th Street near Third Avenue. A metal sign in gothic letters read: "Sandor Kariko, Hungarian Acrobatic Master, Second Floor." The elevator opened onto six middle-aged women in various stages of obesity gyrating and perspiring to the sharp instructions barked by the master. Browning walked past them to the locker room where he put on tight blue shorts and a sleeveless blue jersey.

At 11 a.m., he entered the exercise studio, now deserted except for a short, lithe man with a wrinkled face.

"Ready, Monsieur Browning?"

"Yes, Sandor."

He led Browning through a series of warm-up stretches--arm, leg, and torso extensions. Then came vigorous leg raises, balancing movements, mat tumbles, and parallel bar maneuvers. Rings attached to thick ropes at a height of nine feet were his weakest point. As he somersaulted vertically over and over, his left arm gave way on one complicated turn and a half, and he crashed to the mat below. Sandor moved over to help, but Browning pushed him away. After heavy aerobic breathing, he jumped up again, grasping the rings, now performing more slowly, especially on the upward twists. His movements were awkward, forced. It was near the end of his session, and he was tiring.

Five minutes before noon, the Hungarian led him in wind-down exercises, a slower version of the preliminary ones. Browning gave him a one hundred dollar bill, reserved the same hour for the following day, showered, and left.

After lunch, he kept his customary Monday afternoon appointment with a large German-owned wine firm on lower Broadway, where, in return for a substantial retainer, he advised on taste patterns in the U.S. and price movements in Europe. He talked with an amiable former diplomat named Hugo who poured out glasses of Riesling and made disparaging remarks in a thick German accent about 'predatory' and 'feckless' competitors.

Afterwards Browning went to the New York Public Library, where he browsed for three hours in the small Middle East Room. Recent Middle East history he found to be more than normally confused: civil war in Lebanon, internecine struggle among the Palestinians, Libyan troublemaking, Syrian intransigence, difficulties in the growing rapprochement between Egypt and Israel, differences in perspective between the U.S. and Israel, Saudi Arabia and petro politics, Communist penetration in Iraq and South Yemen. He would return each afternoon for the next few days to scan historical data stretching back to 1948 and beyond. Although he developed a morbid fascination for the subject as a whole, two items above all interested him— Yasir Arafat's personality traits and work habits, and the motives inspiring Browning's potential recruiters.

This job would be his highest paid ever, if it came through. He knew that it would. He was already planning his moves. Browning had turned down the last two contracts, not because the money was bad, but because they hadn't inspired him.

He could afford to be selective. His day job, combined with his extracurricular activities, had already given him a measure of financial security. The Arafat hit, if it came through, would constitute an astronomical payday. Another positive feature was the complicated and dangerous challenge it would pose.

The wine tasting took place in the auditorium of the Explorers and Hunters Club, a marble-columned building on Park Avenue where boar heads protruded from the walls and colorful paintings depicting scenes of elderly gentlemen with handlebar mustaches pointing huge shotguns at cringing foxes or stalwart buffalos graced the oak-paneled interior. A dozen prosperous looking men mulled around a center table containing rows of red wine bottles. They sniffed and tasted samples of Gevrey-Chambertin, Clos Chas-sagne-Montrachet, and Nuits-Saint-Georges, courtesy of the Chateau Pomme-Freres of Burgundy. On another table, also surrounded by growers and connoisseurs, were bottles of Brunello di Montalcino, Chianti Classico, and Montepulciano, courtesy of the leading distributor in Milan. A tall, grey-haired man in a deep blue suit introduced each bottle to the semi-annual gathering of the Chevaliers des Vins. His recitation was then interpreted into French and Italian. Browning whispered into Cynthia Sherman's ear any interesting point made in French or Italian that had not been made in English.

Browning introduced Cynthia as an "aficionada" of their trade. When it became known that she occupied a high position at Sherry Netherlands, a few men with major vineyards in France and Italy passed their cards and made appointments to see her.

After the tasting, Browning drove his Mercedes to a small Italian restaurant in Greenwich Village, where the proprietor, after greeting him warmly, seated them in an alcove by a scene of the Spanish steps in Rome.

"If I haven't told you yet, Cynthia," said Browning, as they dined on pasta, veal, and spicy spinach, "you look stunning." She was wearing a strapless red evening gown and gold pendant. Her lips were blood red, her eye shadow dark blue. Her hair had been frizzed into a thick Afro.

"Thanks, babe. I'm not too hip to accept the occasional compliment."

"You like the meal?"

"It is delish. Except for the wine." They were drinking the house red.

"You're right. No way it compares to the stuff we just had."

"I just don't see you doing it, Charles.

"Doing what?"

"You know. The wine tasting, the wine selling. You are smooth enough, okay, and you know your wines. That I can see. But you just don't seem the type. I picture you more as...a professional athlete or a high-level executive. Something like that."

"Everybody has got to eat, Cyn. I don't see you doing it either."

"Well, how did you get into it?"

He looked at her. "You really want to know? After Vietnam I was bumming around Europe. Had a French girlfriend whose father was a wine magnate. Had a mini conglomerate--vineyards, bottling, distribution, marketing, the whole works. He took a liking to me, probably saw me as his future son-in-law. I don't know. But he taught me every aspect of his business. After I split with his daughter, I returned here and set myself up as an independent wine consultant. Slow going at first, but I made contacts and built my reputation. It's not a bad life. I travel a lot, visit vineyards in Europe and occasionally in California, and attend the major auctions in London, Paris, and Milan. And the bread's good, believe me. You saw the car, and I have a home in Southampton where I spend most weekends."

"You trying to snow me, Charles?"

"Not at all," he said, smiling. "Now you tell me how you got into it."

"Only fair. It was tough growing up in the South. Overt and subtle racism everywhere. I couldn't wait to escape to California. In college and grad school I found I had a penchant for economics. It was either teaching it or making money with it. I chose the latter."

"Wise choice," he said, raising his wine glass and looking directly into her eyes.

"During my last year at the Stanford B School, I got all sorts of offers, but I would be damned if I was going to be any token black woman executive in some big multinational firm. By that time I had wanted to come to New York anyway, and the only offer I got here was from a competitor of Sherry. Stayed three years, then Sherry made an irresistible offer. Good money, fascinating international people coming by all the time, more and more responsibility and status. And so here I am."

"Let's make a toast to wine," he said, raising his glass.

"Why?"

"For bringing us together."

When they were driving uptown, she said: "A cousin is staying at my place."

"We'll go to mine."

His penthouse overlooked Central Park from the west. She lingered on the balcony admiring the view. Then she came into his arms. Slowly they undressed each other, and as her clothes dropped to the floor, he studied her closely. She was big-breasted with a thin waist, shapely legs, and curvaceously rounded posterior. Her skin was smooth and supple to his touch.

"You're gorgeous, you know," Browning said, moving his hands from her breasts to her hips.

"You're not so bad yourself," she said, squeezing his arms and then his butt. "Nice ass, and all those arm muscles. From lifting wine bottles, Charles?"

"Whatever you say, Cynthia. Can we move into my room?"

Hugging each other tightly, they edged towards his bedroom, moving to his large circular bed. He was already erect, and as he touched her, she became wet, with her breath rapid and loud. Standing near the window, they touched each other for several minutes, kissing and looking into each other's eyes.

"Tight, taut, great," he whispered to her, fondling her breasts and the curvature of her rear end, gently easing her onto his bed.

"Mmm," she said almost breathlessly, as he put his left hand on her rear end, and continued with his middle finger of his other hand to explore her vagina.

Then he entered her, and they moved slowly, then more rapidly, as their lips and tongues mingled together. The slow rhythmic movement of their bodies intensified, and he held back as they moved, waiting until she shouted on reaching climax before he permitted himself to come.

"Cynthia, Cynthia, that was amazing," he uttered, as he withdrew from her.

"Definitely not bad, Charles…my first time with a wine stud," she said, smiling at him.

As they lay back smoking cigarettes, she looked at the clock. "Shit, it's past 1 a.m., and I've got a 10 o'clock appointment." She hurriedly put her clothes on.

"I'll call you tomorrow," he said lazily from the bed. "I want to see you again."

"You kidding, Charles? This is a one-night stand. Nothing more."

He sat up, startled. "Hey, I usually say that."

"Then there's no problem." And she was gone.

Chapter 12

The signal came in mid-morning. They arranged to meet at the Alice-in-Wonderland statue in Central Park.

During his acrobatic class, Browning felt especially strong. His turns on the rings went smoothly, the taciturn Sandor even praising his form.

The park was filled with joggers, mothers with baby carriages, and strollers enjoying a sunny summer day that for once was not suffocatingly humid.

"Burger has agreed to your demand," David Arovitch said. "He wants you to proceed immediately."

"Deposit one and a half million dollars at the branch office of the Banque de Montreal at 53rd and Lexington. Use this account number." He handed Arovitch a slip of paper.

"I'll need at least two days," said Arovitch.

"Thursday morning at the latest. I'll be ready to start as soon as the money is there."

"Our sources say that Arafat will be in Beirut for the next seven days preparing a conference of Arab terrorists."

"Freedom fighters, they call themselves," Browning said curtly. "May I assume the money will be deposited on time?"

Arovitch glared at him. "Yes. Just be sure to blame it on his fellow terrorists. We do not want any involvement."

"Of course. I'm not a complete idiot, you know." And he walked away brusquely, leaving Arovitch muttering some obscenities in Hebrew and English.

That evening, unable to concentrate on the psychological sketch of Arafat that he was preparing, Charles Browning picked up the telephone and asked the operator for the number of Cynthia Sherman. "Unlisted" was the response. After hesitating a moment, he dialed an old girlfriend named Louise, an editor at Harper and Row that he hadn't seen in months. She was in and would be delighted to see him, she said. Within minutes of arriving and making desultory conversation over a drink, he led her into the bedroom. Afterwards he looked blankly ahead, making no effort to communicate.

"What's the matter, Charles?" Louise asked. Her crimson cheeks almost matched the color of her hair. She ran her fingers through the mat of sun-bleached hair on his chest.

"You don't seem your usual dynamic self this evening?"

"Did it show in bed?" he asked.

"Well..." She sat up to study his face. He reached over to touch her, then withdrew his hand.

"You know what it is, Louise?" he said, shaking his head. "Met this high-class black chick yesterday. We went out last night, and then I took her back to my place. So what happens later? She ups and splits, saying it's only a one-night stand. What do you think of that?"

"Fuck you, Charles. No wonder you called me out of the blue. You just wanted some quick action, some consoling. No one uses me." Louise turned her back.

He put his hand on her shoulder, but she smacked it away. "I'm sorry," he said. "I was callous. Can I make amends?"

"I should have known you by now, Charles. You're a bastard. A charming bastard maybe, but a bastard nonetheless." She turned towards him. "What's the use? You'll never change. I should know the score when you re-enter my life. Come back here," she said, grabbing him roughly. "I won't heave on you like your smartass black chick."

In her arms he thought of the Thai whore who had held him the same way many years before in Bangkok. After eight straight months in the Delta fighting the VC, the mosquitoes, and the muck, he had needed the rest and recreation in the randy massage parlors in the notorious Pat Pong area and the more sedate Soi Cowboy street off Sukumvit.

It was in Vietnam that he discovered that he had a taste for murder. The moment he stuck a blade into someone's back, he experienced a strange exhilaration. No matter that it was the company sergeant who had ridden them ragged and endangered their lives.

First the tense build-up, then the orgasmic, rejuvenating release in the act itself. It was pure power, an ecstatic high of boundless energy. Thirsting to re-experience this sensation, he volunteered for dangerous patrols. Many in the platoon thought he had a suicidal streak, especially when he signed up for a second term of duty after the murderous Vietcong Tet offensive of February 1968.

After his release from military service in 1970, Browning went to Malaysia, hiring himself out as bodyguard to a local opium dealer. When the boss found him siphoning off some of the booty, Browning gunned him down and took over the business, expanding it beyond the capital, Kuala Lumpur. Soon after, the Singapore crowd moved in, and he recognized that it was time to go.

Before returning to the U.S., he dallied in Europe learning the wine trade which he recognized as an effective cover. For someone of his talents, Browning realized, the quickest way to big money--and an affluent lifestyle--was to hire himself out to the rich and powerful who inevitably would have rich and powerful enemies they wanted to have eliminated. Straddling respectable society and the underworld, and using a variety of pseudonyms, Browning developed contacts, first in the playgrounds of the U.S. (Las Vegas, Palm Beach, and the Caribbean), then in Europe and Latin America. His lifestyle improved dramatically. He ate in four star restaurants, bought his penthouse and the beach house in Southhampton, and slept with beautiful fashion models. Working in the wine trade, he acquired a reputation as a sophisticated, high-living playboy. And he acquired clients in his other trade as well.

His start, ironically, came through the back door. In Montreal for a wine festival, he heard about friction between the leaders of the top French and English-speaking gangs. Asking each gang leader how much he would pay to dispose of his rival, Browning accepted the higher bid and returned home with one hundred thousand dollars in his pocket.

Next he was hired by a Long Island heiress whose husband was threatening divorce and remarriage with a younger woman. A Wall Street executive contracted for the killing of his counterpart at a rival firm. In Paraguay the general in power recruited him to put away the air force commander aspiring to replace him. When on a hot summer evening Browning came to the presidential palace to collect the balance owed him, the country's ruler, ten bodyguards at his side, inquired why he should pay.

"Because if you don't," Browning replied, "five top assassins will come after you pronto. You may surround yourself with a hundred bodyguards if you like, but one day when you are careless, one of them will put a bullet in your back or your head and the Paraguayan people will rejoice." The ruler paid in gold coins.

After that hit, Browning had sufficient funds to purchase elegant furniture for his Hamptons house, travel first-class, and be more selective in the contracts he accepted. In New York he was in great demand as a wine consultant who obtained quality European wines at surprisingly low prices. In the wine trade he was known as an aloof, but consummate professional who revealed little, but always produced what he promised. He had a similar reputation in his other field of endeavor.

On the morning of July 11, 1978, Browning learned that one and a half million dollars had been deposited in his numbered bank account. By noon he was on board the Concorde flight to London, arriving at his suite in the Grosvenor Hotel on Park Lane at 9 p.m. local time. After showering, he put on a blue Cardin blazer with cream slacks and went to Chez Solange in Soho, where he ordered truite meuniere, salad, petits pois, and mashed potatoes, along with Sancere 1964.

Wide awake, he walked the streets along Hyde Park near Marble Arch until 2 a.m. gazing at strolling pedestrians and restaurant workers hurrying to get home and declining the advances of two highly attractive prostitutes of East European origin.

The next morning, before the auction began at Christie's, he stopped by the manager's office for a brief chat. During the auction, he sat at the front left, bemused by the intensity of bidding for Bordeaux reds and German whites. When the Lafite '53 lots came up, the auctioneer prematurely closed out the bidding at the signal of Browning's uplifted catalogue.

"Success at Christie's. Lafite purchased. 259. Charles Browning" read his cable to Cynthia Sherman.

The next morning at Heathrow, he boarded a British Airways jet to Beirut.

Chapter 13

His first week in Beirut was frustrating. For one thing, the truce in the Lebanese civil war, in effect when he had accepted the assignment, broke down. For three days Syrian rockets shelled the Christian stronghold in west Beirut, with the Christian forces taking reprisals against the Moslem quarter. Browning stayed in his hotel, the Supreme, a block from the Mediterranean coast, venturing out only once to observe the shelling when he couldn't stand being cooped up any longer. The hotel manager, Mr. Chamouni, tall with hollow cheeks and a lugubrious expression, termed his fellow citizens "barbarians." "Don't they know they are destroying a civilization?" he muttered repeatedly to his few foreign guests.

Cornering Browning in the lobby one morning, Mr. Chamouni explained why the city had declined to this lamentable state. "Mammon pure and simple. Beirut needs banking money, not oil or foreign aid, to survive, and it is all going out, not coming in. We are finished," he added sadly. "Our clients now bank in Zurich and bathe in Deauville."

Finally, on the day after Israeli planes flew overhead to warn the Syrians against annihilating the Christians, the 59th truce in the civil war was announced. Gradually people edged back into the streets, running for cover only when snipers were detected or army vehicles screeched perilously close.

Posing as a journalist, Browning carried out his ostensible assignment of interviewing PLO leaders for a Los Angeles newspaper. It was hardly worth the effort. In the tense atmosphere, his movements were restricted, and whenever he ventured outside the somewhat elastic neutral zone, cocky youths in battle fatigues nervously waved their guns and asked to see his papers.

As expected, Yasser Arafat's trail was elusive. Ever since a night time Israeli commando raid on a headquarters post had resulted in eleven deaths, the PLO leadership took extraordinary precautions. They changed residences as often as they changed clothes. Scores of bodyguards surrounded him whenever he emerged in public.

Browning asked the help of the U.S. Embassy, and a tall, thin Bostonian named Adrian obligingly drove him around for half a day before bowing out because of the danger. At the News Club where he went daily for drinks and gossip, Browning was given a few contacts by fellow journalists, leading to insignificant interviews with minor officials who exaggerated their role in the PLO hierarchy and laughed in his face when he solicited their aid in obtaining an interview with Yasser Arafat.

He had come up against a stone wall. In this geographically and ethnically divided city, he could not get anywhere close to Yasser Arafat. He questioned his arrogance in accepting the assignment; yet he did not want to admit defeat. However, facts were facts, and he could not touch Arafat in Beirut. Then, unexpectedly, Arafat organized a news conference.

The PLO leader wanted to announce the results of a meeting on "Tactics to Retake the Homeland" which had been held in secret during the last seven days. Journalists were invited to present their credentials to a corps of militiamen at a central point in the neutral zone. Then they were driven in pickup trucks to Liberation Hall in East Beirut for the press conference. Joining the first group, Charles Browning managed to get a seat in the third row in front of the podium.

Yasser Arafat wore his customary green military outfit and a black-checkered keffiyah. He had a rough bearded face and small, smooth hands that gripped the sides of the makeshift lectern during his opening remarks. As he talked, the journalists in the packed hall scribbled frantically on their notepads. Speaking in lightly accented English, Arafat hinted at a broad new political formation within the PLO umbrella group, new alliances abroad, military discussions with certain anti-Zionist states, and a new weapons procurement policy. He announced an imminent trip to "important Middle East capitals."

Then he alluded to the death of Selim el-Nuseury in Geneva the week before. "This despicable act will live in infamy," he said. "Selim el-Nuseury was above all a diplomat. He represented us in the United Arab Emirates, in Tunisia, and finally in our observer delegation at the United Nations in Geneva. He has become another martyr to the liberation of Palestine, another Zionist victim. He served us well and we shall never forget him." Sipping a glass of water, he watched the journalists below wave their hands.

The first question, from the correspondent of the Manchester Guardian, concerned possible motives for the murder.

"To keep us out of international organizations," Arafat said, jabbing the air with his finger. "The Zionists will not succeed. The next session of the General Assembly will confirm that."

"Are you saying, Your Excellency," asked a Kuwaiti journalist, "that you expect a favorable vote in the Security Council on the admission of the Palestinian Liberation Organization to the U.N. General Assembly?"

"By nature I am an optimist. Does that answer your question?"

"Will you be attending the General Assembly, Your Excellency?" the Kuwaiti followed up.

"Surely that depends on the Security Council vote," Arafat answered.

"Mr. Arafat," asked the Middle East correspondent for the Washington Post. "When you speak of a 'broad new political formation' within the PLO, are you suggesting that rejection front dissidents like Barka and Habash will rejoin the movement?"

"We are in contact with them and other so-called dissidents. We would welcome their return to the PLO mainstream movement. Our differences with them, after all, are about means, not ends. Surely reasonable men can resolve such matters when they are united on the larger issues."

Arafat patiently answered questions for the next hour. Then he thanked the journalists for their attention and, bodyguards at his side, went backstage and left the hall. His bulletproof Mercedes, surrounded by a corps of motorcycle guards, sped down the path and took a circuitous route through some Muslim areas to the airport where Arafat boarded a Caravelle bearing the insignia of the Libyan Air Force.

Browning watched the motorcade pass. Then he was ushered into a pick-up with twenty-five reporters. Palestinian militiamen escorted them through the dusty winding streets of the medieval Arab quarter, where masses of people congregated around sidewalk market stalls offering the latest oriental spices and sweets. Hovel-like, confined living quarters were punctuated every few hundred yards by a series of mosques. When Browning had visited Beirut six years before, he had been struck by the astounding visual contrasts—the camel and the Cadillac, the mendicant and the merchant, the mosque and the bourse, co-existing side by side in curious, if paradoxical, proximity. Now only the ancient half, a monument to timelessness, remained. The modern part had been reduced to rubble.

The truck deposited them at the intersection of President Nasser Boulevard and the Rue Charles de Gaulle, the European no-man's land between the Muslim and Christian quarters. Barbed wire strung along the sidewalk, and formerly elegant shops and banks, if not gutted, were boarded up. On one side, Muslim soldiers lounged in the shadow of the huge Barclay's Bank, while across the way, Christian militiamen scrutinized each identity card before allowing the journalists to pass.

Tossing a coin to a mutilated beggar blocking the sidewalk, Browning strolled towards the harbor six blocks away. At ground level he saw apprehensive faces peering out, causing him to reflect on the notion that he, a foreigner, could walk about freely, while the inhabitants whose complexions or rather, religions, were magnets for sniper bullets, were compelled to remain cooped up.

Entering the hotel, he told Mr. Chamouni that he was leaving Beirut. He offered to pay for the entire period reserved, another ten days, but Chamouni refused with dignity.

Browning ate lunch in his room, lamb stew and boiled potatoes, sipping red wine from a bottle of Mouton Rothchild '69. He carried his suitcase to the lobby, where the manager waited with a red-eyed old man displaying blackened jagged teeth.

"This is Abu, the village idiot," Mr. Chamouni said. "He will get you through the lines if anyone will. Both sides feel sorry for him, so they let him roam at will. But do not give him too much; it all goes on drink anyway. And be sure to come back here when you next come to Beirut."

Browning paid the bill, while Abu slung his suitcase into the front seat of a 1957 black Packard. Opening the back door, he bowed ceremoniously for his passenger to step in as if Browning were an English aristocrat out for a drive in the country.

Abu drove quickly along small back roads, slowing down only when soldiers appeared at crossroads. When they saw who it was, they motioned for the car to pass. They arrived at the airport without incident.

After buying a first-class ticket to Cyprus, Browning sat in a comfortable chair with an old copy of Wine World. Though relieved to be leaving Beirut, he wondered how the Israelis would react to his admission of failure.

Chapter 14

From the back garden of his chalet high on a hill outside Jerusalem, a white-haired, thick-necked man in his late seventies watched through a small telescope as a taxi wended its way forward.

"He's coming," Eli Burger said to David Arovitch who was sitting in a white metal chair next to some pear trees.

"He had better have something to say for himself."

"You don't like him very much, do you David?"

"Come on, Eli. He's an anti-Semitic, arrogant goy. I understand why we need him, but I am not obliged to like him."

"True. Just try not to show it."

Charles Browning rang the front bell. An old woman, wrinkled and stooped, escorted him along a stone path to the back garden. Burger and Arovitch turned to face him.

"So you failed," Burger said, without introducing himself.

"Let us just say that I didn't succeed."

"Why?"

"He was too well guarded. No way could I get to him."

"Did you try?"

"The war started up again. The city was chaotic. I didn't know the language, the people, the geography of the city, or the environs. It was a thousand to one shot, to begin with. In Beirut—at this time—it became a million to one. I know an impossible situation when I see it." Then, hesitating a moment, he added: "There is no way I can get to him in the Middle East."

"That's wonderful," said Arovitch. "Why the hell did you accept the job?"

"Because," said Browning calmly, "it's a terrific challenge."

"The money also, Browning," shouted Burger, pacing back and forth. "Don't forget the money."

"Sure," said Browning, smiling. "It's also a good payday."

"So now you have one and a half million dollars of our money," Arovitch said. "What happens next?"

"I will return it minus expenses within a week."

"Not so fast," Burger said. He motioned him to a huge telescope fastened to the ground at the far end of the garden. Leaning over, Browning saw the walls and buildings of one corner of the Old City. He made out the rough-stoned Western Wall, the silver-domed Al Asqa mosque, and the melange of new and old stone surfaces of the partly restored Jewish Quarter to the left. By twisting the instrument slightly, Burger fastened on the Mount of Olives.

"That is close to where I first lived when I came from Poland in 1934," said Burger with a sweep of his hand. "I fought the Arabs, the British, and the Jordanians for that little piece of fallow ground."

Browning's expression showed little interest.

"Have you ever heard of the Irgun?" Burger asked.

"The Irgun Zvai Leumi? 'National Military Organization'. Part of the underground movement in the 1940s; your Prime Minister was once commander-in-chief. You boys got away with a lot of mischief until the Haganah disarmed you when you tried to smuggle in those guns on the Altalena in June 1948—the war of attrition against the British occupation forces in '46 and '47, the 'lash for a lash' campaign…Then the massacre at the King David Hotel."

"What do you mean 'massacre'? We gave them ample warning."

"The message was cryptic. No matter. It shocked the world and hastened the end of the Mandate."

"If you know so much, Browning, tell me who made the phone call to the British to evacuate the King David?"

Browning touched a yellow rose, smelling its fragrance. "Someone using the pseudonym 'Israel Halprin'. They never found him. Most people thought it was Begin."

"He was thirty miles away that day. We couldn't risk his capture."

"Why are you boring me with stories of the terrorist underground? You're still living in the past, it seems."

"'Terrorist underground'?" said Burger, bristling. "We weren't as crazy as the Stern boys, and we were so-called 'terrorists' only to remove the British usurpers."

"I'm not really interested in your politics," said Browning quietly.

"You and your cavalier attitude. If you know your Jewish history back to ancient days, then you know how we fought for our land against overwhelming numbers—against the Romans, the Ottomans, the British, the Arabs in four wars since 1948. Finally in 1967 Israel regained what was rightfully hers. The real terrorists—the Palestinians—are challenging that. Everything is being jeopardized. Even our Prime Minister, my old friend Begin, is making deals."

"I read about that. A lot of talk about a U.S.-brokered deal with Sadat for mutual diplomatic recognition between Egypt and Israel."

"Yes, things are happening and I…we…don't like the way things are going."

And that's where I come in," said Browning.

"Precisely. You say that you cannot get Arafat in the Middle East. Do you have anything else in mind?"

"It is said that he will come to the U.N. in September. New York is my home ground. I will have a much better shot at him there."

"Not sure that I like it, Eli," David Arovitch intervened. "Can Browning guarantee that the Arabs will be blamed for Arafat's death in New York?"

"Why not?" Browning answered. "Arab terrorism is international. It can devour its own as easily in New York as in Beirut."

"David," Burger said softly. "All we want is Arafat's death. There could even be an advantage in your being there to help our friend here."

Arovitch bristled. "I still don't like it, Eli."

Burger turned to face Browning. "I want to discuss the matter with my younger colleague. How long can you stay in Jerusalem?"

"Until noon tomorrow. You know where."

"Of course," said Burger. "The King David."

"One more thing," Browning said. "If you decide in favor, I want a 180 laser sub-machine gun...fully equiped, with bullets. The Israeli army bought hundreds from the American manufacturer. You will have an easier time getting one than I will." Breaking off a rose by its prickly stem, he placed it in his lapel buttonhole and left the garden.

Eli Burger trained his small telescope on the taxi driving slowly downhill. Then he moved to the larger telescope, directing it to a different part of the city below. When it focused on the King David, he let it rest.

"Let's go inside," he said to Arovitch.

En route to his study, he asked the maid to serve them tea.

The study was book-lined, with stone artifacts and decorative plates set up on wrought iron stands on tables and bookshelves. Photos of Burger with Israeli politicians, including David Ben-Gurion, Golda Meir, Moshe Dayan, and Menachem Begin, hung on the walls.

Arovitch sat on a leather chair opposite Burger, who took the rotating desk chair. Glancing at the desk photo of a young couple clowning it up for the photographer, Arovitch asked? "How is Miriam?"

"Suffering. She hasn't really gotten beyond it yet."

"Do you see her much?"

"I get out to Yad Yehudah about every other week."

"I am surprised that she stays."

"She's like me. Stubborn. She was one of the founders of the settlement, you know. Has a strong commitment to make it work...Even after losing her husband in the terrorist attack."

"But all those bad memories, Eli. Also, how is she ever going to meet another husband, stuck out there in the hills?"

"My daughter is not so keen to meet another man and get remarried. She says she will never meet anyone like Moshe."

Arovitch shrugged.

"That is another reason too, David."

"I know, I know."

"Ever since my son-in-law was killed in that PLO attack at Yad Yehudah, I have been obsessed with one thought--how to punish those butchers. When I see Miriam haggard from nights of crying over her dead husband and Yoram, who is condemned to grow up without a father, it has made me into a crazy man. I have seen death before, believe me. But when it's a member of your own family, it's so much more painful." He blew his nose with a handkerchief.

"If only Moshe had had a chance to defend himself," Burger continued. "He was such a fighter."

"Right in the back. No chance," said Arovitch, grimacing.

Burger stood up and then dropped down again in his chair. "Until now I have felt helpless. That is why I cannot let this opportunity pass." He folded his hands on the desk.

"Arafat's death would accomplish many things, as I see it--pay back Moshe, rid Israel of a vicious enemy, throw the terrorists into disarray, wreck the PLO entry into the U.N., sabotage any Middle East agreement detrimental to Israel's interests. The Americans are threatening to slow down weapons deliveries unless Begin becomes more flexible on Egypt and on the settlements policy in the West Bank. So far he is resisting, but how long can he go on in the face of American pressure?"

The old woman brought in tea for them. She poured it out slowly for Burger, then for Arovitch. As she did so, Burger said, "Hannah takes good care of me, don't you, Hannah? She serves me before my guests. I cannot make her learn any manners." Hannah's face did not change expression as she dusted the desk top.

"Begin and I are made of the same stuff," Burger continued. "We sat at Jabotinsky's knee in the old country, came to Eretz Yisroel about the same time. Two dogmatic die-hards from the shettl on the same messianic mission— cultivate the land, fight the British, found the State, protect it from the Arabs, increase it, and above all, never compromise. Turn the other cheek and you will usher in a new Holocaust. Begin supports us in Gush Emunim, although he cannot say so. He believes in the historical necessity of settlements and the complete acquisition of the West Bank. You know, he's writing the introduction to my book on the emancipation of Judea and Samaria." Burger paused. "But he's under great pressure now, and I feel that he might bend if something doesn't happen soon."

"So you think that we should give Browning carte blanche?" Arovitch asked.

"Browning is self-assured, hungry for money, and completely ruthless. He was sophisticated enough to recognize that he couldn't get to Arafat in Beirut, David. And man enough to back down. He will do it if anyone can."

"Okay, Eli. I will go along and help him in New York, if he even wants my help."

"And David, do not let your personal dislike of Browning interfere with the operation. He is the right man, I'm convinced. Go to the King David as soon as you get to Jerusalem this afternoon. Tell him to go ahead. Tell him I will try to get the gun he wants. And David..."

"Yes?"

"Tell him not to fail again."

Burger walked Arovitch to the door of his study. "Call me after you have talked with him. Find your own way out, would you, David?"

Sitting at his desk, Burger opened a drawer and removed a folder. Wedged in at the bottom was a faded piece of parchment. Unfolding the parchment, he withdrew a yellow-streaked paper that he gazed at for the next half-hour.

It read:

June 1946

To Israel Halprin,

The Jewish National State Israel will salute your brave action at the King David. Fraternal greetings.

Begin

Chapter 15

"That is correct, Mr. President," said the tall, lanky man into the telephone. "The special Security Council meeting should take place in mid or late August." U.N. Secretary-General Kurt Waldheim, his angular face pinched and drawn, gazed blankly out his 38th floor window at the New York skyline, bare and lustrous in the late afternoon.

"Of course I realize what a formidable task you have, Mr. President," Waldheim continued, "but let us be frank. You are in the process of developing the framework for an Egyptian-Israeli diplomatic treaty. You have confided in me that negotiations will take place in mid-September at Camp David. What a wonderful accomplishment this will be. Your wisdom and effective diplomacy will live in historical memory. However, I have it upon the highest authority that if the United States does not allow the Palestinian Liberation Organization to become a member of the General Assembly, President Sadat of Egypt will withdraw from your diplomatic treaty between Egypt and Israel. I am saying this to you on a confidential basis."

Waldheim wiped his brow with a handkerchief and then continued speaking. "I will, of course, deny this in public. It looks to me that there is a quid pro quo operating here—the U.S. does not veto the admission of the PLO in the U.N., and then soon afterwards you will have your treaty and, I would imagine, a Nobel Peace Prize for your efforts." Getting up suddenly from his chair, Waldheim paced the room, gathering up the long telephone cord as he walked.

"Mr. President," he said a moment later. "I must ask you directly. So much is at stake here. Can you assure me that the United States will waive its veto rights on the Palestinian issue in the Security Council, as we agreed?" The Secretary-General looked over in alarm at the impeccably attired Indian sitting on the sofa ten feet away. His Chef de Cabinet, Krishnan Katani, pursed his lips and made a gesture with his open palms.

"A few days delay, Mr. President? I guess it will not matter if the results will be beneficial. I will wait to hear from you then. Good-bye."

Replacing the receiver, Waldheim banged his fist on the desk. "Damn it, Krishnan. I thought the matter was settled. Now he's vacillating. Wants some more time to 'sensitize' American public opinion. But I'll be damned if I am going to let my plan be ruined by a vacillating, weak American politician."

"It would be a pity," said Katani in a languid tone, lighting a cigarette from a pack of filtered Marlboros.

"He says that he's concerned about an adverse reaction in the country. So he is going to make a speech or two hinting at a general shift in policy. And see what the reaction will be."

The Secretary-General suddenly looked pensive. Then he said reproachfully: "A president is supposed to lead, to mould public opinion, not be the puppet of an indecisive, fickle public. Democracies...I tell you, Krishnan, sometimes I can see the beauty of dictatorships. You know the trite saying about Mussolini making the trains run on time. Important things get done. No weakness or hesitation with a regime like that."

"Are you advocating dictatorships, Mr. Secretary-General? You musn't forget that I come from the largest democracy in the world. Indira Ghandi is trying to subvert it these days, but she won't succeed."

"No, Krishnan. I'm just frustrated by the absence of a definitive decision on the part of the Americans. Carter may have his Camp David triumph in a month or so, but my triumph, my rightful victory and that of the U.N., is the crucial element for me right now. For the U.S. to play games at this late stage after everything was worked out between Carter and me is particularly galling."

"Typical American conceit," Katani said. "Uncle Sam sets the affair up, activates the other parties, and then hesitates or backs out, to the profound annoyance and detriment of everyone else concerned."

"Let's be fair, Krishnan," Waldheim said in a mellower tone. "Carter does have a hell of a problem in this country now. Petrol queues, inflationary spiral, twelve points behind Teddy Kennedy in his own party. The Jewish lobby is agitating strongly. Carter has got to be cautious now. I can understand that."

"American politics are really beyond my comprehension," said Katani, yawning. "At Cambridge modern history began with the Norman invasion and ended with the ascension of Queen Victoria."

"Drink, Krishnan?"

"Lowenbrau, if you don't mind."

Waldheim opened the portable fridge to the left of his desk. After pouring the beer for Katani, he made a scotch and soda for himself.

"What will you do when you leave this place, Krishnan?" the Secretary-General asked.

"Cheers," the Indian said, raising his glass. "Back to my government. They will give me a District Commission. Part of the deal for coming here on assignment."

"Why not stay on? We could find something agreeable for you. A Director 2 post. Maybe even an Assistant Secretary-General."

"An appealing thought, since an international civil servant works much less than a national one. But I do have family and land back in India, both of them extended."

"My wife tried to get me back to Austria after the first term," Waldheim said nonchalantly. "Sometimes I wish I had taken her advice." He stared out the window at the Empire State Building whose architecture he had always found atrocious. "I confess that some of the criticism has been getting to me lately."

"It is the curse of center stage," said Katani, sipping his beer. "Look at your predecessors. Hammarskjold got blasted by the Russians, U Thant by the Americans. Do you expect to accomplish miracles in this job? The big powers penny pinch to keep the U.N. financially weak. They use the veto to keep it politically weak. You've been remarkably successful, if you ask me. No major wars during your administration. The Third World edging into a position of importance without undue friction. The U.N. under your leadership has gone into environment, women's rights, transnational corporations, eradicated smallpox. You've built the Donaupark in Vienna to house a number of U.N. agencies. You've accomplished major miracles, if you ask me."

"You are being very kind, Krishnan," said the Secretary-General, who was not immune to receiving praise from his loyal subordinate. He believed that Katani, who often challenged Waldheim's notions, was being sincere. "But I have to tell you that all this carping about my not being 'activist' enough...being more 'secretary' than 'general'. That's really galling to me."

"All that verbiage is nonsense. Balderdash. Nowadays the S-G must be a conciliator. And that is what you are par excellence. You do not have the scope of a Hammarskjold running the Congo like a U.N. fiefdom or a U Thant denouncing the U.S. over Vietnam. You are more hemmed in by the big powers and the Third World. You should know this and not let things get to you so much."

"Being criticized as a poor administrator of the Secretariat. That really upsets me, Krishnan." Putting the glass aside, Waldheim rested his chin on his folded hands.

"The Secretariat. That cesspool?" said Katani. "That overblown bureaucracy with its baroque intrigue and competing feudal interests? All those powers and groups agitating for more influence and leverage. The whole U.N. is a hothouse of power competition. The Russians control the Security Council and Political Affairs, the Americans the UNDP and UNICEF, the Brits WHO and Economic and Social Affairs, the French Secretariat Administration and Personnel, the Africans UNESCO and technical cooperation, the Chinese and Arabs now demanding everything else in sight. How can you administer a madhouse when it is run by the inmates"

"It is a perpetual balancing act," Waldheim said angrily. "Just this morning the Latin Americans came to see me about the open directorship at the International Labor Organization. I couldn't tell them that I had promised it to the Arab bloc in return for allowing the Japanese to get Public Information. And the idiot whom the Latin Americans proposed is an incompetent cousin of the president of a second-rate military dictatorship. It makes me sick."

Katani nodded sympathetically. He had heard this litany before.

"I'm sorry. I refuse to be a bloody conciliator par excellence, as you put it. I want to break out of this trap. When my term ends in two years, I go back to Vienna, and I want to be remembered for something more than just keeping the damned ship afloat."

"The 'Grand Design'?"

"Precisely. I now have a chance to make my mark over the Middle East and, more importantly, to gain financial independence for the United Nations. It is time that the U.N. regained some respect, became a strong factor in world affairs again."

And you become President of Austria, Katani said to himself.

"How is the 'Grand Design' proceeding?" he asked. "You have been reticent about it lately. I thought that perhaps you had dropped the idea."

"I know you think that it is preposterous, Krishnan. But it was all being tied together neatly…until a few minutes ago. If Carter backs out, I swear to you that I will leak how U.S. Ambassador Andrew Young is personally supporting the Cubans in Africa. Or how the U.S. is sabotaging the antiballistic agreement with the Russians—the so-called 'SALT' pact--with secret underground nuclear tests in the Pacific."

"Can you prove these things?" Kitani had heard the S.G. mouth off before on unverifiable matters about which he seemed to have no doubts.

"Yes." Waldheim poured himself another drink. "But," he added, futility evident in his voice, "what good will it do me? The 'grand design' must succeed. The future of the U.N. depends on it."

"Where do you stand now?"

"Just yesterday the Arab bloc agreed to vote for the Law of the Sea Treaty if I get the PLO into the U.N. General Assembly."

"Including the section which taxes any seabed raw material by 18% and the tax revenue goes to the U.N.?"

"Yes. If this treaty is ratified, Krishnan, do you know how much the United Nations will benefit? I calculated it the other day. The first year we will get eight hundred million dollars. And the sum will grow exponentially every year. Finally the U.N. will become financially solvent. Removed from the whims of governments--like Russia withholding its contribution to the 1963 Congo operation, the U.S. refusing to pay dues to UNESCO and the ILO because of their anti-Israel positions, the Chinese being assessed far lower than they should be because they will not reveal the numbers of their massive population or their GNP. No longer will the Secretariat feel like a cheap cousin of the World Bank. No longer will we be a prostitute to be haggled over. The U.N. will be able to afford a strong supra-national military force independent of the contributions of the member states."

Katani had heard this spiel before. "It sounds wonderful, but it is a mirage."

"No, Krishnan," the Secretary-General said emphatically. "For once your cynicism is inappropriate. Everything is arranged, I tell you. If I may be immodest this once, I have maneuvered brilliantly. I have aroused fears, provoked jealousies, promised posts, secured privileges. Now 'everyone' stands to gain materially from the passage of the Law of the Sea Treaty and to lose from its defeat. The Russians will get the new Under-Secretary-Generalship in Food and Agriculture and exclusive mining rights in their Baltic zone. The Chinese will obtain Western technology for seabed exploration in the South China Sea; France and the U.S. will get a substantial percentage of minerals extracted for providing their technology. The U.S. will have sole rights up to 100 miles from their Pacific Coast. To say nothing of a new Middle East settlement and a million more barrels of Saudi Arabian oil a day."

"What about the Brits, the Germans, the Asians, Japanese, Latin Americans?"

"The Common Market countries have been given exploration rights in five African mining zones. Japan gets fishing rights and pressure reduced on the killing of whales. Latin America gets an equitable share of American mineral exploration in their waters. The Asians get their zones and percentages increased."

"And the Arabs?"

"High posts in UNESCO and UNDP, a larger U.N. presence in southern Lebanon, and admission of the Palestinian Liberation Organization to the General Assembly. The PLO must gain admittance," Waldheim shouted uncharacteristically, "or both the Arabs and Russians will not accept the treaty."

"You mean to say," said Katani, "that after all these years, you really are close to…"

"Yes, damn it. But only if Carter keeps his word and doesn't veto the PLO getting into the General Assembly. If that occurs, as it MUST, all the pieces will fit perfectly together, and the result will be that the U.N. will become an independent entity free of the financial and political pressures of all of the world's selfish nations and predators, and I can ultimately hand over some real strength to my successor."

"I'm shaking at the thought of what you are telling me."

"Don't shake, Krishnan. Just advise me. What shall I do about Carter?"

Katani walked over and poured himself another beer. "I yield to no one in my anti-Americanism," he said when he had sat down again, "but I think you should sit tight and let Carter 'sensitize' his public opinion. If he fails or professes to fail, hit him with the potential leaks over Andrew Young and nuclear tests. He will go along just to save his political neck."

"I cannot wait very long, Krishnan. The Russians want confirmation that the U.S. will not veto PLO entry. They want to reap credit in the Arab world. Shupelov wants an answer today. He is waiting for my call."

"Then call him. Tell him that Carter is smoothing out a few things domestically. Tell him that you expect no difficulty in obtaining American approval."

"Yes, why not? Best to face him now." He asked his secretary to summon Shupelov.

"Good afternoon, Boris," Waldheim said pleasantly fifteen minutes later to a stout man with wavy grey hair and a prominent mole on his left cheek. As Under-Secretary-General for Political and Security Council Affairs, Shupelov was the highest ranking Russian working at the U.N.

After shaking Waldheim's hand and nodding at Katani, Shupelov inquired, "Any news?"

"Everything is going well," said Waldheim. "We expect to call a Security Council meeting on the PLO issue in..." Katani squirmed in his seat. "... in late August or early September."

"It must be in August, Mr. Secretary-General," said the Russian, shaking his head. "Mr. N'Diaye has cancelled his home leave this month just to preside over a Council meeting." The Guinean President of the Security Council for the month of August was more amenable to Russian influence than his September successor, a West German, would be. "And my staff has prepared all the documents for the meeting," he added.

"The documents can easily be used in September," said Katani quietly.

Shupelov ignored him. "This is very upsetting, Mr. Secretary-General, for reasons we both know." Taking out a large pipe, he stuffed cherry-smelling tobacco in the bowl and lit up. It was Shupelov's express assignment to ensure that the PLO got into the U.N. General Assembly. His government had made deals with three Arab oil-producing states who promised favorable energy exploration rights in return for Soviet leadership in shepherding PLO admission to the U.N. General Assembly. And Shupelov personally was under considerable pressure and surveillance, especially since his predecessor, Arkady Shevchenko, lured allegedly by excessive C.I.A. money, a lucrative book contract, and an American mistress (who, in fact, was writing a book for publication in 1978 entitled "Defector's Mistress" giving intimate details about Shevchenko's idiosyncratic sexual proclivities as well the prostitution trade in Washington, DC where the C.I.A. was 'secretly' housing the Russian) had defected to the U.S. just over a year ago, the highest ranking Russian ever to do so. Although it was considered very unlikely that the austere Shupelov, whose father had been a Red Army commander under Trotsky in the Civil War and who himself had risen through Party ranks to become Commisar of the Kiev region, would succumb to the anti-Soviet temptations of the West (money, sex, and publicity), his phone was monitored and his staff riddled with KGB spies, like all of his Russian colleagues and underlings, just to be sure he toed the party line.

"It is upsetting to me too, Boris," said Waldheim, "but let's be optimistic. President Carter wants a little more time to sell the idea to the American public. He promised to call me in a few days; I'm sure that he will have good news for us then."

"Just tell him," Shupelov said coldly, "that a great deal depends on his fulfilling that commitment." He got up to leave.

"Oh, Boris," Waldheim called out when Shupelov was near the door. "Could you see me tomorrow morning around 10 a.m.? I have decided not to add a Chinese official to the Political Affairs staff. We will review other candidates tomorrow."

Shupelov left the office.

"A real charmer," Katani said.

"Quite a change from Shevchenko, don't you think? Done deliberately, I am sure,"

"Oh, Arkady. That master of subtlety. Purveyor of charm and circumlocution. Vodka on his breath before lunch. Mistress on Sutton Place."

"This one is a Puritan by comparison. Which reminds me of Carter. I'm worried, Krishnan. What can we do to hasten things along? I am thinking of calling Ambassador Young in for a talk right now."

Katani argued against the idea. He advised Waldheim to avoid giving the impression of insecurity or impatience. "Wait a few days. You can always increase the pressure on the Americans then, if you need to," he said to the Secretary-General. Hopefully you won't need to. For now, try to relax. You're becoming a nervous wreck."

"You're right, Krishnan. ... Look at me. I'm sweating and my hands are shaking. It's the 'grand design'. Ach…so much at stake. I had better calm down before I contact Young or Carter again. Let's have another drink."

Chapter 16

"When did you first want to sleep with me, David?"

"The second time I saw you,"

"And why not the first?"

"Because I don't like sleeping with Nazis. When you first introduced yourself to us at the Mission, I thought Himmler had taken over. 'You vill do dis. You vill do dat."

"I had to crack down. The previous ambassador was very lax. What happened the second time?"

"We were in your office discussing a report. Again you were precise, insistent, but when you made a joke about the U.N. producing an abundance of paper but no substance, I knew I was dealing with a human being and not a machine." He leaned towards her. "The more I was around you, the more I wanted you. But you were so remote that I never gave myself much hope."

"And now?"

"I won't let you go," he said, hugging her tightly.

They were in her apartment on the evening of his return from Israel. He had called Sonia from Kennedy Airport to say he was back. Though she seemed distant on the phone, she did not refuse his request to come over immediately. Scarcely in the apartment, he declared how much he had missed her and how deeply he loved her. She put off the inevitable questions about his unexpected trip to Israel.

Sonia Berenson preferred her pied-a-terre on West 68th Street off Central Park to the lavishly decorated rent-free apartment on 79th Street near York Avenue that the Israeli government provided its U.N. ambassador. She chose the furniture herself from antique shops in the Village, terming the eclectic agglomeration "Yiddish colonial." It gave her bodyguard fits, when, a few evenings each week, alleging fatigue or a need for solitude, she would jump into a taxi and disappear. Once he disobeyed her instructions not to follow her. Waiting in the shadows across the street, he observed the Second Secretary at the Mission, David Arovitch, walk up the steps of the brownstone building shortly afterwards. He omitted this information from his report and never followed her again.

Oxford-educated, fluent in five languages, Sonia Berenson had held a succession of diplomatic posts (Mali, Sweden, Italy) before being appointed ambassador to the U.N. three years earlier at the relatively young age of forty-five. Charming, eloquent, tough-minded, she was a rarity in an organization dominated by men.

Married in her late twenties to Yehudi Berenson, a high-raking army officer, she discovered quickly that marriage was no substitute for a career. After a year she resumed her overseas assignments. The couple stayed married more out of lassitude than desire. Release came when her husband burned to death in his tank in the Golan Heights during the Yom Kippur War of 1973. Even before his death, she had had a few love affairs, twice with younger men. A liaison with a handsome military attache at the Greek Mission to the U.N. ended in scandal when his Mission cabled Athens demanding his recall. The Foreign Ministry in Jerusalem advised her obliquely to be more "discreet."

One night while they were working late at the Mission, David Arovitch proposed dinner at a nearby Chinese restaurant. Drinking liberally, they swapped stories about ex-spouses (he was divorced, with a small son in Haifa), and when in the taxi uptown, he suddenly kissed her, she told the taxi driver to take them to West 68th Street. Since that evening, they had carried on a schizophrenic existence—formal colleagues at the Mission, lovers outside. Periodically Sonia Berenson tried to cool the affair, but David would become so miserable that she invariably relented.

Five months before, they had had a crisis when the Foreign Ministry forwarded Arovitch's papers for customary reassignment. He said he would quit and drive a taxi in New York rather than leave her. Exerting pressure, she managed to get him a two-year extension, which they celebrated with champagne and a sensual weekend in a forest cabin in the Poconos. By June1978 they had been together almost nine months.

Lately, though, Sonia Berenson had found him aloof, preoccupied. The sudden trip to Israel had messed up their plans to spend some precious free time together at the beach. She didn't like unexpected disruptions in her life. But she had signed his leave request without making a fuss.

On the morning after his return, she asked him about the trip. He had just finished showering and was drying himself.

"What is to tell? I saw my family—my son, my mother, my Uncle Morty in Beersheba, and my sister in the moshav near Tel Aviv."

"You didn't stop in at the Ministry?"

"Sonia, I only had four days. If I had walked in the door, I would have had to brief everybody and his cousin. It was a personal visit, strictly personal, to see my family." There was an edge of annoyance in his voice.

"David," she said, tossing on her red robe. "I want to tell you something. You are free to do as you please, but I will not tolerate lies."

"What the hell are you talking about?"

"The air of mystery about your trip. Your total silence, as if you have a guilty conscience. You are hiding something from me. I know it."

"For God's sake, Sonia. What are you suggesting? That I had an affair in Israel?"

"You said it, David. Not I."

"This is getting ridiculous, Sonia. I saw my family and a few friends. That was it."

"When you're ready to tell me the truth, David..."

"That is the truth."

Turning on the shower, Sonia Berenson climbed in and thought of her schedule that day—the interview with the New York Times reporter, the meeting with visiting Knesset members, the strategy session with her staff, the calls she would make to D.C., Los Angeles, Cleveland, Boston, and locally to alert prominent Jewish leaders in AIPAC, the Washington-headquartered Jewish organization, about the rumored American switch on the PLO issue at the U.N.

"Sonia, didn't you hear me calling? I'm leaving."

He had opened the door and poked his head in.

"Good-bye," she said matter-of-factly.

"Sonia, I love you. We'll talk later." He closed the bathroom door.

In the mirror she studied the pinched skin under the eyes and the sad expression on her face. She began to brush her flowing black hair. It's ridiculous, she thought. The entire affair with David is ridiculous. Men, they are impossible, all men…But the hell with him… I have too much else to think about today. She went inside her clothes closet to select her wardrobe for the day and evening.

Outside the Israeli Mission at Second Avenue and 43rd Street, a city policeman scrutinized his pass as David Arovitch entered the building. On the 14th floor, a uniformed Israeli guard, holding a machine gun, sipped coffee and read the Daily News.

After stopping in his office, Arovitch walked down the corridor and knocked on the door of the telecommunications room.

An eye looked through the thick bullet-proof window.

The door was unlocked. "Shalom," said a balding, middle- aged man.

"Shalom, Ephraim. Pouch in yet?"

"What do you think? El Al's punctual, not like..." Hearing some static, he rushed back to the transmitter- receiver set and, after putting on the earphones, began transcribing Hebrew code.

Arovitch walked to the mailroom at the back. Rummaging through a huge basket containing the unsorted diplomatic pouch, he found two letters and a package addressed to him. He returned to his office, locked the package in a desk drawer, and read the letters before beginning his work.

As Second Secretary, David Arovitch represented Israel at various U.N. meetings on technical assistance, the environment, women's rights, population questions, and the Law of the Sea conference. Occasionally he stood in for the Ambassador or First Secretary at political gatherings where inflammatory topics such as South Africa, Cyprus, or the Middle East were discussed. A skilled writer, he drafted Mission position papers and prepared the weekly summary of U.N. political and economic issues for the Foreign Ministry. Insofar as he dealt with a host of vital contemporary international issues, the job was fascinating. However, forced to listen to litanies of familiar grievances at interminable, inconclusive meetings and to read page after boring page of baleful bureaucratic prose in U.N. documents, he found much of his job tedious. As he observed the world organization taking on an increasingly anti-Israel tone, he began to detest the place. Rather than suffer constant criticism, Israel, he believed, should simply pull out of the U.N. If it were not for Sonia and the Arafat business, he would request a transfer. In a way he was glad that Charles Browning had failed to knock off Arafat in Beirut two months ago; it would be a pleasure to see the U.N. besmirched by a murder in its halls.

Arovitch waited impatiently for the morning to end. After a meeting with Greek, Maltese, and Italian counterparts to discuss the formation of a non-Arab Mediterranean bloc within the U.N., he attended a staff session called to review methods of combating the "Zionism equals Racism" resolution which had passed the General Assembly a few years earlier (despite being combated vigorously by American ambassador Daniel Moynihan) and was now being proposed at the UNESCO Governing Council meeting in Paris.

Returning to his office, he dialed an answering service, left a message for "Mr. Ambruster," unlocked his desk, removed the package he had retrieved from the diplomatic pouch, and left the building. At precisely 1:43 p.m., he walked into Grand Central Terminal from Lexington Avenue, proceeding to the downstairs men's room. When the far right toilet stall emptied, he deposited a dime and spent an anguished few minutes trying to ignore the odor. He left the package on the right side of the toilet and walked from the stall. Someone wearing a cap immediately brushed past him into the small enclosure. Quickly washing his hands, Arovitch left the men's room and Grand Central terminal and returned to the embassy.

Five minutes later, Charles Browning, package under his arm, emerged from the stall and walked up the stairs.

Back in his apartment, Browning slowly unwrapped the package. From a reinforced cardboard box, he removed the metal parts and placed them side-by-side on the table. They were smaller than he expected—the sawed-off barrel and trigger, the circular bullet chamber, the dual sights and silencer—excellent for concealment.

Invented by Mormons and manufactured in Salt Lake City, the 180 laser submachine gun was the newest thing in small weapons technology. Light, compact, and deadly accurate, the gun made an instant and lethal marksman out of even a rank amateur because of the laser beam in the telescopic sight. As the helium-neon gas laser emitted a pencil-thin beam of red light on the target, a slight depression of the trigger let fly up to two hundred small caliber bullets on the same path as the beam of light. The gun could fire thirty bullets per second, having the same impact as eleven men blasting away simultaneously. It could kill dozens of people within seconds. Or noiselessly annihilate one man from a distance of up to one mile. It had wonderful deterrent powers, for anyone blinded by the red light that preceded the flow of bullets would certainly consider surrender rather than risk certain death.

Called the "super gun with a red dot," the weapon was sold exclusively to U.S. police departments and certain countries favored by the State Department. Israel was one of these countries. Rumored, though hotly denied by the Mormon Church, was the clandestine sale of the weapon to one or more Arab countries. A Swedish journalist reported having witnessed target practice with the laser gun in a PLO military camp.

Fascinated by the gun since reading about it in a weapons magazine, Browning had wanted to use it for a job. Because of its infallible accuracy and easy concealment, he knew it would be perfect for the present assignment.

Fastening the bullet chamber to the barrel, he affixed the sight and practiced training the red light on real and imaginary targets in his apartment. Then, after taking the gun apart, he returned it to the cardboard box that he placed at the back of his clothes closet.

In mid-afternoon Browning kept an appointment at Sherry Netherlands Wine Distributors. The rotund, cigar smoking Jerry took him to the office of the newly appointed Vice President for International Sales, Cynthia Sherman.

She gave a perfunctory nod as they entered.

"Cyn, Charles has a wild proposal for us. He wants to go on commission for the Southby and Parke Bernet auctions."

"That's an absurd idea," Cynthia Sherman said. "The higher the bid, the higher your commission. You would have every incentive to overbid, Mr. Browning. Nothing doing."

"Wait, Cynthia. You haven't heard my idea. I am suggesting an inverse relationship between commission and bid. The higher the bid, the lower the commission. And naturally the reverse."

She smiled at him. "You do think a lot of yourself. Your incentive now is to keep your bid low in order to maximize your commission. What about people outbidding you? "

"That will be my problem," he said, smiling.

"Okay, provided we set some limits each way." They clarified the parameters of the deal, and Jerry left.

"Congratulations on your promotion, Cynthia." He put his hand lightly on her shoulder.

"I deserved it, babe," she said, brushing his arm away.

"I'm certain. See me tonight."

"I have an engagement."

"Break it."

"How arrogant can you be, Charles?"

"Very. Cynthia, straight from the top, I'm dying to see you. After London, I went tramping around vineyards in northern Italy and France. Saw your face on every grape and on every leaf. Decided that one-night stands are highly overrated. Please see me tonight."

"I'm sure that I will regret it," she said, shaking her head, "but I'll see you for a drink around 9."

"Terrific."

They met in a softly lit bar named Odine's on East 48th Street near Third Avenue. A pianist hammered out some '40s blues tunes. They sat opposite each other at a corner table in the semi-dark watching the wick of a red candle slowly burning in oil.

"Gin fizz, like the last time?"

"Good memory, babe." He ordered a glass of Dom Perignon for himself.

"Aside from taking over Sherry Netherlands, what else is new in your life?"

She thought for a moment. "Mother is coming up here from Alabama in two weeks. Her first time in the city."

"What would she think of your associating with me?"

"She probably would have some quizzical thoughts about my associating with a whitey. You would do your best to charm her out of her latent prejudice, but, trust me, she would see right through that smartass, tough guy veneer you put on."

"Does she see through yours?" He took her hand under the table.

"I need mine in this world, babe. You don't."

"You would be surprised."

After a second round of drinks, he suggested that they go to a disco.

At Regine's he flashed a card, and they were waved to a table in the back. He steered her onto the dance floor. The music blared continuously. Pushed together by the packed crowd, they undulated side by side. As she twisted sinuously, his body kept rapid pace with hers. When a slower number came on, he took her tightly in his arms.

As they swayed together, she felt his hardness in her thigh. She dug her fingernails into the back of his neck.

After they had danced for an hour, he proposed that they leave. On the street he asked: "Your cousin still staying with you?"

"Never existed." She hailed a taxi that moved slowly down Second Avenue.

She had a one bedroom place in the East 20s. It was tastefully furnished, with a butcher block dining table, lavender sofa, circular throw rug, and some metal wire lamps.

The walls and ceiling were painted a deep peach.

"This your mother?" he asked, holding up a family photo on the bedside table.

"Yes," she said.

He turned it to the wall. "She looks sweet and open-minded, but we mustn't embarrass her."

They slowly undressed one another. It had been almost two weeks since the first time, and now their lovemaking, still passionate, was more tender, more deliberate. In bed, he touched her softly as her hand worked on his erection with a practiced touch. Suddenly Browning eased himself downward and his hands cupping her breasts, put his mouth on her vagina, slowly working his tongue and lips on her soft spots.

"Charles, Charles," she screamed, as he continued to lick her until she couldn't stop moving, experiencing an explosive sensation of release.

"Oh, my God," she said…."Come, come up to me." He moved his face up to hers and pressed his lips and tongue in her mouth.

"Oh, that was so exquisite," she said. "Shall I do that to you?"

"Next time, Cyn, next time. It will give me something to look forward to." Bracing his arm on the pillow, he gazed into her eyes.

"So what I'm doing already is not good enough for you, Charles?" she said, her face still glowing.

"Cynthia, Cynthia, what you do already is great. I get so excited being with you. You see how hard I get, how excited I am. The music is already beautiful. The oral part is just a variation on a theme."

"Well, you certainly played some incredible music on me."

She hugged him as they lay in each other's arms.

"Come away with me this weekend," he said softly.

"I thought this was a two night stand, babe." Her eyes opened wide, as she looked at him fondly.

"Not enough. I want more time with you. Outside of bed as well."

"I'll think about it. Now either bug out or go to sleep, Charles. I'm exhausted." And she turned over, asleep within a few seconds, leaving him to study the curvature of her upper back and the contour of her neck.

Chapter 17

The Political Surveillance Unit of the Mossad contains an extensive file system on "P.L.O. Subversives." One file, cross-referenced among such categories as "Women," "Intellectuals," "Political—Nonviolent," "Violent," and "Motive--Family Revenge" is that of

AHMED, Lydia Hanfi

Birth: 21 January 1949 at Ben Din refugee camp, southern Syria.

Education: American University, Beirut; The Sorbonne in Paris in Econometrics; refused Ph.D. teaching fellowship from University of California, Berkeley, to accept position with the United Nations.

Occupation (fictional): entered U.N. in 1974 in the Centre for Development Planning, Policies and Projections as researcher for African developing countries. In 1976, following interventions of Syrian, Iraqi, and Libyan ambassadors, Secretary-General Waldheim appointed Ahmed to Department of Political and Security Council Affairs where she prepares background briefs on Middle East and African affairs for the Under-Secretary-General for Political and Security Council Affairs and for the Secretary-General.

Occupation (real): PLO agent at the United Nations, reporting on political affairs and on personalities and issues in the Secretary-General's office. Intimately connected with PLO Observer Delegation (which Mossad has penetrated with ****) TOP SECRET See Ministry of Defense file, category J.

Languages: Fluent in Arabic, English, and French. Personal portrait: 5 feet 5 inches, 120 pounds, black hair, brown eyes, mole on upper right cheek, one inch scar on back of neck, slender fingers. Gives overall impression of attractive, sexy young woman (SEE PHOTOS)

Psychological Portrait: Through superior intellect and strong character, she overcame physical and emotional adversity of refugee camp to achieve first-class education as economist. Politicized at American University, radicalized at Sorbonne through contact with Palestinian and European terrorists. Death of her brother in October 1973 War caused temporary trauma, transforming deep personal grief into bitter hatred of Israel. Considered militant, but not dangerous.

In 1978 Lydia Ahmed was the only Secretariat employee to have personally benefited from direct U.N. refugee assistance in the Middle East. The U.N. Relief and Refugee Organization literally kept her family alive in the Ben Din camp after their displacement from Haifa in 1948. At age 12 in 1961, she escaped her marginal existence when her mother sent her brother and her to live with wealthy cousins in Beirut.

At American University she learned politics from her first lover, a Tunisian professor of political theory, who educated her in Marx, Lenin, and Fanon. She won an Arab League fellowship to study at the Sorbonne, where she spent considerable time debating liberation strategies with other Palestinians in Left Bank cafes. She developed a close friendship with Ulrike Boscheim of the Bader-Meinhoff group, who had exploded bombs in Munich and Cologne and hid out in Paris for a time, but was later killed in a kidnapping attempt on a Cologne industrialist. Although she attended strategy coordination sessions in Amsterdam and Turin with members of the Italian Red Brigades and Japanese Red Army, Lydia Ahmed at this point considered herself an intellectual, a Marxist theorist trying to apply dialectical materialism and the class struggle to the Arab political context, a thinker rather than an activist.

Her brother's death in the Yom Kippur War changed all that. Fighting in a PLO unit alongside Syrian forces, he was killed in an Israeli air attack. Lydia Ahmed returned from Paris to console her mother. After weeks of brooding, she decided to turn down the offer of a teaching fellowship at Berkeley and instead join the Palestinian Liberation Organization. Presenting herself at a clandestine recruiting center in Beirut, she explained her desire to volunteer for dangerous missions where a woman's presence could be useful. After multiple interviews, the PLO decided that this young woman with the Parisian hairdo and Sorbonne education would be out of place in the trenches. Instead they sent her to the U.N. to analyze political and economic affairs and to report privately to the PLO on the political positions of the Israelis and the Americans.

On its side, the U.N. was pleased to recruit a qualified Palestinian woman economist whose nationality was almost nonexistent in the Secretariat. She worked on development economic problems in the West Africa region, joined the tennis and dance clubs, campaigned for equal rights for women staff members (resulting in the U.N. Recruitment Office fostering a policy which stated that if a man and woman of equal merit applied for a position, the woman should be given preference), socialized among the delegates, and submitted monthly reports to the PLO. Yet she chafed at an assignment she thought fundamentally useless in the struggle for Palestine.

In early 1976, at the instigation of the PLO leadership, she transferred to the Department of Political and Security Council Affairs, where she prepared analyses of Middle East and African political affairs for the Under-Secretary-General or for Secretary-General Waldheim himself. Her reports to the PLO contained briefs on the Secretary-General's office. Yet she felt wasted and useless in the struggle for Palestinian statehood.

Furthermore, in late 1976, she detected a shift towards moderation by the PLO leadership, which, under Syrian pressure, removed its militia from southern Lebanon, all but eliminating attacks on Israel. At the U.N., as she saw it, the PLO observer delegate was toning down his rhetoric on the issue of establishing a state for Palestine.

Lydia read PLO reports emanating from Beirut that contained some of the customary harsh language towards Israel, but seemed to backtrack from aggressive action and, instead to ask or even beg the world community to pressure Israel to relinquish the West Bank and Gaza to the Palestinians. Lydia Ahmed, however, considered this approach not only futile and foolish, but traitorous. In her mind, Yasir Arafat was sacrificing the Palestinian claim to all of Israel in exchange for his personal control of the relatively small, strategically weak Gaza and the West Bank. And more painful to her, Israel in these circumstances would continue to exist as a watchdog over any newly contrived puny state of Palestine.

In July 1977 Lydia Ahmed took home leave in Lebanon, where she contacted the outcast Black September militant, Hassan Barka. Blindfolding her, he drove into the hills to an isolated cabin. There he interrogated Lydia Ahmed about her role at the U.N. for the PLO, her disillusionment with Arafat's policies, and her desire to donate her services to Barka.

"How do I know I can trust you?" he finally said. "How can I be sure the PLO. hasn't sent you to spy on me?" He sipped tea, the cup partially obscuring his face.

"I swear on the body of my dead brother," she said. "Does that satisfy you?"

"No. I would say anything to get my way. Why wouldn't you?"

"How can I prove myself?"

Barka mentioned the name of a PLO official. "He has some financial accounts of the PLO in his possession. Kill him, and bring that information to me."

She located the man in Beirut, where he was more than willing to advise her on improving her political performance at the U.N. on behalf of the PLO. Before long, they were in bed, and after a few days and nights together, he casually revealed where he kept his papers. When he fell asleep that night, she went to the kitchen, picked up a large kitchen knife, and returned to the bedroom holding the knife behind her back. Approaching the bed and making sure that he was still asleep, she stabbed him in his chest over his heart. By morning she had copied the information, and by the afternoon she had delivered it to Barka.

He examined the material. "I have found an ally," he said finally, looking at her. He told her about some of his current operations. He confided that he was financed in large measure by a wealthy Palestinian from Kuwait who supported Barka's radical policies.

After the evening meal he took her in his arms. First stiffening, she realized it would contribute to binding them together.

Barka proved a poor lover, single-minded and quick in the pursuit of his own pleasure. Afterwards he talked politics.

"No," she said the next day when he explained that he wanted her to stay in her present position at the U.N. "It's too passive. I'm sick of playing the intellectual."

"Lydia, it's only temporary. I'll bring you back here when we triumph."

"I'm so frustrated there."

"This time it will be different. You will working for me now, for the cause of Palestinian statehood and Israeli destruction. Your assignment is vital, both at the U.N. and outside. When we strike, you will be a valuable, even crucial part of it. I promise you." Grudgingly she agreed.

Before she left, he gave her a present—a silver bracelet with a picture of the Sacre Coeur cathedral. On the inside, she saw the engraved name of a leading Parisian jeweler.

"This is not from the Middle East. Where did you get it?"

He smiled at her. "Yad Yehudah. The spoils of war."

"Then it was you," she said, staring at the bracelet. "We never figured out who was responsible."

"When Arafat called off his attacks, we intensified ours. To discredit him as a traitor."

"He was embarrassed. I can tell you that. He kept denying the Israeli accusations that he was responsible."

Lydia Ahmed returned to her job in New York. Both the PLO and Mossad continued to assume that she reported on the U.N. for the PLO. Unknown to them, she channeled the same information as well as political analyses to Hassan Barka. Again she was bored until one day Barka instructed her to come to Paris to interpret between himself and a man named Robert Sebastian.

Chapter 18

At 10:30 a.m. on August 30, 1978, Lydia Ahmed was called to a staff meeting in the office of her director, the Under-Secretary-General for Political and Security Council Affairs, Boris Shupelov.

"It's official," he said, puffing his pipe. "The Security Council meeting will take place in three days."

"Excellent, excellent," said a smartly dressed Iraqi, the Section Chief for the Middle East Political Unit.

The morning before, Shupelov had used blunt language with Waldheim. He underlined the demand of the Soviet Union and the Group of 77 (non-aligned nations in Africa, Asia, Latin America, and the Middle East) that the meeting on PLO admission take place without further delay. It was already too late to arrange the meeting in August, as the Russians had wished. Waldheim, wringing his hands, had suggested that Soviet Foreign Secretary Andrei Gromyko telephone American Secretary of State Cyrus Vance. By evening Washington had agreed to the Security Council meeting in early September.

Lydia Ahmed already knew this. The previous evening, she had had a drink with the S.-G.'s Chef de Cabinet, Krishnan Katani, who was using his considerable charm and role of purveyor of high-level 'diplomatic secrets' from the 38th floor (the Secretary General's floor) to impress and eventually 'bed' this brainy, bewitching young Palestinian woman. Lydia had no interest in Kitani, but to keep the secrets flowing, she encouraged his flirtations and allowed him to hold her hand and occasionally to kiss her. This modest beginning encouraged his fantasies, and he tried to see her once or twice a week when he wasn't traveling with Waldheim. His revelations, often prefiguring something important, would inevitably appear in her reports to the PLO and to Barka.

"Mr. Har-Nafi," Shupelov said to the Iraqi. "Prepare the draft agenda immediately. Inform the Security Office, Documentation Centre, Conference Services, and all countries represented in the Council, as well as the PLO Observer Delegation and Israel as interested parties. And tomorrow morning, by 10 a.m. at the latest, give me a summary of each Council member's political stand on the Middle East question. Be as thorough as possible with the Americans."

Back on the 37th floor, Har-Nafi distributed assignments to his staff. Lydia Ahmed was asked to begin the political summary, passing it on to a red-haired Canadian named Edgar for annotation.

After working on her assignment for a few hours, Lydia Ahmed gave it to Edgar.

Then, in the privacy of her office, she dialed the extension of the Chilean personnel officer who had recruited her for the U.N.

Carlos Montoya, Assistant Section Chief for Secretariat Recruitment, was surprised to hear Lydia Ahmed say that she would go out with him that evening. Until now, she had always rebuffed his advances. Carlos Montoya was forty-two, short, with thinning dark hair, flabby cheeks, and a paunch. He took her to the Regency Hotel bar for drinks and Le Pavilion for dinner. He entertained her (or at least thought he did) with low-level UN gossip and an exaggeration of his role in the Recruitment Office. In the taxi afterwards, she put her hand on his knee. Delighted with his good fortune, he took her to his apartment for a long lesson in Latin love.

Afterwards she said: "Now you can do something for me, Carlos darling."

"Haven't I already?"

"Something else."

"What?"

"Find a job for a friend of mine. He will take short-term even."

"Nationality?"

"French, with excellent English. He has done a lot of interpreting for the OECD in Paris."

"Why doesn't he stay there?"

"He wants to work for the U.N. in New York."

"Let him try UNESCO or the World Bank."

"Carlos."

"What is your interest in this fellow?"

"He's a friend of my family. Now will you help him?"

"I'm not promising anything." Then, looking at her: "You're not sleeping with him, are you?"

"No, Carlos darling. I'm sleeping with you," she said, her head sliding slowly down in the direction of his crotch.

Chapter 19

August 28, 1978

"Andy, we are concerned about the Security Council meeting tomorrow." Sonia Berenson and David Arovitch sat in the office of U.S. Ambassador to the United Nations, Andrew Young, located on the fifth floor of the American Mission, diagonally across from the U.N. Secretariat on First Avenue.

Andrew Young was a suave, handsome African American from the 'peach state' of Georgia that happened to be the home state of former governor and now President Jimmy Carter.

"I can understand that, Sonia." Wearing a cream-colored safari suit, Young slouched in the leather chair in front of his desk. Next to him, impeccably dressed in a blue pin-striped suit, sat career diplomat Donald McHenry, second in authority at the American Mission and also an African-American who had not been as involved in the civil rights struggle as Young had been.

"Israel is opposed to a terrorist gang entering the General Assembly as full members."

"That's a little harsh, Sonia,' Young said, fiddling with his pen. "After all, they are already observers in the General Assembly. Under discussion now is a measure to raise their status in the G.A. to member level."

Young was short, about 5'7", chunky and slightly jowly. An African-American who had served with Martin Luther King in the Southern anti-segregation struggles, Young had turned to politics after witnessing King's assassination on a Memphis motel balcony in April 1968. An influential member of the House of Representatives, Young had jumped early onto the Jimmy Carter presidential bandwagon, persuading many other blacks to do likewise. Friends advised him to stay in the House rather than accept Carter's offer of the U.N. post, where, they argued, he would be powerless and forgotten. Thinking that he could make friends for America in sub-Saharan Africa, as well as advance his career, Young ignored their advice. It was his first diplomatic assignment. He spoke his mind freely at the U.N., calling Britain and Sweden "racist" and excusing the presence of Cuban troops in Angola. Suddenly there was an "Andrew Young problem" for President Carter. Word came to him from Secretary of State Cyrus Vance to tone down his 'offensive rhetoric'. Young complied temporarily, but he enjoyed being controversial and was capable of remarks that would annoy Americans while delighting his U.N. colleagues.

Many of the long-term ambassadors and diplomats around the U.N. considered Andrew Young to be the most popular U.S. ambassador in a long while. These ambassadors had interacted with some illustrious predecessors: Adlai Stevenson, a John F. Kennedy appointee who had been governor of Illinois and presidential candidate, losing to Dwight D. Eisenhower in both 1952 and 1956; courtly Supreme Court Justice Arthur Goldberg who resigned from the Court at the request of President Lyndon Johnson to take the UN post; and abrasive, ex-academic, ex-ambassador to India, later New York Senator, Daniel Moynihan who in 1975 eloquently challenged the Security Council resolution that proclaimed that "Zionism is Racism." In the eyes of many long-term diplomats, each of these three had lost credibility at the U.N.—Stevenson for misrepresenting to the Security Council in April 1961 that there was no American support to the Cuban anti-Castro dissidents Bay of Pigs invasion of Cuba (Kennedy had lied to him on the matter); Goldberg for representing Lyndon Johnson's Vietnam policies; and Moynihan for constantly criticizing the so-called Third World 'hegemony' in the U.N. (once calling the General Assembly the 'theater of the absurd'). Though a titular Cabinet post, the U.N. ambassadorship quite frequently got shut out of foreign policy-making decisions in Washington. This changed during the tenures of Madeleine Albright (who later became Secretary of State) and Andrew Young.

As Jimmy Carter's friend and protege, Young tried to remain relatively independent of the State Department, successfully walking the tightrope between representing the United States and keeping a cool distance from those policies he found objectionable. He dramatically enhanced America's image in Africa and improved relations with the country's second largest oil supplier, Nigeria.

Young seemed to enjoy his tenure at the U.N., balancing his overeating at the nightly diplomatic receptions with daily swims at the U.N. Plaza Hotel pool and as much tennis on the single court on the hotel's 38th floor as his overcrowded schedule would allow. He had a low-key, relaxed approach to problems that inspired confidence among his more easily ruffled colleagues. He was totally self-confident, unfailingly courteous, projecting a quiet authority. Exactly one year later, Young would be forced to resign his post for asserting that there existed 'political prisoners in U.S. jails and for misrepresenting to the State Department the nature of a clandestine meeting with the PLO Mission head. Young exited with dignity from the U.N. and, totally in character, termed the U.S. policy of no contact with the PLO as "ridiculous."

Picking up on Young's remark to Sonia Berenson that the PLO were already observers in the General Assembly, Donald McHenry noted that the group was also a member of UNESCO, the International Labor Organization, and the Economic and Social Council. When Young resigned in August 1979, McHenry, in the wake of publicity gained from an unsuccessful negotiation at Kennedy Airport with a Russian ballerina whose husband had defected from the Bolshoi Ballet, replaced him. He was the ultimate contrast to Young: reserved, discreet, and cautiously diplomatic.

"But we don't agree that they should be represented anywhere," David Arovitch responded. "A band of militant radicals dreaming of some fictitious homeland and using terrorism..."

"Sounds like the early Zionists," said Young, smiling.

"You might as well admit the Latvian or Serbo-Croatian governments-in-exile," Arovitch continued.

"That's enough, David," Sonia Berenson said softly in Hebrew.

"We sympathize with your views, Sonia," Young said.

"I thought you shared them."

"Come on, Sonia. Be fair. Israel has had no greater friend than the U.S. in this organization and outside..."

"Often the only friend," added McHenry.

"Andy and Donald, Israel wants assurances that the United States will veto the admission of the PLO at tomorrow's Council session."

"Sonia, we denounced the 'Zionism is Racism' resolution. We stopped paying our dues to UNESCO, withdrew temporarily from the ILO because of Arab shenanigans, voted..."

"Andy, I don't need a catalogue of your country's good works," Sonia Berenson said forcefully. "We are grateful for them, truly grateful, as you know. But we are in a different situation now when we need unqualified American support. My government needs to know if you will veto the PLO resolution at the Security Council."

Young sighed. "I cannot tell you, Sonia. I am still awaiting instructions from the Secretary of State."

Arovitch mumbled a Hebrew curse under his breath which Sonia Berenson caught.

"In that case, Andy, my instructions from Jerusalem are to ask you to ask Waldheim to postpone the Security Council meeting until next week."

"But that's impossible," said McHenry.

"And why is it impossible?" asked Arovitch sharply.

Sonia gave David a look of impatience. "Andy," she said, "the meeting has just been sprung on us. The Cabinet needs a few more days to work out its position. Consult with the Labor Party and other political groups."

Young sat back. "Sonia, I don't know what Washington will decide. But off the record, if there is no veto, how about an understanding between us that you tone down the criticism of the administration and we stop pushing so hard on the West Bank settlements? "

"I will mention it in my cable to the Foreign Minister," Berenson said coldly.

"It's only academic, you understand, Sonia. My instructions may be to veto. I don't know yet."

By mutual tacit consent Berenson and Young stood up, signaling the end of the meeting.

As Young escorted her towards the door, Berenson said quietly to him: "Our ambassador is seeing Secretary of State Vance this morning, Andy, to request a postponement of the Security Council meeting. Please pass on my request as well."

"Of course, Sonia. Now on a more pleasant note, how 'bout lunch next week after the storm is over. Say on Thursday?" Young had always found Sonia Berenson physically attractive, and having finished an affair with a high-powered, brainy middle-aged woman from Belgium two months ago, he began to wonder if he could break down the barriers of this tough-minded, alluring Israeli woman.

"Fine, Sonia replied," as McHenry held the door open. "One more thing, Andy. Why don't you alert Waldheim about the postponement? Let the delegates get away early for the long weekend. As a courtesy. Bye now." The Israelis left.

Young and McHenry returned to the comfortable leather chairs. McHenry began filling his pipe with tobacco.

Young took out a Havana cigar. "What do you think, Donald"?

McHenry smiled and said: "What nonsense. Berenson couldn't care less about the delegates."

Young didn't respond. He was thinking about Sonia's curvaceous bosom and ample hips. He wondered if he would stand a chance.

"Any idea what Washington will decide about the veto?"

"Do I know what Washington decides about anything?" Young answered, picking up the telephone and dialing his private number to the President. The President was 'indisposed', he was told.

"Carter's not available. Guess that we just have to wait. Do you want to make a bet, Donald?" Young asked McHenry. "Twenty bucks says that Washington in its august wisdom decides to withhold the veto."

McHenry shook his head. "Alright, Andy. I'll call you. Twenty dollars says that they...."

Suddenly the phone rang. "Mr. Ambassador, Julian Bond is on the line."

Young picked up the phone with a big smile. "Julian, Julian," he said loudly. "You brought your raggedy Georgia ass up to the Big Apple, and I know why. I read that the NAACP is having an executive meeting in a couple of days. Could that be the reason for your exalted presence here up north in our community?"

"You got it right, Young, for once. I'm here with John." Andrew Young, Julian Bond, and John Lewis in their younger days had been cohorts, part of the brain trust of Martin Luther King, Jr. in the anti-segregation struggles. After King's murder, the three Georgians continued their civil rights work, along with fostering their budding political careers. Bond was elected to the Georgia House of Representatives in 1965, but his stance against the war in Vietnam brought opposition in the state and required the U.S. Supreme Court to certify his election.

"Oh, shit, "Young said. "I've got to deal with you two southern gentlemen…
Too much…"

"Andy, cut the crap and listen up. Join us for dinner tonight. Sylvia's in Harlem. You
got the diplomatic clout, and so you make the reservation. We'll see you there at 8."

"Alright, alright. I'll cancel my date with a hot white chick just to be with you two
southern dudes. You'd better be grateful. I'll see you at Sylvia's."

Young was delighted at the prospect of seeing his old friends. He made a mental note
to run by them his thought of coming on to Sonia Berenson. Maybe they would tell him
to keep his mouth shut and his fly zipped.

Young asked McHenry as a courtesy if he would like to join them, but McHenry,
knowing that he would not fit in well, declined.

Chapter 20

"Come back at two, will you, David?" Sonia Berenson said to Arovitch before entering her office. She dialed the New Jersey phone number of millionaire industrialist Sol Reiner.

"Sol, I think we got some breathing space. Could you bring Cohen and Handler here at three? Sol, I cannot explain now. Bye."

Then, in a systematic manner, she telephoned all the major cities in the United States, from Boston to Los Angeles, Chicago to New Orleans, reaching out to American Jewish leaders in the pro-Israeli organization AIPAC as well as outside. She also called a number of Senators and Representatives in Washington. The forty- five calls took two and one half hours, and she finished, fatigued and famished, just before three.

David Arovitch, meanwhile, took a taxi to his apartment at lunchtime. He dialed a number on his phone.

"Eli, it's David."

Burger's voice came clearly over the line. "How are things going there, David?"

"Very well. The candy arrived, well preserved. I gave it to our friend."

"Was he pleased?"

"I don't know yet. I will speak to him tomorrow."

"Any other news?"

Arovitch described the meeting with Andrew Young. "He hinted that the U.S. would not veto PLO admission into the U.N., Eli."

"Good news, David, from our point of view."

"I'm playing such a double game here. Sonia would kill me if she knew. Yesterday with her at the U.S. ambassador's office, I purposely came on aggressively for a U.S. veto. And now with you, I hope that the U.S. abstains so that Arafat comes here."

"Do not be too tough on yourself, David. Strategy and tactics are two different things."

"Okay, Eli. I'll keep cutting myself in two and pretending that I love it."

"David, have a stiff drink when we hang up."

After the call, Arovitch returned to the Israeli Mission. At 3 p.m. he entered Sonia Berenson's office and was surprised to find Sol Reiner, former Irgun comrade of Eli Burger and the man who had introduced Arovitch to Charles Browning one month earlier.

In the hills overlooking Jerusalem, Eli Burger sat at his desk musing over the latest news. Let the bloody Palestinians get invited to join the U.N., because that will ensure Yasir Arafat's visit. Burger was also happy to learn that the laser gun had been delivered, since he had gone to some difficulty to procure it from an army base in the Negev. Alleging a need to dramatize a crucial point in a secret parliamentary debate on defense appropriations, Burger asked the base commander to furnish him with a 180 laser gun. It would assist his effort to obtain more weapons of this sort from the Americans, he stated. Thinking the demand odd, the commander called the Defense Ministry which was afraid to refuse a request from a Knesset deputy and close confidante of the Prime Minister. A mail clerk in the Foreign Ministry placed the package in the diplomatic pouch bound for David Arovitch at the Israeli Mission to the U.N. in New York, and El Al Airline did the rest.

Burger walked out to the back garden, where he saw the lights of the city below. Accidently stepping on a rose bush, he damaged some petals. Twisting the stem, he broke off the flower and held it to his nose. The aroma was strong, but it wouldn't last. A rush of sadness came over him, as he reflected on the fragility of life in flowers, as well as in human beings.

He thought of the pain of his daughter, Miriam, living alone with her little boy, his grandson, at Yad Yehudah, her husband Moshe killed in the attack a year and a half ago. He saw Miriam existing in a state of suspended animation, a living corpse faithful to her husband's memory. She rejected all of her father's pleas to come to Jerusalem where she might meet other men and make more of a life for herself. With his wife dead ten years now, Miriam and little Yehuda were all the family he had left. It was his gift to them that he was arranging the death of Yasir Arafat, the cretin who had planned the Yad Yehudah assault. It had taken a long time to secure the money and find the assassin, but things were moving forward at last.

The sound of an accelerating motor on the hill leading to his home interrupted his reverie. A car abruptly went into second gear and continued its climb. He wondered who was coming here unannounced. He walked to the front of the house.

The Chef de Cabinet of the Prime Minister got out of a black Fiat. "He wants to see you, sir."

"Now?"

"Yes, sir."

"In Jerusalem?"

"No. At his residence in Tel Aviv."

The drive along the highway connecting Israel's two major cities took an hour. The night was warm and clear. Stars shone overhead, and a quarter-moon hung in the sky like a pendulum. After passing some guard posts, they arrived at the residence, a villa near the coast, secluded behind a grove of trees.

Menachem Begin was a short, bald man with a roundish face displaying prominent moles under his right eye and beneath his lower lip. When he smiled, a space showed between his two front teeth, giving him a mischievous elfin grin. Usually dressed formally in tie and suit, he was now in a loose-fitting short-sleeved white shirt, brown gaberdine pants, grey socks, and brown loafers. His face was wrinkled, with bulging bags under his eyes, but otherwise he seemed in excellent health and spirits for someone suffering from a heart condition.

They sat on a huge sofa in the living room. Begin poured the tea.

"So, Moshe, what couldn't wait until morning?" Burger asked casually. "Labor demanding you resign? Syrians storming the Golan? Inflation climbing over 50%?"

The Prime Minister looked at Burger with a gleam in his eye. "Those problems I can handle alone. No, Eli, I need my 'eyes and ears' again." He tapped the side of the sofa rhythmically with his fingers.

Before the Irgun was disbanded at independence, Burger had made many reconnaissance missions for Begin, who nicknamed him his "eyes and ears." Though close friend and collaborator in the Likud Party, Burger had not heard himself referred to in that fashion for many years.

"Another King David?"

The Prime Minister's eyes tensed slightly. "I wish it were that simple. Take matters into our own hands again with no interference. But it's more complicated, I'm afraid. This PLO business at the U.N."

Startled, Burger said: "What..is...the matter?"

"Carter is mad at me over the stalemate in the negotiations with Sadat. He wants to be sure that he can bring Egypt and Israel together in a shotgun wedding. So many negotiations for so long, and Carter needs this triumph. I have committed to go to Camp David in mid-September if certain things occur. To tell you the truth, Eli, it isn't so bad for us to finally have an Arab country recognizing our existence. Yet I'm not too thrilled about the PLO trying to gain admission to the U.N. General Assembly, and I was counting on a veto by the United States. But now Carter is pressuring me to call off the big macher Jewish guys in the U.S. who are agitating for a veto. It is very likely that the U.S. will not veto Palestinian admission to the General Assembly because Sadat will pull out of Carter's scheme if the U.S. does this. I tell you, it is like a game of dice with twelve sides on each piece."

Burger clutched Begin's arm. "How many times have I told you, Moshe, that you cannot trust the Americans?"

Begin shrugged. "Washington agreed to our request to postpone the Security Council meeting until next week. So we have a few days to mobilize some pressure ourselves. I am sending the Deputy Foreign Minister to Washington, and I would like you to go to New York for me as an unofficial envoy."

"Did I hear you correctly?" Burger leaned forward.

"Yes."

"But Sonia is there."

"Sonia is up to her ears in work, and she has to act 'officially' as our diplomatic representative. I need somebody to speak privately to certain people, make our case, scout around, give me a first-hand report. Who better than my 'eyes and ears'?"

"The eyes cannot see very far and the ears don't hear so well," Burger said with a wave of his hand.

"That's not what I am told," Begin said, smiling. "People say that you are still acting like a lion."

"Who is telling you? The Cairo Post?"

"Eli, you will do what you can. Maybe you can arrange a 'diplomatic King David' for me in New York."

"But I've got appointments here, deadlines..."

"Cancel them. For goodness sakes, Eli, it's only for a few days, until after the Security Council meeting. You can stay in my suite at the Waldorf Astoria. Now when can you leave? Tomorrow?"

"Maybe the day after."

"Good. Tomorrow early, see Heimson in Propaganda at the Foreign Ministry. He's coordinating." He moved a piece of paper in front of Burger. "Now let's go over the list of people I want you to see."

"Moshe, before we begin, there is one thing I desperately need."

"What is it, Eli?"

"More tea."

Smiling, Begin cuffed him gently on the back of the neck.

Chapter 21

September 2, 1978

"It's revolting, Krishnan."

"Diabolical, I would say." Shaking his head, the Secretary-General's Chef de Cabinet lit up a cigarette.

"Carter will not commit himself," Waldheim said, fuming. "And the Russians, Africans, and Arabs in consequence are balking on my Law of the Sea treaty."

"Unleash the dogs. Let Carter know that you have got material that could embarrass, even ruin him."

The Secretary-General shook his head. "It isn't time yet, Krishnan. One rash move, and I will wreck everything that I have been working for during my two terms."

Arms outstretched on the sofa back, Katani blew circular smoke rings in the air above his head. "The future of the U.N. is at stake," he said loudly. "If you succeed with this sea-bed business, it will not only be a remarkable coup for you, but it will mean the salvation and preservation of the U.N. becoming independent of the big power wolves."

"That is why I won't throw it away lightly," said Waldheim, suddenly pacing up and down his office. "Carter must come around."

"You don't think it is time to tighten the screws on Carter?"

"Not yet. His Denver speech signaled a shift in American policy. But he has got to hold firm against the inevitable protest."

"He's not exactly the Rock of Gibraltar, you know. What are you going to do?" Katani looked quizzically at Waldheim.

"Remind him emphatically of his commitment to me. The Russians will have to put additional pressure on Carter, as I've already told Shupelov. To keep the Russians motivated, we will revamp the disarmament agenda and postpone the meeting for six months, something that will definitely please them."

"What about the other blocs?"

"I have been thinking about that. We will give the Africans the vacant Under-Secretary-General post in UNICEF and promise to reconvene the North-South talks early next year."

"I thought you promised that post to Latin America," Kitani said emphatically.

"I did, but I'll give them an Under Secretary-General post at the World Health Organization instead."

"Anything new for the Arabs?"

"They just want the PLO in here as a full member of the General Assembly. Then they will vote for the Law of the Sea and seabed clause."

"So it all comes down to the Americans?"

"Yes," Waldheim said abruptly, raising his voice.

"It always amazes me how one country can be such a nuisance to everybody else," Kitani mused.

"The U.S.?"

"No. Israel."

The phone rang. After speaking for a minute, Waldheim hung up. "That was Jensen in Security. He's gotten word of a big Jewish demonstration planned for this Tuesday in Dag Hammarskjold Park."

"Jewish lobby at it again. Timed for the day before the Security Council meeting. They will protest and make a lot of noise, but they will be too late."

Waldheim looked out the window, then back to Katani. "I think that I will call Carter on Sunday afternoon."

"Hoping that church will mellow him?"

"That the Lord will give him strength to honor his obligations."

"To the seabed." Kitani raised his glass.

"And to the admission of the PLO."

Chapter 22

"Gentlemen, I'm sorry to call you in here on Labor Day weekend. It's an imposition, I know, but we expect Yasser Arafat to arrive in about ten days, and we must be prepared."

Four men sat around a conference table in the U.N. Security Office on the first floor of the Secretariat—U.N. Chief of Security Henry Jensen; U.N. Security Detective John Hardy; New York City Police Captain Lester Schwartz; and FBI District Security Director George Bailey.

"Take a look at this document, gentlemen." Jensen passed out photocopies of a thick file entitled 'Security Measures Taken During the Visit of Yasser Arafat to the United Nations, 18-19 November 1974'. "It's both a description and a critique of the security measures at the time of Arafat's last visit here."

The other men began skimming through the document. "Not a bad show, if I remember correctly," Jensen said, offering a pack of cigarettes around the table. A career officer in the Canadian army, Henry Jensen had volunteered to command the Canadian contingent of the U.N. Emergency Force posted to Sinai after the 1956 war. When in May 1967 U Thant complied with President Nasser's demand that the U.N. forces be withdrawn, Jensen was reassigned to the Canadian Mission to the U.N. as military attache. In 1973 the U.N. Security Chief post became vacant, and Jensen was offered the position.

Around the U.N. he was referred to as the 'Colonel', his highest rank in the Canadian army. He was tall, broad-shouldered, impeccably groomed, and sported a thick handlebar mustache. Reserved, prudent, and businesslike, Jensen had few friends in the U.N. community. His job was routine except during the General Assembly when presidents and prime ministers flocking to the U.N. from every continent needed constant protection. In two years Jensen expected to retire to his farm north of Toronto on both Canadian and U.N. pensions, and his sole objective now was to end his U.N. assignment without major incident.

"I remember this document," said Police Captain Schwartz. "The Force got high marks, as I recall." By virtue of commanding the 18th Precinct, bounded east to west by the East River and Fifth Avenue and north to south from 34th to 59th Streets, Schwartz was involved in all meetings concerning United Nations external security. Short and heavy-set, he had a large, jowly face capped by thin, wavy grey hair. He enjoyed dealing with Jensen, a consummate professional who provided relief from the political hacks in City Hall who were always interfering in his work.

"Much of the document is still relevant," Jensen said, "as long as we supplement it with up-to-date innovations. I am thinking of advanced electronic surveillance, minicomputer printouts of security positions, long-range camera detection apparatus, new crowd control methods, and women security officers. They came in, Mister Bailey, after the Year of the Woman in 1975."

"Next year is the Year of the Child, I hear," said Schwartz. "You been interviewing any kiddies for security posts yet, Colonel?"

FBI agent Bailey didn't smile. Tall, thin-lipped, with close-cropped black hair tinged with gray, he had served in a number of FBI branch offices throughout the United States before assuming his present post, considered a plum, six months before. In two prior meetings with Jensen, Bailey had not attempted to conceal his lack of respect for the United Nations, an institution he considered a useless drain on American finances. "I am told, Colonel Jensen, that FBI functions and responsibilities were rather limited in 1974. We would favor an expanded role this time," he said drily.

"I appreciate your interest, Mr. Bailey," said Jensen. "I suggest that we all review the plan and meet in a few days time to finalize our proposals."

But Bailey continued speaking. "I simply want us to have a greater input in the new plan."

"Wouldn't that depend on what is required?" said U.N. detective Hardy in a thick Irish brogue.

"What is required is…"

"We are interested in any ways your outfit may contribute, Mr. Bailey," said Jensen, cutting off a potential argument. "Any suggestions you make about an expanded FBI status will be seriously considered."

U.N. Security Detective John Hardy decided that he would rather be any place but in this room with back-scratching, pompous security bureaucrats. As soon as the meeting ended, he would head for the Green Derby Pub around the corner and then out to Jones Beach for an early evening swim with his Filipina girlfriend, a secretary at UNICEF on East 44th Street across from the Secretariat. A tall Dubliner with bright red hair and freckles, Hardy had come to the U.N. because it was the only way he could remain in the United States. After emigrating from Ireland, he had worked on the Boston docks as a longshoreman. Just before his thrice-renewed visa was about to expire, Hardy visited New York for the first time. On a guided tour of the U.N., he happened to get into a conversation with an Irish-American security guard who asked Hardy to join him after work for a beer at an Irish pub on Second Avenue. Many beers later, the Security officer agreed to introduce Hardy to Chief Jensen. Inventing a long history of previous experience in security work in Dublin, Hardy talked his way into a low-level security officer job—the 'garbage' shift, night duty in the U. N. garage, standing in the small booth in front of the Secretariat in mid-winter, and the like.

Despite the long and unpleasant hours, Hardy was delighted to be at the U.N. Gregarious and outgoing, he joined various clubs, socialized with secretaries of many nationalities, and ran for the Staff Council as Security Office representative and won. As leader of the delegation demanding higher salaries for the General Service staff, he met with Secretary-General Waldheim on a number of occasions. When the opening arose, Waldheim asked Jensen to assign the Irishman to him as his personal bodyguard.

It was a fascinating experience for Hardy who accompanied the Secretary-General all over the world, and virtually lived in his townhouse on Sutton Place when the S.G was in New York. Learning to gauge Waldheim's moods, knowing when to tell off-color stories and when to keep quiet. Hardy developed excellent rapport with the Secretary-General who was sorry to see the two-year period end. Waldheim told Jensen to promote the Irishman to detective, which meant increased pay and status, daytime hours, and suit and tie instead of blue uniform. Jensen protested that Hardy was not due for promotion, but Waldheim insisted.

Many on the Security staff, including Jensen, resented Hardy's quick elevation. On his side, Hardy felt an incredible letdown in the detective job after his glamorous position with Waldheim. Seeing himself ostracized by Jensen and feeling trapped in a boring job, he began to drink excessively and to think of alternatives. There was no way he was going back to Ireland, but he could play on his contacts in Boston to seek a managerial position at the docks. Grim to contemplate, after being in the forefront and even limelight of international affairs at the United Nations for the past three years.

Two days earlier, Waldheim had instructed Jensen to assign Hardy to the detail making security arrangements for Yasser Arafat's visit. Once again Jensen resented the intrusion.

"Gentlemen," the Security Chief said in his most authoritative voice. "Let me summarize the details of the 1974 plan and present my new proposals for your consideration." When he finished, he concluded the meeting by asking Bailey to contact Washington and Schwartz to liaise with the New York City Mayor's office to request the deployment of additional security forces deemed necessary to protect Yasser Arafat during his forthcoming visit to the United Nations.

Chapter 23

Two blocks away at the Israeli Mission, Sonia Berenson and her staff worked non-stop through the weekend helping to organize a demonstration to be held on the day before the Security Council meeting. In telephone calls and strategy sessions with prominent local Jewish leaders, Sonia discussed ways and means of pressuring President Carter to veto PLO admission into the U.N. The Mission coordinated with the Israeli Embassy in Washington which approached Senators, Representatives, Governors, labor union leaders, businessmen, and entertainment figures to lobby the White House and the State Department.

Following church service on Sunday, President Carter flew by helicopter to the presidential retreat at Camp David to spend a couple of stress-free days playing tennis, jogging, strolling the mountain paths with Rosalynn and Amy, and reading Theodore White's book "In Search of History." Mentally exhausted from a summer of gasoline shortages, extravagant inflation, and low public opinion polls, he vowed to keep work at an absolute minimum.

The phone rang. Picking it up, Carter said softly to Rosalynn: "The Secretary of State…What is it, Cyrus? What is so important that you must disturb my peace in the beautiful woods out here?"

"Well, Mr. President. We in State are getting besieged with telegrams and phone calls demanding a veto of the PLO entry into the U.N. General Assembly. Many important American Jewish leaders, Senators, and Congressmen have called. I thought that I should let you know."

"I know, I know, Cyrus. Senators Jackson and Moynihan called me earlier. And I am told that hundreds, if not thousands, of people are gathered for weekend vigils in front of the White House and even on the periphery of Camp David. You know, I think that you should come here tomorrow with Brzezinski to help me strategize. I will get Walter and Andy Young here as well…Okay, Cyrus. Thanks." Carter hung up and banged on the table with his fist, an uncharacteristic gesture for him.

"I am really furious with the Israelis," said Carter sharply to Rosalynn. "During a meeting with Begin two months ago, he promised that if I significantly increased U.S. military aid, he would concede Palestinian admission into the U.N. General Assembly. That is the tacit deal that we made. Now I know that he is under extreme domestic pressure just as I am, but he needs to tell the leading Jews in America that Israel will ultimately accept the measure so that they will calm down. And he hasn't said a bloody word, leaving American

Jews free to agitate against it in the name of Israel."

"That's terrible, Jimmy," Rosalynn Carter replied. "Maybe you should call and remind him of his promise."

"I should, I should, but I don't want it leaked that I am putting undue pressure on the Israeli Prime Minister. This could muck up, even sabotage, the forthcoming Sadat-Begin talks at Camp David which could lead to mutual diplomatic recognition. For me, that's the 'big baby', the major accomplishment in foreign policy that I want to leave as my legacy." The President shook his head and sighed. "I think that silence is preferable now. If the press gets wind of any so-called pressure from me, I will get blasted and the polls will go even lower. Come, let's take a walk and enjoy the beauty of this place. Maybe that will calm me down."

With his popularity already quite low, Carter did not want to antagonize the powerful government, labor, and business leaders demanding an American veto in the Security Council. He needed to find the right balance in a statement or press conference. Before dinner, he telephoned Andrew Young who was vacationing in Georgia, to join the others tomorrow at Camp David to discuss once again the infernal Palestinian question at the United Nations. Then, acting against his own advice, he placed an urgent phone call to Menachem Begin in Tel Aviv. Carter underscored the importance of consummating the Egyptian-Israeli negotiations to be held at Camp David later in September, an event which promised to lead to an Egyptian recognition of Israel. President Sadat of Egypt and Prime Minister Begin had committed to come to Camp David in two weeks to negotiate an agreement. Sadat had made the smooth entrance of the Palestinian Liberation Organization into the U.N. General Assembly as the precondition of his attendance at Camp David, as well as Egyptian recognition of Israel. Carter intended the Egyptian-Israeli agreement to be the capstone of his foreign policy, if not his presidency, and elevate his standing in the political polls, to be reflected in victory in the next presidential election.

At 6:30 p.m. David Arovitch left the Israeli Mission to drive to Kennedy Airport. Using his diplomatic passport to gain entry to the restricted area for incoming passengers, he greeted Eli Burger just inside the El Al terminal. Within twenty minutes, they were in Arovitch's car heading back to the city.

"A stroke of luck, your coming now, Eli."

"Begin insisted. I have plenty to do for him, but tonight I want to see Browning."

"Impossible. His answering service said that he was away for the weekend."

Burger saw the shimmering lights of Manhattan from the approach to the Queensborough Bridge.

Burger cursed in Hebrew. "A fine thing. Has he said anything to you about the job?"

"He says that he is making progress, but he will not give me any details."

"I respect that. He has got to protect himself." Burger rested his head against the seat. "I'm exhausted. So many screaming children on the flight. I couldn't sleep at all."

"How's the Gush?" Arovitch asked.

"The steering committee met a few days ago. Many think that Begin will cave in to American pressure on the settlements. We have three more settlements to propose. The committee wants me to see Begin about it. I thought it best to let the matter rest until my return."

Arovitch nodded. "And Miriam? Is she well?"

"She's a walking zombie. I went out to Yad Yehudah last week. I think I succeeded in persuading her to spend two weeks with me in October."

"That will be good for you both. The Waldorf Astoria isn't too far away now. Sure you won't stay at my place?"

"No. I'll be better off at the hotel. Why don't you stop the car? We shouldn't be seen together."

Arovitch moved to a fire hydrant.

"Tell me, David," Burger asked. "Is Sonia Berenson doing a good job?"

Taken off guard, Arovitch hesitated.

"The P.M. wants my impressions."

"She is...hard-working, forceful, aggressive. It's a hot spot; the ambassador's constantly on the defensive in the U.N. But she defends our position very well. She has excellent rapport with most all the non-Arab ambassadors, especially Andrew Young, and outside the U.N., the Americans love her. I would say that she's a great asset."

"Good. As an old friend of her father, I want her to succeed. Goodnight, David."

Arovitch watched Burger move slowly down the sidewalk to the Waldorf Astoria Hotel.

Returning to the Mission, Arovitch knocked on the ambassador's door. Wearing thick bifocals, Sonia Berenson was reading and furiously making notes.

"I am here if you want me, Sonia."

A half hour later, his phone rang. "I'm leaving, David. Can you come?"

In the street they began walking uptown. The air was cool and fresh, harbinger of autumn a few weeks away. They went into a nearby restaurant.

After desultory conversation, Arovitch finally said: "Sonia, I don't like what is happening. You are far away from me, and I want you closer."

She brought a drink to her lips. "I have been thinking, David. I am not very happy with myself."

"What the hell does that mean?"

"Look at me," she said suddenly. "A woman approaching fifty..."

David waved his hand in the air. "You are barely over forty-five…."

"Here I am approaching fifty," she repeated loudly, "and still as foolish as a young girl. My emotions seriously out of control…"

"You're not making sense."

"Your unexplained trip to Israel threw me. I was really upset when you didn't give me an explanation. I was fuming over it. I acted the part of a jealous lover." Her face became taut. "It's unbecoming."

David Arovitch took her hand under the table. "Sonia," he whispered. "I love you. I'm crazy about you. I want to restore the status quo ante bellum."

"I don't know, David. You've changed somehow since your trip. You're pensive, secretive. Don't deny it. I sense something different in you. My mind plagues me with the possibilities. Why don't you save me this confusion and just come out and tell me what it is."

"There is nothing, damn it," he shouted. People nearby glanced over at them. The waiter brought their food, but neither felt like eating.

"Sonia, believe me. There is nothing that concerns you."

She nodded mechanically and pecked at her food.

Afterwards he said: "I want to come back with you."

"No, David."

"Please," he repeated, with urgency in his voice.

"Give me space, David. Isn't that what you want for yourself?" She got in the taxi and sped away. He was left standing in the street, feeling frustrated and hollow.

For the next few days he ignored her except for the most necessary official contact.

Jerusalem

UN Security Council

Yasser Arafat

President Jimmy Carter

King David Hotel, Jerusaalem

UN General Assembly

UN Palais des Nation, Geneva

First Four U.N. Secretary-Generals

Trygve Lie
1946 - 1952

Dag Hammarskjold
1953 - 1961

U Thant
1961 - 1971

Kurt Waldheim
1972 - 1981

Chapter 24

September 2, 1978

The sun's rays danced off the water onto the crystalline sand. The intense heat induced a kind of torpor, prodding people off the sand into the ocean or away from the beach towards the large imposing houses on the bluff a hundred yards back.

Near the water's edge, a man and woman strolled along, holding each other tightly at the waist. People stared as they passed, for racially mixed couples rarely, if ever, appeared on Southampton Beach. The young woman, dark- skinned with narrow waist, wore a tight red bikini. The man, quite tanned, was blond and muscular.

"Don't, babe. I've just dried off," Cynthia Sherman said, as Charles Browning steered her into the water.

"We'll dehydrate if we don't go in."

"Slower, Charles. It's cold."

"Chicken," he shouted, diving into the waves.

Afterwards he guided her to a wooden ladder that led up to a patch of grass and a large, colonial style house. They went into the living room and sat on a sofa in front of the fireplace.

"Like that wicker chair?" he asked. "Got it last weekend at an antique show."

"Where do you find time to antique-hop, Charles?"

"I make time for things I like." And he leaned over to kiss her.

"Shouldn't we clean up first?" she asked softly.

"No, I can't wait."

They never left the sofa. Later they fell asleep in each other's arms. A barking dog awoke them and they went upstairs to shower. Then Browning prepared a dinner of filet mignon, local corn, zucchini, and tomatoes, which he served with Chateauneuf du Pape 1969 from his wine cellar.

"Delicious, Charles."

"Thanks, babe."

She smiled. "Where are you from, Charles? Where did you go to college?"

His face tightened. "What's the difference, Cynthia?"

"Christ, you like to be elusive, don't you?"

"Oh, cut the analysis crap, Cyn. Let's just enjoy our time together."

"I can see that any time someone gets close to you, you retreat. Is that your basic nature?" She looked through the wine glass at him.

"Can't we discuss something neutral?"

"Fuck you. We screw and keep the conversation light and platitudinous. That's not my style, man."

"Okay, I dig. What do you want to know?"

"Where did you grow up? Is your family alive? What do you think about? What turns you on? Things like that."

"Spanish inquisition had nothing on you," he said. "I was born in New London, Connecticut, because my father was at the naval base. Partly we lived there, partly overseas. In France and West Germany. Parents separated when I was twelve. Messed up my head for awhile."

"Do you have any brothers or sisters?"

"I had a younger sister. She died in a car accident. I treasure her memory. Here is her picture." He took a picture of a pretty young woman off a side table and showed it to Cynthia.

"I am…so sorry," Cynthia mumbled.

"I know, I know. I don't know what else to say now."

"You are doing fine. Keep talking."

"Spent a couple of years at the University of Kentucky until I decided that I would rather fight for my country than die of boredom studying. So I went to Vietnam during the bloody years. A lot of violence, and I don't want to talk about that right now. After Vietnam I bummed around the Far East pushing dope until it got too hairy. Then as I mentioned, I hung out in Europe where I met this French chick whose dad was in the wine trade. He saw a son-in-law; I saw a profitable business. When the lady and I split, I came to New York to make my fortune. You see, Cynthia, we were not very affluent when I was growing up and I don't want to repeat the experience. So I'm devoting myself to the acquisition of filthy lucre. As much of it and as quickly as I can. Then, with luck, I will retire and settle down."

"Can't imagine you ever settling down," she said.

"I was waiting for some smartass comment."

"Then I didn't disappoint you, it seems. More wine, please." She held out her glass.

"Don't push me too fast, Cynthia. Give me some time. You will not be disappointed."

"Okay, Charles. I will expect some pearls, though."

She came onto his lap. Slowly they moved up the stairs to his bedroom.

Very early Labor Day morning, Charles Browning crawled out of bed. Cynthia Sherman slept soundly. He left a note on the kitchen table saying that he was going for fresh bagels and would return shortly.

Starting the Mercedes, he drove off in semi-darkness towards the town of Southampton. On the main highway, he veered right onto a narrow road and drove two miles. Then he turned left onto a dirt road that led into the forest. Within a few minutes he came upon a huge junkyard where stacks of battered, obsolete cars were piled upon each other. Stopping the car, he got out.

By now it was daylight, with the sun just visible on the horizon. Opening the trunk, Browning removed a briefcase and began to walk around the back of mounds of rusted metal hulks, being careful not to stumble over torn car parts strewn about everywhere. Surveying the mortuary of machinery, he looked for some movement— a night watchman, a guard dog—but nothing stirred.

At the back of the junkyard where the forest began, he stopped. Again he listened carefully. Satisfied with the silence, he unlatched the briefcase, removing the separate parts of the 180 laser gun, including the box of bullets. Having practiced in his apartment many times before, he required just five seconds to attach the round bullet chamber to the sawed-off barrel and affix the sight and silencer. But he hadn't yet fired it, and he was more than curious as to its accuracy and power.

Squinting through the sight, Browning trained the gun on a small sapling, aiming for a piece of bark extending from the trunk. When he touched the button controlling the laser, a beam of red light, seen through the sight as a solitary red dot, flashed on the target. Loading the chamber with several bullets, he depressed the trigger gently and immediately heard the whoosh of bullets, followed by the thud of their impact on the tree. The bark disappeared, wood pellets flying everywhere.

He moved closer to examine what remained of his target. The upper trunk had disintegrated, leaving only the base of the tree, a narrow scrawny pole. The gun's power was impressive, but the accuracy wasn't yet perfect. For the next half-hour, he sighted various branches and then small twigs, activating the laser beam, and firing some bullets. He discovered that by twisting the sight slightly upwards, his accuracy improved. With a pliers and small screwdriver, he made the adjustment. Now he had perfect accuracy. Anything he trained the sight on was demolished by bullets flowing in the path of the laser beam.

For a final test Browning aimed at a spot of red rust on the door of an old Ford that had been stripped of its wheels and placed on bricks off to the side. The rat-a-tat-tat of .22 caliber bullets striking metal resounded in the stillness, causing birds to scatter from nearby trees. The door, shattered and split, was no longer a door, but scrunched metal. Browning headed back towards his car.

A dog's bark echoed in the stillness. A huge German shepherd, wakened by the noise, came into an open space thirty yards away. Baring his teeth, he growled softly at the intruder in his domain. Then he barked loudly.

Browning turned to face the dog. Raising the gun, he looked through the sight, aiming the crisscrossing lines at a spot just below the eyes. Uncertain whether to move forward or back, the German shepherd stopped barking, remaining rooted to the spot. His tail began to wag. Hesitating, Browning lowered the gun. Then, realizing that this was the ultimate test, he shrugged, aimed the weapon, and pressed the button controlling the laser beam. The red light blinded the dog. Browning touched the trigger. The bullets severed the dog's head from the rest of his body. Cartilage and blood were strewn about everywhere.

Browning moved closer. Taking a hundred dollar bill from his wallet, he placed it under a severed paw and left.

"What do you really do for a living, Charles?"

They were on the highway returning to the city in mid-afternoon after spending the morning on the beach and eating a delicious lunch on his veranda.

"That's a dumb question," he replied, not changing expression.

"Babe, there is no way you could support your present lifestyle on wine consulting. No way. Unless your French babe's father gave you mounds of Rothchild 1844."

"I do have...some very rich clients."

"And I'm Greta Garbo. Listen, if you do not want to tell me, don't. I don't give a fuck anyway."

"Alright. I'll be honest with you. Aside from the wine thing, I do some deal-making. Putting American capital together with overseas companies. When a deal goes through, I get a big finder's fee."

"That's pretty prosaic, Charles. I imagined you were a spy or a killer. Something more romantic than just another bloody capitalist."

He pulled into a gas station, parking on the side. "Cynthia," he said, taking her hand. "I have to go away soon. For the biggest deal of my career. When this one goes through, I will be very rich. Understand?"

"Not really," she said.

"Trust me. After this deal, I will be in a position to level with you. I have decided that I want you for my woman. We will move in together. What do you say?"

"Flattering. I will consider it," she said, looking out the window. "When will you be back after your so-called 'deal'?"

"In a few weeks. Maybe sooner. I will stay in touch with you."

"Okay, Charles. Remain the mystery man…But I'll tell you this. Once you get back from your 'big deal', you had better level completely with me."

"Definitely, Cyn…..Now let's go. The city awaits us." He drove off quickly, tires screeching loudly.

Chapter 25

During the weekend, Lydia Ahmed waited for Robert Sebastian to arrive from Paris. To occupy herself, she prepared a report on the pros and cons of the PLO resolution passing the Security Council the following week. Everything depended on the Americans who were under serious pressure from the "Jewish lobby" and pro-Israeli Congressmen to veto, and from the Secretary-General, Russians, and Arab bloc to abstain. Rumors abounded that Waldheim had threatened President Carter with revelations of unseemly U.S. behavior inside, as well as outside the U.N., if the U.S. vetoed the resolution. Gossip persisted that Waldheim would resign if the Americans vetoed. The Arab bloc had hinted at the use of the "oil weapon" once again against the United States. Then there was the obscure, confusing rumor of a link between the Security Council vote and the eternally stalled, forever inconclusive, Law of the Sea Treaty.

After recopying the report for Hassan Barka, Lydia Ahmed delivered the original to the PLO delegation headquarters at the Waldorf Astoria Hotel. A Mossad agent reading a newspaper in the lobby saw her enter and leave the hotel.

Back in her apartment, she took a long cool bath and put on a light print dress. Searching in her jewelry box, she took out the silver bracelet that Barka had given her and examined it closely, but decided that she was not in the mood to wear it. Instead she chose a gold crescent ring and a pair of thin gold stick earrings.

Sebastian did not show up Sunday evening or Monday morning. Just before noon, she went to the corner phone, dialed Western Union, and dictated a cable to Barka:

Monday Noon Joyful Not Repeat Not
Arrived Stop Will Cable Later

Happy to be outdoors, she continued to Central Park, to the circular lake where from the rim, children sent sailboats across the water. It reminded her of the Luxembourg Gardens where two months ago Barka and she had initially met Robert Sebastian. Barka's behavior in Paris had disturbed her. First taciturn, he became deliriously talkative about his plans to replace Arafat. In the hotel room, he forced himself upon her, as if to impose his strength and his will. When she cried out, he only hurt her more. At one point he mentioned his intention to bring her to Beirut after Arafat's death. Once she had entertained and welcomed this idea; now it frightened her.

He became furious. "You will do exactly as I say, or else," he had shouted. Lydia realized to what extent she was caught up with him and what power he had over her. She was, after all, his creation and his confidante, the only one who knew of his plan to kill Arafat. He would never let her go.

Around 8:30 that evening, the phone rang. "I am here," a voice said in French.

"Come up."

Robert Sebastian arrived in a rumpled pinstripe suit showing the effects of his flight from Paris.

"Did you have a good trip?" she asked.

"What is the situation?"

"Tomorrow at 10 a.m. you have an interview with Personnel about an interpreting job." She handed him a piece of paper. "Carlos Montoya is a friend of mine, and he expects you. He should be favorably disposed. If you pass the interview process, you should be able to start right away. I've already laid the groundwork with Montoya..."

"That's good," he said. "Is that all?"

"More or less. Maybe we should discuss some details of..."

"Not now," he said, cutting her off.

She noticed that he would not look her in the eye.

"Let me know what happens," she said.

Nodding, he left the apartment.

Afterwards she went to the corner phone booth to cable Barka that 'Joyful' had arrived.

From inside a doorway, Robert Sebastian watched her leave and return to her apartment.

Chapter 26

September 6, 1978

"How do you know Lydia?" Carlos Montoya asked Robert Sebastian. They were sitting opposite each another in his file-lined office offering a fine view of the skyscrapers of Manhattan.

"She is a friend of my family," Robert Sebastian replied in French-accented English.

"To tell you honestly, I am only doing this as a favor to her. There is a job freeze on now because of financial constraints. No recruitment, no hiring. We can get around this constraint for a short period of time. Maybe three months, extension uncertain. Not very secure, I would say. If I were you, I would look elsewhere. UNICEF, UNDP, or the liaison office of UNESCO if you insist on being in New York."

"Three months to begin with is fine," Sebastian said, looking pointedly at Montoya.

"It's up to you," Montoya said drily. "Fill out this personnel form in triplicate. Take a copy to Leopold Aumont in the French Interpretation Section; leave the others here. Good luck." They shook hands.

Sebastian filled out the yellow form as follows:

Name: Sebastian, Robert Antoine
Birthdate: 27 June 1943
Nationality: French
Height: 6'3" Weight: 190 pounds Marital Status: Single
Permanent Address: 33, rue Saint-Andre-des-Arts Paris 6, France
Present Address: Hotel Tudor, New York 10017
Preferred Field of Work: Interpretation (English-French)
Knowledge of Languages: French, English, Spanish
Education: Lycee Louis le Grand, Lyons, France; Ecole des Langues, Sorbonne; Bristol University, Bristol, England

M.A. in Modern Languages. Ph.D. in Preparation at the Ecole des Langues, Sorbonne, Dissertation Subject: "A Comparison of Semantic Variations in Medieval French and Early Modern English"

Employment Record: 1) 1975-78 — English-French Interpretation, OECD, Paris. 2) 1970-77 — French-English Interpretation at Congresses of the International League of the Rights of Man, International Red Cross, and YMCA Conferences.

References: Jean Lapont, Professor, Ecole des Langues, Sorbonne; Samuel Gillard, Professor, Bristol University; Henri Franchet, Directeur, La Ligue Francaise des Droits de l'Homme.

After signing his name, he went for his interview at the French Interpretation Service.

Leopold Aumont was a refined looking, fastidious Frenchman in his mid fifties. He wore a pale blue suit, cream shirt, and red-orange tie. His close cropped grey hair was neatly brushed back; his hands were small, with long and slender fingers and a large ruby-red ring gleaming on his left pinky finger.

"The Ecole des Langues, n'est-ce pas? Going downhill, isn't it?" he said, reviewing the c.v. "Is Faison still around?"

"He is, I believe. I haven't had much contact with the place lately."

Aumont glanced at the written credentials.

"You've got good experience, I see," Aumont said quietly. "OECD. Croix Rouge, etc., etc. Normally recruitment takes ages, M. Sebastian, but in your case we might make an exception. We are a little hard pressed right now. Most of my staff is on vacation, and there is an emergency Security Council meeting coming up. Let's see what you can do." He sauntered towards the elevator, Sebastian beside him.

They went to a large unoccupied conference room in the first basement. Sebastian walked up some stairs to an interpretation booth, where he put on a set of headphones and activated the transmitter. From below, Aumont read into the microphone from a document entitled: "The Current Political and Economic Situation in Zimbabwe/Rhodesia." In his headphone Aumont heard his English prose translated into literate, correct French.

"Descendez, come on down," he finally said into the microphone. "It was good, very good," he said, when Sebastian returned. "You are really quite accomplished as an interpreter."

"Thank you, Monsieur Aumont." Sebastian permitted himself a modest smile.

"I will propose to the schedule assigner that you be put on the back-up team for the Security Council meeting to be held in two days. You might even work."

"I am very grateful, Monsieur Aumont."

"All we can offer you is a three month fixed term contract. But if I am pleased with you, I will see that you are extended," Aumont said, looking fixedly at Sebastian. "Now go back to Montoya. I will call him in the meantime. Report to me tomorrow at 9 a.m."

"Merci et a demain matin, Monsieur Aumont."

Montoya's secretary instructed him where to get his grounds pass. Taking the elevator to the first floor, he walked past the Security Office, turned left, and went into the pass office. There he was fingerprinted and photographed, and his photo affixed to a three-month pass. He was now an official United Nations staff member.

Chapter 27

"Your comments on the report, gentlemen?" Security Chief Jensen held up the document outlining security arrangements for Yasser Arafat's 1974 visit. Around the oblong table in the Security Office conference room sat Assistant Chief Richard Todman, Security Detective John Hardy, New York City Police Chief Lester Schwartz, and FBI District Director George Bailey.

"It's pretty good," said Schwartz. "It covers land, sea, even helicopter logistical support. The area has not changed much since then. A few more key buildings—the U.N. Plaza Hotel, Uganda House—but little else. We blanket everything with security, and a church mouse will not penetrate our lines. The New York City police responsibility calls for several thousand extra men. City Hall grumbled about the cost, as usual, but the men will be released from other duties that day. Here are the figures, Henry."

Jensen studied the paper. "It seems in good order, Les. Mr. Bailey?" The FBI man had raised his pencil.

"Maybe the 1974 preparations were adequate then," Bailey began. "But they are not sufficient today. Terrorism and terrorist methods have developed by leaps and bounds in the last few years. Consider the Red Brigades, the Japanese Red Army, even the PLO. These people work in coherent groups, organized in small cells, using sophisticated weapons, undertaking both short and long-term terrorist acts. If we in the U.S. have avoided such a calamity, it is due only to the fact that we have adopted the most modern methods of infiltration, surveillance, and deterrence. And I strongly urge that we apply those methods here."

"What do you have in mind, Mr. Bailey?" Jensen asked.

The FBI man produced a paper outlining a plan for security saturation within the U.N. complex, including the Secretariat, the General Assembly, and the Dag Hammersjold Library. This plan, Jensen noted, gave the FBI the preponderant role, subordinating the U.N. security staff as an adjunct, if not lackey, to the FBI command.

"Well-conceived and interesting," Jensen began diplomatically, "but it would make it difficult, if not impossible, to carry on normal U.N. work. You are recommending, for example, that for days in advance, we scrutinize passes at all meetings, spot-check staff in their offices, institute video and tele-communications operations far beyond those in existence, use guard dogs, display weapons prominently throughout the building."

"Visible deterrence is the most effective weapon, Colonel Jensen. As for the rest, infiltration and surprise tactics."

"It's too much, Bailey," said Jensen, shaking his head. "I hesitate to use the word 'overkill.' Naturally we will check the identification of everyone who enters. If they have a U.N. pass, we will assume they are staff members. Nobody unauthorized gets in."

"Colonel Jensen," John Hardy suddenly interrupted. "That is the weak point, isn't it? I agree with Mr. Bailey on the question of internal security. The 1974 plan with a few minor adjustments is fine for the outside, but it is lax internally. I do not hold much with the conspiracy terrorist theory. What bothers me is the lone assassin who gets into the building. With a U.N. pass, no less..."

"Look, Hardy," said Deputy Chief Todman, a husky man with an Australian accent who had worked his way up the ranks from fledgling security officer. "The Chief is in control here. All this crap about imaginary...."

At that moment there was a knock on the door, and a big, beefy man with a beer belly and a flabby face stepped into the room. "Sorry Colonel, but there's a demonstration going on. They've chained themselves to the moon rock case."

"Always something," Jensen said, getting up. "Dick," he said to Todman. "Take over. I'll be back as soon as I can."

Jensen walked quickly with Lieutenant Stuart Rosenberg through the passage connecting the Secretariat and General Assembly buildings until they reached the tourist area. From a distance he heard the chants. Approaching, he saw a group of blue-uniformed security officers ringing a half-dozen young people, four men and two women, chained to the moon rock case.

"Jewish Defense League," Rosenberg said to Jensen.

"Who's the leader here?" Jensen shouted at the demonstrators. By now a large crowd of tourists were milling about and watching the scene.

The demonstrators chanted: "PLO Must Go. PLO Must Go."

"Get them out of here," Jensen said to Rosenberg, who gave the order to cut the chains and drag the demonstrators from the building.

One of them, seeing Rosenberg's name on his badge, yelled at him: "You Jewish traitor. Fascist, Yiddish pig. I bet you're not even circumcised." His face scarlet, Rosenberg hit the demonstrator across the mouth with his open palm, but the young man continued to scream insults as he was dragged away.

"Sorry, Chief," Rosenberg uttered. "I lost my cool. I shouldn't have done that."

"It's okay, Rosey. The kid kept shouting, and you didn't break any bones. Let's just say that it never happened."

"Thanks, Chief. I'll go back to my office now."

Wiping his face with a handkerchief, Jensen returned to the conference room. The others looked up as he entered.

"Militant Jews protesting against the PLO" he explained. "A bit ugly, but manageable."

He turned to Todman. "Dick, starting from tomorrow, I want the building closed to tourists. Otherwise we will face this sort of thing every day. Clear it with the Secretary General's office first, will you?"

Then he spoke to Bailey. "I respect your views, Mr. Bailey. I will accept your proposal of more FBI men inside the building, but I reserve judgment on the other ideas. I will call you in the next day or two."

The meeting was over. Bailey, Schwartz, and Todman left, but Jensen motioned John Hardy to remain seated.

"Don't ever do that again," Jensen said, when they were alone.

"What are you talking about?" Hardy asked, startled.

"You saw that I disagreed with Bailey, and yet you took his side."

"That's not true. I didn't take..."

"It is true," interrupted Jensen, his voice rising. "It's bad enough that you are Waldheim's flunkey here. I don't need a turncoat as well."

Hardy's face reddened, and his fist clenched at his side. "I'm asking Waldheim to take me off this detail."

"Don't bother, Hardy. He's got enough to worry about. Just keep out of my way."

"Fuck you, Jensen. Stay off my back," the Irishman said, storming out and slamming the door after him.

Jensen reached in his pocket for his pipe. He told himself to stay calm. It was going to be a rough General Assembly session, and he deeply regretted his decision not to take early retirement a year ago.

Chapter 28

"Hurry, please," the pretty Australian guide said to a few stragglers eyeing the colorful cubist Mexican mural symbolizing 'suffering humanity'. Walking slowly and gesticulating with her arms, she led a multinational group of tourists—Japanese brandishing cameras, somber-looking Swedes, gum-chewing Kansans and Texans—in and out of the Security Council chamber, the Trusteeship Council room, and the General Assembly hall. She offered a brief historical description of each room and then patiently answered questions asked a hundred times before: Why did the U.N. favor the Arabs over Israel? Why couldn't the U.N. agree on a definition of 'aggression'? What did the Trusteeship Council do? Who paid for the emergency troops in the mid-East and in the Congo? How many terms was the Secretary-General allowed? What exactly did UNESCO and UNICEF do? Were the World Bank and the International Monetary Fund in Washington, DC part of the U.N. system?

One of the stragglers was a tall blond man whom the guide took to be Swedish because of his demeanor and because he accompanied the Stockholm Firemen's Marching Band throughout the tour. Giving the trace of a smile as he passed, Charles Browning mounted the escalator behind the others.

During the tour he studied the spatial layout of the building, focusing on areas that Yassser Arafat would presumably visit during his short stay. His purpose was to choose the best spot from which to aim the laser gun at the PLO leader.

In the General Assembly hall, Browning observed the raised stages and the layers of seats for delegates, journalists, and tourists. Glassed-in television and interpretation booths ringed the hall in a semi-circular pattern. It might be possible to kill Arafat here, but how the hell would he get out afterwards?

The guide mentioned in passing some of the restricted areas off-limits to visitors, such as the Secretariat where the main work of the U.N. in such areas as socio-economic development, demographic censuses, mineral exploration, disaster relief, refugee displacement, condition of women, abuse of children, etc., took place; the Delegates Dining Room where Arafat had hosted a luncheon in 1974, and the Press Room where he had given a press conference. It was imperative that Browning analyze and assess every room and place he saw—determine its feasibility for the job as well as the risks to his safety. He had already solved the problem of smuggling the laser gun and himself into the building.

Deep in thought, Browning took little interest in the tour, perking up only twice, once when the guide stopped before a photographic exhibition of Palestinian children in refugee camps--"the unfortunate victims of the war for Israeli statehood," she put it. And from an aesthetic viewpoint, he appreciated the craftsmanship involved in the intricately carved ivory model of the Chengu-Kunming Railway, a gift from the People's Republic of China in 1974 soon after it replaced Taiwan as the Chinese representative in the U.N. system, including the possession of the veto power in the Security Council.

When the tour ended, Browning went to a phone booth near the U.N. stamp display in the basement.

"Hi, babe," she said upon hearing his voice.

"Cyn, I've got a business meeting tonight, but I want to see you afterwards, say about 10 p.m."

"Ring my bell three quick times, Charles. Then I'll know that it's an obscene caller, and I'll let you in."

He hung up, wishing he were in her arms that very second.

After this job, he would take her on a trip around the world before they moved in together. He would tell her tonight.

At 8:15 that evening, Browning entered a brightly lit brick building on West 74th Street. A sign in the lobby said in large letters: "Plato's Retreat," with a smaller sign in bright colors declaring "Leave Your Inhibitions Behind." He walked down a flight of stairs and received a locker number and lock, as well as a white bathrobe and towel from a statuesque woman with bulging breasts and hips. Moving down a different set of stairs, he found his locker, undressed, put on the bathrobe and headed towards a nearby room featuring a heated pool flanked by marble benches on three sides. Vaporized steam issued from vents near the floor.

In the smoky haze naked men and women lounged by the pool, occasionally gliding into the water. Passing a bench, Browning saw two figures casually coupling. A dark-haired woman, feet dangling in the water, gave him an inviting look. Moving one hand slowly between her legs, she beckoned him to join her.

Browning walked by her to door number 3.

"Gentlemen, are you enjoying yourselves?" he asked, closing the door.

"Not much," answered Eli Burger. Slumped in the corner, he was naked except for the towel around his middle. Strands of white hair on his chest stood out against his pale skin. Next to him, bronzed and thin, sat David Arovitch in the same state of undress.

"It's safe here," said Browning, sliding into the seat opposite them. "Did you come all this way to see me?" he asked Burger.

"No. I came for other reasons. But it gives me a chance to ask how you are doing?"

Browning draped the towel loosely over his lap. "I'm working on it. That's all I can say right now."

"What kind of charade is this, Browning?" Arovitch asked suddenly. "You bring us to this den of iniquity on some perverted joke. Then you refuse to tell us anything. We have invested a small fortune in you and we have the right to know what is going on."

Browning looked at Burger. "Your friend's inexperience is showing," he said, not raising his voice. "I would ask you to remove him from my sight before I do so myself."

Arovitch opened his mouth, then closed it.

"David, please," Burger said insistently. "Mr. Browning is under contract to us on a highly dangerous matter. His personal security is involved. If he prefers to maintain his silence, I accept it."

"He has our money. He should not ridicule us like this."

"Mr. Browning is a man of honor. He has half of our money and would like the rest. Isn't that so, Browning?"

"I never take a job without completing it," Browning answered. "This is a very difficult job, and I will need some help. May we get down to business?"

Browning spent thirty minutes explaining what was required from Arovitch. Over and over he repeated the details like a grammar lesson until he was confident that Arovitch understood. After giving him the time and place for their next meeting, Browning told Burger to return to Israel with "peace in your heart" and left the cubicle.

"David," Burger said wanly after a moment's silence. "Try to think of this as a war action."

"This is nothing compared to what I faced in the '67 and '73 wars."

"Some say that our history since 1948 has been peace punctuated by war. I say that our history should be defined as war punctuated by peace. Your action is part of our war effort during this phony peace." Then he added: "But David, I have told you before not to let your dislike of Browning poison your thoughts. Keep your mind focused on the end result."

"What bothers me most, aside from his sheer arrogance, is his total lack of principle. He would kill his mother if the price were right."

"Are we any better?"

"Dammit, Eli, we have a cause. Our country's survival."

"And we further this cause by executing living flesh and blood?"

"Biologically, Arafat is a man. But politically he is a devil to our people."

Burger sighed. "I am getting old and tired, David. Maybe this is the last thing I will have the strength to do for Israel."

"Nonsense, Eli. You are an ageless Irgun warrior."

Burger forced a smile.

"Come back and stay at my place, Eli. You do not belong at the Waldorf. Too many

PLO types running around the corridors. Accept my offer. There is plenty of room."

"It's not a bad idea. I would be freer to operate. Almost had to bribe a Maariv journalist this morning to keep my name out of his story. The P.M. wants me to be anonymous. When do I move, tonight or tomorrow?"

"Tonight," Arovitch replied. "I'll help you. Now get me out of this place before I succumb to the temptations of the flesh. Sonia would love it if a journalist sees me here and puts my name in a juicy article in the morning newspapers."

"You're right. It would also be something if our Prime Minister learned that I am spending my first night in New York at Plato's Retreat. Yes, let's get the hell out of here before I also give in to the fleshy temptations, as you so nicely put it."

Chapter 29

At nine a.m. the next day Robert Sebastian reported to the French Interpretation Unit at the U.N. Leopold Aumont took him to the small office he would share with a Belgian colleague named Lucienne DuChamp.

"Here are some basic documents you should read," said Aumont, pointing to the top shelf of the bookcase. "By the way, I make it a practice of inviting new staff members to lunch. Are you free today?"

"No, I'm afraid not."

"Tomorrow is the Security Council meeting. What about the day after?"

"Certainly, with pleasure."

After Aumont left, Lucienne DuChamp, a striking looking woman with brown eyes and short hair in her 40s, tried making conversation, but upon receiving only monosyllabic replies, abandoned the effort. At his desk Robert Sebastian feigned interest in the documents outlining interpretation procedures and regulations. Resembling those that he had pilfered from UNESCO in Paris, they described booth design, advised on interpretation procedures, and recommended "constructive collaboration" for the interpreting teams of two. According to the Interpreters Association, interpreting work was so demanding that strict limits had to be placed on consecutive hours of work, with liberal coffee rest periods and coffee breaks.

In another life, Sebastian speculated, he would become an interpreter for the U.N.

Halfway through the morning, Aumont came into the office. "As a special favor to M. Sebastian and because we are short-staffed, Lucienne, I have decided that he will work with you tomorrow at the Security Council."

"But I'm used to working with Pierre, Monsieur Aumont," said Lucienne Duchamp. "He is on leave in the city. I can call him and ask him to come in tomorrow. He will do it."

"No, no, Lucienne. Robert will do very nicely. Give him a chance to prove himself." Aumont left the room.

Looking haughtily at Sebastian, she said: "You are hardly very experienced."

"Give me a chance. I will surprise you."

"All right. Let's talk about it." She moved her chair a few inches closer to his. "I'm not easy to work with. I believe in being very organized. Nothing left to chance. There is enough surprise in what is being said."

"I feel exactly the same way," Sebastian said.

At noon, after lunching in the staff cafeteria, he roamed through the U.N. building, studying the interiors of the General Assembly hall, the Security Council chamber, and various conference rooms. He speculated on Arafat's movements in the building. Lydia Ahmed would have to provide him with a specific schedule. Before coming here, Sebastian had worked out a tentative plan. The weak element was how he would get away afterwards.

For Julie's sake, Arafat must die. For Julie's sake, he, Sebastian, must live. His sister, he felt intuitively, wanted him to survive and have a life free of the cloying, depressing thoughts besieging him day after day since her death.

The only way that he could exorcise the destructive spirit that was twisting, contorting him inside his being was to kill Julie's murderer. It would liberate him, permit him to live a so-called normal life again, whatever this would mean.

Every day after lunch, Lydia Ahmed went to the Delegates Lounge on the second floor to see friends, swap rumors, and absorb or spread gossip about the latest political or personal developments around the U.N. Ornate and formal, the Delegates Lounge was graced by one of New York's most illustrious bartenders mixing the best Bloody Mary's in town, as well as a coffee bar featuring the creamiest cappuccino this side of Milan.

On one wall hung a huge green and yellow tapestry of the Great Wall of China, aother gift from that government in 1974, the year mainland China replaced Taiwan in the U.N. For some unknown reason, the artist had placed a few tiny cars in the right hand corner next to the Wall, giving rise to the impression that under the Communists, the Great Wall of China had become a glorified parking lot. On the north side of the room were large bay windows offering an exquisite view of the U.N. rose garden and the East River. Delegates lounged on plush leather sofas and chairs placed strategically close to each other to allow hushed conversations about vital issues of the day, such as the next move of the U.S. vis-a-vis PLO admission to the General Assembly, the Polisaro Liberation Movement seeking the independence of the Western Sahara from Morocco, or speculation on who would be replacing whom in the hierarchy of the Secretariat or UNICEF or UNESCO.

The Delegates Lounge reflected the special cultural flavor of the United Nations. Suavely dressed African diplomats conferred with cigarette-smoking West European and East European counterparts, often congregating according to Cold War divisions. The buzz of diplomacy pervaded the room at lunchtime. The hot topic was naturally the political implications of the pending admission of the PLO to the U.N. General Assembly. Sitting underneath a faded, but still colorful tapestry donated by Romania, Latin American diplomats lobbied Arab counterparts for support of the Peruvian candidate for the FAO directorship; in return, they would vote for the PLO admission to the G.A. Huddling with African brothers, safari-suited Mozambique and Zimbabwe representatives discussed ways to procure more arms for their guerilla forces fighting the power and the sins of colonialism.

At the bar the "regulars"—politicos, journalists, diplomats from the nearby Missions to the U.N., selected Secretariat staff--exchanged the latest gossip about some ambassador's sex life, political events in obscure corners of the world, or their own career possibilities in their Foreign Services, or in the United Nations, if they were staff members of the Secretariat or one of the numerous U.N. agencies located around the world ('international civil servants' was the operative, dignified phrase). Holding court at the far corner was Nick Beloff, the legendary White Russian, his gaunt, wrinkled face a testimony to harsh experience and deep suffering, who regaled anyone who would listen to pungent and melancholy tales of his family's escape from Russia in 1917 or his own U.N. career odyssey, stretching from documents' clerk in 1948 at Flushing Meadows to U.N. Secretary General Dag Hammerskjold's assistant in the glory days, when the U.N. flag flew over Leopoldville, to his present Assistant Secretary-General position in the Population Division of the Secretariat.

"I can't wait to retire from this midget organization," Beloff would proclaim to anyone who would listen. "Let's face it. The U.N. is castrated by the bully boys (translation: big powers) and prostituted by the jackals (Third World countries). Nobody listens to me anymore, despite my long experience with the organization. I have a plan to settle the Mideast problem, but nobody is interested." At this point Beloff would inevitably order another Bloody Mary. "I'm here only because I need three more years to exit with a decent pension. Othewise you would see my aging Russian body on the beaches of the Riviera all year long." Protected by his permanent contract, Beloff spent four or five hours daily at the bar, drinking, socializing, reminiscing, complaining that his retirement was still three long years away. Everyone knew that he could retire the next day on a good pension, but for him, the U.N. was not just a job—it was a womb and a home where he felt both at ease and important. In his mind, when he retired and was forced to abandon his cushy situation at the U.N., he would once again be a lonely exile in a hostile world.

In the Delegates Lounge ambassadors unwound, drank martinis or beers, and carried on occasionally frantic, but mainly leisurely diplomacy. Archbishop Makarios, the leader of Cyprus, and Henry Kissinger, Secretary of State under Richard Nixon, had been recently seen huddling in the Delegates Lounge with their entourages of ambitious young staff members. Voyeurs from the diplomatic missions, Secretariat offices, and the seemingly nonstop U.N. meetings frequented the Lounge to gaze at some of the world's most beautiful women sporting saris, African robes, or the latest Parisian fashions traipsing in and out of the Lounge, stopping to smile and receive compliments from the elegantly dressed, powerful males (ambassadors and diplomats) from many continents. Diplomatic groupies, they were eyed, judged, propositioned, and bedded at the nearby Missions or hotels. The drama of politics and sex played out continuously in the Delegates Lounge.

"Lydia," someone shouted, as she searched through waves of people for the two members of the PLO observer delegation who she was meeting for coffee.

"You look so beautiful, Lydia," said a tall, thin, elegantly dressed African from Senegal. "Come home and fuck me now," he whispered in her ear.

"Go away, Gabriel," she said, laughing and playfully pushing him away.

Seeing the Palestinians sitting across the hall, she walked over and joined them.

"How will the Americans vote, Lydia?" asked an intense looking young man with a round face and thick mustache named Nabil.

She sipped an espresso. "Carter is under strong Jewish pressure." Looking first at Nabil, then at the other Palestinian, Salim, she said: "If Carter doesn't abstain, that is, if he has his ambassador veto the resolution, we should recommend that U.S. targets be hit hard both here and around the world."

Salim laughed. "You've been seeing too many cowboy and war movies, Lydia." Nabil stared around the room people-watching, debating whether to get up and approach a Nigerian who was chief of a unit in the Department of Economic and Social Affairs and who might help him transfer there from his present less exalted, boring position in the Contracts and Procurement Office.

Conservative cows, she thought. It was precisely this attitude that had prompted her to abandon the PLO for Barka. These puny diplomats had traded their guns for three-piece suits and their principles for full bellies. Once Barka came to power, she would have these do-nothing layabouts replaced by militants. Over the last few days, Lydia Ahmed had been mentally reconciling herself to the idea of living with Barka in Beirut. She would discover his weaknesses, learn how to control him in bed, manipulate him outside...

Other Arabs joined their group, and the discussion continued in animated Arabic about the Security Council meeting and the general swirl of mideast politics.

Someone called her name and she looked up at the pudgy, smiling face of Carlos Montoya. She stood up and shook his hand. "Carlos, you were a darling to get my friend Robert Sebastian a job so quickly."

Jostled by the crowd, they moved to the side.

"See me tonight, Lydia," Montoya said with urgency in his voice.

She owed him one more time. "Okay. Come by after 8."

Hearing her name, she moved off to join a group of Algerians.

The two Palestinians, Nabil and Salim, watched her movements and began whispering to one another.

Chapter 30

Washington, D.C., September 5, 1978

"The U.N. is a farce, Mr. President. It isn't worth a bucket of warm spit, as an earlier Vice President said about his own high office during the time of Franklin Roosevelt."

Sitting across the table, Vice President Mondale winced. He, President Carter, Secretary of State Cyrus Vance, and National Security Officer Zbigniew Brzezinski were meeting in the West Wing of the White House with a delegation of prominent American Jews.

"Despite that undeniable fact," the Texan continued, "membership in the United Nations General Assembly confers a veneer of respectability. It would give the PLO a diplomatic forum from which to lambast Israel. There are also rumors, Mr. President, that once in the General Assembly, the PLO will establish a government-in-exile and be recognized by over 100 nations. Now they are at a crossroads. Deny them membership and they will wither away."

"Don't you think," Brzezinski asked, "that outside the U.N., the PLO will only become more frustrated and violent? At least in rhetoric the U.N. dedicates itself to the peaceful resolution of problems."

"With all due respect, sir," said a well-dressed man from California, "you are dreaming if you think that U.N. membership will transform that pack of cutthroats into instant pacifists. They deny Israel's rightful existence in their charter. Let them recognize Israel, and then they will merit admission."

"Absolutely right, Sam," said a New York labor leader. "Those butchers will never reform. If you ask me, all the damn Arabs are a pack of thieves."

"Come on, Abe," said Vice-President Mondale. "What about Sadat?"

President Carter was unfailingly courteous to the group, practicing what one adviser called the "charisma of courtliness," a low-keyed southern gentlemanly approach which sought to disarm critics by convincing them that he was the most tolerant of men, who desired nothing more in the world than to please his guests. But internally he was agitated. Before the meeting, he had met with Vice-President Mondale in the oval office to vent his frustrations.

"Walter, Walter, I feel as if I am between a rock and a hard place, to use a shopworn expression."

"I know what you mean, Mr. President," said Mondale, sipping tea and feeling happy that the president was confiding in him.

"So many pressures domestically and internationally. It's no secret that the price of oil is surging and the economy is limping along. The Three Mile Island nuclear leak is creating fear across the country. The Soviets are making a lot of noise about Afghanistan, and Iran is falling to pieces with the Shah kicked out and the mullahs declaring Iran to be an Islamic state. I can't do much about these problems in the short run, but I can do something really significant in foreign policy," said Carter, staring at Mondale.

"You mean the Begin-Sadat meeting scheduled in ten days at Camp David, Mr. President. A diplomatic accord would constitute a political coup for you and overshadow those other issues, that's for sure."

"But it's being threatened by this U.N. PLO business, Walter. President Sadat has accepted the principle of a peace treaty with Israel, but only after I promised him that I would permit the entry of the Palestinian Liberation Organization into the U.N. General Assembly. Waldheim has also been pressuring me ferociously on that. If I back down now, I will lose Sadat's trust and jeopardize the peace treaty. On the other hand, the Jewish leaders coming here in an hour are going to give me an earful on why the U.S. should veto the Security Council resolution…Begin was supposed to explain the deal to them and keep them at bay, but he hasn't done so."

"Mr. President, if I may be so bold, we cannot forget about the "two ocean strategy" for the 1980 presidential election. We'll need the strong support of the Jewish leaders at that time."

"Yes, Walter. I know, I know,. Let's take a walk in the garden outside and see if that calms me down. So how do we handle the situation? We're between a rock and a hard place, I tell you." The two men walked to the door leading to the back garden of the White House.

As the Jewish leaders spoke out at the meeting, the president thought about the electoral strategy for 1980, formulated in secret by the President, Vice-President, and a few key advisors which stipulated that Carter, confident of the South, would focus primarily upon the populous states on the Atlantic and Pacific seaboards, conceding the conservative Midwest, except for key states like Ohio, Michigan, and Illinois, to the Republicans. This strategy would win him the election, but he desperately needed California, New York, Pennsylvania, Michigan, Illinois, Florida, and Texas, states that the men in this room and Jewish voters outside who had voted 71% for Carter in the 1976 presidential election could deny him.

"Gentlemen," the President finally said after listening to all of the men in the room. "Thank you for expressing yourselves so frankly to Vice President Mondale and myself, to all of us," gesturing towards Vance and Brzezinski. "We will take your opinions fully into account before making our decision. We do have a knotty issue here. It is more complicated than you think, gentlemen." He paused as they looked unhappily at one another. "However, let me reiterate that our commitment to Israel is total." Leaning forward, he lowered his voice to take them into his confidence. "I will tell you confidentally and unofficially of our intention to supply Israel with fifty additional F-16 jet fighters as well as with half a billion dollars of new financial credits next year. Our relations with Israel have never been better. Prime Minister Begin trusts me. I want your trust as well."

He shook their hands as they filed out of the room.

The President looked at the others seated across the table. "What a political mess we may be creating," he said softly.

"You handled it perfectly, Mr. President," said Mondale. "When you conclude the accord between Israel and Egypt, these men will see it as the Red Sea parting once again to ensure the long-term survival of the Jewish people."

Carter smiled at Mondale. "Trust you to come up with a biblical image to lead us to the promised land. I love it when you try to one-up me biblically, Walter. It's so...ironic."

Mondale didn't know whether he was hearing a compliment or sarcasm. So he kept quiet.

Chapter 31

September 7, 1978

Located at Forty-Seventh Street between First and Second Avenues, Dag Hammarskjold Plaza remained one of the few open spaces in the concrete jungle of Manhattan.
Though dwarfed by skyscrapers on three sides, east was the river, and the few trees and
benches in the Plaza gave the illusion of a park, albeit one with cobblestones for grass.
From April to November an enterprising vendor sold plants in the open air. At noon white
collar workers, secretaries, and schoolchildren on their obligatory visit to the U.N. ate
lunch or relaxed on the benches. The Plaza also served as a place of protest for groups
manifesting their grievances in close proximity to the U.N.

Well before noon on September 7, 1978, thousands of people began gathering for
a demonstration called by the Jewish leaders of America and, more discreetly, by Sonia
Berenson and the Israeli Mission. Patiently they waited for the main group to arrive from
their march down Fifth Avenue and across Forty-Seventh Street. On the fringe of the
Plaza, hundreds of policemen stood guard, while First Avenue, with traffic rerouted west
at Forty-Second Street, was deserted except for U.N. security forces and police lines.

Restless in his office, Security Chief Jensen decided to watch a bit of the demonstration. He invited three security officials, including John Hardy, to accompany him. Since
his run-in with Jensen, Hardy had changed noticeably from ebullient extrovert to sullen
introvert. Feeling trapped in an unpleasant situation and not wishing to bother Waldheim
about his problem with Jensen, he took to sulking around the Security Office and drinking
himself into a stupor outside.

Jensen was secretly pleased to have taken Hardy down a peg. He was less pleased with
reports of loose talk around the security office about friction between Hardy and himself.
So in front of a dozen men in the back office, he cordially invited the Irishman to join the
group heading over to observe the demonstration. They arrived just as the main body
began tramping into the Plaza from Second Avenue and 47th Street. Led by a phalanx
of blue-uniformed policemen, the demonstrators advanced ten or twelve abreast in slow
motion—well-dressed, somber-looking dignitaries in front, casually clothed, chatting
masses behind. There were contingents of Jewish War Veterans (ranging from octogenar-
ians dating back to World War I and middle-aged military men of WWII to younger vets
from the Korean and Vietnam wars), Yeshiva University students, Hassidic Jews, Young
Zionists, Hebrew Schools from the tri-state area, unaffiliated men, women, and children.
The last group to pass was a contingent of husky young men carrying the placards "Jewish
Defense League says 'Never Again'," and "PLO Is Murder International."

A seemingly endless swirl of humanity filled into every inch of Dag Hammarskjold Plaza, spilling onto First and Second Avenues. "This ethnic invasion force," wrote the U.N. reporter for the New York Post, "simply appropriated a choice piece of territory for a few hours today, meeting no resistance from the authorities":

New York City, (he wrote), has never witnessed such a vast outpouring of people on its streets in peaceful protest. The crowd of 150,000 gathered in the shadow of the United Nations to demonstrate in favor of Israel and against the Palestinian Libera- tion Organization. It is a warning to President Carter not to allow the PLO to pass into the U.N. General Assembly. It is a collective cry of anger at the world organiza tion for even considering the sheltering of terrorists.

The dignitaries mounted an elevated reviewing stand set up near First Avenue. A tall, gaunt man identified himself as coordinator for the march and introduced a rabbi who gave the religious invocation in Hebrew, followed by a brief sermon in English:

"I thought of chanting the Mourners' Kaddish to signify the death of an ideal, the ideal of world justice at the United Nations. But I realized that as long as people live and breathe, ideals can never perish. We Americans and Jews must aspire to the highest ideals, while preventing their perversion by others."

Israeli Ambassador Sonia Berenson was the next speaker. After referring to the "cos- mic chutzpah" of the U.N., she stated that the "United Nations in its present mood and composition would refuse to ratify the Ten Commandments simply because they origi- nated in Israel." The crowd hooted and screamed approval. Then she quoted from the covenant of the Palestinian Liberation Organization:

"...the establishment of Israel is fundamentally null and void. The liberation of Palestine will liquidate the Zionist imperialist presence and restore the homeland to its rightful owners."

"Make no mistake," she concluded. "The PLO does not want co-existence, but death and domination. Israel will never negotiate with this surly band of gangsters and murderers."

She was followed by Mayor Koch, Senators Javits and Moynihan, Governor Carey, and Henry Kissinger, who said to a cacaphony of boos, "the United Nations is reeking with the shame of blackmail." The loudest cheer was evoked by a Hebrew School boy announcing his intention to complete his studies and then do his military service in Israel.

Standing on the fringe of the crowd on First Avenue, bored by the proceedings, Henry Jensen puffed his pipe as he surveyed the scene. "Well, I'll be damned," he said to no one in particular.

"What is it, Colonel?" asked a security officer.

"See that short, stocky, white-haired man standing over there," Jensen said, pointing with his pipe. "That's Eli Burger, a fanatically conservative Israeli politician. Used to be called the 'Robespierre of the Right'. Met him a few times during my tour of duty in the Sinai. Spent a miserable afternoon in his office being harangued about the Arabs. Perfectly obnoxious character."

"Why is he here?"

"Damned if I know," replied Jensen.

As Hardy and the others watched Burger, they were nearly trampled by part of the crowd rushing towards First Avenue. Struggling to extricate themselves, they saw about two dozen men and women on the opposite sidewalk holding up signs saying "PLO in the U.N." and "American Youth for Palestine."

Jensen spotted Police Captain Lester Schwartz in the middle of First Avenue. "What is it, Les?" he asked.

"Counter demonstration," Schwartz said. "The 'Committee for Improving American-Arab Relations'. They wanted a license to march; we had to give them one."

"Maybe they have the right," Jensen said, "but they picked the wrong day,"

"Oh, they know exactly what they're doing."

On the west side of First Avenue, the crowd hooted and shouted obscenities. They tried to advance, and the thin line of policemen, poised uneasily between the screaming mob and the Arab supporters, began smacking demonstrators with their nightsticks. Two policemen on horseback rode up to block the way. They jerked on the reins, and the horses raised their front hoofs high in the air, menacing the front ranks of the crowd, which now tried desperately to retreat, but couldn't budge because of the mass of people just behind.

Farther up the street, Jewish Defense League youths brandishing knives and pipes broke through the wedge of policemen and ran towards the pro-Arab group. Police sirens blared. A patrol car zoomed forward, knocking down a J.D.L. member and scattering the others. Police reinforcements grabbed the attackers and hustled them into nearby vans.

"Les, get them away," Jensen said, pointing to the pro-Arab group.

"You're right. Screw free speech." He gave the order, and a dozen policemen escorted the pro-Palestinian demonstrators up First Avenue. The crowd hurled taunts as they vanished from the scene.

Jensen and the others walked slowly back towards the U.N.

"Mother of Jesus," Hardy said, shaking his head. "That was real mean."

"No shit, Dick Tracy," said a security officer not fond of Hardy.

"Chief, Chief," someone shouted from a distance.

"Hey, it's fat Rosy," said an officer.

Running towards them, his belly bobbing up and down, was Lieutenant Stuart Rosenberg.

Between puffs of breath, with sweat pouring down his face, he managed to say: "Bomb...inside med...caller said...Meditation Room."

"Get Johannson. Move," Jensen shouted.

Johannson was the principal bomb defuser on the U.N. Security staff. Rosenberg turned and ran back, Jensen following swiftly behind. It was probably a hoax, the Security Chief thought, but every alarming call had to be taken seriously, every bomb threat investigated, especially since the explosion in the tourist area last March that had shredded the arms of a security officer and left a bystander from Pakistan permanently paralyzed from the waist down.

John Hardy took this opportunity to slip away, heading in the direction of the Green Derby Pub for some much-needed glasses of beer and a game of darts.

Chapter 32

Lydia Ahmed left work just before six. With the Security Council meeting scheduled for the next morning, her unit would be working half the night. She feigned illness in order to come home to see Carlos Montoya, as she had promised.

She lived on East 83rd Street in a one bedroom apartment in a renovated brownstone building that she thought overpriced. Not that she lacked for money. Her U.N. salary was reasonable, and the PLO paid her a stipend each month. In addition, Barka deposited funds for her in an account in Damascus. He wanted her to feel part of a solidly financed organization, not a struggling rebel group.

Turning the key in the lock, she opened the door and stepped into her apartment. In the half-light, his face and body barely visible, a man sat across the room staring at her. Her heart pounding in her throat, she did not know whether to scream or run.

A voice said in French: "Don't worry. It's me."

Lydia felt her legs waver as she gave a pang of relief. Relief turned to anger. "How could you do that?" she cried. "If I had a gun, I would have…"

Flipping the light on, she saw Robert Sebastian shrug. He was sitting at the table sketching with pencil and ruler on some paper.

Coming closer, she saw a scale diagram of the U.N. interior—the Secretariat, General Assembly, Security Council, conference rooms, and connecting passageways drawn to scale and accurately detailed. Sitting in a chair opposite him, she lit a cigarette and asked: "Why are you here?"

He was absorbed in his work. She repeated the question. Again no reply.

"You will have to leave. Someone is coming soon."

"He raised his head. "When?"

"At 8."

He looked down again.

"Please leave. I have some things to do."

"Not yet." He continued penciling.

Lydia looked at Sebastian whose expression was intensely focussed as he worked. The features were not bad at all, she thought, but his face was a mask, a studied blank that made it impossible for her to know what he was thinking. She tried to relax, but was too nervous to do so.

Putting down his pencil, he looked at her. "Tell me about the U.N. I want to know everything—the Secretary-General's personality, the different political bodies, what happens on the day the General Assembly opens, the nationalities that participate in the

Security Council, the Security Office and measures it takes, what happened when Arafat came here the last time. Tell me everything."

"It's impossible," she said, shaking her head. "There is not enough time."

"We have over an hour. Begin."

She saw that it would be useless to argue with him. As she began talking, she hoped that Carlos Montoya would arrive early. Sebastian looked away, closing his eyes a few times as she spoke. Often he asked questions about small details.

Ten minutes before 8, she got up abruptly. "I must get ready. You will have to leave."

He nodded as if in a daze. Gathering up his drawings, he walked past her towards the door.

Suddenly he turned and grabbed her left wrist. "Where did you get this?" Twisting her arm, he yanked her wrist up to her face.

Lydia cried out in pain. "What? What?" she yelled.

"The bracelet," he said, twisting harder.

She saw a look of menacing hatred in his eyes and knew he would kill her if she didn't tell him the truth. "Barka," she said. "Barka...gave it to me. Now let me go..."

He released her arm, and she backed away. His face was twitching uncontrollably. She forgot her own pain at the sight of Sebastian. Removing the bracelet, she flung it at him and shouted: "Take it, you bastard. Take it and leave. Leave. Leave." She ran into the bathroom and locked the door, leaning against it to hear him go.

Bending down, Sebastian picked up Julie's bracelet. The Sacre Coeur Cathedral gleamed on the front and Julie's name on the back. He examined it lovingly as if it were the flesh of his sister. Then, feeling pain in his head, he slowly left the apartment, holding onto the bracelet so tightly that it cut into his finger.

Chapter 33

The twice-postponed Security Council meeting finally took place at 10:30 a.m. on Wednesday morning, September 8, 1978. By 10 a.m. every available seat in the tourist area of the room was occupied by Secretariat staff and diplomatic mission personnel. Security officers directed the press to a remote corner of the upper visitors' gallery. Aside from the five great powers permanently represented on the Security Council--the United States, Soviet Union, Great Britain, France, and China-- the ten countries currently serving two-year terms were Bolivia, Canada, Czechoslovakia, Gabon, West Germany, India, Nigeria, Pakistan, Romania, and Venezuela.

The Security Council chamber in appearance looked like an old-fashioned conference room, something that could have been transplanted from the 1920s/30s League of Nations, the U.N.'s ineffectual predecessor. Dominating the chamber floor was an imposing wooden horseshoe table in the center of the room. The decor of the hall was old-worldly, faded—the dull grey carpet, muted blue-gold curtains, and the huge mural at the back of the chamber symbolically depicting humanity's ascension from pre-United Nations ignorance to post-U.N. enlightenment. In the mural, somber-faced men and women grasping a precipice or trapped in a cave reached upward to heights of human brotherhood and sisterhood, musical sensibility, and scientific discovery. A huge grey-black bird, species unintelligible, stared ominously at the Security Council representatives below.

Delegates of the fifteen member nations flanked the outer rim of the table, while stenographers and précis-writers worked at desks in the center. High above the hall at the front were two levels of glassed-encased booths for simultaneous interpretation in the six official U.N. languages (English; French; Spanish; Russian; Chinese; and Arabic which had been added in 1976). Television, radio, and film studios lay adjacent to the interpretation booths.

Andrew Young, along with Donald McHenry and three other U.S. Mission staff members, entered the hall and began chatting with the portly British ambassador, Sir Ivor Richards, sitting next to him.

Secretary-General Waldheim came into the Security Council chamber last, accompanied by the President for the month of September, the West German ambassador to the U.N., Hans Bleiburg. Waldheim's placid demeanor concealed his inner turmoil. Everything hinged on the upcoming vote for PLO admission to the General Assembly which would generate enough positive votes for the Law of the Sea Treaty whose seabed clause would guarantee both the U.N.'s financial future and Waldheim's political future in

Austria. The vote could assure him of a glorious place in the annals of the United Nations, silencing the carping critics of a "do-nothing administrator," and eliminating the unfavorable comparisons with his predecessor, U Thant, around whose Buddhist head hung a mystical halo of perfection. (Waldheim did not completely accept the historical record, remembering U Thant as someone whose interest in geopolitical and personal power was less than saintlike.) While he knew also that there would always be unfavorable comparisons to his predecessor, the success of the Seabed Treaty could go a long way in changing this perception. Unfortunately all this rested on theAmerican vote, and neither Carter nor Young had revealed their intentions.

High above the Council floor, interpreters for the six official U.N. languages took their places in their respective booths, including Lucienne DuChamp and her co-interpreter, Robert Sebastian, who were responsible for interpreting English into French.

In the crowd below, Lydia Ahmed stood near an entranceway thinking about Sebastian's inexplicably violent behavior towards her the previous evening. Why had he gone berserk upon seeing the silver bracelet on her wrist? She thought of telling Barka, but he would probably distort the whole thing and blame her. He was as unpredictable as Sebastian. Things were getting out of control, and the quicker that Sebastian completed his assignment, the better she would feel. She vowed not to be alone with him again.

At the two principal entrances, U.N. Security staff checked identification cards. Eli Burger, using an Israeli diplomatic passport, moved into the chamber with a number of international officials. Security Chief Jensen, along with Deputy Chief Todman, was watching to see that everything proceeded smoothly. John Hardy, without any specific assignment, came into the hall. Moving through the crowd, he was jostled into a small man climbing the stairs at the side. Hardy uttered a brief word of apology, but the man had moved away. Hardy recognized the right-wing Israeli whom Jensen had pointed out the previous day at the Jewish demonstration.

A gavel pounded for silence. "The meeting will come to order," Security Council President Hans Bleiburg shouted from the base of the horseshoe table. The crowd quieted down. "Because of today's topic," Bleiburg continued, "the delegations of Egypt, Israel, Jordan, Syria, and the Palestinian Liberation Organization will be present at this meeting." One by one, the ambassadors and their entourages came into the chamber. Spontaneous applause greeted the arrival of the PLO observer team, led by Zehdi Terzi, a heavy-set, white-haired man with side whiskers and a curly half-beard. The President gaveled for order.

Sonia Berenson, David Arovitch, and two other staff members of the Israeli Mission to the U.N. took seats opposite the Arab delegations. Only a half-hour before, Berenson had put the finishing touches on the speech teletyped from the Foreign Ministry. Her intervention, she knew, would be irrelevant. Governments invariably made decisions in advance, decisions that were almost always irrevocable. Still, U.N. protocol had to be followed, and this debate had more mystery than most, since the U.S. had not yet shown its hand.

Secretary-General Waldheim was the first speaker. To the surprise of many who considered him to be the quintessence of detached diplomacy never showing emotional involvement, he made an uncharacteristically impassioned plea for the adoption of the agenda resolution. "The admittance of the Palestinian Liberation Organization," he concluded, "is an essential part of the peace-making process in the Middle East. The admission of the PLO to the U.N. General Assembly will benefit the evolution of what I might call the 'inevitable two-state solution'. Dialogue, as always, is preferable to weapons. As Winston Churchill once said: 'To jaw jaw is always better than to 'war war.' I urge you to admit the PLO to the United Nations for the intensification of 'jaw jaw' and the abandonment of 'fight fight'." Waldheim sat down amidst many delegates murmuring and whispering with their entourages and those sitting on either side.

Then, in succession, the Arab ambassadors attacked Israel for human rights violations and for intransigence on the Palestinian question. They championed the P.L.O. as the "legitimate and sole representative" of the Palestinian people, well deserving to be admitted to full membership in the U.N. General Assembly.

During these speeches lasting well over an hour, a few people left the chamber floor. Seeing an empty chair ten feet below, Eli Burger moved down to have a better view of the proceedings. Sonia Berenson looked up from her notes and saw him. She wondered why the Foreign Ministry had not routinely informed her about Burger being in New York for the Security Council meeting.

John Hardy also saw Burger change his seat. Acting on an impulse, he went up to Jensen. "Chief, there's that Israeli again," he said, pointing out Burger. "Shall I keep an eye on him?"

"Don't be ridiculous, Hardy."

Irritated, Hardy walked away and left the hall.

Following the last Arab speech, Security Council President Bleiburg called upon Israeli Ambassador Sonia Berenson.

In interpretation booth 3, Lucianne Duchamp passed the microphone to Robert Sebastian to interpret from English to French. Many Arab delegates walked out of the chamber.

Grasping the microphone, Berenson leaned forward and looked directly at Andrew Young, who was sucking on the tip of his pencil and gazing off enigmatically into space.

"I am aghast," she began, "that the United Nations is considering admitting a terrorist faction whose sole political purpose is to destroy a member state of the United Nations. Israel, as always, favors universal membership in this organization, but only for bona fide sovereign states. Would anyone seriously recommend the admission of Corsican and Breton nationalists, the Irish Republican Army, the Baeder-Meinoff gang, the Japanese Red Army, or the Tuperameros of Uraguay? Yet all these groups, like the PLO, wish to 'liberate' their homelands from supposed oppression." She paused for a moment, then continued. "If this resolution is adopted, it will signify the end of the United Nations as a force for good. Israel hopes and expects that for the sake of the U.N. and for the cause of peace in the Middle East, the resolution will be soundly rejected."

There was scattered applause as she finished.

Bleiburg called for a ten-minute recess to allow for the return of delegates who had left the chamber floor during Sonia Berenson's speech. John Hardy wandered in with them, accompanied by a U.N. plainclothes security detective, a Jamaican named William Smith, who was technically under Hardy's jurisdiction. Pointing discreetly at Eli Burger, Hardy whispered into Smith's ear.

When the session reopened, Security Council members spoke one by one in favor of the agenda resolution, their comments ranging from unqualified support for the PLO from China and Russia to grudging acceptance, tinged with sympathy for Israel from England and France.

The United States ambassador was listed as the last speaker on the agenda. As Andrew Young cleared his throat, the room fell deadly silent. Kurt Waldheim, hands folded on the table, uttered a prayer in German. Across the way, Sonia Berenson and David Arovitch strained to hear. In the French booth, Robert Sebastian prepared to translate Young's speech into French. Charles Browning was also in the room, anticipating Young's comments.

"Mr. Secretary-General, Mr. President, distinguished delegates. The United States government has been the foremost proponent of peace in the Middle East. Later this month two former adversaries, Israel and Egypt, will be meeting at Camp David to discuss their major differences and hopefully agree on an accord. We sincerely hope that additional parties to the dispute will soon follow their lead.

"Yet we harbor no illusions that the way to a comprehensive peace will be easy. The most intractable problem is the Palestinian issue, where mutual animosity is intense. But so it was between Israel and Egypt. As the great American civil rights leader, Martin Luther King Jr., with whom I was privileged to be associated, once said: 'It is easy to throw a stone or shoot a bullet. But what a hard, lonely, and courageous thing it is for men who despise one another to sit across the table and speak the language of sweet reasonableness.' That language and all that it means must be utilized in the Security Council and in all councils concerning the Middle East.

"Therefore, because my government believes first and foremost that the only hope for mankind is to talk—not to throw stones—and second, that the United Nations must be a universal forum, I announce my country's abstention on the agenda resolution. Thank you, Mr. President."

There was a split second of silence, then an outburst of shouting and clapping. Delegates ran up to congratulate Terzi and the PLO observer delegation. Several people hugged and kissed Lydia Ahmed. There was bedlam on the floor. Hans Bleiburg banged his gavel futilely for the resumption of order.

Sonia Berenson frowned at Andrew Young as she left the chamber, followed by David Arovitch and the other Israelis. Young gestured sympathetically to Berenson while accepting handshakes from delegates and then from Kurt Waldheim. He would do his best to mollify her at their scheduled lunch in two days, while pursuing his personal agenda of artfully asking her to consider commencing a relationship with him.

When order was restored, Security Council President Bleiburg confirmed that the resolution had passed unanimously with one abstention. Then he called upon a beaming Secretary-General Waldheim who announced that PLO leader Yasser Arafat would come to New York the following week to attend the admission of his organization into the United Nations General Assembly.

Chapter 34

"It was a good try, Sonia. Don't take it personally." In mid-afternoon Eli Burger, making a courtesy call to the Israeli Mission, found Sonia Berenson disconsolate after the morning's Security Council vote. "Think of how your father would have reacted."

She gave a mock smile. "He was full of bittersweet platitudes, wasn't he, Eli? 'It's only a battle, not the war.' 'Hit them harder the next time.' And then, 'never give up.'"

Burger leaned forward in his chair. "He was a man who had seen the abyss, but refused to fall into it. We can all learn many lessons from him." Sonia Berenson's father had been Burger's comrade in the Irgun who then "defected" to a rival anti-British nationalist group, the Palmach, after the King David incident.

"What brings you here, Eli?"

Burger smiled. "The P.M. wants me to see a few people and give him a personal assessment of the situation."

"Begin has never liked conventional channels, has he?"

"Sonia, Sonia, don't feel slighted. In Israel there is always "balagan', our Hebrew slang for 'chaos', the storm before the calm. Begin is in the middle of balagan with this blasted Palestinian business, and Carter pressuring him to undertake diplomatic relations with Egypt. I think that he wants me to bring him a little ammunition to keep the National Religious Party in line on both of these issues." He showed her a piece of paper from his pocket. "Here is a list of the people I am supposed to see." The list contained six names, one-third the actual number Burger intended to contact.

Suddenly the door opened and David Arovitch came in.

He hesitated when he saw who was there.

"It's alright, David," Sonia Berenson said. "Come in and meet one of the heroes of our independence. This is Eli Burger. Eli, this is our Second Secretary, David Arovitch. He's got a great diplomatic career ahead of him, if he wants it." They shook hands.

"I heard you speak once," Arovitch said.

"Where was that?"

"In Jerusalem. After the massacre at Yad Yehudah."

"How is she, Eli?" Sonia Berenson asked.

"Not so good, Sonia," he said, his face darkening. "Still suffering."

"I'll come back later," Arovitch said, walking towards the door.

"Come in half an hour, will you, David?" she said, ushering Burger towards the couch. "Let us see that list, Eli. Maybe I can suggest one or two other names."

Forty minutes later, Burger left the Mission and walked up Second Avenue, unaware of a man half a block behind following him wherever he turned.

Chapter 35

September 9, 1978

Security Chief Jensen sat in his office examining the schedule of Yasser Arafat's projected movements in the U.N. building. The PLO leader would spend a total of seven hours undertaking the following activities: breakfasting with Arab delegates, conferring with the Secretary-General, speaking in the General Assembly, hosting a luncheon in the Delegates Dining Room, and holding a press conference. Jensen intended to enforce the tightest security measures in U.N. history both inside and outside the building. He picked up the telephone to call Schwartz and Bailey to arrange another meeting on combined security activities.

Before he could dial, John Hardy knocked twice and came into the room.

"What is it?" Jensen asked coldly.

"You won't like this," Hardy said, "but the Secretary General just called me. He would like your report on security measures relating to Arafat's visit by three this afternoon."

"Dammit, Hardy. Are you his private errand boy or something? Why doesn't he call me directly?"

"I don't like it any better than you."

"Well, tell him so."

"He'd be insulted," Hardy said. "Believe me, it's no slight to you. When he is busy like this, he rings me up to do favors for him. The request to call you was sandwiched between one to buy some shirts for him at Bloomingdale's and another to arrange reservations for his wife's dinner with women delegates at Le Cirque tomorrow evening."

"I don't know, Hardy. You have always presented it as if you've got this special hot line to the S.-G. which you are exploiting to the maximum. Pulling rank, etc."

Hardy's face blanched. "How can you..."

"Let's not get into this again," Jensen interrupted. "Just tell Waldheim the report will be on his desk by three." He picked up the phone. "I need to verify some figures from Schwartz and Bailey," he said dismissively.

In the corridor, Hardy, fuming, vowed to quit if Jensen did not retire early in 1979, as rumors were circulating. He doubted that he could even last that long. He decided to look for another job in the U.N., an administrative position far away from the Security Division. The more distance between Jensen and himself, the better things would be. He decided to see his friend, the Staff Council Chairman, to discuss the matter as soon as this PLO business was over.

Turning the corner, he bumped into Security detective William Smith. "Just coming to see you, man," Smith said.

"Not here. Let's get coffee."

"I've shadowed the old Israeli Burger since yesterday noon, just as you asked," Smith said in a slow Jamaican drawl, when they were seated in the cafeteria at a window table overlooking Roosevelt Island and the East River.

"And?"

"Here is what he did." Smith read from his notes. "Lunch midtown diner; visit Israeli Mission; visit Governor Carey's office; visit Kidder Peabody investment banking firm; visit World Trade Center; dinner Katz's Delicatessen on the Lower East Side with two old men wearing those funny black hats on their heads. Then 'bout midnight, he went to an apartment on the Upper East Side where he spent the night. That man has more energy than someone half his age."

"Where is he staying?" Hardy asked nonchalantly.

"92nd Street, near Madison. I checked the name when the third floor front apartment light went on. 'Arovitch.' Mean anything to you?"

"Israeli Mission official," Hardy said, gazing out the window at a garbage barge floating down the East River. "He's in their Secret Service. They all are, you know."

"The old man was out by 7:30 a.m.," Smith continued, checking his notes, "Breakfast Regency Hotel. Then the Circle Line pier on the Hudson River where he met a much younger man. They both took that boat trip around Manhattan 'bout..." Smith verified his watch. "...a half hour ago. It takes three hours, so I got plenty of time to get back there to meet the boat."

"That's good work, William, but it is pretty vague. Doesn't tell us much, except that the old guy is either sightseeing like crazy or visiting everyone and his cousin in town. And tailing him is taking all your time."

"I don't mind," said Smith who would get good overtime pay for the extra hours.

"I may have a better idea," Hardy said, looking out the window again. "A long shot, but if something funny is happening..."

"What is it?"

"Chief might skin me alive," Hardy said softly. "But what he doesn't know won't hurt him. And if I'm right..." It would prove to the arrogant bastard Jensen that I can do something right, Hardy was thinking.

"Hey, maybe we shouldn't..." said Smith, alarmed.

"Let's move," Hardy ordered.

They went down to the second basement to the telephone repair shop. Hardy found Harry Parker, a squat man with bushy black eyebrows, sitting at the back desk looking at a copy of Playboy. He explained to Parker what he had in mind.

"Yeah, could be done," said Parker, going to fetch his toolbox.

Driving uptown, William Smith had a moment of concern. "What if the police catch us?"

"Relax, William. We're United Nations international civil servants and therefore immune to prosecution under United States law."

"I still don't like it," said Smith, clenching his fists tightly.

Parker sat in the back smoking a thick Cuban cigar. He was happy to do Hardy a favor, since the Irishman had fought so hard in the Staff Council last year to obtain salary increases for the maintenance crew.

Shortly afterwards, three men in overalls wearing Bell Telephone hats arrived in front of David Arovitch's building. Smith waited outside in the car.

Hardy explained to the super's wife, a young Hungarian woman with a rudimentary knowledge of English, that they needed to repair telephone wiring in a few apartments. They would need to check the system in the basement because of problems causing multiple conversations on single party lines. Busy feeding her baby, she handed him the master keys.

In David Arovitch's apartment Parker examined the wall phone, noting the wire type and number. After locking the door, they went down to the basement. Attached to the back wall was a metal box containing a cluster of interconnected telephone wires. While Hardy trained the flashlight, Parker made a slight cut in Arovitch's numbered wire and attached a magnetic clip from which he ran a thin silky wire. He moved it along the top of the window rim, fastening it tightly with metal stops, then spliced it to another wire connected to a small magnetic device that he placed on a dusty shelf behind some old books. The connecting wire, in turn, was attached to the underbelly of a small tape recorder placed in a dark hole a few feet from the back door.

"When the telephone receiver in his apartment is picked up," Parker said laconically, "it activates the magnetic clip on his wire which then transmits a current to the magnetic device. The recorder switches on automatically, taking the message down verbatim. As soon as the receiver is hung up, it shuts off the recorder. It works the same for incoming or outgoing calls."

"Brilliant," said Hardy. "Now let's return the keys and get the hell out of here."

Chapter 36

"Your performance at the Security Council session was impressive," said Leopold Aumont, lifting a glass of red wine towards the face of Robert Sebastian. "I toast your success and your future with the U.N."

"Merci infiniment, Monsieur Aumont. I wouldn't mind at all making my career here."

The Delegates Dining Room was packed with Secretariat staff and delegates. Set elegantly over the East River, the Delegates' Dining Room was open to the public for lunch when the General Assembly was not in session. Every week a new cuisine from around the globe was featured. This week was Moroccan, next week Thai. The New York Times food critic gave three stars to the Dining Room for its food, service, and ambiance. The room was packed with well-dressed international types, mainly ambassadors and staff from the country missions to the U.N.

"Don't tell me that you are one of these latent idealists," Aumont said, smiling wryly. He was chubby, with pale skin, thinning hair, and bony cheeks.

"I like the idea of working in an international milieu where national loyalties do not count for so much." It was the line Lydia Ahmed told him to use if anyone asked his motive for wanting to work for the U.N.

"Let me tell you something, Robert," said Aumont, leaning closer, his voice barely above a whisper. "Thirty years ago I was just like you. Puffed up with naive expectations. I was a young man in my 20s, delighted to be in the U.N. which was going to solve all the problems of the world--eliminate war, feed the starving peoples across the globe, transcend the national state and move towards world government. But it was all merde. As the philosopher Charles Peguy once said: 'tout commence en mystique; tout finit en politique'. ("Everything begins as a mystique; everything ends in politics.") That was the dream at the beginning. But what is the reality now? The U.N. has become an encrusted bureaucracy stifling initiative, with old men like me lording it over younger ones like you, with nepotism and continual political pressures from the big powers or the non-aligned states. Nothing is pure. Everything is corrupt, just as in the outside world."

"Why do you stay if you are so cynical?" Sebastian asked, slowly eating his filet mignon and pommes frites. He ordered a second glass of Mouton Cadet.

"There are many reasons, many positive reasons, for me to stay at the U.N...my shrinking, yet still present idealism, my continual hope for international cooperation, the special atmosphere here, so many intelligent colleagues from all over the world... And then on the personal side, the decent salary and reasonable vacation time and, I must not neglect to mention the paid home leave to France every two years. I am human too, you know. I respect and even adore the positive aspects of the U.N. After all, I have made my entire career in the United Nations."

"That is quite an achievement, I would say." Sebastian looked at Aumont's face which had a puckish expression.

"But I cannot overlook the negatives," Aumont continued. "I was here at the beginning and I can tell you that this place has gone downhill from the great hopes of the 1940s. When we first started—at Lake Success in Long Island, Hunter College located then in the Bronx, and then here in the heart of Manhattan, after the Rockefellers donated land on Turtle Bay which had been an abattoir for slaughtering animals.* We initial staff members had an incredible sense of purpose and vitality. Of course it was just after World War II, when everyone was exhausted by the war and its horrors. Early on, we staff members worked like dogs. We would do anything to avoid another destructive war like World War II. We felt that we were laboring for world peace and universal brotherhood, but our idealistic spirit didn't last very long. The Cold War started up, and all you heard in the political meetings was name-calling—'capitalist lackeys'; 'communist puppets'; and so on. And once Israel got its independence in 1948, the Arabs attacked and when they were defeated by the Israelis, they never accepted the reality of the state of Israel, and they have kept making wars or terroristic actions ever since. But..I...I'm talking too much, Robert. I hope that I'm not boring you," Aumont said, placing his hand on Sebastian's arm.

"Non, non, Monsieur Aumont. It is fascinating to hear about the U.N. from one of the originals. An original true believer…"

"A fossil, maybe, and not much of a believer anymore. I think that for me it was the Korean War that made me realize that the U.N. was pretty useless to prevent hostilities. It was June 1950, and I was working in the refugee relief organization in Geneva. North Korea invaded and was sweeping down through South Korea. The U.S. became even more paranoid about communism and appealed to the U.N. Because the Russians happened to be boycotting the Security Council on the day of the crucial vote, the U.N. was able to create a military force that fought on the South Korean side. Led by the Americans, of course, but nevertheless, a 'U.N. emergency police action'. So I have seen it all, Robert, and much of it has been pretty ugly." Aumont raised his wine glass to his lips, but did not drink. He shook his head sadly and resumed speaking.

---

*A rumor, never proven, stated that the Rockefellers and Zeckendorffs, wealthy real estate families, secretly bought up the surrounding property beforehand and made a killing when the U.N.was built and the surrounding property in Turtle Bay skyrocketed in value. Most people believe that their motive was strictly humanitarian, a gesture that would ensure that theUnited Nations would be established on U.S. soil in perpetuity.

"I guess in the end that we human beings are incapable of acting unselfishly. We group ourselves into nationalities and then fight other nationalities. Here in the Delegates Dining Room, all we see are nationalities. See those Africans two tables away. They are Kenyans, belonging to a former British colony. Next to them is a table of Chinese nationals, able to be here only because Mao's 'People's Republic' replaced Taiwan in 1974. When these people come here, do you think that they shed their nationality and acted 'internationally' just because they had joined the U.N.? Nonsense. They compete here for political and private gain just as they do in the outside world."

Sebastian looked around at the sea of black, yellow, and white faces. "Still, I..."

"Do you like being French?" asked Aumont sharply. "The older I get, the more I cling to it."

"You never lose your nationality," Sebastian said, a little defensively. "But there must be a 'world view' that one gains here."

"Yes and no," said Aumont. "For us French, nothing can match our ties of culture, language, history." He sipped his wine, licking his lips. "Oh, Robert, I cannot tell you what a comfort it is for me to speak French to a highly intelligent young man like yourself and to tell you about my history at the U.N."

Sebastian listened, but he was thinking about the bracelet. Lydia had said that Barka had given it to her. Where had Barka gotten it? Since it was the PLO that committed the murders at Yad Yehuda, and Barka hated Arafat and the PLO as it is, could a PLO terrorist have given him Julie's bracelet? Or could Barka have been responsible for...? A sharp pain seared through his head. Barka had hired him to kill Arafat, and he had agreed because of Julie. He had to keep going to achieve his original purpose. He couldn't deviate now. But once the present matter was concluded, he would have to find out about the bracelet. Or maybe before...if he could.

Seeing Sebastian's eyes were glazed, Aumont spoke his name. "Robert."

"Yes?"

"Do I intimidate you?" Aumont stared at him.

"No, Monsieur Aumont."

"Good. Because I like you. You are very handsome and very understanding. And very intelligent. It is charming for me to see a young idealist beginning his career at the U.N." He rested his hand on Sebastian's arm for a few seconds. "Do you know what I am talking about?"

"I think so," said Sebastian, taking another sip of wine.

"There is a whole world I want to introduce you to in the U.N., a select world of masculine sensuality. We are a regular Mafia here, French, Italian, American, Filipino, Thai. We socialize together, party together, sleep together, protect each other. I would like to bring you into this world, if you will let me." Aumont pressed hard on Sebastian's arm.

Robert Sebastian remained silent.

"I do not expect you to answer now. Think about it."

"I will, Monsieur Aumont. May I ask you one thing? When will I interpret next?"

"Oh, you are so work conscious, so diligent even. It's charming." Aumont paused. "The General Assembly opens next week. There will be plenty of work for you over the next few months."

"But it would be such an honor for me to interpret at the opening," Sebastian said. "I would do anything for that." He smiled and looked directly into Aumont's eyes and put his hand on Aumont's arm.

"Would you?" Aumont asked, staring at him and placing his hand on top of Sebastian's. "The others would fume—that foggy-eyed Simonet, that simpering idiot Lagrande. Mmmm...I could propose it to Stanislaw who arranges the schedules. Let me think about it. Maybe you and I could talk about it in my apartment some day soon."

"Any time, Monsieur Aumont," Sebastian answered.

After lunch, they separated near the Delegates Lounge. Aumont gave a long handshake as if concluding a pact.

Walking along a corridor on the second floor, Sebastian opened a door marked "G.A. Private." He passed through a back room and then onto the stage of the General Assembly hall. With the hall deserted, he had the impression of being inside a huge amphitheater. The hall extended upwards over 300 feet to the ceiling, where a cupola, supported by metal girds, allowed light to filter in through a circular glass panel. Straight ahead, behind the semicircular desks of the delegations, ascending tiers of tourist seats spread over several hundred feet.

Sebastian stood at the speaker's rostrum as if addressing the 151 delegations and a full audience. Looking around, he saw the raised dais for the President of the General Assembly and the Secretary-General, organ-shaped gold bars flanking a huge metal seal of the U.N., a globe surrounded by a peace symbol. Above the stage, on either side, the names of member states were arranged in alphabetical order, including the recent addition of "Palestinian Liberation Organization."

Moving down the stairs, Sebastian strolled among the desks trying to get the feel of the place. Helping himself to a glass of water at Poland's seat and a piece of paper from Peru, he began diagramming the interior of the hall at the desk of Tanzania. When he heard the noise of a tourist group in the visitors' gallery, he got up abruptly and left.

In the corridor he took an elevator to the third floor and walked up some steps to a narrow passageway lined by successive doors. Those marked "B.B.C. News," "NBC T.V.," and "French" were locked, but the handle turned on a door marked "Arabic." In the booth he had a perfect view of the General Assembly hall below—the delegates' desks, the stage, the speaker's rostrum. The layout was similar to the Security Council interpretation booth—three chairs, two desks, overhead lamps, microphone, headpieces, and control buttons and switches for language selection, volume, and monitoring of transmission.

The angle of sight was perfect, but how would he be able to protrude a rifle through the walled-in glass front? He might cut the glass, but no matter how quickly he did it, interpreters across the way and delegates below would notice, and Arafat, upon receiving a warning, would have time to drop down behind the marble speaker's rostrum out of sight. After glancing again at his diagram, Sebastian absent-mindedly placed it on a chair, while continuing to touch along the glass and metal partitions. There seemed no way, without eliminating the element of total surprise and without incurring undue risk to himself.

Sebastian suddenly felt dizzy. His heartbeat increased noticeably. His mind began to wander...He had taken on this assignment for his sister, for Julie...But the bracelet meant that...If Barka...Feeling languid and woozy, he sat down.

He stared at the red and green light buttons on the interpreting panel. Then he saw his diagram on the floor just in front of the chair. That was strange, he thought, since he should be sitting on it now. His breathing became more even. All of a sudden he understood. This booth was located off a cramped passageway with no windows. However, air must be circulating, the air that had blown his diagram off the chair and was reviving him now. He dropped to his knees to look.

Under the desk, a six-inch square air-conditioning portal was attached two feet off the ground to the metal wall frame. Bending down, Sebastian observed that it was held in place by four screws which could be removed with a Philips screwdriver and give an opening of about four square inches directly to the hall. He saw through the connecting glass window that the adjoining French interpretation booth had the same portal in the same relative position.

Now he must ensure that Aumont assign him to interpret on the opening day of the General Assembly. He was close to completing the task he had vowed to do for Julie. An unpleasant thought came into his mind about what he must do to induce Aumont to assign him to interpret, sexual acts against his nature, but something he would do without hesitation for Julie.

Chapter 37

David Arovitch sat in his office at the Israeli Mission to the U.N. reviewing the 101 items on the General Assembly agenda. Every year, he thought, there were more issues to discuss, more meetings to attend, more documents to read. The Secretariat employed 8000 people from 151 countries, had a budget of half a billion dollars, and in 1977 had generated seven hundred million pieces of paper. Arovitch laughed silently about the committee formed to recommend ways of reducing the paper proliferation which itself had produced a report of over 300 pages. Given the incredible mix of nationalities, the endemic political and ideological conflicts, the economic disputes, and the language diversity, he was amazed that anything ever got done at the U.N. But an immense amount did get done, he realized, primarily in economic and social areas which never made the headlines. Politics at the U.N. had the sex appeal and received the major publicity in the world press and television, but given the political divisions in the outside world which were inevitably reflected in the U. N., the organization could only look its worst in the political arena and therefore was subjected to the most blatant accusations of impotence or irrelevance. On the other hand, if the U.N. miraculously managed to do something useful politically, this would inevitably provoke allegations of watered-down compromising or cynical deal-making.

This situation had driven many a Secretary General and other high U.N. officials to despair and/or to drink, Arovitch had heard from several UN and Diplomatic Mission sources. It was a rare person both in the U.N. and outside who understood the true nature of the world organization, its hopes and its limitations. Arovitch had prepared a private analysis of the U.N.'s strengths and weaknesses in Hebrew that he intended to publish after his career in the diplomatic service. He had concluded that when observers became frustrated and cynical about the inadequacies of the U.N., they didn't understand that this was exactly what the big powers wanted. They wanted to use the U.N. for their own narrow purposes, keeping it on a tight leash where it could do little damage to their interests. Possessing the veto power in the Security Council, each of the 'Big Five' could prevent the intervention of the U.N. in its messy business—the French in Algeria, the Americans in Vietnam, the Chinese in Tibet, the Russians in eastern Europe and later Afghanistan, and the British in Ireland. And during this era of the Cold War, the interests of the U.S. and Europe differed radically from those of the Soviet Union and the People's Republic of China. And so the intrigue and the balancing act continued nonstop, as each country played the political game to the hilt, hoping that the results, however mixed or ineffectual, would benefit its national and political interests.

Arovitch understood the true nature and limitations of the U.N. But as an Israeli, he was rankled by the treatment often meted out to Israel by the toady states sucking up to the Arab oil-producing countries. He put Japan, South America, and some western European states in the toady category.

Sitting in his office facing a large map of Israel and the conquered territories, David Arovitch saw that the first item on the General Assembly agenda was the ceremony to induct the Palestinian Liberation Organization into its midst. After Arafat's assassination, would the world community simply carry on business as usual, as the Olympic Games had done after the massacre of Israeli athletes in Munich in 1972? Although he could not admit it to himself, Arovitch knew that Arafat's death would not prevent the P.L.O. from entering the U.N. General Assembly.

But the murder, to be blamed on Arab militants, could weaken, perhaps irrevocably, the Palestinian revolutionary movement, and it would show the terrorists that they were not immune from violent death anywhere. And, finally, in Arovitch's mind, it would humiliate the U.N. which so often seemed to work against Israel's interests. Charles Browning was serving Israel's well-being in many ways.

Earlier that day Arovitch had met with Browning to review the details of the American's plan. Finding Browning's arrogance insufferable, the Israeli fantasized leaving the assassin to be captured or killed in the U.N. after he murdered Arafat. The thought that he had life-and-death power over Browning, power that he could conceivably use, gave Arovitch immense satisfaction.

The phone buzzer rang. Sonia Berenson asked him to come into her office.

"David," she said, once he had seated himself on the chair next to her desk. "I have been thinking. We've been under so much pressure lately. And then, with the General Assembly starting next week, it will be nonstop activity after that."

"I know, Sonia. I know. I dread it."

"Let's get away, David, before some new hell descends on us. We need to relax. Let's go away from the city this weekend."

He thought for an instant. Burger would be gone. Browning would be in place. "Wonderful, Sonia. Where shall we go?"

"The lake in the Poconos?"

"Marvelous. I will make arrangements." He pressed her hand and returned to his office.

"Eli," he said on the telephone. "I saw our friend. We made plans for tomorrow."

"Good, David. You asked me earlier if I'm free for dinner. I'm not. I've got to go to Brooklyn. We will talk tonight." They hung up.

Chapter 38

September 9, 1978

Hassan Barka read Lydia Ahmed's coded message one more time:

Further cooperation with Sebastian impossible. He had violent fit for unknown reason when he saw bracelet you gave me. Apparently does not want or need my assistance further.   Lydia

Barka took a walk in the foothills near the cabin to digest the message and decide what to do. He recognized Sebastian as a violent individual with twisted emotions, but there was no earthly reason for the bracelet to have set him off. Did Sebastian have some connection with that girl at Yad Yehudah? Or was there something else involved that Lydia had neglected to mention? Had Sebastian tried to seduce her? In Barka's view, Lydia should give him anything he wanted. Nothing must interfere with the murder of Arafat.

Barka cursed this new development. Everything else was proceeding smoothly. According to both the press and his friend Shukri Kamal, Arafat planned to leave for New York in six days. It was a bad omen that Lydia and Sebastian were no longer collaborating. One thing was certain, Barka decided—she had provoked Sebastian intentionally or inadvertently. She was the weak link who could foul up Barka's plans. Furthermore, she was, after all, the only person besides Sebastian who knew of his intention to murder Yasser Arafat. Out of anger, spite, fear, or stupidity, she could use her knowledge against him. He had always felt uncomfortable about Lydia having this power over him. He must think and decide what to do, even if he decided that the best plan was do nothing right now.

A car slowly came up the mountain path, stopping outside the door where two of Barka's men, brandishing machine guns, waited in readiness. Barka stayed in the shadow of the hut.

Shukri Kamal got out of the car and greeted the bodyguards.

Barka approached him. "For Allah's sake, Shukri, why did you come here unannounced? What if you were followed? For a cautious man you act stupidly, you know..."

"I had to see you, Hassan," Kamal said, taking Barka's arm and leading him away from the house. "Read this."

Barka studied the envelope which had the seal and signed inscription of the PLO leadership. Ripping it open, he read:

My Dear Hassan: We, the Palestinian people, are at a favorable crossroads in our history. Having gained world recognition, we will soon gain our objective of entering our homeland, Palestine. For a long time, unfortunate fraternal divisions have driven us temporarily apart. In this moment of triumph, we must heal all wounds, overcome splits, and speak and act as a homogeneous movement and a unified people.

By the authority vested in me and following the pronouncement of the Supreme Council, I am forming a government of national reconciliation which will embrace all patriots and men of good will. My dear Hassan, I have grieved at our split, and I want you to lay aside past conflicts and to join this government in a most important position. As Minister of National Economy, you will direct the economic fortunes of our people, oversee the treasury, and plan the economic reconstruction of the return to the homeland. I solemnly wish to restore the collaboration and friendship that existed between us. Let us work together now for the mutual benefit of our people.

Please convey your answer to me within twenty- four hours. I trust and hope that it will be positive.

Yours in friendship,

Yasser Arafat

"It's a lie," Barka said.

"No, Hassan. It's the truth." Kamal rested his arm loosely on Barka's shoulder.

As he reread it, the letter had the effect of a hammer blow, stunning him as much as if his dead father now appeared in the path. "It's just not possible, Shukri," he said distractedly.

"But it is. For weeks now we have been discussing the notion of a government-in-exile. Arafat felt it would give more solidity to our purpose."

"And more prestige to him."

"The idea has come up before, but always the divisions among the Arab states made it impossible. This time, with U.N. recognition imminent, Arafat got their approval one by one. He is forming our government and will announce it officially on the General Assembly stage."

"Don't you see, brother?" Barka said heatedly. "It is just another tactic to gain respectability. All these 'respectable' moves do not advance our cause one meter. It is pressure, constant pressure against the Zionists that we need. If I were leader, I would..." He did not finish the sentence.

"Hassan, nine-tenths of your opposition comes from personal dislike of Arafat. He does not understand that. He thinks that your alienation from him is purely political, ideological. He thinks that you will be able to submerge your militant stand within the new group when you join."

It was too ironic, Barka thought. The man he was planning to kill was now offering him an olive branch.

"How do I know that it isn't a trick?"

"Take my word. We have discussed it in the Central Committee. He thinks highly of you, Hassan. He insisted on your inclusion in the new government despite some opposition. He asked me to come and appeal to you."

"Who else is being appealed to?" There was a sarcastic lilt to Barka's voice.

"Everyone in the rejection front. They will all agree. Except perhaps Habash."

"Because he sees it correctly—as hypocrisy designed to promote Arafat and blunt strong action. I could refuse too."

"Where would it get you? You would remain the perennial outsider, always in exile. Whereas if you come in, you will wield significant power in an organized government that will soon be recognized by the great majority of countries in the U.N. We will have money, allies, power. We will finally be able to do something for our people. Don't you see?"

Barka shrugged his shoulders. Walking in a circle, they approached the car.

"He wants an answer promptly," Kamal said.

"He will get it."

"Try to accept, Hassan," Kamal added before driving away. "It would save me coming this distance every time I want to see you,"

Barka went into the hut, now darkened by late afternoon shadows. He sat on a chair, threw his hands up in futility, and moved to look out the window. His bodyguards were smoking cigarettes and sharing a joke. In the background, the rolling hills undulated as far as the eye could see.

What was on Arafat's mind? Barka wondered. Had the PLO leader guessed at Barka's ambition or his bruised reaction to the humiliation of three years ago? It was unmitigated arrogance on Arafat's part to expect Barka to shed his resentment as a chameleon changes colors and pretend that nothing had happened. The wound was too deep. He had suffered insult and pain from Arafat and had determined to remove him from the face of the earth and replace him as the new leader of the PLO.

He began nervously pacing the room, confused and in turmoil. He must not lower his guard, let moderate words and blandishments seduce him into weakness or passivity. How could he find out what was behind Arafat's offer? The time was too short to send out his agents to analyze the situation behind the scenes.

Suddenly a sharp knock at the door. A guard poked his head through. "Ahmed is here. Says that it is urgent."

"Send him in," said Barka, hiding the letter in his pocket.

A young man in military uniform with bushy hair and clean-shaven face entered the hut.

"Why did you leave your post?" Barka asked sharply.

"I thought you would want to see these newspapers, Excellency." He thrust three Damascus newspapers, two in Arabic, one in English, in Barka's hands. The front page story in all editions was similar. Yasir Arafat was setting up a government-in-exile, a unity coalition, bringing in important Palestinian dissidents, including Hassan Barka, who was being offered the post of Minister of National Economy. The other ministerial posts were being offered to individuals of different ideological persuasions, from extreme left to extreme right, with Arafat retaining the posts of Prime Minister and of Defense. These details tallied with Kamal's pronouncement just before.

"Thank you, Ahmed," said Barka quietly,

"Will you take up the offer, Excellency?"

"I haven't decided."

As he left, Ahmed said: "Be careful, Excellency. Arafat is a viper."

After reflecting for some time, Barka sat at the table and wrote a brief note to Yasser Arafat.

*   *   *   *   *

The meeting took place in neutral territory in the foothills of the Lebanese-Syrian border near the tiny village of Qum Al-Iriat. Each man arrived in two cars filled with bodyguards.

As the cars approached each other, Barka was beseiged by a welter of contradictory feelings. Yasser Arafat, after all, was the man who had converted him from raw guerrilla fighter to mature political leader. Nothing was irrevocable. He could still have Lydia Ahmed call off Robert Sebastian. But the moment Arafat emerged from his car, Barka felt an almost physical revulsion.

"Hassan," Arafat said, smiling broadly. "How good to see you." He embraced Barka. "I cannot tell you how happy I am that this terrible thing is over between us."

"Yes, Excellency," said Barka, releasing himself from Arafat's grasp. "It was poisonous—to ourselves and to the cause."

"Thank Allah," said Arafat, with a sweep of his arm, "that after today we will never need bodyguards when we meet."

"Inshallah," said Barka, forcing a smile.

Arafat offered a cigarette to Barka who declined.

"I am delighted that you have accepted my proposal. A key post, perhaps the most important one after my own."

"But, Excellency, I have no training as an economist."

"Hah," said Arafat, gesturing with his hand. "You will have advisers who do. I am thinking of assigning as one of your team a young woman who has been serving as our agent at the United Nations. Her name is Lydia Ahmed. She has a brilliant economic background, I am told." Arafat paused a moment, not noticing Barka's flushed face. "No, Hassan. Aside from economic and financial matters, I will be leaning on you primarily for political advice, using your organizing abilities, soliciting your judgment on a variety of matters."

"You flatter me too much," said Barka.

"You were always the best I had. That is what made our split so regrettable; let us bury it and move forward. Come, let us walk." They strolled off the road onto a path that led to a cliff giving a panoramic view of the valley. "You will come to Beirut, Hassan. Your organization will be amalgamated into the PLO, your military wing disbanded. Good posts will be found for your top men like Hussein and Abu Barem." He walked to the edge, Barka a step behind.

Barka saw that with one swift motion he could push Arafat over the cliff. He visualized himself doing it. He became dizzy. His common sense told him that while he would have an immediate visceral satisfaction, his plans to replace Arafat would come to nothing. In a few minutes he would be dead or a hunted man forever.

Barka moved a step back, and the two men began to walk in the opposite direction.

"Here is the final form of the cabinet," Arafat said, handing Barka a sheet of paper. "What do you think?"

"It is a remarkable achievement, Excellency," Barka said, after a pause. "A true unity coalition. Except for Habash." He was relieved at the omission of Habash who had clearly refused Arafat's offer to join his cabinet.

"The fool. I will crush him. He will be more isolated than ever now." Arafat removed his sunglasses. "I have a surprise for you, Hassan. I am taking you, Ali Ben Buda, and Shukri Kamal to New York with me. I am going to introduce you three as the key members of my new government from the General Assembly stage.

Barka turned to him. "What? You intend to..."

"Don't you think it will be a dramatic and effective move?" He studied Barka.

"Y...Y...Yes. Dramatic and imaginative certainly."

"It was your friend Kamal's idea. To show that we are a collective movement, not a dictatorship. It will illustrate how broadly based we are—you a militant, Kamal a Moslem nationalist, Ben Buda a Marxist. You three photographed with me in the General Assembly will speak louder than any newspaper reports or flattering words from me."

Barka's mind raced. After Arafat's death, he would be the senior member of the delegation at the U.N. He would make an impromptu address, hold the fragilely constructed new regime together, and call for a congress to ratify his leadership. "When do you want me to come to Beirut, Excellency?" he finally asked.

"In one or two days. I have prepared the house on Golani Street for you."

"Near yours, Excellency." He wondered if Arafat intended to keep close watch on him.

"We will have much to discuss, Hassan. But if there is nothing else now, let us say good-bye. We both have a lot to do."

They embraced and returned to their automobiles.

Chapter 39

On the way back to his mountain retreat, Barka felt uneasy. It was happening too quickly and too easily. Was it a trap? He would speak to his guards and keep them in place.

One matter troubled him deeply. It concerned a potential enemy, someone who had a certain power over him. He weighed the pros and cons. By the time he reached his hut, he had made a decision.

Within an hour, he had eaten lunch, packed a small suitcase, and was driven along the road to Beirut. Stopping in a medium-sized town en route, he made a phone call to Livorno, Italy. At the airport outside the capital, he boarded an Alitalia flight to Rome, arriving in the late afternoon.

The dark-haired, pock-marked man known as 'the Sicilian', who had done a 'try-out' job for him in Geneva during the initial phase before Barka had recruited Robert Sebastian, met him at Fiumicino Airport. They huddled in a corner of the lounge for thirty minutes. Towards the end of their conversation, Barka gave the Sicilian an envelope containing a photo, some papers, and fifty thousand dollars. The Sicilian then left to have a glass of sherry before booking his flight to New York.

Barka, meanwhile, decided to return that evening. He waited in the lounge, staring blankly at the never-ceasing movement of people before him. At 8:15 p.m. he boarded his return flight to Beirut where his driver was waiting. They drove to his mountain dwelling. Tomorrow would be a busy day. He would be preparing his move to Beirut.

Lydia Ahmed, writing busily at her desk, looked up as Krishnan Katani, the Chef de Cabinet of Secretary-General Waldheim, came into her office.

"The S.-G. would like an analysis of the consequences of PLO admission on all outstanding Middle East and African political questions at the U.N., Lydia."

She removed her glasses. "I am already working fourteen hours a day on other material for him, Krishnan. Give it to someone else, will you, please?"

Katani smiled. He put his hand on her shoulder." You made the mistake of impressing him with your last report, Lydia. He specifically asked for you."

"When does he want it?"

"In two days."

"Impossible. Make it after the weekend."

Katani nodded. "I will arrange it. In return, how about dinner in the next couple of days, Lydia? I know how much you like Indian food, as well as my fascinating conversation."

Smiling at him and touching his arm lightly, she said: "Your invitation is enticing, Krishnan, but the truth is that I will be free in about a year unless the S.-G. abolishes our overtime work."

"Since I have a personal interest, I will try to lighten your work load," he said "If I succeed, will you have dinner with me very soon?"

"Yes, Krishnan. Now I must work. Go and twist Waldheim's arm now, and let's see if you get anything more than screams of pain in Viennese German."

Alone, Lydia Ahmed returned to the document on issues coming up before the Security Council that she was editing.

The phone rang.

"It's me, Lydia."

"Again, Carlos?" It was the third time he had called that day.

"I cannot concentrate on my work. Your silky presence two floors above distracts me no end."

"Carlos, I am busy. You know how much I have to do with Arafat coming here in a few days. I am working day and night."

"Come on, Lydia. How about tonight?"

"No."

"Please…"

She wanted to tell him he was a fat, simpering slob and slam the phone down, but she had to keep him quiet until after Robert Sebastian killed Arafat. "If I see you tonight, will you leave me alone for awhile?"

"What time?"

"Nine-thirty."

At 1:30 p.m. she left her office to go to lunch. Walking down the corridor towards the Delegates' Lounge, she saw Robert Sebastian coming from the other direction. She froze, then passed by without looking at him. Her wrist still hurt from the twist he had given it the other night when he saw the silver bracelet. She wondered if Barka would reply to her message about the incident.

In a corner of the Delegates Lounge, eating a cheese sandwich and sipping cappucino, she speculated about what lay ahead. After Arafat's death, Barka would insist that she come to Beirut. The prospect both pleased and alarmed her. Pleased, because she desperately needed a change from her stultifying existence at the U.N. In Beirut she would insist on participating in military actions against Israel. In Beirut, she would be closer to her mother, who, according to a recent letter from her cousin, was suffering from pains of arthritis and stomach problems. Yet in Beirut there would be Hassan Barka who could be aggressive, if not tyrannical. Dealing with him would take subtlety and strength. She was under no illusions.

During the afternoon she worked on the Security Council document and made notes for her report to the Secretary General. At one moment her phone rang.

"We are meeting tonight. At nine," said Sabri el-Deudri, a member of the PLO observer delegation. "To finalize arrangements for His Excellency's visit."

She hesitated, then said: "Good. See you tonight."

Before hanging up, she telephoned to cancel her date with Carlos Montoya who begged for the following evening. She agreed.

At 6:30 she left the Secretariat. Taking the bus up First Avenue, she got off at 78th Street, where she browsed in an antique shop, bought some groceries in Gristede's market, and headed for her apartment. Burdened by her briefcase and the overfilled grocery bag, she slowly walked up the stairs. Arriving at her door, she fumbled in her purse for the keys. Suddenly she heard a light footstep behind her. Before her head could turn, a hand pressed over her mouth, and she felt something sharp stick into her back.

"Go in," a man's voice said.

Her hand trembling, she unlocked the door. He shoved her forward, locking the door behind them.

Turning around, she saw a dark-haired, pock-marked man with small eyes pointing a gun at her.

Slowly the Sicilian reached in his pocket and took out a photo. Without saying a word, he glanced from the photo to her face.

"What is it?" Lydia asked in a shaky voice." What do you want?" Her instincts told her it was not a mugging or a rape, but something worse.

"Please, please...don't do it. I will do anything, anything, for you." She talked nonstop, pleaded, whined, cajoled. The Sicilian just stared, his eyes looking coldly into hers. She opened her arms, offering herself. For an instant he looked admiringly at the curves of her body. Then the blank stare returned, and sensing her pleas as futile, the man's purpose unswayed, Lydia Ahmed sobbed pitifully. "Tell me why you are doing this. Please, I beg you," she said, breathing deeply.

The Sicilian gave a slight shrug.

"Who is it?" she sobbed." The Israelis? Who?"

"Barka," he said softly.

The bullets silenced her screams, as she slumped to the floor, her eyes glazed and opened lifelessly. The Sicilian bent down and placed his ear over her heart.

Satisfied, he got up and left the apartment, the door locking behind him.

Chapter 40

"Robert darling. I'm all aglow." Leopold Aumont brushed his lips against Sebastian's cheek and then lay back on the pillow. "It makes me shudder to think what you just did to me. Your hands, your mouth…I cannot tell you about the sensations. I feel, how shall I say it, so alive." Holding onto Sebastian's hand and staring at his face, Aumont asked: "Tell me, precious. What shall I do to you? There is nothing I could deny you now. You command and I am your willing slave." He began to move his hand teasingly downward on Sebastian's body. "Let me, my precious, let me."

Sebastian, expressionless, held tightly onto Aumont's hand, preventing any further motion. "Leopold, I'm fine. I think that I'm tired now. Next time I will not stop you, I promise."

"Mon cheri," the older man said, sighing. Aumont's fingers started tracing soft circles on Sebastian's chest.

"There is something I would like, Leopold," Sebastian said, holding Aumont's hand fixed against his waist.

"Anything, Robert, anything. I want to make you feel even a tenth of what I did." Aumont's breath quickened.

"Let me work the General Assembly opening. It would mean everything to me."

Aumont sat up. "You are incorrigible to speak of work at a moment like this." He shook his head. "You are so ambitious, Robert. It isn't good. You must learn to relax, to let yourself go, as you just did with me. You put me in heaven. I could do that to you."

Sebastian put his hand up to Aumont's face. "Maybe you could teach me, Leopold."

The older man hugged him. "That was beautiful, Robert. I will teach you if you will let me." He resumed touching Sebastian. "Perhaps you will relax more now if I consent to your wish. I have said that I would deny you nothing. There. Does that help?"

"Yes," said Sebastian.

Afterwards Sebastian got out of bed and began to dress.

"Are you sure, dear boy, that you cannot come to dinner with me?" Aumont asked almost pleadingly.

"Leopold, I told you earlier that I have an invitation from some friends of my family. They know that I am in New York and I have to see them this evening."

"Alright, alright," said Aumont, feigning a hurt expression. "Abandon me, if you must. See if I care."

Sebastian came over and sat on the bed. Looking into Aumont's eyes, he said "Don't worry. I will not abandon you."

"Dear one," said Aumont, embracing him.

After a few seconds, Sebastian gently extricated himself and left the apartment.

That same evening, using an Israeli Mission limousine, David Arovitch took Eli Burger to the airport to catch his return flight to Israel. Back in Manhattan, at precisely 10 p.m., Arovitch backed the limousine into a dark alleyway on East 78th Street next to an empty building. A man moved out of the shadows, climbed into the car trunk, and slammed the door shut from the inside. Arovitch drove onto the East 79th Street exit to the F.D.R. Drive and headed downtown.

A couple of minutes later he saw the overhead sign "48th Street, United Nations Garage, Next Right." Making the turn, he headed towards the mouth of the garage. A U.N. Security Officer and two city policemen stepped in front of the car before he had proceeded thirty feet.

"Where you going, bud?" asked a burly cop waving a flashlight into the car.

Holding out his Israeli Mission identification card, Arovitch said calmly: "Late for a meeting, officer."

"You got Diplomatic DPL plates; go park in front."

Arovitch hesitated a second, then said: "The meeting is going to last half the night. I don't want to clog the driveway."

The policeman went to consult a U.N. security officer on duty inside the small office in the mouth of the garage. "All right. Go ahead," he said.

Arovitch drove along the passageway, turned sharply right after 200 yards, and went up a ramp to the second level. He parked behind a huge pillar that obscured the rear end of the car. Stepping outside, he looked around cautiously.

The garage was empty except for a few scattered cars. After a silent minute of watching, he unlocked the trunk of the limousine and threw it open wide. Charles Browning stepped out holding a thick brown corduroy bag.

Browning did a few knee-bends, straightened his rumpled clothes, and then without a word, walked to a door fifty feet away marked "U.N. Entrance."

Arovitch waited in the limousine reading Hebrew newspapers for two hours before driving out of the garage.

Browning, meanwhile, took the elevator to the now deserted tourist level 1B of the General Assembly building. Passing the souvenir gift shops, U.N. post office, and UNICEF card and gift stall, he opened a door marked "Emergency Exit" just beyond the guides lounge. Descending two flights of stairs, he entered a passageway on level 3B where he stopped to check a diagram. Proceeding down the corridor, he reached his destination, a door marked "MAINTENANCE."

Browning let the door slide quietly behind him. As expected, the room was empty, the evening shift still at work and the night shift not due before 11 p.m. Opening a locker, he hung his jacket, removed faded blue jeans and a fireman's shirt from the bag, changed his clothes, and shut the locker door. He fitted a combination lock into the small hole in the door, and closed it. Then he sat down on a wooden bench to wait.

Twenty minutes later three men noisily came in. "Well, what's this?" asked a short man with bulbous eyes and protruding stomach.

"I'm starting tonight," Browning said. "They assigned me to this shift."

"New guy, huh?" asked a dark, thin man rhetorically. "We got too many as it is." Banging open a locker door, he slung his coat inside.

"Yeah," said the third man, grunting agreement.

"Don't pay any attention to these creeps, sonny," said the short, stocky man. "What's your name?"

"Joseph Palowski," answered Browning, shaking the other man's chubby hand.

"Polish boy, eh? I knew you was okay. I'm Stanislaw Kaminski, crew foreman. And this here is Luigi Bendetti and Bob Hawthorne."

"Hi," Browning called out. The other two nodded.

"You all set up, Joe?" Kaminski asked. "You got your card?"

"Yeah. A temporary one. Tomorrow I'll get the regular card."

"That's good," Kaminski said, putting on thick black rubber soled shoes. "You call me Stan. Everyone does. Even these charmers here." He smiled, revealing yellow and black stained teeth. "Hey, Joe. Why's you working here? A good-looking kid like you. It ain't the most elegant job, you know."

"Well, it's like this, Stan," said Browning. "Things are pretty tough out there these days. When this opportunity came along, I grabbed it. Help me to get on my feet again."

"You done right, kid. Listen, you and me..." Six or seven men entered the room, and after making introductions, Kaminski resumed talking to Browning: "...as I was saying, Joe, let's go upstairs and I'll show you where they keeps the mops." He ushered Browning through the door. "I'll give you a guided tour, so to speak. If you forget about the hours, the job ain't so bad. We get the same six weeks' vacation time as..." The door shut behind them.

During the night Browning mopped floors, washed windows, polished brass fixtures, and emptied trash barrels. Although the work was infinitely boring, the crew changed tasks frequently, and Browning considered it a good physical workout. The major problem was Kaminski who, having befriended him, talked his ear off about the U.N., the "old country," the Church, and Polish food. Browning finally got some peace by agreeing to come to Kaminski's home to meet his wife and eat a tasty Polish home-cooked meal. He cursed himself for not having the foresight to choose an Italian name, since the thin, sour-looking man, Bendetti, seemed to resent Browning's presence and kept his distance.

Studying the men in the maintenance crew, Browning saw them as a reflection or microcosm of the United Nations: Pole, Italian, Americans, Asians, blacks. However, these were the lumpen-proletariat, the universal losers, dumb, misshapen men working for a pittance, while the classy delegates and permanent staff upstairs received far greater money and attention. Still, the maintenance men, as Kaminski explained, got the same vacation time as the professional staff and a decent salary for their manual labor.

When the night shift ended, the crew returned to the locker room. Browning joined a group lined up at the shower stalls, making certain that he was last.

"Hey, Joe," Kaminski shouted. "Why don't ya come with us for some breakfast?"

"Can't today, Stan. Gotta wait around to get my pass."

"Yeah, I forgot. Take care, kid. I'll tell the missus you'se coming to dinner sometime real soon."

"Right." After showering. Browning put on his original clothes, stuffed his workman's outfit in the locker, refitted the combination lock, and slipped out the door.

That evening he repeated the process. Quickly enough the work became drudgery. Kaminski carried on his insufferable monologue. Bendetti shunned him as before. Three hours mopping the floor under Kaminski's watchful eye and shrewish tongue gave Browning a splitting headache. Feigning illness, he asked Kaminski to allow him an hour's rest. Though it violated his sense of duty, the foreman reluctantly agreed. Browning took the escalator to the second floor where he found a couple of chairs in an isolated place, took a brief nap, and awoke refreshed.

Chapter 41

September 11, 1978

At 2 a.m. Henry Jensen reached over the sleeping form of his wife to answer the telephone.

"This is Terzi of the Palestinian delegation. I am sorry to disturb you, Chief Jensen, but one of our members of the Secretariat has been killed."

Forty minutes later Jensen arrived at Lydia Ahmed's apartment where he found Terzi and a group of Palestinians. The apartment was in shambles—silverware on the floor, chairs upturned and mutilated, sofa cut up, papers strewn everywhere. On the living room floor, blood dripping out of the corner of her mouth, lay Lydia Ahmed.

"This is horrible," said Jensen.

Terzi led him to the window and talked in a hushed tone. "She never showed up for a meeting last night, so we investigated and found her like that."

"Poor woman," Jensen said shakily, sitting down woodenly on a chair. "She probably discovered someone robbing her flat. Just look at the mess."

"No," said Terzi, sitting opposite Jensen and folding his hands. The other Palestinians huddled in the far corner whispering. "You see, when we arrived, the place was impeccably neat. Lydia was lying dead on the floor, but there was no evidence of robbery or rape. True, her pocket- book was open, but the wallet contained a few hundred dollars. Her clothes were not disheveled in any way." He talked slowly, logically, like a lawyer building his case. "My first reaction was identical to yours, this being such a violent city. I remember vividly the 'Summer of Sam' killings last year. So I did not discount a gratuitous killing, a madman with no motive whatsoever. But it was all too neat, too perfect. The door was locked from the outside, and she might not have been discovered for days had it not been for our meeting. I am convinced that her killing was premeditated."

Aching from fatigue, Jensen blinked rapidly. "By whom? For what reason?"

"First I thought it was the Israelis," Terzi went on. "Miss Ahmed, you see, worked for our organization. Our enemies most likely knew this. With our leader coming next week, they would like nothing better than to sabotage our efforts at the United Nations."

"But why her?" Jensen asked. "Was she so important?"

"An Israeli action was my first thought, as I said, and I have not entirely excluded it," Terzi said. "But now I believe the situation even more sinister. We searched everywhere for clues, you see, and found this in the bottom drawer of her desk." He showed Jensen a piece of paper handwritten in Arabic.

"It is Lydia's writing. I will translate it for you. The title is 'Why Yasser Arafat Must

Die at the United Nations'."

"What?" shouted Jensen.

Terzi repeated the title. "She begins: 'In the Palestinian context, Yasser Arafat is an arch-compromiser, a conservative possibly able to lead a peacetime state, but unsuited to wage war against an implacable foe that is determined to hold on to conquered Arab land.' Next line, Colonel Jensen: 'Arafat is an intellectual nullity, unable to grasp complex political theory and incapable of inventing it. He wants to be a Lenin, but ends up a Nixon, a hollow man clinging to power, as to a first love, until the end'. Next line: 'Ideologically suspect, if not reactionary.' Next: 'Weak, vacillating, craven, corrupt. He deserves the capital punishment he is about to receive.' And more of the same. The last lines are particularly interesting: 'Our new leader is ideologically pure, politically radical, and courageous in battle. The murder of Arafat is an existential act completely justified in the existing political context'. "

Terzi looked up and Jensen saw that his eyes were bloodshot. "But what does it all mean?" the Security Chief asked.

"It means that she was a traitor. To our leader and to our cause. Everything that she did for the Palestinian cause was pretense."

"But why did she die if she intended murder herself?"

"You are the detective, Colonel Jensen. I leave it to your ingenuity. Perhaps something went wrong with the heroic 'new leader'. Maybe she was changing her mind, and he struck her down." Looking at Lydia Ahmed's body, he added: "Frankly, I think she got exactly what she deserved."

Jensen telephoned Schwartz and Bailey, and within the hour, the police and FBI arrived. Autopsy experts began examining the body. A finger printer and police photographer worked around the apartment. Two FBI men sifted through her belongings. Terzi reread the note, as a stenographer took it down in English.

Jensen, Schwartz, and Bailey moved into the bedroom to talk.

"This is a bitch," said Bailey. "According to that note, there is a plot against Arafat which will culminate at the U.N."

"It could be a forgery," said Schwartz, "or maybe just expressing the girl's private views. For me," he added, pointing a finger at his chest, "I'm not going to discount a mugger or even a jealous lover who panics and bang, he shoots her and runs away."

"I'm afraid, Les," said Jensen quietly, "that I cannot ignore the contents of her writings."

"Of course not, Henry. You would be derelict in your duty, if you did. Arafat is coming into your jurisdiction. All I am saying is that we have no hard evidence to back up any conspiracy theory. At least right now."

They agreed that the FBI would interrogate the PLO and other Arab delegations, the police would question neighbors and people in the area, and the U.N. security staff would contact Lydia Ahmed's colleagues and friends in the U.N. The three forces would pool information later in the day.

On the way to his office, Jensen reflected that in his seven years at the United Nations, this was the first actual murder case connected with the U.N. There had been two dramatic suicides: one, a young American who, after removing his clothes and proclaiming himself the Secretary-General, jumped from his 27th floor Secretariat window; the other, a middle-aged Turkish secretary who, apparently involved in an unhappy love affair, put cyanide in her coffee and slumped over onto her typewriter in front of her amazed office-mates.

Just after 8 a.m., Jensen took the elevator to the 38th floor. He reported to Secretary-General Waldheim what had occurred.

"Tragic," said Waldheim, his fingers clasped together. "Just tragic." He paused. "A highly intelligent woman," he continued, looking at Jensen. "She would have had a great career here. She was working on something for me now, in fact."

"What was that?"

"A political analysis. Speak to Katani about it, if you wish."

"There is one more thing," Jensen said. "The PLO found a note in her desk. Here is an English translation." He passed it to Waldheim.

After a moment the Secretary-General said: "This is very bad. What are you doing about it?"

"The police and FBI are working on it outside, and we are investigating internally here. I will keep you closely posted."

"Please! Colonel Jensen." They shook hands and Jensen left. Waldheim turned back to the document he was composing, entitled "TRANSFER OF SEABED TAX REVENUE TO THE UNITED NATIONS: REGULAR BUDGET: FINANCIAL SECURITY FOR DECADES."

Chapter 42

John Hardy arrived at the U.N. after visiting a synagogue on the lower East Side, where an old rabbi translated the Hebrew portions of the taped conversations on David Arovitch's telephone. During his stay in the apartment, Burger had spoken with the Israeli Mission, arranged a number of appointments, and confirmed his return flight to Israel. Nothing was remotely suspect.

Hardy went to see the phone repairman, Harry Parker.

"A big fat zero, Harry," he said." When can we remove the bugging mechanism?"

"I'm all tied up today, John. So many blasted phones out of order in the Secretariat. Can it wait 'til Monday? I would appreciate it."

"Sure, Harry." Hardy went upstairs to punch in his card indicating his arrival time at the U.N.

"Chief wants to see you," the desk officer said.

"Hardy," Jensen began, after the Irishman had sat down. "You are going to make yourself useful for once. Now listen closely." He related the facts of Lydia Ahmed's death and showed him the transcript of the anti-Arafat notes found in her desk.

"Drop whatever you are doing," Jensen continued, "and start making inquiries. Speak to everyone who knew her. Begin with her office, Political Affairs. Grill Shupelov, grill everyone there. Find out what she did during her working day, check out her personal life, see if she behaved strangely recently. Konda and Ramirez will join you later. Don't let on about the note to anyone, since it may turn out to be a dud. Here is her U.N. file. Now get moving."

Hardy went to the Political Affairs Division on the 37th floor. "He is busy," said Shupelov's secretary, a grim-faced Polish woman.

"Not for me he isn't," Hardy said, opening the door.

"I beg your pardon," Boris Shupelov said from behind his desk. His foot moved automatically to the buzzer on the floor linking his office to the KGB bodyguard a few doors away.

Hardy showed his U.N. security badge.

"One of your staff members is dead. Lydia Ahmed. I want to ask you about her."

The grey-haired Russian relaxed his foot and removed his glasses. "Will you repeat that, please?"

"I am sorry to inform you, sir, but Lydia Ahmed is dead, and I am investigating on behalf of the U.N. Security Office." Hardy gave a few details of the death.

Shupelov shook his head. "It's terrible, terrible. Such a fine, beautiful girl. Such a hard worker. Ahh, it is unbelievable." Hardy asked him to describe her work habits. Shupelov answered every question about Lydia Ahmed's friends and personal life with repetitive "nyets."

One by one, Shupelov's staff came into his office to be questioned by John Hardy. Lydia's secretary, a comely, dark-haired Brazilian woman named Rosita, left after a few seconds crying hysterically. Hardy elicited nothing of value. Everyone considered Lydia an intelligent, efficient worker who was cordial, if not particularly friendly, to him or to her. She was discreet and even mysterious about anything unrelated to office work, and more than one person suspected that she was spying for the PLO. Deeply committed to the Palestinian cause, she spoke frankly of her disdain and even hatred for Israel.

Krishnan Katani came down from the 38th floor on a routine matter and saw a number of staff members rubbing handkerchiefs on their reddened eyes. "What is it?" he asked someone innocuously.

"Lydia Ahmed. Dead. Killed apparently," said a Swedish political affairs officer.

"What? Are you sure, Christian?" Receiving a nod, Kitani could not prevent himself screaming: "No no, it can't be true…"

Hearing the commotion, John Hardy emerged from Shupelov's office and went up to Kitani. "Easy, man. Easy…Are you okay? You obviously knew her…."

"Yes, yes," Kitani said in a muffled voice. "From work…I can't believe it."

"None of us can," replied Hardy. "Do you have any knowledge of who might have killed her?"

"No, no," said Kitani, rubbing his eyes and moving to the stairs to return to his office where he closed his door and tearfully began to mourn for Lydia. He thought about his recent flirtatious remarks to Lydia which she had always gently rebuffed. All this was irrelevant now, as he visualized her pretty face and flowing black hair, and he could not refrain from sobbing bitterly.

After questioning the Political Affairs staff, Hardy returned to his office and began to make notes for his report to Jensen. At 1 p.m. he went to the Delegates Lounge to speak to the Arab clique. Unanimously they blamed the Israelis for her mysterious death. Returning to his office to include their opinions in his report, he then passed it on to Jensen's secretary.

Chapter 43

Arriving in his office at 10 a.m., Robert Sebastian telephoned the three-star French restaurant, La Cote Basque, to reserve a table for two at 12:30 p.m. Then he settled back into his chair to read a copy of Le Monde that was floating around the office. Across the way, Lucienne Duchamps looked up from her document detailing the upcoming General Assembly schedule.

Fifteen minutes later, Sebastian's phone extension rang. It was Leopold Aumont. "I have just been called to a meeting which threatens to go on until one or one-thirty. I swear that I will leave by 1:15 p.m., no matter what. Can we postpone our lunch a bit?"

"Of course. I will make it for 1:30 p.m. If you come a little later, no problem." Sebastian called to change the reservation.

"I am bored, bored," Lucienne DuChamp shouted, throwing the document on the floor. "Let's go and have coffee Robert."

"Why not?" Sebastian said.

In the cafeteria DuChamp took two huge pastries and coffee. "I will begin my diet again next week," she said smiling and gobbling down one of the creamy pastries. Sebastian accompanied her to a table near the window, where they talked about Paris and Brussels, comparing the citizenry and the food. "For reliability," DuChamp said pontifically, "there's nothing like a Bruxxelois; for excitement, a Parisian. And you may disagree, Robert, but the Common Market has brought some wonderful restaurants along with its lumpy bureaucrats to Brussels." She licked the chocolate from her fingertips.

They got up to leave. Approaching the newspaper stand just outside the cafeteria, they saw a huge crowd forming.

"What's this?" DuChamp asked, as her way was blocked by a pocket of people huddling around someone reading a copy of the *New York Post*, delivered ten minutes before. Pushing his way through, Sebastian caught a glimpse of the headline: "PALESTIN-IAN WOMAN SLAIN. U.N. STAFF MEMBER." Underneath was a photograph. Lucienne DuChamp, momentarily caught in the midst of the crowd, stopped to read over someone's shoulder. Finally extricating herself, she looked around for Robert Sebastian, but he was nowhere to be found.

"Chief Jensen, my name is Carlos Montoya." The small, chubby Chilean entered Jensen's office without knocking. He was holding a copy of the *New York Post*.

Jensen had just hung up from a conversation with Police Captain Lester Schwartz.

Everything was still confusion about Lydia Ahmed's death.

"I am pretty busy right now, Sir," Jensen said. "You need to make an appointment with my secretary."

Montoya sat down slowly on the chair opposite Jensen's desk. He looked deathly pale.

"I say. Aren't you feeling well?"

"I was a close friend of Lydia Ahmed," Montoya said, taking out a handkerchief and wiping tears from his eyes. "I may be able to help you." He composed himself. "Recently she asked me to do her a favor. She wanted me to find a job for a friend of hers, a Frenchman. He came and gave me the usual spiel about wanting to work in the U.N. He was polished, even charming. Yet there was a core of toughness about him. When I asked questions about his background, he was very remote."

"What is his name?" asked Jensen, playing with his pen.

"Robert Sebastian. I put him in contact with Aumont in French Interpretation who was looking for someone short-term. He is working there now," he said, shaking his head, tears forming again. "Lydia used me, I know. But I loved her." He buried his face in his hands.

"Go back to your office," Jensen said. "Write down your office number, and we'll come and question you later." Taking his revolver from the desk drawer, Jensen rushed to the pass office down the hall and pulled out Sebastian's photo. After showing the photo to four security officers lounging in the hall, he told them to accompany him.

They entered the French Interpretation Section. "Where is Robert Sebastian's office?" Jensen asked a secretary. She pointed down the corridor. Outside an office door they saw a makeshift sign with Sebastian's name on it. Holding his gun, Jensen pushed the door open quickly.

"Mon Dieu," gasped Lucienne Duchamp.

"Where is Robert Sebastian?" Jensen said loudly.

"I...I...don't know. We had coffee this morning, but I haven't seen him since." Pointing to the left, she added: "Ask Aumont, our chief. They were going to lunch together, I think."

Aumont's door was open a few inches. Behind the desk staring blankly ahead, sat Leopold Aumont, his face flushed, his hands folded stiffly on the desktop. He barely reacted as Jensen and the security officers approached him.

"Mr. Aumont. Are you all right?"

Twisting his head slowly towards Jensen, Aumont asked angrily: "Who are you to come barging in like this?"

"Security Chief Jensen. We are looking for one of your staff members, Robert Sebastian."

"Oh, where is he?" asked Aumont rapidly. "The dear boy never showed up for our lunch date at La Cote Basque. I waited and waited. Completely lost my appetite."

The four security officers looked at one another.

"We want to question him in connection with the death of a staff member."

"Oh, that Palestinian girl. Everyone is talking about it. Was Robert involved in that?"

"We don't know. But we definitely want to ask him. What can you tell me about Sebastian?"

Aumont swiveled his chair and looked out the window. "Accomplished interpreter, gifted even. Precise, cool under fire; with some practice, he could be the best one here." Hesitating for a moment, Aumont added: "Very ambitious too. Always eager to work."

"What did he say about himself?"

Aumont's jaw tightened. "Very little. He was the quiet type. Would not talk much about himself or his personal life before coming to the U.N. And, God knows, I tried to get him to open up." Turning towards Jensen, he asked: "Do you think that he is a criminal, that he killed the Palestinian woman?"

"We don't know yet, but we will damn well find out. Mr. Aumont, you've given us a sketchy picture. Can't you recall something more substantial?"

"Only that...he was a...beautiful person." Then, haughtily, Aumont said: "I think you are after the wrong individual, and that is all that I am going to say to you."

"Look here," Jensen said, pointing his finger. "Oh, never mind. We'll be in touch with you later."

After posting two security guards in Sebastian's office, Jensen interrogated everyone in the unit about the Frenchman. Then he went to see Carlos Montoya, who under pointed questioning, revealed that Lydia Ahmed had asked him to find a job for Sebastian after she had gone to bed with Montoya.

By late afternoon Sebastian had not returned to his office and Jensen was convinced that he would not do so. At a meeting with Bailey and Schwartz, he reported what little he knew about Sebastian. They studied his U.N. curriculum vitae and photo.

"What do we know?" Bailey asked rhetorically. "First, he's French. Second, Lydia Ahmed, whom we suspect of having harbored strong anti-Arafat feelings, screwed around with this personnel officer to get Sebastian a job in the U.N. as an interpreter. Third, his fag chief had a crush on him. Fourth, he has disappeared. Not much to go on but it stinks to high heaven."

"But why the hell did he kill Lydia Ahmed just before Arafat's arrival?" asked Schwartz. "It brought needless attention to himself."

"Maybe she was double-crossing him," said Jensen, puffing on his pipe. "Maybe they quarreled about money. Anything could have gone wrong. Rash, though, I will admit."

"I will have to notify Washington about this," Bailey said. "It is getting outrageously out of hand." Turning to Jensen, he continued: "Colonel, you should pass on the photo and c.v. to French intelligence."

"I have already put in a call to Prioleau, their head agent in New York. He is calling me back."

"There is a faster way," said Bailey. "If you use our facilities, you can get Paris on a direct hook-up."

Jensen accompanied Bailey in a taxi to the FBI regional headquarters at Third Avenue and 70th Street. The Communications Center, located in a large room on the fifth floor, contained telephone installations, computer data bank, radio-video transmitters, and audio-visual equipment. Lifting a phone receiver, Bailey requested clearance from Washington to communicate directly with Paris on the radio-video transmitter. "Go ahead, New York," the message came back.

Jensen wrote out a statement for the operator to keypunch:

HIGHEST PRIORITY GRATEFUL PROVIDE INFORMATION REGARDING FRENCH NATIONAL GIVING NAME ROBERT SEBASTIAN POSING AS INTERPRETOR UNITED NATIONS SUSPECTED INVOLVEMENT PALESTINIAN TERRORISTS SEEKING ASSASSINATE YASSER ARAFAT STOP U.N.CURRICULUM VITAE BELIEVED ERRONEOUS AND PHOTO FOLLOWS IMMEDIATELY STOP YOUR MOST URGENT ATTENTION GEORGE BAILEY FEDERAL BUREAU INVESTIGATION NEW YORK AND HENRY JENSEN UNITED NATIONS SECURITY CHIEF

The operator then transmitted the information on Sebastian's U.N. file.

Bailey pressed the "video" button. He fed Sebastian's miniature U.N. photo into a slot for enlargement to 8 1/2 by 11 inch size. The blow-up was visible on the verifier screen.

"What do you think, Colonel?"

"Most interesting technology," replied Jensen, puffing on his pipe.

Bailey pushed the transmission button. "Works by microdots," he explained." Within seconds the reproduction will appear on their receiver screen. Then it's up to them."

Chapter 44

In Paris Pierre Jobin scrutinized the file and picture that had been brought to him minutes before. A thin-lipped, bony-cheeked man in his early fifties, Jobin was the Chief Inspector of the Violent Crimes Unit of the International Section of the Deuxieme Bureau, the French Secret Service. Twice-divorced, Jobin was now 'married' to the Bureau, colleagues said of their assiduous Chief Inspector, who routinely worked fourteen hour days, often through the weekend. His only known hobbies were skiing and golf which he pursued as frequently as his work schedule permitted during their respective seasons.

Jobin had never heard the name 'Robert Sebastian' or seen the photo before. The terminology FRENCH NATIONAL and ASSASSINATE YASSER ARAFAT suggested that a professional assassin of French nationality was being used in a scheme to murder the P.L.O. leader. It was a potentially spectacular crime undoubtedly involving a highly accomplished professional. After asking an associate to investigate the validity of the information on Robert Sebastian's United Nations c.v., Jobin obtained the files of French professional hit men and of unsolved murders having the earmarks of an assassin. In reviewing these files, Jobin weeded out those individuals where an extant photo was radically dissimilar to that of Sebastian (although he understood that photos could be altered); where the individual concerned was in prison or dead; and where, in Jobin's judgment, the qualities required for such a difficult operation were seriously lacking. Three files were left, all of them problematic, but he asked his colleagues to check out the individuals concerned.

Then Jobin turned to the files of high-level unsolved murder cases in France and in Europe that had the traces or suspicions of a possible French involvement. In the last ten years these included the murders of the cousin of the Crown Prince of Saudi Arabia in Zurich where a French assassin's involvement was rumored; a restaurant owner in Lyon; the supposed murder/suicide of Senora Albornoz in Seville where Spanish police reported a mysterious Frenchman placed in the vicinity of the Senora's apartment just before her death; a Senegalese general vacationing in Nice; a business partner of an important Nouvelle Vague film director; and the sister-in-law of a wealthy pharmaceutical distributor. Probing the files, Jobin noticed that the film director and distributor frequented a well-known casino on the Ile Saint-Louis in Paris run by the notorious Milachi brothers. He rang for the files of Armand and Bernard Milachi from the Internal Nonviolent Crimes Unit which included the subjects of 'gambling' and 'illicit casinos'.

In Bernard Melachi's file, a memorandum had been filed a month earlier noting the testimony of one Rene Simperoni, a heroin pusher in Marseilles, who, turning state's evidence to reduce his jail sentence, mentioned that he had passed on the name of Bernard Melachi to two individuals of Arab descent inquiring about a professional assassin. Speaking with the chief of the Internal Nonviolent Crimes Unit, Jobin learned that Bernard Melachi was currently under investigation for cocaine peddling. Jobin instructed Deputy Inspector Schneider, a burly ex-rugby player whose nose resembled uncooked cauliflower, to bring in Melachi.

"What's going on here?" shouted Bernard Melachi as he was pushed into Jobin's office two hours later. "No warrant. No warning. I'm a respectable businessman, Inspector, and we still live in a Republic. I could sue. I could have your ass, and I will, unless there is a really good explanation for this high-handed, blatantly bad behavior by you and your men."

"Sit down, M. Melachi," said Jobin quietly.

"I must tell you that I protest in the strongest..."

Reading from a piece of paper, Jobin said: "Bernard Melachi, birthdate: 23 May 1930, Dijon. Arrested, petty thievery, Marseilles 1946, two years' suspended sentence; bank robbery, Dijon 1950, three year jail sentence; suspected complicity, murder of Samuel Levy, Paris 1955; drugs, Marseilles..."

"Cut it, Inspector. That's all past history, accounted for and over and done, and you know that."

"Then I will jump to the present. You are owner with your brother, Armand Melachi, of the Casino Royal, Ile. Saint-Louis, which caters to professional gamblers, members of the film world, and certain disreputable politicians."

"What do you mean 'disreputable'? They are Gaullists, Giscardiens, Socialists..."

"The point I am coming to, M. Melachi, is that they will not use their influence to protect you against the charge of peddling large quantities of cocaine, charges now being investigated."

Bernard opened his mouth and closed it.

"Let me turn to a different subject though. Do you know this man?" Jobin showed Melachi the photo of Robert Sebastian.

"Never saw him in my life."

"Do you know the film director Jean-Louis Gaupin and the pharmaceutical distributor Georges Plaudit?"

"I believe they come into my casino from time to time."

"It has come to our attention that you are on close terms with a professional assassin who killed persons connected with Gaupin and Plaudit. I believe you have made certain other contacts for this assassin." Jobin looked at him squarely in the face.

"Inspector, I..."

"The name of the man in this photo is Robert Sebastian. Ring a bell?"

"I...want...to consult my lawyer."

"Melachi, unless you talk very quickly, I am going to personally see you go behind bars for the rest of your natural life which has been known to shorten in such circumstances. We have convincing evidence on the drug issue—tapes, photos—you are dead right there. And we are close to apprehending Sebastian. Do you think that he will keep quiet about you?"

Bernard Melachi, taut-faced, straightened his tie. "Alright, Inspector. What do I get if I sing?"

"If what you tell us is valuable enough, we will overlook the cocaine charge, or at most, issue a public reprimand."

Bernard nodded.

"Schneider," Jobin said. "Call for a stenographer."

Chapter 45

Henry Jensen knocked on the Secretary-General's office door. It was 8:30 a.m.

"You are making a habit of early morning visits, Colonel Jensen," Waldheim said coolly.

"We have discovered who 'Robert Sebastian' is, Mr. Secretary-General. French Intelligence just passed this on to the FBI which rushed it over to me." He handed over a file which Waldheim began to read.

Jensen continued while the Secretary General looked at the file. "The name is the alias of a professional killer, highly accomplished, responsible for a number of murders. Two Arabs—a man and a woman resembling Lydia Ahmed—hired him to kill Yasser Arafat."

Waldheim looked up when he finished. "The description, while vague, seems to fit Lydia Ahmed. And the man?"

"French and FBI checking further. A common description; no name. Not much to go on."

"So what happens now, Colonel Jensen?"

"Unless Sebastian is caught very soon, the French will advise us to call off Arafat's visit. I agree."

Waldheim looked sourly at him. "You want me to call off the visit of the leader of the Palestinian Liberation Organization precisely when his organization is entering the U.N. General Assembly? The PLO representative Terzi would ridicule me openly, and he would be right."

"You will do it if you prefer not to have a murder on your hands and your conscience."

Waldheim nervously lit a cigarette. "Colonel Jensen, even if a professional assassin is going after Arafat, are not the combined security forces that are being mobilized here sufficient to prevent this assassin from getting close to the U.N. building?"

"The security measures and forces are awesome," Jensen replied. "And I am going to double them, if you don't call off the visit. But all the security forces in the world may not be effective enough to..."

"Come now, Colonel," Waldheim interrupted. "An awesome display of force would deter any sensible man. And who is more sensible than a professional assassin who wants to live to spend his hard-earned money? Strictly speaking, they are businessmen, not kamikaze pilots sacrificing their lives for emperor or country. With the proper precautions, I shouldn't think that we have a thing to worry about. Carry on, Colonel Jensen, and keep me informed. Goodbye."

Jensen returned to his office in an sour mood. He telephoned the PLO observer delegation, requesting that Terzi come immediately to the Security Office.

"You should know, Dr. Terzi," Jensen said grimly, "that very recently a woman resembling Lydia Ahmed in the company of a man described as an Arab arranged for a professional assassin to murder your leader at the U.N. The assassin, named or pseudo-named Robert Sebastian, undoubtedly caught wind of the security forces bearing down on him and has disappeared. Here are some photos you may have of the man."

"This is dreadful," Terzi said. "Does Secretary-General Waldheim know?"

"Yes. I just saw him."

"What did he say?"

"That we should intensify security."

"And I say that you should catch the man. What if he is still walking around free when our leader comes?"

"My personal recommendation to you, Dr. Terzi, is to tell your leader to cancel or at least postpone his trip until we find this 'Sebastian'."

"How can you be sure of finding him?"

"We have distributed his photo everywhere."

"And if he disguises himself?"

"That has occurred to me."

"I am going to see the Secretary General right now," Terzi said, leaving the Security Office.

During the next hour Jensen telephoned the chief agents of seven national secret services, summoning them to attend a meeting in his office at 4 p.m. that afternoon. Each of them initially expressed reservations which were overcome by Jensen's seductive statement that all the others would be in attendance. The ploy worked, and after the seven men had filed into the room within a few moments of each other, Jensen began the meeting.

"Gentlemen, it is unprecedented that, although you all know one another or about each other, you should ever come together like this." He looked around the table at the principal operatives in the United Nations of the world's major secret services: William "Billy" Harrington of the CIA, whose official U.N. cover was Liaison Officer of the Rome-based Food and Agricultural Organization outpost in New York; Vladimir Andreyev of the KGB, ostensibly Section Chief of the Audio-Visual Office in the Department of Public Information; Fui-yao Yang of the People's Republic of China, Assistant Secretary-General, Chinese Translation Service; Sir Basil Batchforth, M.I.5, Deputy Chief Middle East Section, United Nations Development Program; Maurice Prioleau of the French Deuxieme Bureau, Deputy Director , Technical Assistance

Personnel Office; Shehzad Czachur of the Iranian secret service who was posing as a journalist for a Tehran daily and would go into forced retirement after the Shah's fall; and Zev Moscowitz of Mossad, Deputy Director of Personnel in UNICEF. The seven men sat tensely around the table, refusing to acknowledge the presence of the others and wondering if they had erred in coming to the meeting.

"Gentlemen," Jensen continued. "A monumental crisis has arisen, requiring the cooperation and possible assistance of everyone here. I wanted you all to be present so that I can talk openly and avoid harmful rumors, unwarranted conclusions, and possible allegations that I said one thing to one service and something else to another. And finally, by acting collectively, we may avert a terrible crisis."

He passed out files to the seven men.

"The man whose photo you see," Jensen began, "is a professional assassin of French nationality who has been recruited to execute the head of the PLO, Yasser Arafat, who is coming here next week. Let me tell you how we discovered the plot." He related the story of Lydia Ahmed's murder, Carlos Montoya's involvement in getting Robert Sebastian a U.N. job, and the subsequent discovery by the Deuxieme Bureau of Sebastian's recruitment and intentions.

"This is the essence of what we know so far, gentlemen. The typed pages are a verbatim record of what the Deuxieme Bureau passed on to us. I need not tell you the potential consequences of the assassination—political instability internally and externally possibly leading to conflict, pressures upon stable Middle East regimes, terrorist violence, disruption of the oil supply, big power confrontation. I may exaggerate, but you will agree that it is in all our interests to prevent an assassination."

Jensen wiped his forehead with a handkerchief. "Specifically, I want to enlist your services to help us catch, or at least, neutralize, the man known as Robert Sebastian. You all have resources and sources of information lacking to us. Please help us in any way you can." He cleared his throat and sipped some water.

Yang of China raised his pencil. "What precautions are you taking in the U.N., Mr. Jensen?"

"First, Mr. Yang, let me say how grateful I am for your attendance here today." Since its admittance to the U.N. in 1974, the People's Republic of China had steadfastly refused to acknowledge, even privately, that it had any political or intelligence operatives working on the U.N. staff or in the Chinese Mission. Though aware of his role, the others had been shocked to see Yang at the meeting. To them, the fact that China was "going public" was almost as significant as what Jensen had just revealed.

Jensen continued: "The FBI and police will have massive forces in operation on the day Arafat comes here. We in Security are planning unprecedented measures which we will inform you about when they are finalized."

"Colonel Jensen?"

"Yes, Mr. Harrington."

The CIA man, who came from Louisiana, spoke in a deliberately slow drawl. He was thin, with graying black hair and wire-rimmed glasses. His last assignment had been Belgrade, and before that, Saigon. "I want to make a statement to the others in this room." They all studied him.

"Some of you have cooperated with me before; some of you have been on the other side of the fence. Now we are all in this together, and we must think of each other as friends, or at least temporary allies, on this single operation. I share Colonel Jensen's concern about the dire consequences of this Sebastian succeeding in his nefarious plot. We in the Company will do everything we can to prevent it. If any piece of knowledge or information comes to our attention, we will immediately share it with everyone else. It is just possible that another service may pick up on it and carry it further. Do I have your agreement to do the same, gentlemen?"

"Jolly good idea," said Batchforth. "We in the U.K. agree."

The Russian Andreyev, steely-eyed with close-cropped hair, stirred in his chair. "You always speak so calmly of cooperation, Harrington, and then you stab us in the back."

"Mr. Andreyev," Jensen said, startled.

"We know the situation now," Andreyev continued, "and the Soviet Union will look to its interests." He got up and left the room.

"Cold War idiot," Yang said to Harrington who nodded.

Prolieu spoke. "We concur in the gravity of the matter and most certainly agree to Mr. Harrington's proposal."

"Thank you, Monsieur Prolieu."

One by one the others agreed to share any vital information that came their way.

"Alright then, gentlemen," Jensen said. "Let us keep in the closest contact with each other. I will see what I can do about bringing Mr. Andreyev back to the fold, so to speak."

They stood up and filed out of the room.

Chapter 46

From their cabin they saw the lake sparkle in the early morning light against a background of evergreen trees merging together on encircling hills. They took long walks on narrow, winding paths, enjoying the fresh air and cool mountain breezes.

"Oh, David," Sonia Berenson said, as they strolled hand in hand by the lake. "We must come here more often."

"It's idyllic, Sonia. Nothing matters here but us."

Yet he felt edgy, unable to stop thinking about Browning and Arafat.

On the morning after their arrival, David Arovitch woke very early, went outside, and drove to the nearest town for breakfast. At the luncheonette his eye caught the headline of the local newspaper: "ARAB GIRL SLAYER STILL AT LARGE." He bought a copy.

Entering the cabin, he saw Sonia stirring in bed.

She gave him a warm smile and stretched her arms out towards him. Holding her tightly, he said: "Brought you some coffee and a Danish pastry. Interested?"

"Very." She sat up in bed, the sheet folded around her.

"What do you make of this killing?" he asked, showing her the newspaper.

She sipped the coffee. "Lydia Ahmed was a PLO agent, as we know. Maybe a grudge Palestinian killing."

"Strange, though, coming just before Arafat's arrival."

"David, really. I thought we vowed not to mention the U.N. up here."

"Sorry, darling. Finish up, and we'll go for a walk around the lake. It's a marvelous day."

"Wouldn't you rather join me here, David?" she asked, moving the sheet away.

The time passed quickly, and on Sunday evening, they reluctantly drove back to the city. The nearer they got, the more tense David Arovitch became.

Sitting next to him, Sonia Berenson was extremely happy. The weekend had dispelled her doubts and brought them close together again. Now she felt that she knew David very well and that they could have a future together.

Chapter 47

September 14, 1978

Eli Burger sat in the back seat of the government car taking him to the annual ceremony honoring the memory of slain Irgun comrades. Begin had reminded him of the event near the end of their debriefing session relating to his New York visit two days earlier. During the session, Burger described the drama of the Security Council meeting leading to PLO admission into the U.N. When Burger uttered Andrew Young's phrase "abstain," Begin's lips formed the word "treachery." Begin used some choice Hebrew slang to convey his point.

"Now, like a pack of goniffs expecting their leader," Burger replied, "all the U.N. awaits Arafat. Maybe," he added expressively, "the chief butcher will get his head blown off, while the others get their asses kicked in."

When Burger concluded his recitation, the Prime Minister thanked him for his efforts. "My 'eyes and ears' didn't fail me," he said, as he shuffled away, seeming quite low in spirits. Burger knew that Begin had serious trouble in the Knesset, where a no-confidence motion on the government's relations with her chief ally, America, had been tabled by the Labor Party.

When Burger next saw him at the commemoration ceremony, Begin's mood had changed dramatically. He was in his element, at ease. He gave a stirring speech, evoking the camaraderie of the old days, when they had blasted the hell out of the British and the Arabs. Seventy men, most very old, many in wheelchairs, listened wet-eyed to his stories of heroism and triumphant struggle. A rabbi, formerly of the Irgun, chanted the Kaddish in memory of their departed comrades. Then Burger briefly paid tribute to their former leader, now Prime Minister, who, he asserted, "would never compromise before Israel's sworn enemies."

Afterwards they sat around tables filled with pastries and cups of tea, reminiscing, and inquiring about each other's health. They were fewer and fewer each time they met, Burger noted with sorrow, and he wondered how long it would be before these meetings ceased altogether, the Irgun's exploits appearing only in history books.

At one moment Begin beckoned him with his finger. Arm draped around Burger's shoulder, the Prime Minister led him outside for a stroll around the grounds. Stars flickered overhead, and the night was still. From the tail end of an elliptical-shaped cloud, the moon appeared slowly, illuminating the far edge of the lawn.

"You are a prophet, Eli. I thought you would like to know."

"Know what, Moshe?"

"Your remark the other day about Yasser Arafat getting his head blown off. Well, it may come true. He may not survive the trip to New York."

"What do you mean?" Burger asked, stopping in his tracks, certain that Begin was referring to Browning.

"Before leaving the office tonight, I got a cable from Mossad in New York. They say an assassin is after Arafat in the U.N."

"What..."

Begin ran his hand over the hedge. "It seems that the Palestinian girl who was murdered was double-crossing the PLO. She was apparently scheming with an assassin to bump off Arafat at the U.N. The Security Chief there asked for Mossad's help..."

Burger's knees buckled, and he fell sideways on the grass.

"Eli, Eli, are you alright?" Begin shouted. "I will get help."

"No, no," yelled Burger, panting heavily. "I'm okay. I tripped. That's all. Help me up."

Begin helped him to his feet. "You sure you do not want to see a doctor? At our age...

"No, please. Let's keep walking."

They strolled towards the end of the lawn. Begin glancing anxiously at his friend.

Burger recovered his composure. "I'm okay, Menachem. Forget about it. What were you saying about Arafat?"

"Somebody, they do not know who, is after him. A Frenchman, it seems. At least it's the meshugenah Arabs who are doing it. God knows how the Americans would react if we were responsible for Arafat's death on their soil."

"Arafat is an unrepentant criminal. He deserves execution."

"Maybe so," said Begin, turning back, "but personally I hope he survives. He is friendly with Sadat, and who knows, a worse fanatic, like Habash or Barka, might replace him. And, Eli, with or without Arafat, the PLO is coming into the U.N. General Assembly. There is no way we can block it now. And I will tell you this, Eli, we are not doing too badly with the Americans. Carter has got a guilty conscience for what he did in the Security Council. The American ambassador told me this morning that the U.S. is going to double our military allotment for next year, including the latest fighter jets." They had arrived back at the reception hall. "But enough of this political Scheiss (shit). You have got to promise me that you will see your doctor, Eli. I cannot afford to lose you now."

"I promise," said Burger.

When he arrived home, Eli Burger locked himself in his study, lit a thick red candle, and gazed hypnotically at the flame flickering in the darkness. It relaxed him.

The death of his son-in-law, Moshe Leibowitz, at Yad Yehudah over two years ago which had traumatized his daughter Miriam had impelled Burger to conceive his plan of assassinating Arafat.

On the personal side, it was biblical justice, a life for a life. Until this evening it seemed logical politically also. Now Menachem Begin, his former comrade in arms and lifelong friend, had shaken his confidence. Burger wanted Arafat dead, but could he jeopardize new weapons for Israel for the sake of a personal grudge?

And had he ever given a moment's thought to the notion of someone worse replacing Arafat? Burger anguished at the thought of abandoning his plan, so near to fruition. He felt like an ineffectual old fool. There were two consolations: the Arabs might do the job for him, and he would save a great deal of money. Having gone deeply into debt to finance Browning, he would recoup and potentially save a small fortune.

At six in the morning Israeli-time, he dialed New York, but there was no answer. Half an hour later, he tried again.

"David."

"Eli. How are you?"

"I have been up all night, David. Now listen closely. Begin told me yesterday that the Arabs have an assassin loose in New York against Arafat. A French killer hired by that slain Palestinian woman and other Arabs."

"You mean there are two...Impossible..."

"Yes, David, there are two, Burger said, pausing. "David, I hope that you are sitting down. Now listen to me very closely. I have given this a lot of thought. The PLO is coming into the General Assembly, even if we kill Arafat. They will get another leader, maybe a worse one, from Israel's point of view. Begin made that point very clear to me."

"It doesn't matter, Eli. We are ridding our country of a cancer."

"Begin told me confidentially," Burger went on, "that the U.S. is giving a lot of extra weapons as compensation for its treachery in the Security Council."

"Eli," said Arovitch, wary now. "What are you leading up to?"

"If the U.S. found out that Israelis arranged for the killing of Arafat in the U.N., maybe they wouldn't give us the weapons." Then he said it. "We must call off Browning."

"Eli, there is no way the Americans will find out. The Arabs will be blamed. We will get away with it."

"Nothing is foolproof, David..."

"Eli, you are tired. I don't see..."

"You have been my loyal, trusted friend, David. Trust me now. I know what I am doing. For us to try to kill Arafat is senseless and dangerous to Israel. My eyes have been opened. I was acting only for personal vengeance...Because of Yad Yehudah and Miriam and Yoram...I have been burning with hatred ever since Moshe was killed, and this propelled me forward. However, I must put the interests of Israel far above my own. And therefore you have got to stop Browning. Tell him he can keep the advance. It will be a pretty good payoff for doing nothing."

David Arovitch was stunned, too choked to speak. Finally he managed to say:

"So Arafat lives."

"Yes...unless the Arabs and their French assassin get him."

"Okay, Eli," Arovitch said resignedly. "It is your operation, your money..." But he felt misused, a pawn manipulated by a fatuous master operating according to some arbitrary personal logic or illogic...What a waste of time, of planning, of purpose, of money. Though he was seething inside, he contained himself.

"Go see him now, David, and call me back."

Arovitch put down the receiver. Breathing heavily, he smashed his fist against the wall, causing a picture to fall off its hook to the floor. He poured himself a drink. Coughing, he wiped the liquid off his chin with his shirtsleeve.

Ignore Burger's order, he thought. Say nothing to Browning. Let him go through with it. He wrestled mentally with the consequences of disobeying Burger. Then, thinking that this was a miserable way to end his beautiful weekend with Sonia, he went out the door and drove to the U.N.

Showing his pass at the night gate, Arovitch gained entrance past a group of security officers and policemen. Once in the building, as he headed for the third basement, he was confronted on the stairs by two maintenance workers, one thin and dark-haired, the other short and bulky.

"Where you going, man?" Luigi Bendetti asked.

"You know Joseph Palewski?" Arovitch asked.

"Joe. Sure," said Stanislaw Kaminski. "What ya want with him?"

"He's a friend of mine. You know where he is?"

"Yeah. Try the General Assembly lobby."

In the lobby Arovitch saw Browning off in a corner mopping the floor. As the Israeli approached, Browning gave no sign of recognition, but once Arovitch came alongside, he whispered: "You stupid fool. What are you doing here? You're going to ruin the whole operation."

"It's finished, Browning. Burger has called the operation off."

"The fuck it is. You gone crazy, you stupid bastard?" Down the hall Kaminski and Bendetti stopped to watch.

"Burger just phoned me from Israel. He told me to stop the operation. I am only passing on his orders. He said you can keep the money we have already given you."

Standing up straight, Browning glared at Arovitch.

"You just tell your buddy over there that the operation is continuing. This is not a movie reel you can stop and start at will. When I do a job, I finish it. Always. No exceptions. I'm going ahead, and if there is any messing around, any at all, you and your friend are dead. Now get the hell out of here." Browning moved away with his mop, swishing it aggressively back and forth across the floor.

"Eli, it didn't work."

"What do you mean 'it didn't work', David?"

"I gave Browning your instructions. He insists on completing what he started."

"We have got to stop him. There is too much at stake. I am flying over."

"Eli, it's a waste of time. Browning is all wound up. He will not stop for anything. He threatened to kill us if we interfered. He is a crazy man, obsessed."

Burger's voice came through shakily. "I don't know what to do, David. I must think. I...I will call you later. Will you...be home after work?"

"Now I will."

Chapter 48

John Hardy opened Henry Jensen's door. The Security Chief was meeting with two of his lieutenants.

"Not now, Hardy. I'm busy."

"It cannot wait, Colonel. It concerns the matter we are investigating, the assassination attempt on Arafat."

Jensen sent the others away. "What is so urgent?"

Hardy smiled nervously. "Arafat is very popular. There is another assassin after him too."

"Hardy, I don't have time for your feeble jokes."

"Jensen, you have made me feel like dirt here. I've got some dynamite information for you, and if you're not interested, frankly I don't give a flying fuck. It will be your head, and Arafat's."

Jensen glared at him, breathing heavily. "Alright, Hardy. What is your great revelation?"

"Colonel Jensen, I felt that I had to prove something to you. I'm not sure exactly what—maybe to show you that I was competent, that I didn't kiss Waldheim's ass to get a promotion and my position here. Anyway, when this Burger guy kept popping up all over the place, I had a hunch. So I had him tailed. I planted a bug on the phone where he was staying, in the apartment of an Israeli Mission guy named Arovitch."

"You did what?" Jensen was ready to explode.

"You heard me."

"On whose initiative and responsibility?"

"My own." He paused for a split second. "You would have never heard about it if I hadn't hit paydirt. I checked on things on Friday, but nothing unusual. Then this morning as I was removing the bug, I thought I would get a final reading, just for the fun of it. Since the tape is mostly in Hebrew, I went downtown to have a rabbi translate it for me. He's old, not so clear-headed. Did not understand much of anything, but I gave him an extra hundred to keep his lip buttoned. I typed out a transcript of last night's conversation between Eli Burger and David Arovitch."

Jensen looked at the sheet of paper. "I don't believe it...This means...It's preposterous," he said, shaking his head as he read.

"It's the bloody fact, Colonel. Two, two assassins chasing Arafat."

"My God. And after what I just learned about Sebastian."

"What is that?"

"French Intelligence located his mother."

"His mother?"

"Yes. Don't ask me how, but they did it. She is in a nursing home in northern France, apparently a physical and mental wreck. Here is the report." He handed over an "eyes only" envelope.

"Jumping Jesus," Hardy said, looking up at Jensen. "His sister died in this settlement called Yad Yehudah in a PLO attack a couple of years ago. So to avenge her, he's taking it upon himself to kill Yasser Arafat, the PLO leader. He was hired by Lydia Ahmed and an Arab man, but now that his cover is blown, he will continue to hunt Arafat because the whole matter is entirely personal, a way to avenge his sister's death."

"That's what I think also," said Jensen. "I figured that once he was discovered and we then saturated the U.N. with security, Sebastian would realize that he couldn't succeed and he would abandon the effort. But from everything that I have been reading, we are dealing with a desperate, obsessed man who is on a personal mission."

"We gotta find him then."

"How, Hardy?" Jensen permitted himself a smile. "And now you bring me this other news about...what is his name...Browning."

"If you will permit me. Colonel Jensen, we know...or rather, Arovitch knows where this Browning is located. I suggest we act quickly to eliminate him. Then we focus on Sebastian."

"Sounds reasonable." Jensen telephoned Sonia Berenson at the Israeli Mission, informing her that he was coming there immediately on an urgent matter. She agreed to cancel her next appointment.

Fifteen minutes later, Jensen and Hardy sat in her office. As she listened to the Hebrew tape, she was stunned. Too upset to reply, she asked them to repeat it. When it finished, she shook her head in frustration. "This is terrible, terrible. One a respected political figure in Israel, the other, my...my Second Secretary."

"So you recognize the voices and can confirm the accuracy of this translation?" Jensen passed over the transcript.

"Yes," Sonia Berenson said after scanning it. How could David do this? she kept thinking. It showed how little she knew him. This is what he had been concealing from her.

"With your permission, Ambassador Berenson, I would like to call Mr. Arovitch in here."

For a moment she wanted to warn David to flee. But she answered "Of course" and buzzed her secretary.

As he entered, David Arovitch was surprised to see Jensen and Hardy, whom Sonia coldly introduced to him.

"Sit down," Jensen said. "We want you to listen to something." He pressed the tape recorder button.

First Eli Burger's voice came on, confirming an appointment with Mayor Koch. Then the incriminating conversations relating to Charles Browning. David Arovitch's face turned scarlet. He glanced over at Sonia Berenson who was biting her lower lip and staring out the window.

"Well, what do you have to say?" Jensen asked, when the tape finished.

Arovitch just shook his head. What hurt most was Sonia knowing. She seemed so shocked. "I...I...Oh, what's the use?" And he sat back, arms folded.

"I will tell you the use," Jensen said angrily. "For some crazy, misguided reason, Burger and you arranged to have Yasser Arafat killed at the U.N. Now Burger wants to call it off. But your assassin, this Browning, refuses. Right? Right?" Jensen glared at him.

"Yes," Arovitch finally said.

"And in the meantime, we have another assassin floating around trying to do the same dirty work. It's a fine mess."

Hardy came up and whispered in Jensen's ear.

"It's essential to neutralize both assassins," Jensen continued. "Since our friend here knows where Browning is, we will tackle him first. Where is he?"

Arovitch did not respond.

"Where is he?" shouted Jensen, grabbing Arovitch's shirt tightly in his fist. "Tell me, you bastard, or I will beat it out of you."

"Colonel Jensen," Sonia Berenson said, startled.

"You don't frighten me, Jensen," Arovitch said, knocking his arm away. "I've been in an Arab prison camp; this is nothing to me."

"David, you never told me that," Sonia Berenson said in Hebrew.

"I never told you a lot of things," he answered.

"Let us stay calm. Colonel," Hardy said, pulling Jensen's arm away from Arovitch.

Jensen sat down.

"So you won't tell us where Browning is?" Hardy asked Arovitch.

Stalling for time as he thought, Arovitch said: "I do not like sending anyone to his death who hasn't harmed me."

"And Arafat?"

"That's different. He is a malevolent Arab."

"David," said Sonia Berenson, a pained expression on her face. "How can you be so blinded by hate? So politically naive?"

"Don't lecture me, Sonia," he snapped at her in Hebrew. "That is how I feel.

And so should you."

"Wait a minute," interrupted Hardy. "Just a minute. I'm getting an idea. What if... what if...Listen, listen a second. Even if we get rid of Browning, we still have the threat of Sebastian." Turning to Arovitch, he asked: "Just how good is this Browning?"

"He came with the highest recommendation," said Arovitch. "He's very tough. He's well organized, highly intelligent, seems to have good judgment...I find him very arrogant, but I recognize his qualities. He tried to get Arafat in Beirut, but backed away when he saw that it was impossible. That is why the U.N. came into the picture."Arovitch paused a moment. "But he is relentless. Nothing, nothing, will stop him now unless you kill him."

"Then we will kill him," Jensen said emphatically,

"No, Colonel. Hear me out," said Hardy, waving the air with his hands. "Browning was hired at great cost to assassinate Arafat. He wants to complete the contract. Very admirable. We will let him carry on, but with one slight change."

"What is that?"

"We will redirect him against Sebastian."

Chapter 49

Eli."

"David, I was going to call you. I have decided. I am flying over tomorrow morning."

"It will not be necessary, Eli."

"You stopped him?

"No, not yet. There is...something else that has occurred."

"Tell me.

"My phone was tapped from the time you stayed in the apartment. They know. They know about us and Browning."

"Who is 'they'?"

"The U.N. Security Office. And now Sonia."

"David, what are you saying? Tell me directly."

"They have a tape of our conversation last night. So they know that we hired Browning to kill Arafat and that we are now trying to stop him. They want me to see Browning this evening...to send him against the other assassin. Ironic, isn't it? We got caught, not trying to kill Arafat, but trying to head Browning off."

"David...you said Sonia knows about us. That means... Begin will know also?" Burger's voice changed into a whisper.

"I don't see how Sonia can keep this quiet. You can try and appeal to her, if you want."

There was silence on the other end of the line.

"I'm sorry, Eli," Arovitch continued. "We are both in hot water now. Maybe they will go lightly on us if I cooperate with them on Browning. What else can I do?"

"Goodbye, David."

"Goodbye, Eli. You try to relax. I will call you after I see Browning."

Burger slowly replaced the telephone receiver. He walked out to his garden. In the distance, the lights of Jerusalem flickered like stars in the firmament. Since his arrival in 1923, Eli Burger had witnessed the city's metamorphosis from medieval village and historical site to metropolis. After a few minutes of hypnotic staring, he suddenly realized that the cool breeze was chilling him. He went inside the house to his study. He looked at the photo of his daughter and grandson on the desk. Tears came into his eyes; he wiped them away with his stubby fingers. He thought of his action at the King David Hotel long ago in 1946. Then the face of his ancient friend, Menachem Begin, the Prime Minister, came into his consciousness looking shocked, even aghast, at Burger's inexplicable plot to kill Arafat. Burger anticipated the disappointment, the shame...How could he bear it? Opening the desk drawer, he took out his revolver, placed the gunpoint to his temple, and pulled the trigger.

Charles Browning reported to work in a foul mood. He has barely survived the monotonous maintenance job, the vapid chatter of Kaminski, and the sullen stares of Bendetti, bearing some unspoken grudge towards him or towards the world at large. But would he survive the inept games of Burger and Arovitch? They had made him uptight when he should be loose, diverted his attention when he should be focusing it unimpeded on the task ahead. Cursing their stupidity, he debated whether he should call the whole thing off, as they now wanted, and walk away with half their money.

In the General Assembly lobby Browning strolled past the large bronze statue of the muscular ancient Greek mythical figure of Poseidon. Feeling himself watched, he turned around abruptly and saw Luigi Bendetti standing twenty feet away.

"Nice statue, eh?" Browning said.

Bendetti did not respond.

"Guess that I'll change now." Browning started to move away.

"Kid, I don't care what the fuck you do."

"You don't like me much, Bendetti, do you?"

"You don't fool me for a second, kid. You ain't no maintenance worker."

Had he been deficient in something maintenance men do? he wondered. "You're right," he said slowly. "I'm just doing this to get myself together. Once I save a little capital, I'm gone."

"Cut the act, kid. You fooled the other jerks, specially that gullible idiot Kaminski. But you didn't fool old Luigi here." Smirking at Browning, he said: "I picked your lock."

"You what?"

"You heard me. Went right in when no one was around."

"What the hell did you do that for?" Browning's mind raced over the possibilities.

"To find out what was cooking. I was suspicious of you right away. I got good instincts about people, and you weren't the maintenance type. Also, nobody here uses a lock. We leave our valuables at home or check 'em upstairs."

"Christ. I was new here. How was I supposed to know that?"

"I found that funny gun with the round barrel and the silencer in the locker. Found the diagrams and papers too. That's a real funny language. Arabic, ain't it?"

Browning didn't answer.

"I knew you was up to no good. Specially after I seen you with that guy the other night."

"So what?"

"So you're in here to do a job. You're after that big Arab guy coming in a few days from now. Go ahead. Deny it."

Browning moved closer to him.

"You got two choices, kid. Either cut me in or I go straight to the cops. Lots of 'em roaming round here. They would be interested in what I got to say."

"What do you want?"

"How much they paying you to do the job?"

Hesitating, Browning answered. "One hundred grand."

"Give me half. Fifty."

"That's hardly fair. I'm taking all the risks."

"You still got a pretty good payday, kid. With my fifty, I can quit this miserable hole. If you don't come across, I go straight to the police. You hear?"

Browning sighed. "Okay, you win. But you keep your mouth shut, or you're in big trouble.:

"Kid, I swear I'll leave town, and you'll never see me again. Now where is the bread?"

"I got some downstairs."

"Let's go. And no stalling."

Moving through the door marked "Emergency Exit," they proceeded down the stairs.

"You're one smart guy, Luigi," Browning said over his shoulder. "You had me pegged from the beginning, eh?

"It takes a lot to put one over on me. I've had some bad luck lately, but that's all changed now."

They passed level 1B. "How far to go?" asked Bendetti when they reached the second basement level.

"Almost there. Two more flights down."

"Is it stashed in the locker room?"

"Nearby."

At the third basement level, Browning led Bendetti down the corridor. He opened the door of the boiler room. Both men began perspiring immediately.

"So it's in here," said Bendetti.

"Yeah. Behind that storage case. You gotta admit it's a good place to hide dough. Nobody would have found it in a million years if it hadn't been for you."

Bendetti leaned over to look behind the storage case. "Hey, I don't..." He never completed the sentence. Browning hit him with a powerful karate chop on the back of his neck. Though the blow traveled only twelve inches, it cracked the spinal column. As Bendetti slumped to the floor, Browning began dragging him down the metallic steps towards the boilers. In front of a huge boiler, Browning tugged on the handle of the furnace door, but it wouldn't budge.

Spying a wooden crate nearby, he moved it next to the boiler and stood on it to get a better grip. The furnace door creaked, then opened, instantly emitting sparks from the raging fire inside. Ducking to avoid burning his face, Browning leaped off the crate and lifted Bendetti's limp body. Extending his arms as high as he could, he heaved the body into the furnace. Sparks danced out from the open furnace door. Browning slammed the handle shut.

Then he went up to the maintenance room where he changed into his levis and black boots. The rest of the crew tramped in.

"Where's Luigi?" Kaminski shouted across the room.

"Dunno," said a Mexican worker on his crew.

Browning worked by himself, avoiding any contact with other crew members. For an hour he mopped the Secretariat lobby floor near the Dag Hammarskjold Library. Then he was startled to see David Arovitch approach.

"Motherfucker, didn't I tell you not to come here?"

"I had to, Browning. They know. The authorities know. U.N. Security bugged my telephone. They heard Burger and me discuss you."

"You bungling son of a bitch. For two cents, I would..." Browning raised his mop.

"Don't panic. They are not interested in you alone. There is another assassin after Arafat."

"What the hell are you talking about?"

"Just as we did, some Arabs have hired a pro to kill Arafat when he comes here. A Frenchman."

Browning looked incredulously at him. "This can't be true..."

"It is! Furthermore," Arovitch continued, "U.N. Security knows that I tried to stop you and that you refused."

"I suppose they followed you here as well."

"No," said Arovitch, looking directly at Browning. "They are holding back because they want you to go after the other assassin—for the same money."

"The idea stinks. Tell them so."

"What are you going to do?" Arovitch asked.

Browning looked away. "I don't know. I was a fool to get mixed up with asshole Israelis. Whatever the money..."

"Take the security chief's number. Call him. What do you have to lose?" Arovitch gave him a small piece of paper and walked away.

A half hour later, Security Chief Jensen's office phone rang. "Is this Browning?" asked Jensen. He signaled Hardy to take the extension.

"Your friend delivered the message. Talk. You've got thirty seconds."

"I'm Security Chief Jensen and I'm here with Detective Hardy who is on the other line. You're a professional, Browning. As a reasonable man, you know that it is now impossible for you to carry out the Arafat contract now that you've been exposed. However, we have learned that another professional like yourself may be acting against all reason or preventive security measures. So we propose that you kill him for the same payoff."

"Who is putting up the new money?"

"That is our worry. We will get it."

"What guarantees do I have?"

"Any you want."

Browning thought for a few seconds. "I want a hundred thousand down. Four hundred thousand more when he dies. If he lives, but doesn't succeed against Arafat, then I want only one hundred thousand more for my preventive efforts."

Jensen looked at Hardy who nodded affirmatively.

"Okay, we agree."

"I will tell you one thing straight, Jensen. You fuck with me, and you're dead. So are Hardy and the Secretary-General..."

"No one is fucking with you, Browning. We are making a serious proposal, and we expect results. We will need some time to get the money. Call me at noon sharp, and we will make arrangements for delivery."

The phone clicked. Jensen returned to his office and sat down slowly behind his desk. He was extraordinarily tired. The tension over for the moment, he put his hands behind his neck and yawned.

"Where do we get our hands on that kind of money, Colonel Jensen?"

"I am surprised at you, Hardy," Jensen said, smiling. "Now that I know what a clever fellow you are, I would think that you could figure out something like that."

"The Israelis?"

"Yes, and..."

"And who?"

"Our mutual friend."

"Who is that?" Hardy asked.

"The Secretary-General."

Kurt Waldheim frowned when he saw Jensen, whose unexpected presence these days presaged trouble.

"Well, Colonel Jensen. How is the Sebastian investigation proceeding?"

"Good and bad, sir. We have some unexpected developments." He told Waldheim about Sebastian's sister.

"We thought that Sebastian would be deterred from trying to kill Arafat, but now," Jensen said, "we think he will stop at nothing." He passed over the Deuxieme Bureau report.

"I have enlisted the help of the secret services at the U.N. And," continued Jensen, "I have also arranged an additional weapon against Sebastian. This will sound fantastic, so I had better start at the beginning." He related how John Hardy, to prove his "competence" to Jensen, had bugged Arovitch's phone when he learned that Eli Burger was staying with the Israeli Second Secretary. "Here is a transcript of the Burger-Arovitch conversations after Burger returned to Israel."

"I don't believe it," Waldheim said, shaking his head." A second assassin. It's impossible, incredible."

"Unfortunately it's true. Arovitch admitted everything, and we decided, on Hardy's suggestion, to deflect Browning from his original target to..."

"Sebastian?"

"Yes. And he has agreed. However, we have a problem about money."

"What problem?"

"Browning insists that the terms of his Arafat contract be fulfilled. He is owed $500,000, and he will accept that amount to go after Sebastian."

"That is a small fortune."

"The Israeli Mission has agreed to come up with half of it. So, Mr. Secretary-General, I have to ask you for the rest of the money. Only $125,000 is needed now."

"You are joking, surely," said Waldheim.

"I couldn't be more serious."

There was a moment's silence, finally broken by Waldheim. "It's preposterous. The United Nations now finances assassins? What if this sordid business got out? The world powers would have my head, and the U.N. would be ruined."

"It will not get out. The Israelis clearly do not want this publicized. That leaves only Hardy, you, me...and Browning."

"How do we know that Browning will not blackmail us later, saying he will reveal the plot if we do not give him several million dollars?"

"We don't," said Jensen. "But I have the strong impression that he will take his money and run, and we will never hear from him again."

"And how do I put my hands on $250,000 without the Controller's Office, which scrutinizes everything with a microscope, finding out?"

"There must be a way," said Jensen.

"It is not possible. We have to find another alternative."

"There isn't any. We have two choices, Mr. Secretary- General—kill Browning or hire him. Each choice is risky. In the first, we have to find him. We have no idea where he is. On the phone I heard him threaten Hardy, me, and you if...if we mess him about. Also, we would still be left with the problem of Sebastian."

"You have put me in an awful position, Colonel Jensen. What choice do you leave me?"

"You always have a choice."

"I will get the money," shouted Waldheim. "But the next time you make decisions in my name, bloody hell, consult me first."

"I will need $125,000 by early afternoon and the rest in reserve tomorrow.

"You will have it. Now, goodbye."

Telephoning the branch manager of the Chemical Bank on the fourth floor of the Secretariat, Waldheim asked him to deliver in person $250,000 in cash by noon from a U.N. special account that was automatically replenished to the level of half a million dollars. Waldheim knew that this account was never audited by the Accounts Division or the Controller's office on the understanding that the S.-G. needed a reserve fund for "miscellaneous expenses" to oil the engines of diplomacy, as his best judgment and the 'objective needs' required.

Waldheim cancelled his morning appointments. He needed time to think. This assassination business was now unbelievably messy. It could easily jeopardize his seabed tax plan that he believed more and more would be the financial and even political salvation of the United Nations. Should Arafat be killed in the U.N.—a deed too horrible to contemplate—-the Arab bloc, as well as Russia, would not feel bound to vote for the Law of the Sea Treaty with its Seabed Clause, and this would destroy his carefully planned initiative to make the United Nations financially and politically self-sufficient. It could also undermine or even destroy his future political career in Austria.

The phone rang. His secretary put through President Carter.

"Mr. Secretary-General, I have just received an FBI report about some French assassin named Sebastian operating in the U.N. against Yasser Arafat. Is this true?"

"He was operating in the U.N., Mr. President, but we believe that we have frightened him off. In fact, I am quite certain of it."

"I need not remind you, Mr. Waldheim," Carter said in dulcet tones, "that the assassination of a foreign leader on American soil is unthinkable."

"Let me assure you, Mr. President, that everything is under control. Extraordinary measures are being taken to protect Mr. Arafat on the international territory of the United Nations. This is international soil, as you are aware, but I can assure you that we are treating this situation with the utmost gravity and concern."

"Nevertheless, I would feel more comfortable sending up a detachment of White House Secret Service agents. They are awfully good. I see here that this Sebastian has some revenge motive against the PLO leader. His sister, isn't it?"

"Mr. President, I will speak to my security chief about your Secret Service men coming here. Whom shall he contact at the White House about that?"

When he hung up, Kurt Waldheim was visibly shaking.

Chapter 50

September 11-12, 1978

In Beirut, Yasser Arafat met non-stop with his newly formed cabinet. He defined responsibilities, delineated lines of authority, assigned specific tasks, and prepared the strategy for the PLO entry into the United Nations General Assembly. Despite considerable jockeying for influence, a surprising spirit of harmony prevailed. Superficially at least, Arafat had succeeded in reconciling dissidents like Barka, Salim Sherati, and Abdul Kalaba and bringing under one umbrella the most disparate and seemingly irreconcilable ideological elements in the Arab camp. Sensing the drift, the ideological extremist George Habash pledged benevolent neutrality. Under Arafat's lead, the cabinet decided that a demand would be made at the United Nations that the PLO become a member of the International Court of Justice where it could present its grievances against Israel. On a practical level, the PLO would further insist that the Israeli government set a timetable for the 'liberation' of the West Bank of the Jordan River and the Gaza strip which would comprise the minimum territory for the new Palestinian state. Simultaneously, with an eye to exerting maximum political and economic pressure upon the so-called 'friends' of Israel, PLO representatives were dispatched to Libya, Saudi Arabia, Iraq, Kuwait, and the United Arab Emirates to urge these countries to invoke the oil weapon, if necessary, as a means of pressuring the United States, Western Europe, and Japan against Israel.

"It is all cosmetic, Shukri," said Barka one afternoon to Kamal. "Sweet stories and pretty pictures, but useless in a practical sense. We say 'please' and 'thank you', but nothing will change. The petrol states, with the possible exception of Libya, couldn't care less about us. Their investments are tied up in New York, London, and Houston. So why would they pressure the United States or the U.K.? And look how Sadat and Egypt are now taking steps to recognize the Zionists. This can only reassure and boost the aggressor state. Why would Israel relent and give up its illegal territories unless we pressure the shit out of them? With constant attacks first and diplomacy last. Arafat talks eloquently, but his words are hollow. They lack substance. They lack power. His moves and his policies are the wrong moves and policies at the wrong time by the wrong man."

Kamal shook his head. "If you feel so strongly about it, Hassan, why in heaven's name did you join the cabinet?"

"A certain close friend of mine pressured me," Barka said with a vague smile on his face. "Don't deny it, Shukri. However, there is something that I want to ask you. If one day we should find ourselves without the great Arafat, would you support me as the only one who can hold this movement together, prevent fraternal battles, and unite all of the different elements against the Zionists?" In Barka's mind, his old and dear friend, Kamal, the Minister-designate for Social Welfare, was to be the link between the old and the new regimes, the conciliator who would support him unequivocally and rally the other cabinet members, particularly the potentially recalcitrant ones, to Barka's leadership.

Shukri Kamal walked to the window, then came slowly to his chair. "We go back a long way, you and I, Hassan. I know better than anyone what a dangerous dreamer you are. Nothing you do would ever surprise me. If something is going on, for Allah's sake, do not tell me. But if that hypothetical situation you have just described ever takes place, you can count on me. How could you think otherwise?"

Barka had already decided who would live and who would die in the new regime after Arafat's death. Those who had gloated over his former banishment from the PLO would be killed. So would the "unreliables"—those deemed ideologically unsound and those who could be hostile to his future leadership. Shukri could work on fence-dwellers deemed to have good will, while those considered irredeemably disloyal were marked for death. Meeting individually with five loyal members of his entourage, Barka assigned each of them a murder. "You will take action," he said, "if Arafat disappears or dies. You will wait for my signal and only then you will move. Understand?" All five nodded assent.

The waiting period in Beirut made Barka uneasy. He wondered how Robert Sebastian was faring. Since Lydia's death there had been no communication. He decided to contact Sebastian by means of the telegraphic phone code they had agreed upon.

The day before the PLO departure to New York, Arafat called a cabinet meeting in his air-conditioned bungalow. The ministers sat around a large table in the study. After reviewing some minor policy issues, Arafat suddenly mentioned Lydia Ahmed. "She was a traitor," he said. "A note was found in her apartment denouncing me and my policies. What is more, we believe that she was part of a plot to assassinate me when I arrived at the United Nations."

"What did you say, Your Excellency?" someone shouted. "This cannot be true." Many uttered loud exclamations or hushed words around the table.

Hassan Barka almost fell off his chair. Had Lydia been so stupid as to leave incriminating evidence linking him to the plot? He looked at the door fifteen feet away. He would be cut down even if he did get outside. He waited for the axe to fall.

"Some of you look shocked," said Arafat. "Do not be naive. I live in the shadow of death all the time. What choice do I have?" Smiling enigmatically, he took a sip of lemonaide.

"What is the exact situation, Excellency?" someone asked.

Arafat put down his glass. "A potential assassin is on the loose in New York. He is being pursued, but has not been caught yet."

"Then you should not go," said Mohammed Rasheed, the Minister for Occupied

Territories. Others shouted their agreement.

"I must go," Arafat replied. "It is our moment of triumph. If I am not there, I am little better than a coward."

"Nonsense," said Rasheed, a white-haired man in his sixties known for plain speaking. "Terzi will stand in for you. You can announce the new government from here."

Arafat shook his head. "It is not the same."

"It is common sense and prudence, Excellency," continued Rasheed. "I beg you to reconsider. If something happens to you, this fragile peace among us may collapse. We'll be set back ten years. The Zionists will benefit; no one else."

Arafat looked around the table. His eyes stopped at Barka. "What do you think, Hassan?"

Barka wondered if Arafat knew and was playing a deadly game with him. Rather than appear indecisive or counsel prudence, Barka decided to play it forcefully. It was his only chance, he thought. "With all due respect to our venerable Minister for Occupied Territories, I do not agree with him. Which one of us has not lived with the fear of death—by the Zionists or by a treacherous, so-called brother? We have chosen a violent life as our calling," he continued, glancing around the room. "As part of it, we may die violently, as His Excellency says. Until now we have been outcasts, nonentities fighting a savage struggle against superior, if not overwhelming, forces. Finally, Allah be praised, the situation has changed. The entire world community, including our enemy, the United States, is welcoming us on a level of equality. Every new nation that enters the United Nations goes in proudly, triumphant over the colonialism that oppressed it. A sovereign head of state accepts in person the sacred trust of the United Nations. For us the event is magnified by the fact that our state will be officially born in the General Assembly when our leader announces the new government."

Looking at Arafat, Barka said softly: "His Excellency is precious to me. I cannot tell you all how happy I am that I had not died before becoming his brother once again. I would gladly volunteer to take any bullet meant for him. But I cannot believe that all the resources of the United States and the United Nations will not create a fortress of protection to dissuade even the boldest assassin. That is all I will say for now." Barka sat back, closing his eyes.

Sitting next to him, the Minister of Justice patted Barka on the shoulder, while across the way, someone shouted: "Bravo."

"That was well put, Hassan," said Arafat. "Your thoughts echo mine completely. I must go to New York. Our Arab brothers expect it. I am confident that the Americans will protect me; we have been in communication with them about it. Yet, Gentlemen, this threat has brought home to me the need to look to the future. Our movement to establish the state of Palestine must survive. We must go forward, not retreat into confusion. So I have decided that before leaving Beirut, I will make a political testament, designating one of you as my successor. I want you all to swear now on the Koran that you will be loyal to this person should I vanish from the scene." Reaching for the holy book, he passed it around for them to swear loyalty to his soon to be designated successor. Then he dismissed them.

Back in his residence, Barka thought of one thing—-would Robert Sebastian go ahead or would he be deterred or possibly even caught beforehand? As for Arafat's statement about nominating a successor, Barka dismissed it as sheer bravado, if not outright hypocrisy, given Arafat's insatiable love of power and proven reluctance to relinquish it.

During the night a soft knock woke Barka. Holding his revolver, he moved to the door. "Who is it?"

"Shukri. Let me in."

Opening the door, Barka rubbed his eyes. "In heaven's name, Shukri," he said, once Kamal entered. "What is so urgent that could not wait until the morning?"

"He has done it, Hassan. He has written his will. And left a copy with me to disseminate in case of his death. Though he swore me to confidence, I couldn't help breaking the seal to look."

Barka snapped to attention.

"You will never believe who he has named as his successor."

"Who, Shukri? Who?"

"You."

Chapter 51

In his apartment Charles Browning cleaned and loaded his revolver. Then he opened the large-size U.N. manila envelope that John Hardy had passed to him an hour before in darkness in Central Park. After counting the money, he locked it in the wall safe behind the Calder lithograph, mixed a gin and tonic, and began reviewing Robert Sebastian's dossier.

Though the information was scanty, Browning noted that Sebastian's credentials were roughly identical to his own—approximate age, height, and weight, an international reputation as an assassin, with some important hits to his credit. Browning felt a shiver in his spine—he was pursuing an alter ego, an equal. It was his most significant professional challenge, even the pinnacle, of his career. Luckily Browning had the advantage of knowing about Sebastian, while the Frenchman knew nothing about him.

While the two might be superficially similar, Browning saw how differently they operated. Browning's cardinal principle was to demand increasing sums of money from one job to the next, a natural progression enabling him to achieve financial security and potential early retirement from an obviously dangerous way of life. This job was a huge financial step forward for Browning, perhaps the coup de grace that would propel him into retiring from his career as a hit man. Sebastian, on the other hand, was erratic—the alleged amounts of money he received varying enormously from one job to the next. In 1975 he supposedly received 150,000 Swiss francs for a hit, while in 1976 he accepted 85,000 French francs—a substantial decline—for another. It made no sense to Browning. Didn't the Frenchman have any professional pride? Was it simply catch-as-catch-can, Sebastian arbitrarily accepting any contract no matter the remuneration? Was the bastard that unstable?

Secondly, Browning prided himself on dominating any given situation. Unless he was in absolute control, he refused a contract. Only once had he made an exception—the present operation—where because of the exceptionally high payoff, he had accepted the job even though he had to rely excessively on David Arovitch's help. And what had happened? The situation had almost backfired. It could have been catastrophic for Browning. The FBI, police, or U.N. Security could have stepped in and terminated Browning's mission, if not his life.

In contemplating the variables, Browning realized that his cardinal philosophy until this job had been never to deviate from basic principles. Never alter or compromise... and never depend on the help of another party or person. He would remember these lessons for the future. However, there would be no future for him as a professional assassin.

Browning had made a promise to himself that he would pack it in after this job. He had promised Cynthia that he would curtail his traveling in order to be with her.

He began to ruminate about Cynthia. Cynthia, Cynthia Sherman, his brown beauty. As soon as this job was done, he would stick to his innocuous profession of wine trader. He would have enough money to live very comfortably with her. He would take her to Europe, to Asia, to Australia. He suddenly missed her very deeply.

Picking up the phone, he dialed her number. It was daytime, and she was at work at Sherry Netherlands. "Hi, Babe. Hi, Cynthia," he said to the voicemail recorder. "It's Charles. I miss you terribly. I am far away now, but I am finishing up my work, and I will come back to you very soon. Cannot wait to be with you. Cannot wait to be in your arms. Be patient, Cyn. I promise you that we will have a glorious future together. See you as soon as I can. Love you…." He slowly hung up the phone.

He turned his mind back to his prey…Robert Sebastian. It was hard to figure him out. Unlike Browning, Sebastian did not seem sufficiently self-contained or even exercise the necessary caution. Some might even call him reckless. He got involved in high risk situations such as the Arafat job where he depended unduly on Lydia Ahmed and doubtlessly killed her for that very reason. In 1976, as Browning saw in the Deuxieme Bureau file, Sebastian got involved with the casino owner Bernard Melachi, who rather quickly provided a number of contacts and then very recently betrayed Sebastian to protect himself. Sebastian, Browning concluded, needlessly courted danger, sought it out almost. He was reckless to the point of abandon.

Finally, at bottom, Sebastian was highly emotional, if not sentimental. He had befriended this Algerian boy Bekir, who told the Deuxieme Bureau about the dinners in the bistro, the nocturnal walks by the Seine, the trip to the Pyrenees, and Sebastian's help in getting him a job at the Galeries Lafayette. Browning observed that after that interview, Bekir disappeared and was being sought by the French police. An unsuspected quality of naivete and innocence in a professional who, down deep, was festering with hate and disdain for Arabs. There was also a report on an interview with a French woman named Denise Fouchet who had been a close friend of Sebastian's sister and may have been his mistress. She confirmed how upset Sebastian had been about the death of his sister, saying that he had basically disappeared afterwards, with her seeing him only once, very briefly, at the café Les Deux Magots.

Browning now fully understood why Sebastian acted irrationally, took extreme risks, considered money unessential, and, above all, had agreed to work with Lydia Ahmed to kill Yasser Arafat at the United Nations. It was because his beloved sister had died at that Yad Yehudah settlement at the hands of the PLO The man's motives clearly transcended money. He was acting to avenge his younger sister.

Browning had to laugh. This Sebastian was so emotionally involved in pursuing

Arafat and his judgment so clouded that he would continue beyond rational limits. Sebastian saw Arafat in terms of pure hatred. Since his sister's death, he was acting in a bizarre manner and would undoubtedly continue doing so until the PLO leader's death or his own demise. Now, ironically, it was Browning's job to see that Arafat lived. The poor bastard Sebastian didn't stand a chance. Browning would see to that.

He poured himself another drink and reviewed Sebastian's file for the seventh time, searching for something he might have missed. He didn't find anything that he had not probed endlessly before.

One thought had been crystallizing in his mind since early morning. Even if possessed by demons, Sebastian would want to survive after killing Arafat. He would therefore factor his own safety into the calculations; minimizing the risk and ensuring his subsequent escape would be critical elements of any plan.

In this light, Browning studied his map of the U.N. interior, analyzing Arafat's every potential move, calculating the relative degree and duration of his exposure and estimating the proportionate risk factors for Sebastian. The best spot to assassinate Arafat, Browning concluded, was the General Assembly hall where Arafat would be spending considerable time in the open. But having posed as an interpreter once, would Sebastian, now discovered, be so foolish as to try it again? He would more than likely choose some other spot and assume some other guise in that hall. But, Browning reasoned, Sebastian in disguise might very well gravitate to an interpretation booth, an area that he knew well from his assignment at the Security Council meeting that had approved the admission of the PLO to the General Assembly. The news conference and luncheon with Arab ambassadors were also possibilities. As before, Browning analyzed the safety factor, time element, and Arafat's accessibility. As he ruminated, he concluded that it boiled down to two or, at most, three elaborate, though terribly risky, alternatives.

Browning knew that he, too, would be taking great risks. He did not put it past U.N. Security trying to dispose of him in order to ensure silence and save the big payoff of money due to him. He knew that his freedom of action in the U.N. was severely restricted, and he had to calculate the escape factor for himself as well. He therefore altered his face, adding a grey mustache, eyebrow color, and gray tint to his hair, as well as artificial flesh to enlarge his nose and ears. Once he was satisfied with his new appearance, he took a photo that he grafted onto the U.N. admission pass he had previously used to gain entrance as a maintenance worker.

Once or twice he thought of staying home and doing nothing. If Sebastian were frightened away by the security forces, Browning would collect another $100,000 for Arafat's mere survival. Yet deep down, Browning knew that Sebastian would go forward against Arafat because of his obsession with exacting revenge for the death of his sister. Browning also knew that nothing would keep him away from the U.N. today. His pride would not let him abandon the challenge, whatever the risks or odds involved. It was his chance to show that in confronting potentially the best professional in the world, he, Browning, would prove to be even better.

Chapter 52

September 14. 1978

The plane taxied to a halt in semi-darkness on a remote airstrip of Kennedy Airport. Federal marshals and airport security police immediately surrounded it. As portable steps were rolled in place, Under-Secretary-General for General Assembly Affairs Harrison Dodd, a tall, jowly-cheeked ex-Congressman from Michigan, moved forward to greet the arrivals. A Nixon appointee, Dodd had intended to occupy the highest American post in the Secretariat, the position formerly occupied by the revered American diplomat of the late 40s and early 50s, Ralph Bunche, as a capstone to his career as governor of Michigan and congressman in Washington, DC To his surprise, he found himself agreeably caught up in the maelstrom of U.N. politics and prevailed upon President Carter in early 1977 to allow him to remain in his U.N. post for another four years. Although his position lacked any real power, Dodd reveled in being at the center of international affairs at the U.N. and globally, and he enjoyed the prestige of proximity to Waldheim on the General Assembly stage. It compensated for the disagreeable task of being Waldheim's protocol errand boy assigned to meet high-level diplomats before turning them over to the Secretary General for the real business at hand.

The plane door opened, and three bodyguards, cautiously peering at the group below, took tentative steps forward. Arafat and his entourage followed down the stairs. Arafat was dressed in his customary green military uniform, with a checkered keffiyeh headdress. The other Palestinians wore conservative business suits.

"Mr. Arafat," Dodd said, introducing himself. "The Secretary-General is waiting for you at the United Nations."

"I am pleased to meet you, Mr. Under-Secretary-General," said Arafat softly. "I would like you to meet some members of the new government of Palestine. This is Mr. Ben Buda, Minister of Foreign Affairs; Mr. Sidoli, my personal assistant, Mr. Barka, Minister of National Economy, and Mr. Sherati, Minister of Social Welfare."

Dodd shook their hands. "We had better not delay, sir. For security reasons, we are going by helicopter. If you will just follow me." Dodd escorted them to the helicopter parked fifty yards away.

Airborn, Dodd tried making light conversation, but all the Palestinians, including Arafat, seemed pensive, replying only in monosyllables. They rode the rest of the way in silence, broken by intermittent chatter of Ben Buda and Sidoli who were in New York for the first time. Dodd pointed out some buildings of the Manhattan skyline, already visible in the early dawn.

Arafat, sitting between his bodyguards, worked on the speech he would give to the General Assembly later that morning.

Hassan Barka, though tired by the nighttime journey from Algiers, remained in a state of feverish excitement. By noon he expected to be the head of the Palestinian Liberation Organization and by extension, the new Palestinian government. Arafat's naming him as successor would only facilitate the transition. It would defuse potential opposition and reconcile any skeptics or resisters not marked out for execution by Barka. The plan was simple. After Sebastian killed Arafat in the General Assembly, Barka would have Kamal show the other ministers a copy of Arafat's political testament designating him as successor, claim his inheritance, and then deliver the speech accepting the PLO's induction into the U.N. General Assembly.

Barka had already outlined his address. First would come a grief-stricken eulogy to the martyred Arafat; next, the announcement of the new government of Palestine; thirdly, mention of a solicitation for Palestinian membership to the International Court of Justice in The Hague; and finally, an ultimatum to Israel to surrender usurped Palestinian land or face the consequences. The entire plan, Barka knew, depended on Robert Sebastian's timing and efficiency. Two days earlier, Barka had telephoned Sebastian who assured him that that everything was proceeding as planned, even though Sebastian knew that he had been identified and was being pursued. To Barka's surprise, Sebastian alluded to the silver bracelet worn by Lydia Ahmed, saying that Lydia had stated that she had received it from Barka. "A lie, a complete lie," said Barka. "I have no idea what she meant or what bracelet she was referring to." Sebastian didn't comment, slowly hanging up the phone.

Suddenly the helicopter swooped down, hovered thirty feet over the U.N. garden, and gently landed on soft dirt beside a bed of rose bushes. U.N. Security officers and F.B.I. agents lined up on four sides. As Arafat's feet touched ground, Arab delegates spontaneously surged forward to embrace him and the other Palestinians. They milled about, talking excitedly until the Jordanian ambassador whispered into Arafat's ear that the Secretary-General was waiting nearby. Breaking away from the crowd, Arafat approached Kurt Waldheim who was standing stiffly fifteen feet away. Just behind stood his Chef de Cabinet, Krishnan Katani, Henry Jensen, and John Hardy.

"I am delighted to see you, Mr. Secretary-General," said Yasser Arafat, smiling broadly. A U.N. photographer took shots of the two men warmly shaking hands. It was not the first time they had met since Arafat's visit in to the U.N. in 1974. After conceiving the interlocking steps of his "Grand Design," Waldheim had secretly sounded out the PLO leader in a hotel room in Damascus on a summer night one year ago. Their initial talk had led to a meeting of the minds: Waldheim would pave the way for the Palestinian entry into the U.N. General Assembly, while Arafat would line up a number of nations in the Middle East in favor of the Law of the Sea Treaty. Their collaboration, while personally beneficial to each of them, would transcend the personal and alter significantly the world's view of the PLO and of the United Nations.

"How was the journey, Your Excellency?" said the Secretary-General, towering over the diminutive Arafat.

"Fine, fine. We are happy to be here. The day that we have planned for has finally arrived."

"Everything is ready for you. Can you come to my office now for some coffee and croissants?"

"Of course."

Accompanied by a dozen security officers, including Jensen and Hardy, Waldheim led Arafat into the U.N. building. Barka and the other Palestinians went to the Delegates Lounge for a breakfast reception sponsored by the Arab League. Trailing behind the Secretary-General's group until they reached the elevators, Jensen and Hardy branched off to the Security Office.

Waldheim and Arafat rode in silence to the 38th floor with six security men. Since his arrival, Arafat had kept his right hand inside his jacket, Napoleon like, resting on the barrel of a revolver fit into a holster strapped to his chest. Now he let his arm dangle loosely by his side. The revolver would give him mental assurance and protection against any would-be assassin lurking in the U.N.

Kurt Waldheim was extremely agitated, though he concealed it well. In the "world's toughest job" the norm was bad enough. The frantic pace of meetings, lunches, dinners, and receptions during the General Assembly was nerve-wracking, beyond the physical endurance, mental, and emotional capacity of most men. Just the other day, Katani had remarked that a Secretary-General, to succeed, "must have the strength of Sampson, the patience of Job, the guile of Tallyrand, the intelligence of Einstein, and the affability of an American politician."

The pressures this year were overwhelming. Admittedly much was self-imposed, the inevitable accompaniment of his plan to make the U.N. financially self-sufficient and secure himself a prominent political place in Austria's future. Exhausted by a month of sixteen-hour days, he was on a regime of black coffee, pep pills, sexual abstinence, and irregular eating. But if this little man to his left in the Arab headdress survived until night-fall, it would be worth it.

When they were alone in his office, Waldheim showed Arafat a copy of his schedule for the day.

"When is the press conference, Mr. Secretary-General? Is the omission an oversight?"

"We eliminated it for security reasons, Your Excellency. We want you exposed as little as possible."

"But I must get our message across to the world's press."

"You need not worry," Waldheim said, nervously lighting a cigarette. "The newspaper and television coverage are riveted on you."

"I have not included everything I want to say in my General Assembly speech. It is essential that…"

"Your Excellency," Waldheim interrupted. "Let me be frank. This French assassin Sebastian has not been apprehended yet. We believe that he has been scared away by our extraordinary security measures, some of which I am not at liberty to mention. Today the U.N. is an armed fortress." Feeling his voice and blood pressure rising, Waldheim sat back and sipped his coffee.

"It seems that you have thought of everything, Mr. Secretary-General," said Arafat quietly.

"Everything. I assure you."

"Then why not the press conference?"

Against his better judgment, Waldheim agreed to restore the press conference.

Chapter 53

"Are you certain? I need to see you, even for five minutes."

"No. Too dangerous."

Barka was disappointed. He hated using the telephone in this instance. But Sebastian seemed adamant.

"Is everything ready?"

Sebastian did not volunteer more.

"One thing has become crucial. You must do it either before or early into his speech in the General Assembly. Can you assure me of that?" Barka was sweating profusely.

"Nothing is certain." A pause. "But I can manage it, I believe."

"The rest of the money will be delivered afterwards, as agreed. In Paris."

"Yes. Now I have a question for you. Are you sure that you know nothing about that silver bracelet Lydia Ahmed was wearing?"

"I told you. I know nothing about it. Lydia lied if she told you that I gave it to her."

Sebastian hung up the phone. He remained silent, visualizing Lydia in pain and anger throwing the bracelet to him, shouting that Barka had given it to her. But Barka denied that he ever gave it to her. If so, why would Lydia have made this allegation? Was she lying or was Barka? Whoever had killed Julie had taken the bracelet. It had then ended up in the hands of Barka and Lydia, and Lydia was now dead. Who had killed her? And why? Confused and uncertain, Sebastian took several deep breaths, sifting through the alternatives. The Israeli press, along with everyone else, put the blame on the PLO for the attack on Yad Yehudah. The PLO had denied responsibility, but that meant very little. Could Barka have instigated the attack in order to embarrass Yasser Arafat? If so, he was Julie's murderer. But he categorically denied knowing anything about the bracelet. How could Sebastian find out? He now had a chance to avenge Julie by killing the leader of the PLO. But what if Barka …Sebastian's head suddenly throbbed with pain, and he sat down in the dark for over an hour to alleviate the stabbing pain. Finally he emerged from the dark room with the pain subdued, even though he still had a complete absence of clarity about the big question tormenting him.

In front of the U.N. building five thousand policemen stood on guard. All traffic had been barred north of 42nd Street. Three thousand more policemen were deployed on side streets off First Avenue, including five hundred in front of the U.N. Plaza Hotel, where the Palestinians, except for Arafat who was leaving by plane in the late afternoon, were scheduled to spend the night. Coast guard launchers with scuba divers patrolled the East River, a precaution designed to prevent a repetition of 1964, when Cuban refugees tried to shoot mortar at the U.N. from Queens while Che Guevara was addressing the General Assembly. Police helicopters hovered overhead. Sharpshooters were stationed in nearby buildings. Policemen with dogs went into the underground manholes in search of would-be hidden assassins. The security forces marshalled that day were unprecedented—more massive than for Nikita Khruschev in 1958, Fidel Castro in 1961 and 1963, the Pope in 1965, and Yasir Arafat in 1974. Inside the building, hundreds of FBI and Secret Service men equipped with guns and walkie-talkies ranged in designated areas. U.N. Security officers, uniformed and plain clothed, stationed themselves in assigned spots. A mass of protesters in Dag Hammerskjold Park were hemmed in by the surrounding police forces which blocked them from coming any closer to the U.N. All of the security forces inside and outside the building carried a photo of Robert Sebastian.

At 7:30 a. m., Jensen, Hardy, and Bailey met in the UN Security Office looking for loopholes or weaknesses in the security preparations. They walked through the building scrutinizing every detail. In the General Assembly hall, they saw security officers examining seats, desks, interpretation booths, and TV rooms.

"It's airtight," said Bailey. "No one in his right mind would try anything here today."

"Sebastian is not in his right mind," Hardy said.

"He doesn't stand a chance," said Bailey.

"I wish I could be so confident," said Jensen, puffing on an unlit pipe. He had not informed Bailey about the recruitment of Charles Browning as added insurance against Robert Sebastian.

Before returning to the Security Office, John Hardy telephoned David Arovitch and told him to come to the U.N. Security Office. Arovitch, after all, was the only one who could recognize Browning.

Chapter 54

Back in his hotel room, Robert Sebastian glanced at his image in the bathroom mirror and saw a youngish man of dark complexion, heavy jowled with slight skin discoloration. The cheeks were paunchy, and a dark, bushy mustache appeared under a fleshy, bulbous nose. His hair was dyed jet black. The skin color on his face, neck, and hands had been darkened with a skin pack and odorless cream. With his new appearance, including nondescript black-rimmed glasses, even Julie would not have recognized him now.

Moving to the camera set up on a tripod across the room, Sebastian set the self-timer mechanism, depressed the shutter release button, sat on a chair eight feet away, and waited for the take. The film developed in thirty seconds. Trimming the edges of the photo, he affixed it to the U.N. pass once issued to Robert Sebastian, but now officially made out to "Nassan Berlin."

Then he went down to the street and took a taxi to an address in the East 20s. Entering the vestibule of a narrow white-brick building, he opened the front door with a key made earlier for the occasion and took the elevator to the seventh floor. Pressing the rear apartment bell, he made it ring continually.

Finally someone scuffled towards the door, asking in a sleepy voice who it was.

"Georges, it's me, Sliman. Your fellow interpreter…Open up…Please. I must see you.

"Sliman. Why...so early?" He undid the latch and opened the door.

A dark skinned man dressed in tight blue underpants found himself bowled over onto the floor looking up at a gun. Sebastian closed the door behind him.

"What the hell, mister?" Georges Amafi asked shakily.

Sebastian pulled Amafi up by his arm. "Your bathroom. Where is it?"

"It's, it's...that way."

"Go there. Quick."

Amafi protested in a fumbling voice. Sebastian dragged him roughly to the bathroom.

"Into the bath. Now." Amafi climbed into the gleaming white bathtub. Sebastian yanked him down into a sitting position. Then he turned the hot and cold shower faucets on fullblast, drenching Georges Amafi, who started to scream. Placing the gun behind Amafi's ear, Sebastian fired twice.

Blood trickled from the spot, and Amafi slumped down motionless.

Robert Sebastian turned off the faucets and left the bathroom. Finding the apartment keys on a bedside table, he double locked the door from the outside and took the elevator to the street.

An hour later Sebastian joined a group of Secretariat staff walking through police lines at First Avenue and 42nd Street. Both at the gate and at the entrance to the Secretariat building, he held out his pass for security men to check his identity. Since the face resembled the photo on a genuine U.N. grounds pass, they let him go into the building.

Limousines threaded their way through the police lines to deposit their passengers by the Delegates Entrance. After identifying themselves at the door, delegates proceeded to the General Assembly hall which began to fill up well before 10 a.m., the scheduled hour for the session to begin.

Since the 150 country delegations were organized alphabetically, one could see within any given ten square feet a representative admixture of the world's skin colors, nationalities, sartorial styles, and political ideologies. Friend sat next to friend or foe depending on the first letter of its national name (although one nation changed its U.N. name simply to distance itself from its alphabetical neighbor).

The General Assembly met each year in New York from September to December—a cosmopolitan circus of conflicting cultures and nationalities matched only for its universality and pageantry by the Olympic games. For the next three months, one hundred fifty delegates would sound off successively on topics or grievances that concerned them—from Cold War politics, colonialism, capitalist or communist political or economic encirclement and the danger of the proliferation of nuclear energy to the redistribution of the world's wealth from the affluent countries to the poorer, marginalized ones, defense of whales, and the innumerable small power animosities against their neighbors, rivals, or the big powers. Cynics called it the "silly season," defenders the nearest thing to world democracy that existed—one country, one vote in a forum where oratory replaced belligerence and verbal steam was vented over major contemporary issues, even if very little, if anything, was ever done about them.

Above the hall, in two glass booths on the left side, NBC and BBC crews, watched by security officers, moved their TV cameras in place. In adjoining booths, interpreters in the six official languages sat with their earphones on.

Shortly before 10, Sonia Berenson and the Israeli delegation without David Arovitch entered the General Assembly hall. Andrew Young came over to offer greetings and a word of consolation. As always, Berenson was courteous, though her face was somber. She was not thinking about today's session that she knew would be bad enough politically for Israel. She was sick at heart about Eli Burger's suicide, and preoccupied with David Arovitch's attitude and behavior.

She had passed from anger to sympathy to confusion to sadness over David. She doubted whether she could ever trust him again. She had decided he must leave the

Mission, and she would tell him so later today. She would be sad, maybe very sad, but she was a survivor and she would move forward without him. Then, quite unexpectedly, she thought about her lunch two days earlier with Andrew Young who began by explaining apologetically why the U.S. had suspended its veto on allowing the PLO to enter the U.N. General Assembly. Then Young began to show more than diplomatic interest in her.

"Sonia," he said. "I have always admired you, not just as a fellow—I am not sure of the feminine term—ambassador, but also as an attractive, even beautiful and brilliant woman."

"Andy, why all these compliments? What are you saying?" She looked directly at him.

"Sonia," he said wanly. "I work my butt off at the Mission and outside, but I am a lonely man. My marriage ended some time ago, and I need female companionship. I know that you lost a husband quite a while ago, and as a fellow workaholic, I would imagine that you can be lonely sometimes as well." He paused for a moment. "Maybe we are kindred souls." He put his hand on hers for an instant, then withdrew it.

Berenson looked at him and said: "Andy, Andy, you sly devil. I confess that I have always considered you a charming and attractive colleague, a fellow diplomatic traveler, so to speak. But nothing more. Am I correct in thinking that you are suggesting something more than our current political cum diplomatic relationship?"

"You said it, Sonia, not me." Young was smiling.

"I'm flattered, Andy, but let's take it slowly. Let's get through the General Assembly meeting, and if you still feel the same way, invite me to dinner and we can see how the wind is blowing."

"That's perfectly fine, Sonia. You will hear from me a day or two after the Arafat business…" He raised his wine glass in a silent toast to her.

The thought flickered through Sonia's mind that an affair with Andrew Young might be the perfect tonic for her after David left the Mission and her life.

Charles Browning in disguise showed his U.N. maintenance pass to gain entrance to the tourist entrance of the U.N. complex. He entered a stairwell that descended three stories to the boiler room level. Emerging on level 3B, he walked away from the boiler room to a storage area filled with tools and metal equipment. Wedging his hand behind a group of shovels, he located a small brown paper package that he had put there three days earlier. He quickly unwrapped the package, gently placing the small pistol into his inner coat pocket. Then he walked up two flights to the level of U.N. stamp and tourist shops, now deserted, and headed towards the basement area of the General Assembly building which was packed with delegates making their way to the General Assembly hall.

Browning had put himself mentally in Sebastian's place and imagined that his quarry would assess the trade-offs between risk-reward, proximity, and visualization of the target. It was clear to Browning that Sebastian would avoid the open, exposed General Assembly hall, and instead find a peripheral place that would allow a set amount of time within which to accomplish his task. This would mean either the television/radio booths or the adjacent interpretation booths that spanned the General Assembly hall, each booth affording a clear look at the podium where Yasser Arafat would speak. He decided to mount the stairs to explore the TV booths first and then, if necessary, move to the nearby interpretation booths. Identifying Sebastian would be difficult, because he would surely be in disguise, as was Browning. Yet Browning felt a strong inner confidence that if Sebastian had come to the U.N. today, only he, Browning, had the psychological and professional qualities to identify him and, more importantly, to stop him. In a way, Sebastian was his Doppelganger, his spiritual and even physical double, recruited for the same mission of killing Arafat and who would see the task through to completion because of his determination to avenge his sister. If necessary, Browning ruminated, he would use Julie's name and memory as a means to confound and defeat his adversary.

Chapter 55

Close to 10 a.m., the seats of 150 delegations were already filled with ambassadors, staffs, and alternates. Above the hall, in two glass booths on the left side, NBC and BBC crews, watched by security officers, moved their TV cameras into place. In adjoining booths, interpreters in the six official languages sat with their headphones on.

As the hour of 10 a.m. approached and passed, the atmosphere became electric. Anticipating the imminent appearance of Yasser Arafat, the delegates spoke in hushed tones. At five after the hour, the door at the side of the podium opened.

A security officer carrying a pitcher of water and glasses walked into the hall and placed them on a table next to the podium.

Behind the podium in the antechamber to the hall, Secretary-General Waldheim, accompanied by Under-Secretary-General Dodd and the President of the General Assembly for the current session, Maximilian Zafougar, the Foreign Minister of Iran, waited for Yasser Arafat and his entourage. A lean, distinguished-looking man with wavy grey hair, Zafougar had been Iran's representative to the U.N. years before and was now General Assembly President for 1978 because of geographical rotation and as a reward for faithful service to OPEC. In his mind, the present session would be historic, not only because of PLO admission, but also because he intended to press Third World claims to the hilt.

Waldheim looked up as Security Chief Jensen and John Hardy entered the antechamber. He moved to a corner with them.

"Everything is in place," Jensen said. "The surveillance is...extraordinary."

"What about your man Browning?"

"He is here, undoubtedly in disguise," said Hardy. "We just don't know where."

Waldheim shrugged, a mixture of disdain and resignation.

"Mr. Secretary-General," said Jensen. "Can you arrange it that after Mr. Arafat finishes speaking, the session be suspended so that the Palestinians can leave for the second floor lounge? It would be less exposure time."

"I will mention it to Zafougar."

Jensen and Hardy then went into the General Assembly to take up their positions.

Throughout the hall Security officers stood on alert. Hardy wondered, nevertheless, whether it would not come down in the end to a contest between Sebastian and Browning. Instructing David Arovitch to point out Browning if he could identify him, Hardy gave the Israeli a security badge to enable him to roam more freely. Standing on the right side of the hall, Arovitch gazed at the different delegations and invited guests at the back. Jensen, Hardy, and he had discussed the fact that since Browning would be in disguise, the probability of Arovitch recognizing him was small. Nevertheless, the Israeli kept looking discreetly in all directions.

The PLO delegation, surrounded by security officers, arrived in the antechamber shortly after ten. Arafat stopped to exchange a word with Zafougar whom he had met before.

One of the Palestinians approached Waldheim. "Mr. Secretary-General," Hassan Barka said smiling. "We met in the Rose Garden this morning."

"Yes, yes. Of course." Waldheim shook Barka's hand firmly, although he had forgotten his name.

"I want to express my profound gratitude to you. You have spared nothing to make us welcome. We will be eternally grateful to you,"

"Thank you," said Waldheim. "We are doing our best."

"It is excellent, excellent. Perhaps we could have a private chat later. I am Hassan Barka. Remember the name, Mr. Secretary-General." He walked over to the PLO group.

Kurt Waldheim stared after him, thinking Barka quite a decent fellow, as well as a perceptive observer of the Secretary-General's efforts.

Waldheim walked over to Arafat, still chatting with Zafougar. Arafat appeared confident, jaunty even. "Ah, Mr. Secretary-General. Are we ready now?"

"In a few moments, Your Excellency. Normally we have a number of formalities at an opening General Assembly session—an address by the outgoing President summarizing the last Assembly's achievements, an homage to him by this year's President, and so forth. But this morning we will dispense with all that. Our distinguished President, Mr. Zafougar, will introduce you immediately. You will then come forward to make your speech. The President will induct the Palestinian Liberation Organization into the United Nations General Assembly. Then the session will be suspended to permit you to withdraw to an adjoining lounge."

"Mr. Secretary-General, I wish to remind you that I intend to announce the formation of our new government and present the leading ministers."

"That is your privilege, Your Excellency," Waldheim replied coolly. "But in the interests of security, please keep your address brief."

"I understand," said Arafat.

"I think we can commence now," said Zafougar with a flourish. After final handshakes, he walked to the podium door, followed by Waldheim and Dodd. A security officer opened the door, and the three men walked onto the podium.

The packed crowd immediately quieted down.

Zafougar took his seat in the center of the raised dais. Waldheim sat on his right, Dodd to his left. After pouring a glass of water for himself, the Iranian offered one to them. Dodd accepted, but Waldheim, tensely looking out at the audience, refused with a curt nod.

At 10:20 a.m., Zafougar raised the wooden gavel and banged three times. With a glance at the interpreters, he leaned towards the microphone and said loudly: "The 35th meeting of the General Assembly will now come to order."

High above the dais, in interpretation booth 6, the Lebanese Arabic interpreter, Sliman Mamoud, had become extremely nervous. As the hour of 10 approached, he checked his watch every few minutes and wondered why his Tunisian interpreter colleague, Georges Amafi, usually so punctual, was late today. Last night, when the interpreters' grapevine informed Mahmoud that the G.A.would begin early today—at 10 a.m. rather than the customary time of 10:30 a.m, he had immediately phoned Georges. They had joked about Arafat requesting an early session in order to be back in the afternoon to lead the assault on Jerusalem. What could have happened to Georges? Mahmoud wondered. If necessary, he could carry on alone, though the rules stipulated two interpreters must be present for every session, one spelling the other every half-hour.

At five after ten, Sliman Mahoud checked his watch once again. If Georges did not show up within five minutes, he decided, he would leave the booth to telephone the Arab Interpretation Section. But the door handle suddenly turned, and Mahmoud breathed a sigh of relief.

Robert Sebastian, in disguise, entered the booth.

"Who the hell are you?"

"Nassan Berlin," Sebastian said, closing the door. "Georges Amafi called in sick. I am his replacement."

Mahmoud studied Sebastian. "Why haven't I seen you before?"

"Just transferred from Geneva." He sat at the front left, placing his briefcase on the floor, next to his leg.

Mahmoud accepted the story. With Arabic services rapidly expanding, the U.N. recruited and moved interpreters around the system all the time.

Sebastian gave his nationality as Iraqi. Mahmoud began speaking Arabic.

Sebastian uttered some elementary words in Arabic and than asked: "Do you mind speaking in English? I need the practice."

After chatting for a few moments about Geneva, a city Mahmoud had visited frequently, the Lebanese agreed to Sebastian's request that Mahmoud begin interpreting first.

Sebastian put on his earphones to hear Zafougar's booming voice: "...a soldier and statesman who symbolizes the political aspirations of his people..." He lowered the sound until it was barely audible.

"It's perfect," he thought, looking at the rostrum below. Forty-five degree angle to the podium. He will be in my sight; the gun will do the rest. He closed his eyes. "Julie, Julie, it's almost over."

Chapter 56

At ten-foot intervals around the perimeter of the General Assembly hall, security officers watched the delegates in the center and the journalists congregated in the back in the area normally reserved for tourists. John Hardy stood nervously at right side of the hall. A short distance away was Jensen, arms folded, pensive. Next to him, David Arovitch.

"Sonofabitch Israeli," Hardy thought, glancing over. "He had better be right about Browning. Not all the U.N. security, not the fucking feds, not even the bloody IRA, could stop Sebastian now. But another pro… Send a pro after a pro and pray…"

Hardy's eyes traced an arc from the sea of faces on the General Assembly floor to the stiff, angular presence of Secretary-General Waldheim on the raised dais. Waldheim surveyed the scene below, his impassive face betraying little. On his left, Under-Secretary-General Dodd gazed intently ahead, while on his right, Zafougar continued his introductory oration.

"As commander-in-chief of the Palestinian revolution, he has used a gun, yet fundamentally he is a man of peace." Pausing, Zafougar reached for a glass of water.

Charles Browning, climbing the back stairs to the TV-interpretation level, first surveyed the three TV studios, finding technicians focusing their long-range cameras on the General Assembly podium below. There were photographers and stenographers in each studio. Successively entering each studio, Browning gave a big smile each time, jerking his arm to indicate that he had entered the wrong place and was going to the adjacent studio. He silently made his way past the TV studios and entered the area where the interpretation booths were located.

Sitting in the middle of the auditorium below, Sonia Berenson doodled in Hebrew on her notepad. Delegates nearby thought she was taking notes. Once she looked up at David Arovitch; his eyes were elsewhere.

"When he last addressed us in 1974," Zafougar continued, "the only precedent for an individual addressing the General Assembly whose country was not a member was His Holiness, Pope Paul VI, who in 1965 blessed the United Nations as an earthly agent of divine peace.

"That event casts its living light on today's session. The U.N. has covered itself with glory by conferring membership to the General Assembly upon the Palestinian Liberation Organization. I now introduce the leader of the PLO, a man who stands for justice as well as for peace, His Excellency Yasser Arafat." As he retreated, Zafougar signaled with his right hand.

From a door at the back of the rostrum, a Security officer brought in the high-backed oaken chair reserved for heads of state. He placed it by the speaker's lectern below the president's dais. Other security officers placed three chairs on the right of the rostrum. A plush red carpet was rolled from the door to a point near the lectern.

There was a half minute's silence. Then, as a slight figure in a green military uniform and headdress advanced slowly across the carpet, a cry went up. The Saudi Arabian ambassador was the first to stand. Other delegates jumped to their feet, clapping loudly, waving fists in the air.

"Keep your eye on them," Jensen said to John Hardy, pointing to a cluster of Arab delegates moving noisily towards the front.

Hardy's hand tightened on the gun in his pocket.

Arriving at the rostrum, Arafat clasped his hands together above his head, acknowledging the applause. For a second, his bright windbreaker opened, revealing a light blue shirt and a holster buckled to his body. Holding one fist up, Arafat deftly buttoned his jacket with his other hand.

In the audience U.S. Ambassador Andrew Young caught a glimpse of the holster.

"Do you know that he is carrying a gun?" Young said to the PLO press spokesman nearby.

"You are mistaken, Sir." was the reply.

Yasser Arafat stretched his arms forward as if to embrace the audience. Arab, Third World, and Communist bloc delegations stood cheering. The American, European, and some of the Latin delegates sat quietly, tapping pencils. The applause became deafening when Zafougar walked down the steps to hug Arafat.

As planned, Sonia Berenson and the other members of the Israeli delegation rose and left the hall.

At that moment three men came through the open door at the back, moving to the chairs on the rostrum. Taking the seat closest to the lectern was Hassan Barka. Next to him were Shukri Kamal and Ben Buda.

"Look," shouted an elated Sliman Mahmoud in interpretation booth 6. "Arafat's going to announce his new government. It's wonderful, isn't it?"

"Wonderful," replied Robert Sebastian.

Peering into the English interpretation booth, Charles Browning heard the applause intensify, then die down. He was calm. Having examined Sebastian's dossier and studied the photo, he felt he had understood the man's psychology and motivation. The Frenchman was operating with an obsession. Money was not important to him, as it was to Browning. The bastard was hunting Arafat purely for revenge. He moved to the next booth, French interpretation, where Sebastian could likely be. Browning removed the pistol from his inside coat pocket, holding it in his right pants pocket.

At the lectern Arafat looked at his audience and began his speech. In the Arab interpretation booth, Sebastian silently opened the latch of his briefcase. Mahmoud was preoccupied translating the Arabic to English.

"Mr. Secretary-General, distinguished delegates, good friends. The admission of the Palestinian Liberation Organization to the United Nations General Assembly is a monumental victory for the Palestinian people who have suffered ignominiously in exile for thirty years."

Barka, sitting a few feet away, glanced at Arafat. May Sebastian be quick, he thought to himself.

"In 1948 the United Nations took the decision to admit a Zionist entity into its midst. At the time the U.N. was a small, unrepresentative body dominated by colonialist powers. Today, with almost universal membership, the United Nations is charting the course for a new world, one free of the taint of imperialism, colonialism, and racism in all its forms, including Zionism."

In the Arabic interpretation booth, Robert Sebastian moved behind Sliman Mahmoud who was busy interpreting. His palm cupped over Mahmoud's mouth, jerking the head rapidly back. As Mahmoud fell, Sebastian plunged a knife directly into his heart. The interpreter died with his mouth open, as if he were about to ask a question. Sebastian took the headphones from his head and laid him gently on the carpeted floor.

In the General Assembly, the Arabic to English interpretation suddenly stopped, total silence replacing Mahmoud's animated voice. The British ambassador called over a security officer and asked him to investigate. Before the officer was a few steps away, the ambassador shouted that the interpretation had resumed.

Standing nearby, John Hardy heard the exchange. He looked up at the interpretation booths above the hall. His eyes moved from booth to booth. Each was occupied by interpreters. Sebastian had posed as an interpreter, he thought, as he moved towards Jensen.

Chapter 57

As Sebastian undid the four screws of the air-conditioning panel located at the front of the booth, he "interpreted" into the microphone from a typewritten paper taped to the wall. His words had little to do with Arafat's speech. The PLO leader spoke moderately:

"I, a child of Jerusalem, the ancient city of peace, have come to the United Nations with a liberator's gun and a dove of peace. Do not let the dove of peace soar away. Do not let the hawks of war swoop down to replace it."

But Sebastian's prose was far more aggressive, proposing that the Arab people unite to fight the Israeli 'predators' with their planes and tanks in an endless battle to "liberate" the Palestinian people from the servitude imposed by the Zionist enemy.

Hearing the English translation, Andrew Young whispered to an aide: "truculent little bastard, isn't he?"

Browning edged his way along the interpretation booths. Glancing into the French language booth, he saw that the two interpreters were women. So he moved to the adjacent Russian booth where a woman was busily interpreting. The back of the man sitting next to her was husky and it could be Sebastian. Browning opened the door of the booth.

"What are you doing?" the man uttered shakily, startled by the appearance of this stranger.

"I am looking for an interpreter," Browning said.

"What do you mean?" the man interjected. "We are all interpreters."

Browning studied his face and mannerisms. Could it be Sebastian posing as a Russian interpreter? The woman interpreter gave Browning a dirty look. So he asked the Russian to step outside.

"Please tell me," Browning said when they were outside the closed door of the booth. "How long have you been interpreting at the U.N.?" He held tightly onto the pistol in his right pocket.

"I beg your pardon, sir," answered the Russian, speaking English with a pronounced Russian accent. "But who are you to be asking me this question"?

"I am a security officer.   Your name, please?"

"Andre Volkov. Again, I ask you. Why do you ask me these questions?"

"Are you Robert Sebastian?"

"Are you crazy? I just told you that I am Andre Volkov." The Russian, with no trace of nervousness, looked disdainfully at him. "Look at my pass."

Browning's instinct told him that the Russian was telling the truth. Although he did not want to waste any more time, Browning decided to ask one or two more questions until he was completely satisfied.

Several yards down the hall in the Arabic interpretation booth, Robert Sebastian looked through the four inch square opening that he had created and saw that he had a perfect line of sight to Arafat on the rostrum below. Out of the corner of his eye, he could see Barka, listening solemnly to Arafat's discourse. Barka, the successor.

From his briefcase Sebastian removed the rifle parts. After clipping the magazine to the barrel, he clasped the barrel onto the base and affixed the telescopic sight.

His hand caressed the gun.

He removed the headset. The "interpreting" stopped. Again, delegates tuned into English were disconcerted. Arafat, unaware of any technical problem, continued speaking.

On the floor of the hall, Hardy told Jensen about the earlier interruption of the English interpretation.

"I'm going up there," he said, suddenly seeing at the same moment a thin beam of light coming from one of the booths. Hypnotized by the flickering light, Hardy saw it waver slightly. Was he imagining it? No, the light moved a fraction in one direction, paused, and then edged back. What was going on in that booth? he asked himself. He tried to blink it away, but it stayed, now resting on Yasser Arafat's right cheekbone.

"Christ," he shouted, pointing. "We blew it."

Hardy ran towards the side door leading up to the interpretation booths, Jensen and Arovitch several paces behind.

When the light struck his face, Arafat, momentarily blinded, stood perfectly still. Having survived so many assassination attempts, he had developed, he believed, a kind of immunity against violent death. But the red light now proved him wrong. He was suddenly afraid to die.

Through the lines on the sight, Sebastian saw Arafat freeze. All he had to do was press the trigger. Thirty bullets would rip out Arafat's brains. But in Sebastian's mind her face reappeared. And he reached in his pocket to touch the silver bracelet, saying her name. "Julie."

Arriving at the Arabic interpretation booth, Browning peered in and saw Sebastian pointing the rifle. He threw open the door and shouted: "Sebastian. Julie's dead. Don't do it." Browning reached into his pocket for his pistol.

Sebastian's face twisted when he heard Julie's name. He hesitated as he saw the target appear in the sight, and then disappear. Each time the gun fixed on its target, it wavered. His muscles strained to control it. His arms shook as he thought of Julie, of the way she had died. He struggled to keep the gun steady long enough to fire. The light beam fluttered left, right, back the other way.

Then his finger touched the trigger.

The General Assembly hall reverberated with machine gun fire. The burst lasted four seconds, the sounds echoing for several moments. Blood flowed into the carpet, making it a deeper shade of red.

Behind the marble lectern, Yasser Arafat lay perfectly still, a toppled statue. His face was ashen; he appeared lifeless. Then his right arm moved, reaching for the revolver under his jacket. Reassured, he opened his eyes. Blood flowed around him, staining his black and white robe. One hand still holding the gun, he moved the other, touching blood. Slowly he lifted his head to find its source. He saw half of Hassan Barka's face, the half that had not been shot away. And he closed his eyes, wondering what had saved him.

Browning had his pistol trained on Sebastian's head. "You killed Arafat, didn't you?"

Sebastian looked at Browning and said: "No, I killed the man who killed Julie...."

"I'm sorry for what I have to do, but I'm a professional, like you. I was hired to do this. Put your hands up."

Breathing heavily, Sebastian didn't react. He tried to absorb the fact that Julie was now avenged.

Just then Hardy crashed into the booth, gun pointing skyward.

Sebastian quickly spun the machine gun around.

Shots rang out from two pistols. Sebastian fell.

"You can take credit for it, Hardy," Browning said, putting his gun in his pocket and hurrying out of the booth.

A few seconds later, Jensen and Arovitch, guns in hand, appeared in the booth.

Jensen stumbled over a body at the side near the entrance.

"Interpreter," Hardy said. "He's clean. Probably been here for years, poor bastard."

Jensen had already turned his attention to the other man lying face down on the floor. Slowly peeling away the mustache and false skin, he saw the resemblance to Sebastian.

"It's him. See the photo." They stared at the photo which Jensen removed from his jacket pocket and then at the man on the floor.

Two days later, in his office, Security Chief Jensen completed his report to the Secretary-General, utilizing information supplied from the Deuxieme Bureau and from Mossad. The dossier read as follows:

Robert Brown: aliases: Beulieau, Green, Lepardieu, Michales, Sebastian.

Birthplace: Lyons, France. 1942 American father, French mother.

Childlhood spent in Lyon, Paris and New York.

Education: Lycée Léon Blum, Paris; University of Virginia; Ecole des Langues, Marseilles.

Languages: French and English perfect. Working knowledge of German, Italian, and Spanish.

Military Service: French army, 1962-1966.

Professional Cover: Business Investments in U.S. and Europe; car racing; martial arts.

Criminal activity: responsible for nine known or assumed murders in Europe and Africa from 1971 to present (see footnote 2, names).

Sister (Julie Brown Ben-David) killed in attack on Israeli settlement Yad Yehudah, West Bank, January 1977. Initiated by H. Barka (see footnote 3A re Lydia Ahmed).

Two items in the file had been retrieved from Robert Sebastian Brown's pockets. One was a silver bracelet, the other a snapshot of an attractive young blond woman, a big smile on her face, posing against a pillar in the Palais Royal in Paris. Gazing at the bracelet, Jensen saw the gleaming image of a cathedral on the front and the name "Julie" on the back. He ruminated for awhile, playing with the idea of giving the bracelet to his own daughter Julie who was living in Toronto. Shuddering at the thought, he placed the bracelet carefully in an envelope. Holding up the photo, Jensen saw the word "Julie" scribbled on the back. He studied it for a moment, then placed the photograph in the envelope, and closed the file.

Chapter 58

A week later, near the end of September, Southampton Beach was deserted except for an attractive couple, arms encircling each other, meandering along the shore. Every so often they would embrace, kiss passionately, and then resume their stroll.

"Charles, you came back to me," Cynthia Sherman said. "I had my doubts whether you would." She was wearing a black bathing suit and slim gold necklace that Browning had given her.

"I can understand that, Cyn, but I told you that I would come back and take you around the world." He picked up a flat rock and threw it sidearm skimming into the ocean.

"Slow down, Charles. You're going too fast for me. Let's get to know each other again before we skip out of town."

"Okay, Cynthia. Whatever you say. I have to emphasize to you that I made the great deal that I was talking about, and so now I have the means to give up my other 'profession' in order to avoid excessive travel and have more time with you."

"Charles, I do believe that you have lost some of your insufferable arrogance on your recent 'business trip'. I definitely like the new sweeter you better than the old angry, narcissistic individual you were."

"Then I will obliterate the old me, Cyn. The new Charles must admit that he likes himself better this way too. I am calm, unstressed, even euphoric. I'm a happy man, because I have nothing more to prove except my love and affection for you.

"Oh, Charles…." She held his head gently and kissed him on his forehead. "Let's talk about that trip tonight. Can we start in Alabama to see my mother?

"Of course, Cynthia."

They resumed their stroll down the sandy beach.

Postscript

The events depicted in this story are fictitious Some of the characters are based on real individuals who have retained their names--Kurt Waldheim, Yasser Arafat, Jimmy Carter, Walter Mondale, Andrew Young, etc.--but the words they speak and the events attributed to them are likewise fictitious, the invention of the author.

The time frame in this story is the middle and late 1970s when the author worked at the United Nations. It was an era when the U.N. Security Officers did not carry weapons (September 11, 2001 changed all that), when the telephone and the telegraph were the mechanisms of global communication in the U.N. system (before computers and e-mail), and when the U.N. was considered humanity's last, best hope for an orderly and peaceful world. The 'colonial era' had, in the main, ended in the 1950s and 1960s, with newly formed nations in Africa and Asia swelling the ranks of the U.N. General Assembly. It was, nevertheless, a turbulent era, with Cold War animosities at a high pitch, and the fall of the Berlin Wall and the dismemberment of the Soviet Union twelve to fifteen years away.

The one constant spanning that era and our own was and remains the Middle East, in particular, the Israeli-Palestinian problem which takes on different leaders and different forms, but seems intractable, if not insoluble. The terror of that era is dwarfed by the proliferation and expansion of terrorism in the current period (Taliban, Al Queda, ISIS, Boko Haraam, Somalian terrorists, etc.). Nevertheless, the hostilities and 'terrorism' of that era were extremely intense, with military actions, killings, and reprisals, with words like 'PLO murderers', 'intifada', 'racism', 'Zionist imperialism', and 'apartheid' the currency of Middle East semantics. "Plus ca change, plus c'est la meme chose" is an overused truism, but it is perfectly applicable to the Israeli-Palestinian conflict which antedates the establishment of the Israeli state in 1948 and seems to go on forever. Hence the hope that the novel will not be dated by its placement in the late 1970s, but will have a relevance and immediacy for today.

The geography of this novel roams in a non-linear way from the West Bank to Paris to Nairobi to Tel Aviv to Cyprus to Beirut to Geneva to New York. Eventually it settles in New York because of the plot's assassination attempt at the United Nations. It is hoped that the partial focus on the global and internal politics of the U. N. will have both interest and appeal in a period when the United Nations seems a marginal player.

A film made in 2007,"The Interpreter," has a plot line about a potential murder of an African dictator in the United Nations by a female interpreter whose brother was killed by cohorts of the dictator in a fictitious African country. With the agreement of the then U.N. Secretary-General, Kofi Annan, the filmmaker, crew, and actors (including Nicole

Kidman and Sean Penn) were able to use the General Assembly hall and other locales on several Sundays to do the filming inside U.N. premises.

The plot of the film, along with the characters, is completely different from DIPLOMACY AND DEATH AT THE U.N. The author could not have borrowed from or been influenced by anything in "The Interpreter," since he wrote this novel in the period 1978-1981, when, as a dedicated international civil servant in the United Nations, he decided to suppress the novel rather than risk losing his job, since anything that a staff member writes for outside publication requires approval by the internal authorities of the United Nations. A novel 1) featuring two professional assassins roaming around in the interior of the U.N. and 2) professing to have inside information of the Secretary-General manipulating political leaders and historical events in order to create a super fund to enable the United Nations to become financially solvent and politically independent, as well as to ensure his election to the presidency of Austria (well before the revelations of Kurt Waldheim's clouded Nazi war past), would never have been cleared for outside publication. So the author put the novel aside for many decades, keeping his job until retirement from the U.N. in 1999. A year or so ago, he decided to take it up again and revise it, adding some new features (such as the marriage of Julie and Danny in Cyprus) and new characters (such as Denise, Robert Sebastian's love interest). In the main, however, the plot and principal characters remain the same as in the earlier edition.

As mentioned above, the entire plot, as well as the opinions attributed to the novel's characters, is purely the invention of the author.

Acknowledgements

I owe a huge measure of gratitude to a number of individuals who encouraged me to complete the revision of a novel that I originally crafted over thirty years ago as a staff member of the United Nations. Anya Taylor, my companion, first suggested that I dig out the manuscript from my storage space and consider revising it. After reading the draft with fresh eyes as a U.N. retiree, I deemed it satisfactory to give to Anya, a former college literature professor, to offer her judgment as to the merits of revising it. Anya answered in the affirmative, and so I decided to instill life in my sleeping manuscript. As with the initial writing of the first draft many decades ago, I thoroughly enjoyed refining and refashioning the plot, deepening or adding instrumental characters, and introducing stylistic innovtions.

Along the way, I showed successive drafts to family members and friends, several of whom made excellent suggestions to consider incorporating into the novel. Noel Edelson, for example, proposed that I move Danny and Julie's marriage from Israel where secular Jews cannot easily get married to Cyprus where Israeli marriage is a "cottage industry," as I have Danny tell a reluctant Julie. I also thank Noel and Leah for proofreading the manuscript in its final stages.

Many people offered encouragement and support, including my children Alissa, Steven, and Jonathan, and my grandson, Andrew, as well as my sister, Nancy Weintraub, nephews Adam and Josh Weintraub, my son-in-law, Joel Isaacson, future daughter-in-law, Katelind Root, and cousin Judy Brew. Important also to mention are Amit Bhattacharya, John Bing, Hamid and Sigrid Bouab, Michelle Cohen, Richard Dannay, Myra Gordon (who was present at the creation), Noel and Leah Edelson, Alison Gardiner, Cathy Gay, David Godshalk, Myra Gordon, David and Emily Kales, Eric Kruger, Nick Lekas, Bob Lewy, Ferdie Lyn, Sam Mani, Tony Miller, John O'Leary, Bill Ryan, Bob Salpeter, Charles Salzberg, Claude Schostal, David Smith, Nina Smith, Will Swift, Anya Taylor, George and Sydney Torrey, Lynn Visson, and Richard Young, many of whom read the novel and offered ideas and support. I owe a hearty thanks to them all.

I would like to thank my close friend and tennis partner Bob Salpeter for offering his incredible design skills in the service of designing the cover and the interior of the book.

Finally, I thank Jonathan Gordon, Bob Salpeter, and Anya Taylor for helping me to come up with an acceptable title once I learned that my original choice of "Deadly Diplomacy" had been used in Australia in the 1990s.

Praise for Diplomacy and Death at the UN

An historical thriller with a fast-paced plot and fascinating characters doing the unexpected in a dramatic way. I am proposing this novel to my book club.

Judy Brew

This fast paced story produces an unexpected series of incidents that intrigue and fascinate the reader. I enjoyed the international aspects of the plot, and I particularly enjoyed learning about the role of the United Nations where much of the action takes place. A fine suspense thriller.

Michelle Cohen

Romance, intrigue and derring-do emanate from the roiling Middle East to Nairobi, Paris, Geneva and New York. All coalesce in a plot to assassinate Yasser Arafat at the United Nations. President Jimmy Carter and Secretary-General Kurt Waldheim have cameo roles that add historical credibility to this tale of love, murder and diplomacy. "Diplomacy and Death at the UN" is not just a page-turner, it's a re-read.

Noel Edelson

An action-packed thriller, informed by a keen eye for setting and the world of diplomacy. Never have the workings of the UN and its behind-the-scenes drama been so vividly captured. The final pages will leave you breathless!

Emily Fox-Kales, Ph.D.
Author, Body Shots: Hollywood and the Culture of Eating Disorders

Intrigue, romance, politics, suspense, diplomacy, and murder...Richard Gordon has it all in his fast paced, can't put down thriller. The novel is set in the late 1970s and early 80s, when President Jimmy Carter's peace endeavor between Egypt and Israel hangs in the balance. Globe trotting around the world, ending at UN Headquarters, the reader is on a whirlwind tour to find out who lives and who dies.

Cathy Gay
Catherine Gay Communications

What an exciting story. I decided to psyche out the assassin as he/they pursued the targeted political leader who was theoretically "impossible" to approach and kill. I understood perfectly the mentality of both the perpetrator and the victim, since I have been in that position more times than I can say. The word 'verisimilitude' comes to mind as a descriptive catch-all term to confirm the reality of what the author has accomplished. He has written a novel with an intriguing, even catchy, title, but he could have labeled his work as non-fiction.

GS

Professional Assassin

Lime heat-seeking rockets from different warring factions, all focused on the same targeted individual, intense motives abound in this fast-paced narrative set on a global stage in the 1970s. The author jets us to Paris, Israel, New York, Kenya, Peru, Lebanon, and finally the United Nations in New York as the deftly drawn characters, minor as well as major, pursue their ineluctable ends. As the prose races and pauses, the hidden motives of the characters are gradually revealed. Dear Reader: Prepare for a wild and colorful ride, with a stunning surprise at the end.

Eric Kruger

Political Economist

An engrossing tale with engaging and timely intrigue that takes place in the late 1970s, but has immediate relevance to our present turbulent era. A page turner that I highly recommend.

Dr. Robert Lewy

Former Senior Associate Dean, Columbia University Medical Center

The complex Middle East politics become very personal as the action spans continents and becomes a cat and mouse thriller in the United Nations. This thriller took me onboard immediately and wouldn't let me go. Subtle twists and turns throughout. A great read. Couldn't put it down.

Tony Miller

Ex-Air Force Officer; a major gardener who understands a great plot

"Diplomacy and Death at the U.N." is a page-turner in the tradition of "The Day of the Jackal." Not only do we get to know the principal figures and their conscious and unconscious motivations, but we also get the thrill of the many twists and turns occurring along the way. A thoroughly enjoyable read!

Dr. John O'Leary,

Psychoanalyst who understands the dark side of human nature, including borderline, paranoid, and depressive personalities.

Because of my work, I can identify with many aspects of the assassination plot—careful assessment of whether to accept an assignment or not; importance of understanding motives and factors other than money; deep analysis of the psychology of the recruiter, the assassin, and the designated target; meticulous preparation of the linked steps in the evolution of the plot, including the murder weapon; relentless, if cautious pursuit of the target; identifying the factors which can maximize or impede the chances of a successful hit; and the need to create a foolproof escape plan. Gordon seems to know all this, as well as the inner workings of a killer's mind. Is this pure speculation on his part, or has he…..?

R.R.
Professional Assassin

A great way to learn the history and traditions of the United Nations—while being entertained by a page turning mystery.

Bob Salpeter
Graphic Designer, Salpeter Ventura, Inc

An imaginative novel of many parts—historical thriller; political drama; fascinating characters, ranging from professional assassins to major political figures; wide geographical span from the Middle East to Africa to Europe and to New York to the Security Council and General Assembly of the United Nations. A revenge plot of a brother pursuing the murderer of his sister and willing to go to the ends of the earth to settle accounts.

Anya Taylor
John Jay College of Criminal Justice, CUNY, Professor of English

Two assassins, each unknown to the other, are hired to kill Yasser Arafat, leader of the Palestinian movement, the PLO. Within this broad outline, we encounter various characters motivated by their human emotions—revenge, love, sex, money, political power. Much of the action takes place at the United Nations which the author knows in great detail, having worked there for many years. The plot is driven by personal and political intrigues. The suspense builds, and we wonder with great anticipation how it's all going to end. A must read; difficult to put down.

Dr. George Torrey
Ph.d. in Literature

Middle Eastern politics, the workings of the peace process, hidden assassins, revenge for murder, passionate love scenes, financial plots and intrigues at the United Nations – Richard Gordon has them all in his novel "Diplomacy and Death at the U.N." This suspenseful and intriguing international thriller whips the reader at top speed across oceans and continents. A great read for those who enjoy page turners featuring international plots, assassinations, complex psychological personalities from a wide range of countries, and passionate love stories. The author, a retired UN employee, has inside knowledge both of the workings of the organization and of the dozens of countries to which he traveled while working there.

Dr. Lynn Visson
U.N. Interpreter (retired)

Made in the USA
Middletown, DE
15 December 2019